Fragile Brilliance

My dearest Victoria,

Thank you for

Everything!

The Timber Wolves Trilogy:

Destiny Binds
Time Mends
Fate Succumbs

Timber Wolves Companions:

At First Sight
All We See and Seem

FRAGILE BRILLIANCE

A SHIFTERS & SEERS NOVEL

Tammy Blackwell

Published in
the United States

Content editor: Gwen Hayes of Fresh Eyes Critique
Copy editor: Leslie Mitchell of G2 Freelance Editing
Cover Designer: Victoria Faye Alday of Whit & Ware Designs

Cataloging Information

Blackwell, Tammy
Fragile Brilliance/ Tammy Blackwell - 1st. ed.
340 p. ; 22 cm.
Summary: Maggie McCray has worked her whole life for the opportunity to attend Sanders College. It's her one chance at becoming a world-renowned artist, and she's determined nothing will get in her way. But when a murder brings Maggie and her powers to the attention of the Alpha Pack and the tragically handsome Charlie Hagan, her carefully planned future hangs in jeopardy.

ISBN 978-1493658435
[1. Werewolves - Fiction. 2. Kentucky - Fiction. 3. Colleges and universities - Fiction. 4. Paranormal.]

For Samantha Newman,
because she stood strong
when many would have broken.

CHAPTER 1

By the second day of college, Maggie McCray was already bored with naked people. She found this more than a little surprising since she hadn't actually seen a naked body besides her own until she moved into the dorms last Friday.

"Oh my God, can you believe that just happened?" Reid St. James grabbed Maggie's arm, her eyes opened so wide Maggie worried she would dry out a cornea. "My mother would absolutely die if she knew they allow streakers on campus."

"I don't really think they 'allow' them. He did get tackled by the campus police." It was all rather dramatic with the guy in a Darth Vader mask racing out of Rooke Hall, screaming the words to the national anthem without a stitch of clothing on his body. A cop burst through the doors of the building mere seconds later, yelling for him to stop. He didn't, which resulted in the cop taking the guy to the ground in the grassy commons where most students congregated between classes. The scene caused foot traffic to come to a complete standstill on the sidewalks.

"Did you see the triangle with the black dot drawn on his belly?" Reid asked as Maggie tried to wind her way past a group of guys encouraging the cop to "whip out his Taser". "That was the symbol for the LSH society. They're like the most exclusive club on campus. Most people don't even know they exist, and no one other than the members knows what LSH stands for."

Reid was very into Sanders University's secret societies. The Greek system was abolished from campus in the 1980s after a rivalry between two fraternities ended up with two dead kids and a mob of angry parents. According to Reid, there were a few societies that existed on campus before then, but with the sororities and fraternities gone, they really began to flourish. Now everyone who was anyone was invited to join one.

Since Maggie was a no one, she didn't pay much attention to the whole thing, but Reid was very much a someone. Or at least, she thought she was. Her dad was the CEO of some security company that went by letters Maggie couldn't remember, although Reid recited them as if she were announcing her family was in line for the British throne. The St. James family was absolutely dripping with money, as Reid's Mercedes and closet full of designer clothes could attest, but at Sanders, money wasn't enough. The school catered to the wealthy, and Reid was finding herself to be a very small Marc Jacobs wallet in a sea of Salvatore Ferragamo purses.

That didn't stop Reid from making every effort to become one of the important someones on campus. She was like a repository of information on the popular students. She practically stalked well-known upperclassmen, hanging out at all the spots they were known to frequent, certain one of them would look over, see her sheer awesomeness, and invite her into their inner circle.

It wasn't a bad plan, except for the whole sheer awesomeness part.

"Can you believe someone would do that? I mean, who agrees to run around naked in front of the entire campus?"

Reid pushed her Rainbow Dash-colored bangs off her forehead with emerald and ruby-ringed fingers, giving Maggie an unobstructed view of her rolling eyes. "I would never do that. Ever. Not that I'm ashamed of my body, because I'm totally not, but I respect myself too much to streak across campus like some... some..."

"Streaker?" Maggie suggested.

"Attention whore."

Maggie bit her lip to keep the laughter trapped inside. Reid was chiding someone else for not wearing clothes and seeking out attention? Did she not know people who pranced around in glass dorm rooms in nothing but sheer lace undergarments shouldn't throw stones?

And the way Maggie saw it, anyone who obsessed over secret societies and enjoyed having long, involved conversations about the bubble-like quality of her butt and pertness of her boobs would probably pay someone for the chance to do an initiation streak across campus.

A spattering of applause and wolf-whistles drew Maggie's attention back to Darth Vader and the poor police officer trying to help him back on his feet. Once Darth was standing firmly, he turned toward the crowd and triumphantly held his shackled hands above his head. The entire quad erupted in cheers. Maggie found herself clapping and laughing along with the others despite herself.

"Moron."

And just like that, Maggie was no longer in the mood to laugh.

"Davin," she said with a slight nod of her head before quickly averting her eyes, not because he and Reid were actually doing anything, but because after just a few days, it had become habit.

Maggie met Davin shortly after getting settled in on move-in day. She had taken a shower to wash away the I've-been-carrying-boxes-in-hundred-degree-weather funk, and when she returned to the room wearing only her bathrobe and shower shoes, she found a very naked and very sweaty Reid and Davin testing the springs in Reid's new mattress. The situation was awful enough, but then the couple decided to go ahead and finish their activities instead of calling it game-over. Since she was awfully close to naked herself, Maggie was forced to hide in the bathroom until the noises finally stopped. When she ventured back into the room, Reid, who was still lacking clothes, made the introductions. Still, it took Maggie a few hours to figure out naked boy's name was Davin since Reid only referred to him as "my boyfriend," as if it was his given name.

In the beginning, Maggie made an effort to befriend Boyfriend despite their unfortunate introduction. He was a sophomore metalworking independent study student, and as a freshman independent study student in the art department, Maggie was eager to find out more about the program. He would have been a great resource... if he ever deigned to speak to her.

Maggie tried to not let Boyfriend's lack of communication get to her. As far as she could tell, he was only capable of monosyllabic responses to Reid's nonstop chatter and the occasional Neanderthal comment, like the remarks Maggie could hear him making to Reid about the size of the streaker's genitals.

Boyfriend was a world-class douche, and because Maggie had the best luck on earth, he also happened to be in the Anthropology class she was unfortunate enough to have with her roommate.

She wondered if it was possible to get a schedule change. It wasn't as if she really needed Anthropology. It sounded like a made-up class anyway.

Fortunately, things started looking up the moment they walked into the classroom. Reid gave a middle-school worthy squeal, grabbed Boyfriend, and took off for a pack of girls decked out like a Guess ad, leaving Maggie blissfully alone. She picked out a seat on the opposite side of the room and pulled out her notebook. She was doodling in the margins when a hush fell over the room. She looked up, expecting to see Professor Suddeath ready to start the class, but the instructor wasn't the focus of everyone's attention.

Harper Lee "Scout" Donovan stood at the front of the room, glaring at one empty seat and then another. Pale blue eyes clashed with Maggie's and Maggie dropped her gaze, embarrassed. She told herself she wasn't going to gawk, but when Scout Donovan planted herself in the desk next to hers, she couldn't stop her eyes from wandering over.

Not staring at someone who looked like Scout was impossible. She reminded Maggie of some long-lost mythical Scandinavian princess. Her skin was like freshly glazed ceramic, a pure, unblemished white; her eyes were just a few shades darker, a hint of blue to distinguish the irises from the whites; and her hair was wild tuft of short, silvery locks sticking out in an artful arrangement atop her head. She was beautiful in a disturbing sort of way. Still,

Maggie tried hard to not let her gaze linger any longer than necessary. Being the 4'11" daughter of a half-Japanese, half-Scottish mother and African American father, Maggie knew all too well what it was like to have people pay too much attention to the way you look. It was annoying enough for Maggie. She couldn't imagine how much worse it had to be for someone as well known as Scout Donovan.

Two years ago, Scout had been all anyone could talk about. She'd been kidnapped by domestic terrorists and since her grandfather was a US Senator, every media outlet in the world covered the story from every possible angle for weeks on end. If the media went a little crazy over her disappearance, then it completely lost its mind over her rescue. The story was like something from a movie. A family friend, who happened to be a cop, refused to give up on the search, even when everyone else believed she was dead. He dug and dug for information until he finally found a credible lead. Because of his tenacity, the FBI let him come along when they raided the hideout where she was being kept. Toby Hagan was only supposed to be there so Scout would have a familiar face to put her at ease, but then something went wrong. As he was leading Scout from the building, a hidden operative for God's Army of Defenders shot him in the back of the head, killing him instantly.

On the television and in newspapers, the focus was on the tragic tale and heroic death of Toby Hagan. But on the Internet, the story took on a different life. There was only one tiny bit of footage of Scout after the incident. She was leaving the hospital when CNN managed to get a shot of her walking across the parking lot. Maybe if she'd looked small and defeated the world would have pitied her, but

Scout didn't look like a girl to be pitied. The muscles lining her too thin frame gave the bruises dotting her pale skin the look of battle wounds. There was no defeat in the way she held herself. Watching her walk across that parking lot, the world knew she wasn't someone you wanted to mess with. In no way did she look like an innocent young girl who had just been rescued from the bad guys. Instead, she looked like she'd fought her own way out, taking down anything and anyone who got in her way. Less than five seconds of footage and it spawned a dozen different memes. At first they were complimentary. One of the most popular had Scout Photoshopped onto the cover of video games and action movies. But then people got mean, as they often tend to do when they don't actually have to look the person they're tormenting in the eye. A year passed and Maggie still couldn't go online for long without seeing a picture tagged with "Whiter than Scout?"

While Conan O'Brien, sweater vests, and rugby were all considered a yes, paper, chalk, and snow didn't make the cut.

Maggie risked another glance at the pale figure to her left and caught Scout staring back at her. She was about to apologize when Scout asked, "Who are you?"

"Me?" Maggie looked around to make sure there wasn't someone of importance standing just over her shoulder. "I'm Maggie. Maggie McCray."

"McCray? I don't know any McCrays."

"Sorry...?"

Scout pushed a piece of her short, spiky hair behind her ear. "You really should have informed us you were going to be here. I mean, I don't care really, but Liam gets a little worked up over this type of thing. I've tried to tell him it's not like I can't take care of myself, but he's a guy, which means his ears don't work when a female speaks."

"Liam?" This conversation wasn't making any sense whatsoever. No one mentioned Scout coming away from her abduction with a brain injury, but Maggie supposed the girl was entitled to a mental issue or two.

Scout's eyes narrowed until only a tiny slice of arctic blue could be seen. "Don't you dare get all weak-kneed and terrified because I mentioned Liam. We're equals. He's not more badass just because he's a guy. I'm just as scary as he is. Promise."

Maggie would've happily told Scout she couldn't imagine anyone more terrifying than a crazy Mila Jovovich, but Dr. Suddeath chose that moment to start lecturing. While he went over the syllabus and explained the college's academic integrity policy for about the millionth time, Maggie tried hard to ignore Scout, but it was hard since Scout showed no signs of ignoring her. Maggie could feel her eyes on her through the entire class and wasn't at all surprised when the other girl loomed over her desk the instant they were dismissed.

"Who are you?"

Again Maggie glanced over her shoulder to make sure there was no one standing behind her.

"Maggie McCray," she repeated.

Scout leaned in, crowding Maggie's personal space. "Why didn't you answer me?"

"I... I just did." Definitely a brain injury. "Are you okay? Do I maybe need to call someone for you?" Surely Senator Harper didn't let her just wander around like this. There had to be a secret service detail or nurse or something to keep her from roaming into the middle of the street and getting run over, right?

"The hustings is this weekend," Scout said, sliding something onto Maggie's desk. "I expect you to be there." And with that, she turned and walked out of the room.

Maggie sat and stared at the business card sitting on the middle of her desk. It was plain white with a black paw print and address printed on one side. She flipped it over to find the other side blank. "What the...?"

"Oh. My. God." Reid was immediately at Maggie's shoulder. "Did you just get tagged? By Harper Donovan? How freaking cool is that?"

Maggie flipped the card over again as if some sort of explanation would magically appear. "Tagged?"

"That was Harper Donovan. She's like a rock star."

"She was kidnapped by terrorists. That's not the same as selling out the Staples Arena."

"What did she say to you?" Reid's fingers clamped onto Maggie's arm hard enough to leave bruises. "Did she give you something?"

Part of Maggie wanted to be bratty and just slip the card in her pocket, but she handed it to Reid instead. "She invited me to some party or something. I think she was confused."

Reid's eyes narrowed on the card. "Obviously." Reid rubbed her finger over the embossed paw print. "Mind if I keep it?" she asked, cutting her eyes at Boyfriend as if asking his permission. "You know, since you don't need it?"

Maggie probably should have been offended by the obvious cut, but she wasn't. She didn't really care what Reid or Scout thought about her, and the last thing she needed was to get caught up in some rich kids' club. Unlike her perpetually bored classmates, she had better things to do with her time than following esoteric rules just so someone would pretend they liked her. For example, she only had five minutes to make it to the other side of campus before her drawing lab started. With any luck, today's nude model would be somewhat less wrinkly and smelly than Old Man March from yesterday.

"Take it," Maggie said, throwing the strap of her satchel over her shoulder. "It's yours."

Reid bit her bottom lip and snuggled the card against her chest. "Thanks, Mags. You're the best."

She wasn't. Not yet. But that was why Maggie was at Sanders College. One day, she would be the best, and then people like Reid would be clamoring for her attention and acceptance. Until then, she was on her own. But it was okay. Alone was all she'd ever known.

CHAPTER 2

Charlie Hagan scanned the nearly two hundred faces staring up at him, his fingers tapping out an impatient rhythm. After his third sweep of the room, he dug out his cell phone.

"Where are you?"

He waited thirty seconds for a reply. When none came, he typed out the same question again and hit send. He sent the message five times before Layne sent back a response.

"Jesus. Can I not take a piss w/o u getting all up in my business?"

"Not when you're supposed to be attending a hustings," Charlie typed back. "Get your ass in here now."

The last thing Charlie needed was to be dealing with his nephew when Shifters and Seers from all over the world were wandering around to see just how spectacularly the newly minted American Alpha Pack was failing, but he didn't have much choice. Since his brother died last year, Charlie had become Layne's legal guardian, which meant he had to deal with the thirteen year old's crap no matter how inconvenient it was or how ill equipped Charlie might be.

"Any sign of Scout's unregistered Seer?" a voice asked from over Charlie's shoulder at the same moment Layne slipped through the door and found a seat in the back row. Even if he hadn't recognized the voice, Charlie would have known it was Joshua by the smell of chocolate clinging to the Stratego. Somehow Joshua managed to smell like chocolate even immediately after taking a shower. Charlie figured he'd eaten so much of it over the years it was somehow permanently embedded in his chemical make-up.

"None," Charlie said, not bothering to hide the irritation in his voice. "Did Michelle get any hits in the Archives?"

"No, and I didn't find anything when I poked around the innerwebs." By which Joshua meant he hacked into every database he could find and traced her digital footprint back to birth. Joshua could do things with a computer Charlie didn't know were possible and were most certainly illegal. The popular belief in the Alpha Pack was Joshua's computer prowess came from actually building the internet with his own two hands. The guy might look eighteen, but he had been born back when Model T's were still chugging up and down the streets. Eternal youth was just one of the many advantages of being an Immortal. "Want me to send Makya out to bring her in?"

"The Alpha Female said to let her be for now," Charlie said even though he really wanted to disobey the order. Most Shifters would have shrugged off an unregistered Seer, thinking they were harmless. They assumed since Shifters were the who could Change into a wolf - or in Charlie's case, a coyote - they had nothing to fear from girls who could See the future, someone's thoughts, or whatever their particular power might be. But Charlie knew you didn't have to grow fangs and claws to tear a person apart. As far as he was concerned, anyone who wasn't aligned with the Alpha Pack was an enemy.

Which unfortunately meant he had a lot of enemies.

There was some commotion to Charlie's right, and he turned to meet a pair of eyes the exact same shade of green as his own.

"I see news of my beauty has traveled far and wide," Jase Donovan, Charlie's cousin and closet friend, said. "You think we might have to build onto the barn to accommodate my ever-expanding fan club?"

The Alpha's farm sat on 1800 acres, 800 of which were wooded. The main house had three floors and eight bedrooms. Four other small houses also sat on the property, which meant the majority of the American-based Alpha Pack could cohabitate without having to invest in bunk beds. And then there were the barns. Charlie grew up in western Kentucky where barns were small affairs that either housed a tractor and its various accessories and maybe some hay, or they were a place where you strung up tobacco leaves and smoked them before taking them to market. If western Kentucky barns were a pick-up truck, then central Kentucky barns were stretched limos. Their property housed twenty different barns. A handful of those were actually old tobacco barns, but most were either six or ten stall horse barns, and a few of them boasted places for humans as well as horses to sleep. But the biggest barn, the farm's crowning glory, was a 2700 square foot building with a vaulted ceiling and hand-carved stone covering the exterior. It didn't look so much like a barn as it did a cathedral, which is why it now served as the location of the Alpha Pack's summer hustings, a time when any Shifter or Seer could seek audience with the Alphas.

The barn currently held over two hundred people.

"Surely to God we won't have this many people every time," Charlie said. This wasn't even the first hustings they'd held since the new Alphas came into power over a year ago. The other two had attracted even larger audiences. "You can only gawk at Scout so many times before it either gets old or she stabs you in the eye."

Talley Matthews, who was sitting on the other side of Jase, looked up from her Tablet. "Who is stabbing what?"

"You," Jase said, grabbing her hand and placing it on his chest. "You're stabbing my heart with tiny arrows from Cupid's bow."

Talley's blue eyes slid back to her device. "Nice try, but you're still not forgiven."

Since Jase and Talley were disgustingly in love and Talley was generally acknowledged as overly kind and forgiving, Jase had to have done something rather remarkable.

"You know, I got hit in the head during my workout yesterday. Hard. Hard enough to cause brain damage."

"You don't have brain damage," Talley said to her mate, flicking her finger across the screen of her device. "You just forgot."

"I didn't forget. I just failed to remember."

Talley frowned, but even Charlie could tell it was just an attempt to keep from smiling. "That's the same thing."

"Did you forget your mating ceremony anniversary?" Charlie guessed, knowing the two had completed the ritual that bound their lives together forever and always as mates last August.

"I got a dozen roses, a two pound box of chocolates, and a necklace," Talley said, fingering what appeared to be a ruby surrounded by a bunch of diamonds.

"Pick that up at Wal-Mart, Jase?"

"Tiffany's, actually. The store. Not Tiffany, the crazy lady with all the cats who used to live next to Gramma. Did you know they actually put their stuff in little blue boxes? I thought that was just in the movies or something, but it's true."

"Good to know you went for low-key and subtle."

"Well, it's only the first anniversary. I'm saving the extravagant stuff for five years."

While Jase was talking, the room, which had been filled with the buzzing of over two hundred voices speaking at the same time, grew eerily quiet. Charlie didn't have to look up to see what - or, more accurately, *who* - caught their attention.

"Well, we're here now," Scout said, stomping up to the table. "Don't worry, Jase. Liam and I just walked on over. It's a lovely day for it." A small puddle was forming around her. She peeled off her raincoat and tossed it in a heap behind her.

Charlie closed his eyes. "You forgot the Alphas?"

"I don't like the word 'forgot'," Jase said. "It makes me sound careless."

"You forgot the Alphas, and then didn't go back to get them?"

"By the time I remembered I was supposed to drive them over, they were already trudging through the field."

"She will kill you, and I will let her."

"Nah." Jase smiled out at the crowd before them, and Charlie was pretty sure he actually heard a few of the Seers sigh. His cousin had that effect on people. Charlie had too once, but that was a long time ago. "Half of these idiots are going to piss her off so bad she'll not even remember I made her walk through the rain and mud."

And half of those idiots were dominant enough to be able to hear Jase's muttering even though it was the new moon, the time when their powers were at their weakest. If he'd said the same thing five minutes before, Charlie would probably be sporting a bloody nose and a few broken bones by now. If they were a real Alpha Pack, then no one would even think about it, but everyone knew how big of a joke they were. Instead of pooling together the strongest Shifters in the world, Scout surrounded herself with her friends and family when she became Alpha Female. Charlie tried to explain how coyote Shifters weren't really Alpha Pack material - the gig was pretty much reserved for the more dominant wolves - but she was stubborn and one of the two most powerful Shifters in the world, so she got her way. Charlie's cousins now sat in the majority of the seats facing the audience, and the others were occupied by a hodgepodge of Seers ranging from kick-ass (Talley) to... well, to a woman who didn't actually See anything (Michelle, the glorified librarian).

The only thing keeping them from being torn to shreds by a hundred other Shifters wanting to be in power was the guy rubbing a towel over Scout's wet hair. At an imposing muscle-corded 6'3", Liam Cole radiated a power even the most nonmagical person in the world could feel. There hadn't been a Shifter of his dominance in known history. While most Shifters had to wait on the full moon to Change into a wolf or coyote, Liam could go furry whenever the mood struck. After he rose to the Alpha Male, a few Shifters were stupid enough to Challenge him for the position. It didn't take long for even the most ignorant of their kind to realize it was a very bad idea.

Everyone was scared of Liam. Even Charlie, whom Liam considered one of his closest friends, was a little intimidated by the guy. But what very few people realized was Liam wasn't the biggest threat in the room. There was one Shifter whose dominance was equal to, if not greater than, his. And while Liam had very little patience for the idiot Shifters of the world, the girl he bound his life to had even less. In fact, she was just as likely to punch you through a wall as shake your hand.

"Chuck," Scout said, taking her seat next to him. Some may have thought sitting at the Alpha Female's right hand was a sign of prominence, that Charlie was some kind of super-important member of the Alpha Pack, but that was about as far from the truth as you could get. Charlie had a pity position, but he wasn't a total waste of space. He'd made a vow to protect the Alpha Female at all costs, even his own life. Hence his spot at the table.

It was much easier to take a bullet for someone when you were only inches away.

"Your majesty," he teased because it was what was expected of him. "Might I say, you look especially professional today."

"I do what I can," Scout said as she zipped up the dry Green Lantern hoodie Liam had dug out of his gym bag. "Anything I need to know before we get started?"

Charlie acknowledged the Alpha Male with a nod of the head as Liam took the seat next to his mate. "Nothing new since Joshua forwarded our report to your iPads an hour ago."

"And this Maggie person?" Liam asked.

Charlie shook his head, and Scout cursed.

"I can send Makya—"

"No," Scout said. "She's probably just scared. God knows people have had a reason to fear the Alpha Pack before."

"But we're different."

Scout looked him in the eye, and it took everything he had not to look away, scared of what she saw swimming in their depths. "Yes," she said with a hint of sadness in her voice. "That we are."

CHAPTER 3

The hustings was an opportunity for Pack Leaders across the world to bring issues before the Alphas, who were basically the king and queen of the Shifters and Seers. Growing up in a pack that typically kept to themselves and hadn't sought audience with the Alphas in more than four generations, Charlie always assumed their world was a fairly small one. It didn't take long for him to realize he was wrong. Michelle, who had access to every piece of information on every pack in existence, told him there were over seven hundred registered packs in the world, and nearly two hundred of them lived in the United States.

The tall, dark skinned Shifter now standing in front of the Alphas was from a small Mexican pack that numbered only three Shifters and two Seers. Until he attended his first hustings, Charlie hadn't even considered the existence of Mexican Shifters.

"Your Highnesses," he said, sinking to one knee as his daughter curtsied.

Liam checked the list of appointments. "Mr. Guzman. What can we do for you today?"

"It's not me," Mr. Guzman said. "It's my girl here. She has something to tell you." The girl in question looked like she would much rather turn around and run as fast as she could out into the rain than tell them anything. She just stood there, eyes wide and lips trembling slightly, until her father pushed her forward.

"What's your name, honey?" Talley asked, sounding like a sweet old grandmother instead of a nineteen year old.

Even with the prompt, it still took an encouraging smile and nod from Talley for the girl to answer.

"Gus," she said so softly even those with enhanced hearing had to strain to understand her. "No, Augusta. I mean, my real name is Augusta, but people call me Gus... sometimes."

Scout, who wasn't quite as maternal as her best friend, propped her elbows on the table. "Well, Gus Sometimes, is there something you needed to tell us?"

"Y-y-yes, ma'am. I... ummm..." Gus swallowed, the sound louder than her sotto speaking voice. "My sister Saw something."

"Was it that I would be cast as the next Doctor? Because I've got my fingers crossed." Jase held up his hands to illustrate the point. "I think it's my time."

Charlie kicked his cousin under the table, but instead of bursting into tears like he'd feared, Gus actually smiled. "Sorry, but no. Aurora is in favor of a lady Doctor. And anyway, she only ever Sees evil."

"Evil?" Scout echoed.

"Evil," Gus confirmed. "Tragedies. Blood. *Death.*"

Charlie didn't like the way too familiar path where this was heading.

"Whose death?" Liam asked, leaning forward.

Gus twisted her hands together.

"Gus, whose death does your sister See?"

"There was an angel," she said, eyes fixed on the floor in front of her. "One of those beautiful angels that are almost too pretty to be a guy. He had giant wings and a sword in his hand. And below him, piled on the ground, were the bodies of those he'd slain." She looked up and met Scout's eyes. "Yours was on top."

"Where is your sister?" Liam asked.

When Gus continued to study the floor instead of answering, Liam turned to her father. "Mr. Guzman, where is your other daughter?"

"She died four years ago, Your Highness," Guzman said, his fingers fidgeting with a ring hanging from a gold chain around his neck.

Liam narrowed his eyes in concentration.

"Was your daughter a future Seer?"

"Yes, Your Highness."

"And she had this vision before she died?"

"No, Your Highness."

A wave of murmurs passed through the crowd, the sound accented with snorts of disbelief and annoyance.

The crowd wasn't alone in their skepticism. Scout's mouth opened, and Charlie braced himself for whatever snarky remark she was about to let fly, but Jase saved them all.

"Is anyone else confused? Because I'm confused."

Robby, one of Charlie's distant cousins, raised his hand. "I second that confusion."

Charlie tried to ignore the they're-all-idiots chuckles coming from the audience as Guzman turned to his daughter with pity in his eyes. "Explain it to them, my corazoncito."

"They'll think I'm crazy."

"Don't worry," Scout assured her. "This is the Alpha Pack. We're all mad here."

Gus squared her shoulders and took a deep, steadying breath.

"Aurora was my twin. Two weeks after our twelfth birthday, she received her Sight." Her voice was still soft, but it carried throughout the large room. "It was horrible. She woke up in the middle of the night screaming about the children covered in blood. No matter what we did, she would not stop crying. The next night the news reported a bus carrying a group of children to the local zoo was involved in a head-on collision. Eight kids were seriously injured. Two died. They showed the crash site on the television. It was what Aurora had Seen.

"It went on like that for three years. Over and over, Aurora Saw blood and death. Eventually, she couldn't take it anymore. She ended her life with a razor blade."

Gus's expression hadn't changed, although her father was clearly struggling to hold himself together.

"I thought I was latent, and I was okay with that. I knew what being a Seer was doing to my sister, and I wanted no part of it. But then Aurora died, and I discovered what I can See."

"What do you See?" Talley asked, her face pale.

"I See Aurora."

Charlie wasn't sure he was following.

"Aurora. As in your dead sister?" Jase asked.

"Yes."

"Can you See her right now?"

Gus nodded to the empty space between her and her father. "Yes."

Okay. So he was following. Good to know.

"So this vision of Scout and the angel... Aurora saw it recently. As in after death?"

Excellent. Liam was following too.

"Yes, Your Highness."

Scout leaned forward, disbelief etched into the lines of her forehead. "Mr. Guzman, has she relayed visions from her dead sister before?"

"Yes, Your Highness."

"It's 'Scout', not 'Your Highness'," she said for at least the tenth time that day. "Have any of these from-the-grave visions of the future come true?"

"She Saw a white wolf take down the former Alpha Female in field surrounded by the dead and the wounded."

Scout's pale face managed to get even whiter. "Have *all* of them?"

"Yes," Gus said, finally gaining enough confidence to answer for herself. "In one way or another."

Scout screwed her eyebrows together. "I'm going to get stabbed to death by an angel?" She looked down the table where Joshua sat. "Do you have you something you need to tell me?"

Charlie's mind had made the same leap, but even as it did, he knew it wouldn't happen. Joshua was an Immortal and believed he was chosen by God to be an eternal warrior for heaven. That sounded kind of close to an angel. Add in how he liked to kill things with swords, and you had to wonder. That was, you would if you didn't actually know Joshua. As far as avenging angels went, he was pretty low key. And not only had he allied himself with the Alpha Pack in a way no Immortal had before, he'd actually joined their ranks. Liam had sworn him in as a Stratego, and Charlie considered him a friend. No way would he try to kill Scout.

Or at least, Charlie didn't think there was any way he would try to kill Scout. He had been wrong about who might kill whom before.

"I know you," Gus said, staring at Joshua. "You were there."

"Was he the angel?" Jase asked. From the corner of his eye, Charlie could see his hand inching towards the gun strapped to his side.

"He was dead." Gus's gaze roamed around the table. "And so were you," she said to Liam. Her eyes locked with Charlie's, and he felt himself flinch. The light brown eyes set off by thick, black lashes and tanned skin would have been startling enough without the added touch of crazy lurking there. "And so were you," she told him before moving on to Jase and Talley. "And you. And you. And—" Gus gasped, and her entire body started shaking. Charlie followed her unfocused gaze over his shoulder to see what could have possibly terrified the girl so much. What he found was Makya.

"Keep him away from me." Gus's voice was shaking even harder than her body.

Makya, who had been told at least a million times to never speak during a hustings, shot Scout a look. "What the hell is she talking about? I haven't done anything."

Scout ignored him. "Gus?"

"You have to promise me." She was inching backwards. Her father, who had been standing patiently at her side up until now, didn't look so much worried as resigned and embarrassed. "Promise me you'll keep him away."

"I promise." To prove it, Scout turned around and addressed Makya, who served as the Alpha Pack's Omega. "As your Alpha, I forbid you from getting close to this girl.

Consider it a Shifter Restraining Order. Get closer than 500 feet, and you'll be punished."

"But I don't even know that girl! I haven't done anything!"

Scout gave Makya a look that clearly said, "*I know you didn't do anything to the crazy girl. Just shut up and go with it.*"

By the time Scout turned back around, Gus was already gone. She'd finally followed her initial instinct and ran out the door, her father trailing closely behind.

Liam and Scout locked eyes. Neither of them did anything but look at the other, but Charlie knew they were communicating through their bond as mates. He wasn't exactly sure how it worked since the only explanation anyone would give him was, *"with your mate you just know"*, but there were times when he was certain the two of them were having entire conversations without either ever uttering a single word.

Of course, with Liam's laconic tendencies, that probably worked out for the best.

Talley nodded, a sure sign Scout was using her ability to speak directly to any Seer through the mind-to-mind connection usually reserved for Seers and Shifters during the full moon. Then, Talley looked at Jase and they did their own mate-to-mate silent conversation thing.

Six months ago the entire Alpha Pack gathered in Romania for the winter hustings. While there, Charlie had ventured into town on his own. He'd been surrounded by people who didn't speak a word of English, and he didn't understand a word of Romanian. He'd felt completely detached, almost as if he was a ghost roaming the streets of a place that wasn't just a different country, but a whole new world.

And yet he'd felt more connected to what was going on there than he did when everyone around him started their wordless communications.

Finally, after what felt like forever to Charlie, Liam called the next person forward.

Five hours later, things were finally starting to wind down, although you wouldn't have been able to tell from the red-faced man calling Scout every name in the book for telling him his daughter didn't have to marry the Shifter he'd promised her to when she was only four.

"Listen, I understand you made a promise, but one, this is twenty-first century America. We don't do arranged marriages," Scout said, annoyance shining in her pale blue eyes. "And two, she doesn't even like guys. Forcing her to marry one just so you can have access to..." She flipped through some papers. "Nevada? Seriously? This territory doesn't even have Vegas in it."

The man let loose a long line of four-letter words to describe his feelings towards Scout while his daughter looked like she would like very much to crawl into the nearest hole and disappear until the apocalypse hits.

"Mr. Mandel." The command was quiet and held absolutely no inflection, but the man stopped mid-sentence all the same. Liam had that effect on people. "We've reached our decision."

"She's my girl," Mr. Mandel spit out. "She will do what I tell her to do."

"Imogen," Liam said, speaking to the Seer instead of her father. "You See sickness, right?"

Imogen pointed to Aunt Rachel, who sat at the far end of the table. "She's running a low grade fever."

The old lady, who had been uncharacteristically quiet the entire day, waved away the comment with her hand. "It's a cold."

"It's bronchitis," Imogen said. "And if you're not careful, it's going to turn into pneumonia. I would go get some antibiotics soon if I were you."

Aunt Rachel glared, but didn't say anything since she was too busy coughing. As Liam passed her a bottle of water, he and Scout shared a look. At Scout's nod, he flashed a quick, small smile before turning back to Imogen and her irate father.

"Miss Mandel, we would like to extend to you an invitation to become an Alpha Pack Potential." Imogen's hazel eyes widened at the same moment the matching set her father possessed narrowed. "If you accept, you understand you will have to leave your current pack and move in here."

"My daughter isn't going to become one of your—"

"I don't have much. I can be ready to move to Kentucky in a matter of days," Imogen said, stepping away from her father. The look he shot her was enough to make her flinch, causing Charlie's gut to scream out a warning.

"You'll require an escort," he said, speaking up for the first time since the official hustings began. He normally didn't like to talk or draw attention to himself at these things, but he understood the body language of their new Potential and her father. If they let Imogen go alone she would be sporting some new bruises and possibly broken bones when she returned. "A member of the Alpha Pack will accompany you and help you move your belongings back here."

The relief and hope in her eyes was enough to make Charlie know he was right.

"Really? You guys don't have more important things to do than help me move?"

"Makya doesn't," Scout said. Makya audibly huffed, but Scout didn't even look in his direction. "He would be happy to help out, unless you were planning on making me promise he would stay the Hades away from you, which I wouldn't blame you if that's the case."

Imogen shook her head with so much enthusiasm her light brown braid flipped up onto her shoulder. "I would be happy to have Mr. Makya help out."

"Fantastic," Scout said, leaning back in her seat. "It's all settled then."

All this time, Mr. Mandel had been reaching new heights of anger. He stalked up to the desk, well beyond the line of what was considered a safe and respectable distance from the Alphas. Liam and Scout pretended like they didn't notice, but Charlie knew without looking he wasn't alone in putting his hand on his gun. Jase and Joshua were also ready to perform their duties as Stratego.

"You arrogant piece of trash," he said through clenched teeth. "You think you're so high and mighty for stealing something that never belonged to you. Well, know this, your time is coming. The fall of the Alphas has already begun. And I, for one, will dance on your graves."

CHAPTER 4

Maggie didn't belong at Sanders College. Never was that point more abundantly clear than when standing at the counter of the school's cafeteria.

The choice between gougeres and bourguignon would be so much easier if I had any idea what either of those things are, she thought as a woman in a pressed grey uniform waited not-so-patiently for her order.

"Bourguignon?"

"With or without?"

With or without what?

"With, please." *And I'll just hope that's with an unhealthy dose of cyanide.*

Maggie had saved money for three years, worked hard her entire way through high school, and sat through three interviews just to get into this school, and now she was hoping to be poisoned just so she wouldn't have to endure another day. Maybe her mother was right. Maybe she should be careful what she wished for.

The tiny part of her brain that was calm and understanding realized this was probably how a lot of people felt as they tried to adjust to college life, but Maggie wasn't in the mood for calm and understanding. She was in more of an overwrought and despair frame of mind, so she stuck with that train of thought, allowing herself to feel the full emotional blow of knowing there wasn't a single table in the cafeteria where she would be welcome to sit. At that moment she knew exactly how her ancestors must have felt standing in the middle of a whites-only restaurant. Except this time, it wasn't her dark skin setting her apart. There weren't a lot of black kids at Sanders, but she wasn't exactly the only one. She was probably the only one, though, who was here on a full scholarship and wasn't set to inherit more money than you could earn working sixty hours a week at McDonald's for the next fifty lifetimes.

You normally wouldn't expect to see a tiny unaccredited college in the middle of Kentucky filled with rich kids, but Sanders College wasn't a normal school. Sure, students declared majors and earned grades, but with a pass-rate of over ninety percent, it was obvious Sanders wasn't exactly known for its rigorous curriculum. What set it apart was an award-winning faculty. You could take English from a National Book Award nominee or Biology from the writer of multiple *New England Journal of Medicine* articles. No one was quite sure how Sanders attracted all-star professors, but after walking through the faculty parking lot and seeing how few classes they each taught a semester, Maggie thought she had a good idea.

But Maggie's experience over the past week taught her most Sanders students couldn't care less that their professor was the former CEO of the largest communications firm in the nation. They were just there to get their piece of paper and network so they would have someone to play golf with when they inherited their daddy's Fortune 500 company.

As Maggie watched a girl slide her hand up a guy's shirt, she amended that thought. Walking away with a piece of paper and a few more friends wasn't quite as important as getting a MRS degree for some of the girls.

Dating. Yet another entitlement of the rich.

Maggie was the exact opposite of rich and the thought of dating the progeny of a Real Housewife made her queasy. So what was she doing here?

She'd been working towards this ever since Ida York came to speak to her art camp in the eighth grade. Maggie had won a statewide art competition and the prize had been a full scholarship to a weeklong camp at the University of Tennessee. All one hundred of the eighth graders in attendance had sat enraptured as Ida talked about getting her art shown at the Museum of Modern Art in New York and the Tate Modern Gallery in London. She spoke candidly of her life as a world-renowned artist, dropping names of famous celebrities and f-bombs as she prattled on. A dozen different rings caught the light as she waved emphatically, and since they'd been studying textiles just the day before, the whole group could tell that she was draped in a high quality silk dress. When the time for questions came, Maggie, who had always sat quietly in the back of every classroom she'd ever been in, raised her hand.

"How did you become you?" It wasn't the most eloquent of questions, but Ida understood. Maybe she'd noticed Maggie's second-hand Wal-Mart clothes or the hungry look in her eyes, but Maggie knew Ida understood.

"I became me by working my ass off," Ida said. "I suck at book learning, but I did everything I could to make good grades in school, and I worked on my art every single day. Every. Single. Day. I missed every school dance and every house party because I was too busy working. And it paid off, because I was accepted as an independent study student at Sanders College on scholarship. And once I got there, I kept working my ass

off." She held her arms out to the side to indicate the collection of her artwork sharing the stage with her. "Did these take talent? Of course they did. But talent isn't what makes a great artist. Lots of people have talent. What will make you great, what will make you successful, is hard work."

Maggie had taken Ida's words to heart. By the end of her freshman year of high school she'd gone from being a C-student to having a 4.0. She started volunteering at the rec center the week after she got home from camp and was teaching art classes by the time she was fifteen. Even when she started working part-time at The Dollar Store, she kept up her grades and spent every available minute at the rec center. And Ida was proven right. It had paid off. She had gotten into Sanders and was studying under one of the most respected ceramicists in the nation.

The day she'd received her acceptance letter to the program, she'd cried. Knowing she would get the opportunity to study what she loved with some of the best minds in the industry was too much emotion for a girl who never believed she would be able to go to college.

She'd gone from ecstatic over being accepted to wishing she could leave so quickly it gave her whiplash.

"You don't want to eat that," a voice said from behind her. She turned to see Scout Donovan eyeing her tray with a crinkled nose. "I think they killed a horse, covered it in swamp water, and then gave it a fancy name so poor college students would be tricked into eating it."

"This is meat?" Maggie felt like kicking herself for not being brave enough to ask what the hell it was she was ordering.

"Only in the vaguest sense of the word." Scout stuck her finger in the glop sitting atop the mystery meat and gave it a poke. "What is this?"

The girl who had been standing at Scout's elbow smacked her friend's hand like she was a misbehaving child. "You can't just go around touching people's food."

"I'm not sure the USDA would actually qualify it as food," Maggie said, not minding at all that some strange girl had touched the contents of her plate. It wasn't like she was going to eat it anyway. Remembering her manners, she looked at Scout's friend and smiled. "Hi, I'm Maggie."

"Talley Matthews," the girl said, stretching out her hand. The tray was a little hard to balance with one hand, but Scout solved the problem by snatching it away. "Please ignore Scout," Talley said. "She was raised by wolves and has no manners whatsoever."

Talley didn't look like the kind of girl Maggie would have imagined as Scout's friend. Scout had all the cold beauty of a supermodel, and from what she could see, the bluntness of someone who had been so pampered her whole life she expected the world to simply bend to her will. Talley was just as beautiful, but in a much more normal, girl-next-door way. She was a little on the heavy side, her figure reminding Maggie of Duane Bryer's Hilda. The contrast of her dark hair, blue eyes, and freckle-dusted skin weren't as startling as Scout's complete lack of contrast, but compelling all the same. But the part about Talley a person immediately noticed was the kindness shining out of her eyes. You couldn't help but feel all the warm fuzzies when she was nearby.

Maggie hadn't realized the opposites attracting thing applied to friends.

"It's really nice to meet you, Maggie," Talley said, still holding onto Maggie's hand. Since Maggie hadn't really shaken many hands in her life, she wasn't quite sure, but she felt like this one had been going on for much longer than necessary.

"Same here," Maggie said, trying to free herself. For someone so sweet and innocent looking, Talley had one heck of a grip.

At some point during this exchange, Scout had somehow managed to get rid of Maggie's tray. Since it wasn't sitting on a nearby table, she could only assume Scout had handed it off to one of the staff people who worked in a waitress-like capacity. Without the tray to keep her hands otherwise occupied, Scout was able to cross her arms to complete her closed-off, forbidding look.

"You didn't come to the hustings," Scout said.

"Yeah, about that..." Maggie frantically tried to think of a way to tell the most well-known student at Sanders to leave her alone without sounding like she was telling her to leave her alone. "I'm honored, really. But I'm an independent study student. I don't really have time to be in your little club."

"You don't have time for my *little club*?"

Yeah, that probably wasn't the best word choice. Too bad life didn't come with a gum eraser.

"I'm sure it's really... amazing." Was that what secret clubs aspired to be? Amazing? Or was *really pretentious* a more appropriate compliment? "And I would love it if I could find the time or money to join, but as it is..." She shrugged, leaving off the obvious.

"Little club? My *little club*?"

Good God. What did she want? Did she think Maggie would fall to her knees, thanking her for sparing her a glance?

"Ignore her." Talley placed a hand on Maggie's arm. "She gets a little overwrought about 'the society'," she said, adding air quotes and a roll of the eyes. "But it really is amazing. At least we have real food." A girl in a tight dress and heels walked past them so closely Talley had to take a step to the side to avoid getting plowed over. "And no one wears Prada," she added, her eyes following the girl whose tray boasted a well-balanced lunch of an apple and bottle of water. "With the exception of Scout's desire to control the entire universe, we're a pretty laid back group."

Maggie had to admit Talley seemed more like her kind of people. She was wearing a pair of well-worn Old Navy jeans and a vintage Coca-Cola shirt. Once she stopped to think about it, Scout didn't exactly have the rich kid look going on either. In fact, the cut-off jean shorts and plain black tank top looked like they could have come from Wal-Mart. Maggie hadn't noticed how much Scout's clothing stood out from the typical Sanders fare until Talley pointed it out, probably because Scout didn't need two-hundred dollar jeans to convince people she was better than them. Her instantly recognizable scowl did a fine job of that all by itself.

"We're having a barbecue this afternoon." Talley moved the hand that had been resting on Maggie's forearm to link into the crook of her elbow. "Hamburgers, hot dogs, chips, and an entire freezer full of Grater's ice cream. Some honest-to-shiny real food with real people wearing real clothes."

"That sounds nice, but..." Maggie knew she should stop letting Talley lead her to the door, but the picture Talley was painting was so tempting.

"We live just outside of town," Scout said from somewhere over Maggie's right shoulder. "Lots of grass. You can get away from campus and actually breathe a little. No obligation. We just want a chance for us all to get to know each other a little better."

Maggie turned to meet Scout's pale blue eyes. "But why? Why would you want to get to know me?"

Scout's eyebrows rose just a fraction of an inch. "Because you're special."

CHAPTER 5

While Scout and Talley might have dressed like normal, middle class people, the vehicle waiting for them just outside the cafeteria gave away their true Rodeo Drive roots.

"Ladies." A wannabe Gap model opened the door to the shiny black Escalade dramatically.

"Excellent timing," Talley said, leaning in to give him a kiss on the cheek. Not satisfied with the fleeting contact, the guy turned and kissed her fully on the mouth long and hard enough Maggie had to look away, her cheeks flaming. They didn't stop until Scout made a comment about the strength of her gag reflex.

When Maggie finally looked their direction again, Talley's lips were red and swollen and little lights danced in her eyes. "Jase, this is Maggie. She's joining us for dinner. Maggie, this is Jase."

Jase's arm was snagged around Talley's waist. They were a pairing that didn't really look like they belonged together - Talley was too curvy to be a Gap model and Jase was too athletic and self-assured for a sweet girl-next-door type - but there was no denying they were in love. Maggie was a little surprised by the twang of jealousy she felt. She didn't have the time or desire to join the rest of her classmates in a boyfriend hunt, but she would have to have a heart of steel to not want someone to look at her the way Jase was looking at Talley.

"Glad to see you finally came to your senses," Jase said, nodding his head in acknowledgement of the introduction.

"I was starting to think we were going to have to send Liam after you since Scout forbade the rest of us from doing anything."

"Am I supposed to know this Liam guy?" They all said his name as if he was a Marvel superhero or something.

"Liam Cole." Jase waited for a reaction. Since the name didn't ring a bell, a quizzical expression was all she could muster. "She doesn't know who Liam is?"

His question was aimed at Scout, but Talley answered. "Maggie wasn't really looking to join any of the school's secret societies. Scout is recruiting her."

"Secret society?"

"Secret society," Scout said. "You know, the thing you're going to get kicked out of if you don't stop making out with your girlfriend in public and start getting me back to the farm?" Her eyes darted around the small campus. "All these people are making my skin crawl." When Jase didn't immediately move, she made a shooing motion with her hand. "Yip-yip."

Jase's eyes narrowed as he released Talley and moved out from in front of the open car door. "I am not your air buffalo."

"But everybody's got an air buffalo," Scout said, climbing into the backseat. "Mine is fast, but yours is slow."

"Where did we get them?"

"I don't know. But everybody's got an air buffalo."

Talley scrambled up into the passenger's seat and gave Maggie, who was crawling in beside Scout, a sympathetic look over her shoulder. "Ignore them. These two have taken twin language to an art form."

Maggie looked back and forth between the girl beside her and the boy getting into the driver's seat. Thanks to all the news coverage surrounding Scout's disappearance, she knew Jase was Scout's brother, but she couldn't see even a trace of resemblance. Scout was long and lithe, her appearance and attitude reminding Maggie of a beautiful but deadly icicle. Jase had a more rangy build and everything from his sun-kissed skin to sparkling green eyes brought to mind warm grassy fields.

"Go ahead and say it," Scout said.

"Say what?"

"We don't look like twins. It's okay. Everyone says it."

Maggie thought about it. Sure, she'd been cataloging their differences, but she would have never pointed them out. "I'm not everyone," she finally said. "I figure you guys know what you look like."

"It's okay," Jase said. "Scout already knows I'm the good-looking one. You don't have to tip-toe around it."

Scout reached over and flicked her brother on the ear. "You know, it's days like this I'm glad we don't share DNA. I don't have to worry about my future children turning out like you."

Maggie looked back and forth between the Donovans, trying to figure out what was going on. She felt like she'd accidentally skipped an important episode in this story arc.

"They're not biological twins," Talley explained, saving Maggie's poor brain from exploding. "Their parents got married when they were babies, and as they grew up, they somehow forgot they didn't have any shared blood and became the most twin-like twins you've ever seen."

Maggie muttered something about things finally making sense, but inside she was having a sappy, sentimental moment. Choosing your twin sounded like the most beautiful thing she'd ever heard. No wonder the two of them seemed so confident. How could you not be when someone picked you to be their other half?

It didn't take long for the town to fall away and give way to rolling hills. Maggie's grandfather had driven her straight to the school when he was moving her in, so she hadn't been able to explore the area surrounding the small town of Chinoe where Sanders was located. The fields were emerald green, rising and falling until they disappeared into a line of trees. Horses dotted the landscape, and even knowing nothing about thoroughbreds or the racing industry, she knew she was looking at animals who cost more than the fully quipped luxury SUV she was riding in. You could tell where one giant farm ended and the next began by the color and style of fence lining the road. When a black fence gave way to one made of stone, Jase slowed down.

"Fenrir Farm?" Maggie asked as Jase punched a code into a gate marked as a service entrance.

"Apparently when a farm costs over a million dollars, you have to name the stupid thing," he said as the gate swung open. "Liam thought it would be a good idea for Scout to name it, and Scout thought Fenrir Farm would be hysterical. This is just one shining example of why we encourage the Alphas to not think."

Something in Maggie's gut clenched at the mention of Alphas, but then the car turned off the main drive and she caught her first glimpse of the main house.

Once, in fifth grade, her class took a field trip to an actual southern plantation. The house was one of those grand white affairs with big windows and sprawling porches begging you to put on a sundress and enjoy some ice-cold sweet tea. The only differences between that house and the one at Fenrir Farm was the one she was looking at now was made of stone and wood and was at least twice the size of the one she'd seen in fifth grade.

Jase brought the Escalade to a stop by a pond so big it might qualify as a lake. The wooden dock was at least forty feet long, and it didn't come close to reaching quarter-of-the-way-across mark. A pavilion built in the same style as the house sat near the edge of the water. A fireplace filled the back wall and a bank of grills lined the far side. A guy who looked like he could be a professional quarterback was standing in front of one, flipping burgers, while a few other people lounged on the collection of picnic tables.

"This is beautiful," Maggie said, meaning it. Her hands itched with a desire to commit the scenery to paper. "Who lives here?"

Scout's face said she'd asked a stupid question. "We do."

"We who?" From the maps they'd flashed on CNN, she thought that Scout and Jase lived in another part of Kentucky.

"We," Scout said, spinning her finger around in an all-encompassing circle. "This is The Den. Well, the U.S. branch of The Den. The real one is still in Romania, obviously."

"Obviously," Maggie agreed, although she wasn't sure what she was agreeing to. This was Scout's secret society's version of a frat house? No wonder everyone wanted to join. Even though most of the school's population came from wealthy families, she doubted they all grew up in places like this. The freaking pavilion probably cost more than her family had seen in her lifetime.

"So... do you want to get out, or do you plan on sitting here and staring at my house all day?"

Maggie felt heat creep into her cheeks. "Sorry," she said, grabbing ahold of the door handle. "I've just never seen a house this big before. My home could probably fit in your garage." There was no use lying about it. If Scout and her fellow club members were really interested in having her join, then they probably knew all about her anyway. Wasn't that the way these things worked?

Even though she was surrounded by strangers and was so far out her comfort zone she couldn't find it with a telescope, Maggie calmed the moment her feet hit the ground. The storm the day before had left perfect late summer weather in its wake. The sun was warm, but not so much you felt like your skin was baking. A slight breeze danced over the perfectly manicured lawn making the whole place smell like a bottle of fabric softener. Maggie slid a toe off the edge of her sandal, a smile creeping up on her face from the feel of the soft grass and damp earth.

"Where is everyone?" Jase asked, hopping up onto the top of a picnic table and snagging a handful of potato chips.

A girl who stood taller than most every guy there made a big production of looking over both of her shoulders, her waist-long blond hair swishing back and forth from the force of the motion. "We're here," she said with a thick Eastern European accent.

Jase crammed a few more chips into his mouth. "Charlie isn't."

"Charlie hardly counts as 'everyone'." Maggie couldn't tell if she was actually disgusted with Jase or if her accent just made her sound like she hated the fact he was ever born. From the look a girl with orange hair and freckles shot Mother Russia, it was the second.

"He's out looking for Layne," said the orange-haired kid, who looked all of twelve.

What kind of college group was this?

"Where has the little demon run off to this time?"

The question came from Scout, who was predictably standing apart from the crowd, hovering somewhere between where everyone was gathered on the tables and the quarterback at what was really more of an outdoor kitchen than a line of grills.

Jase leaned back on his elbows and shot his sister a superior look. "If Lizzie knew where he was, Charlie wouldn't be out looking for him, now would he?"

Scout's oh-so mature response was to stick out her tongue.

"I don't suppose you can See lost things, can you?" The kid, who was apparently named Lizzie, asked Maggie.

"Lost things?"

"Sorry, we've been rude," the giantess with the accent said. "I'm Mischa, and this is Lizzie. We serve under Talley. Aunt Rachel, Michelle, and Marie," she nodded at an old lady and two girls who appeared to be in their late twenties, "also serve, but they don't normally stay here. They run the Archives, but they came in for the hustings." A head tilt in the other direction took Maggie's attention to another girl in her twenties. This one had a very pin-up look going on with her pouty lips and sexy curves, and she looked as socially uncomfortable as Maggie felt. "That's Imogen. She's new."

"Hi," Maggie said, trying to make sense of anything Mischa just said. At least she understood the names, even if there were more of them than she could remember. "I'm Maggie."

"Yes, we know," Mischa said. "You know, you really should have attended the hustings when Scout requested your presence. Trust me, I served under Sarvarna. I know what used to happen when someone disobeyed the Alpha Female. Thankfully, Scout is a bit more forgiving."

"Actually, guys..." Maggie thought that came from Scout, but she couldn't really hear over the words 'Alpha Female' repeating over and over in her head. "...Maggie isn't a Seer."

Lizzie's face lit up. "Another female Shifter? Awesome! No wonder you were avoiding us."

Maggie took a few steps backwards, but then her knees buckled and she couldn't move another step. From her count, there were thirteen of them. Thirteen. And one of them was the Alpha Female. Her eyes flicked to the guy who had abandoned the food to stare at her along with everyone else. Everything in her said this was the Alpha Male. There was literally nothing she could do. If it was only one or two, and if they weren't the most powerful one or two Shifters on earth, then maybe, but as it stood, she was completely defenseless. She couldn't outrun them, and she sure as hell couldn't fight them.

She was as good as dead.

That thought propelled her. She ran, kicking off her sandals as she went so she could move faster. If she could only make it to one of the barns she might be able to barricade the walls. It was a long shot, she knew it, but it was better than just standing there and waiting for the worst to happen.

She hadn't truly been watching where she was going, spending more time looking over her shoulder at the wolves who were still standing in place, giving her enough of a head start to make the chase fun.

Thank the heavens for arrogant mistakes, Maggie thought, finding just enough energy to quicken her pace. A second later, she realized that thought should have been directed at herself as she collided into another body with enough force they both went flying. Long arms made a cage around her; one hand sprawled over her head as they crashed to the ground.

Even before she could draw a breath, she was struggling.

"Shhhh.... It's okay," a male voice said in her ear. "No one here wants to hurt you."

Maggie might have laughed if she wasn't so close to the edge of hysterical tears. No one wanted to hurt her? Of course not. After all, Shifters were well known for inviting her kind to their dens for a friendly cookout.

Right. And Hitler invited the nice Jewish family from down the street over for the holidays.

"I swear on an allegiance older than time that my sword and the full power of the heavens will protect you."

Maggie stopped resisting, not so much because she felt safe, but because her brain was too busy trying to process what he was saying.

An age-old allegiance. Sword. The heavens.

She was being held down by an Immortal? An Immortal who was in league with the Shifters?

What. The. Hell.

"We come in peace," said a voice she recognized as belonging to Jase. She tilted her head, and sure enough, most of the Shifters and Seers had caught up to them and stood in a loose circle around where she was still trapped beneath the Immortal's body. Any fight left in her quickly jumped ship. There was no chance of escape. Either the Immortal was right, or she was dead. Whichever it was, there wasn't a thing she could do about it. She released a shuttering breath and said, "I would like to get up now."

"No running?" The Immortal asked. She shook her head and he pulled back just enough to look in her eyes. She took a second to note how young he looked. "I mean it," he said. "No one here is going to hurt you."

He did seem sincere, and knowing that made Maggie relax just a little.

A relaxation, which lasted all of two seconds.

"Don't make promises you can't keep, Joshua," said an unfamiliar male voice. As Joshua disengaged himself from her body, she could see the quarterback standing on the edge of the group, his body standing protectively in front of Scout.

Joshua stood and offered her his hand. "The moment she realized what you mangy mutts are, she freaked out and started running. I hardly think she's here by choice."

The quarterback's hard eyes didn't leave Maggie's face. She fought the urge to pull Joshua back on top of her as a shield.

"She entered the Alpha Pack's territory. Not a smart move for a Thaumaturgic."

"I didn't know." What came out was more of a croak than a voice, but Maggie was surprised anything at all had managed to make past her lips. "I... I didn't know I wasn't supposed to be here. I just wanted to go to school." The realization she might never see the campus again made her feel a strange sense of affection for the tiny clump of buildings. "I just wanted to go to school," she said again, this time tears evident in her voice.

She'd been discovered by Shifters. It was a fate all Thaumaturgics feared. No matter what their gift - an affinity for earth, wind, fire, or any other element or object - Thaumaturgics were no match for Shifters.

How did things go so horribly wrong? Was she getting what she deserved? Is this what came from wanting something too much, so much you were willing to sacrifice everything else to have it? For wanting more than what you have with such fierce longing you can't even consider failure?

"Liam," Talley said from her spot slightly behind Jase. When no one responded, she said it again, with more force. "Liam!"

The quarterback finally tore his eyes from Maggie and directed his intense gaze at Talley, who didn't flinch like Maggie would have. "The hamburgers are burning," she said calmly.

Liam blinked, looked back at the grills, then at Maggie, and finally settled on Scout.

"I don't like mine well done," she said. "The ends get all crunchy and gross." He didn't move, so Scout poked him in the arm. "You're scaring the poor girl, and I'm more than capable of taking care of myself and my people. If you keep insinuating I can't, I'm going to get irritated and throw you into a tree. Again."

Liam leaned down so his face was only inches from Scout's. "What makes you think that you're going to be less scary than me?"

Scout's eyes widened. "What? Me? Scary?"

The corner of Liam's mouth kicked up.

"Only when I want to be. I can be very nice and affable. After all, I got Maggie to come here, didn't I?"

"I'm going to go out on a limb here and guess that *Talley* got Maggie to come here."

Scout looked around Liam's shoulder, a scowl on her face. "Maggie, am I scary?"

"Terrifying," she answered honestly.

"More or less scary than Liam?"

Maggie took a moment to think about it. Liam looked like he could and would rip her apart with his bare hands. But the thing with Liam was, you would know he was coming. Scout was just as lethal, it was written in the muscles lining her body and the intensity in her gaze, but she would be subtler about it. If Scout wanted you dead, you would still be dead, but you might not know it until after the killing blow was delivered.

"More," Maggie decided. "But less intimidating."

Scout wrinkled her nose. "That doesn't make sense."

"It does if you've met the two of you," said Jase. "And for the record, those hamburgers are officially beyond salvation." He jerked a thumb towards the grill where flames were licking up towards the roof of the pavilion. Liam barked a four-letter word and took off running.

Talley caught Scout's eye. "You know he's probably going to do something stupid, like forget we have a fire extinguisher, and burn himself, right?"

After muttering something about men and their stupidity, Scout also took off, which left Maggie with... a bunch of Seers and Shifters.

Still, it felt like an improvement.

"Sorry, they can be a little intense sometimes," Talley said. "They don't mean to be. It just comes with being Alphas."

Maggie nodded as if that made perfect sense, although not much was making sense to her. She didn't know much about Shifters and Seers, only what her grandmother had told her when she was a little girl. At the time, she thought they were merely stories. Even a six year old knew boys couldn't really turn into wolves and girls couldn't really see things that weren't there.

But then she'd received her gift and learned magic does exist. When she asked her grandmother about the Shifter and Seer stories from her youth, she'd said, *"But of course they were true, Maggie-Chan. Why would I make up such a terrible thing?"*

The stories her grandmother told her really had been terrible. The Seers in the story would find where "our kind" was hiding with their abilities, and then the Shifters would come and pull them out of their homes to hold trials. At the time, Maggie thought "our kind" referred to humans in general, but she later found out differently. The word Thaumaturgic literally means "someone who can do miracles", but for some reason the Shifters translated it as "evil witch". Thus, the trials they held were actual, honest-to-Arthur-Miller witch trials, and more often than not of the stake and flames variety.

"I thought the Alphas would be older," Maggie said to Talley, fastidiously ignoring the others gathered round. True, they all looked more eavesdroppy than murdery, but Maggie knew if she acknowledged their presence, her fight or flight response would kick in again.

"Yeah, usually the Alphas are older and a little less Scout-like, but..." Jase shrugged off the end of the sentence, which left Maggie wondering about what had changed. "Listen, I know this went all sorts of wrong, but despite anything Liam might have said, we aren't going to hurt you. Really. We didn't even know you were a Thaumaturgic until like five minutes ago." He tilted his head to the side and gave her a once-over. Even if Talley hadn't been standing there, tethered to him by their interlocked hands, she would've known he was sizing her up instead of checking her out. "You are a Thaumaturgic, right? You're not like some other crazy supernatural person running around that we've never heard about, are you? Because I'm not really ready to accept anything else at this point in my life."

"You have to promise me, Maggie-Chan. No matter what, this is our secret. This is a truth only the bearer can know. Your grandfather is a good man, but the power doesn't live in him, so he doesn't know it exists. Do you understand?"

"Yes, Sobo," Maggie said, and at the time, she really thought she knew what she was promising. What did a twelve year old know about keeping a lifelong secret? "I won't tell anyone."

"I know you won't," her grandmother said, placing her wrinkled hands on either side of Maggie's face. "You are Sobo's good girl. It's why I've given you this gift."

Maggie didn't answer Jase. Her promise wouldn't allow her to confirm, but she felt like it would have been just as much of an insult to her grandmother to deny it. So, instead of saying anything, she concentrated on the way the sun filtered through his hair.

"No comment?" Jase guessed.

"Is pleading the Fifth an option?"

Joshua looked down at her, a smile on his lips. "For now. But you know I know, right?"

Of course she knew. The bond between Immortals and Thaumaturgics wasn't the same as the one between Shifters and Seers - Maggie's grandmother said the two couldn't exist without the other - but the ancient treaty between the two groups had become ingrained in the DNA of Immortals and Thaumaturgics. Maggie hadn't met an Immortal until Joshua tackled her to the ground, but she'd known deep in her soul what he was the moment she saw him. She could only assume it worked the other way.

Maggie tilted her head up, having to look pretty much straight up to see his face clearly. "I know that you promised to protect me."

"I did," he said, his big eyes solemn. "And I will. I swear my never-ending life on it."

CHAPTER 6

The hamburgers were beyond redemption. It didn't bother Maggie as much as it did everyone else. For one, she was still so freaked out she wasn't able to eat much anyway. And for another, she was a vegetarian.

"You don't eat meat at all?" Jase looked at her like she'd just announced a deep, passionate hatred of sunshine, sugar, and the Muppets.

"None at all."

"No cheeseburgers?"

"Nope."

"No hot dogs?"

"Nuh-uh."

"No steak? No chicken? Not even fish?"

"No meat." She couldn't believe this was throwing him even more than the fact she was a Thaumaturgic. Apparently, Scout had felt a "vibe" from her and they'd all thought she was a rogue Seer until Talley told them otherwise. How Talley knew, she wasn't quite sure, but for all of her gentle meekness, Maggie was pretty sure Talley was a kick-ass Seer. "I don't eat the flesh of animals."

Jase shook his head. "What about milk and cheese and ice cream. For the love of God, please tell me you eat ice cream."

"Vegetarian, not vegan." Being vegetarian was hard enough. She wasn't quite sure how vegans ever found something to eat. "It's not an animal rights thing for me. I just don't like the way meat feels in my mouth."

Jase made a noise, which might have been the start of a laugh, but he was drinking a Mello Yello at the time, so the noise that came out was more of a strangled cough. By the way his face was turning red, it might have been actual strangulation. Scout hit him on the back a couple of times, but the swats were fairly ineffectual since she was doubled over laughing.

Maggie took a sip of her water as if she had no idea what the hysterics were about.

Talley caught her eye from across the table. "You did that on purpose," she accused.

Maggie struggled to maintain a look of innocence. "Maybe."

She still wasn't comfortable, but then again, rarely was Maggie comfortable around a large group of people she didn't know. But it was her experience that with the exception of a handful of people (Jase quite possibly among them), most people felt that way. At least she was at the normal I-don't-like-people-I-don't-know level of discomfort instead of the lamb-among-wolves place she'd been before. Everyone seemed to be making a big production of being super-nice to her and putting her at ease. Even Scout and Liam were putting in an effort, although they had to be reminded on occasion to not scowl.

Actually, once she thought about it, she realized this was the most comfortable she'd been since pulling out of her driveway a week ago.

Semi-comfortable while eating with a pack of Shifters. Maybe this was one of those trippy dreams she had when she took too much allergy medicine.

"See? They're not so bad," Joshua said as if he could read her mind.

"They're the nicest Shifters I've ever met."

Joshua laughed, and it was the exact sort of laugh you would expect from a guy who was all big eyes and long limbs. The noise startled a bunch of ducks who squawked back at him as they left the pond en mass.

"How did you get tangled up with the Alpha Pack, Joshua?" Shifters didn't persecute Immortals like they did Thaumaturgics, but it was still strange to see one interacting with a pack of them like they were friends.

"You can pick family, but not your friends."

"I think you said that backwards."

"Oh. Right." He offered her an Oatmeal Cream Pie from the snack cake assortment on his plate, and she took it. "These guys here," he said, indicating the rest of their company with a wave of his hand, "are the good guys. Recently, they had to stand their ground against the bad guys, and since I'm not particularly fond of bad guys, I helped. It worked out so well, they offered me a position, and I accepted."

Maggie blinked. "You're Alpha Pack?"

"I'm a Stratego. Do you know what that is?" Maggie shook her head. "It's like a general in the army. Most of these guys are at the same level of Shifter hierarchy I am, but no one outside of this group is above me." She didn't know what to say. Was he trying to scare her? Let her know he wasn't really on her side after all? "Maggie, I'm an Immortal, and I'm one of the top ranking people in the Alpha Pack. This ain't your mama's Alpha Pack. Things really are different." He looked around and Maggie did the same. No one was paying attention to them. They were all too busy talking and laughing... and in the case of Jase and Scout, arguing. "You could be a part of this," Joshua said.

"I'm not a Shifter, and I'm not a Seer," she said, her attention caught by the older lady who was giving a man a firm talking-to. He was a good four inches taller than her and had at least fifty more pounds of muscle, but his expression was a blend of chagrin and fear. "I don't have a place here." And she didn't want one. Not really. Her place was at Sanders College. Her *future* was at Sanders. That was more important than a place where she might be able to breathe and be her true self.

As people began to finish their food, Maggie could tell something was wrong. She caught Jase, Joshua, Liam, and Scout all checking their phones with regularity. Conversation at the table where she was sitting started dying off, everyone's attention somewhere beyond the horizon. Even though she didn't possess enhanced hearing or sight, she knew the moment something changed because everyone else got to their feet at the same time. About ten seconds later, a boy popped over the hill behind the pavilion. He looked young, maybe thirteen, but he was running like an Olympian. He skidded to a stop a few steps in front of Liam and Scout. Maggie had never seen him before, but she felt certain his face wasn't normally such a sickly shade of white.

"The gym. Dead." His words came in whooshing pants. "He's dead." And then he broke down into tears.

Maggie decided she must have reached her shock quotient for the day because her only thought was that of all the reactions she was considering, taking off all her clothes wasn't one of them. Scout, on the other hand, tore off her tank top and shorts before the boy had even stopped speaking. Her underclothes quickly followed, and before Maggie could mentally note how her lines differed from the selection of other naked bodies she'd seen over the last week, Scout was gone and a wolf stood in her place.

The horizon dipped and wavered in front of her.

"Deep breaths." Joshua's voice came to her from the other end of a tunnel. "Breathe in through your nose for four counts, and then out through your mouth for eight. Come on, Maggie. Stay with us."

Maggie tried to breathe. She really did, but there was a *wolf* standing where Scout was supposed to be.

"You Changing, too?" Jase asked.

"No, it'll waste too much time," Liam said. "I'm still not as fast as she is. I'll run down with you guys. If she needs backup once we're down there, then I'll Change." He grabbed onto the hair at the back of Scout's neck and crouched down in front of her. "We're coming behind you in the truck. Don't do anything stupid until we get there."

She growled and the sound went straight to Maggie's spine where it crawled around like a million little ants. And then Scout broke out of Liam's hold and was off, sprinting across the field.

"Jase. Talley. Joshua. Truck. Now." Liam's face and voice were completely devoid of emotion. His eyes, on the other hand, couldn't hide the fear and anger raging inside him.

Jase pulled on Talley's hand, but she stayed rooted to the spot.

"Tal, come on. Liam needs us."

Talley's eyes were filled with tears when they met Maggie's eyes. "I'm sorry," she said. "You need to come with us."

"I need to what?" Maggie didn't want anything to do with a dead body. "No, sorry." But Jase didn't let her refuse. He grabbed onto her arm and dragged her along behind him and Talley. She knew better than to try to pull away. The relaxed, cooler-than-cool Jase was gone. The person shoving her into the back seat of the Escalade was one of the highest-ranking members of the Alpha Pack. He expected his commands to be followed, and Maggie didn't want to find out what would happen if life didn't meet his expectations.

Liam had the vehicle in gear and moving before Jase even shut the door. They took off across the field just like Scout had, ignoring the paved paths and damage they were surely doing to the carefully manicured lawn. Scout was fast, but the Escalade was faster. They got there just in time to see her slip in between the doors that had been left slightly ajar. Liam didn't even cut the engine. He just jumped out and trailed after her. Jase was reaching for the door handle when Talley said, "It's not Charlie."

"You sure?" Joshua asked.

"Positive."

Jase closed his eyes and took a deep breath. When that didn't seem to help, he took another.

"It's okay." Talley said quietly, her hand rubbing slow circles on his back. "It's not him. It's okay."

"Where the hell is he?" Jase asked through clenched teeth.

"Probably still looking for Layne. Don't worry. We'll find him. Soon."

Maggie had no idea what was going on. Well, she was pretty sure there was a dead body somewhere and Talley didn't think it was their friend, but beyond that, she was lost. Did this happen often with the Alpha Pack? Were dead bodies just a regular part of day-to-day life? Was this some elaborate scare tactic they were using on her? Were they just setting her up? Maybe planning on pinning some random dead body they'd already killed on her so they'd have an excuse to tie her hands and feet together and throw her in their lake or pond or whatever in the hell it was?

She should leave. They were all distracted for the moment, so much so she decided they either were really upset a dead body was found on their property or they were the best actors she'd ever seen. She wasn't sure enough to risk her life, and that is what she would be doing by staying there. She knew the smart thing to do was to jump back into the Escalade where Liam had conveniently left the keys, and drive as fast and as far as she could, but instead of being smart, she followed along behind Joshua as he led them into the barn.

Maggie had grown up in the south, but she was a city girl. Not that Monarch was really all that much of a city, but she hadn't spent her childhood running around farms or anything, so she didn't have a really good working knowledge of barns. She'd always thought of them as little wooden buildings with dirt floors and some horses or cows. The thing she walked into was at least twice as big as the house she grew up in, and there were no horses or dirt in sight. Instead, it looked like an exclusive, posh gym you might find on the upper west side of Manhattan. Or at least, it was exactly what Maggie assumed exclusive, posh gyms on the upper west side of Manhattan looked like. Brand new weight benches, stationary bikes, treadmills, and machines she couldn't even fathom the purpose of filled the bottom floor. The loft - or what would have counted as a loft if this was an actual barn - only went about halfway across the length of the main level and had a glass wall so whoever was doing whatever it was they did up there with their wall full of medieval looking weapons could look down on the rest of the building.

Or if you were on the bottom floor, you could look up and see the dead man suspended above the matted floor.

CHAPTER 7

Whenever Charlie found his nephew, he was going to kill him. His entire day had gone to hell the moment Lizzie sent him a text to say he needed to tell the teachers it was okay to let her grab Layne's homework. He'd done as she asked, and then he'd gone out to find where in the hell Layne was if he wasn't at school.

Not that Charlie knew what to do with the kid once he found him. Most days Charlie felt like he wasn't old enough to take care of himself. There was absolutely no way he was capable of taking care of a punk-ass thirteen year old with more issues than a former Disney Channel star.

Over the past three hours Charlie had trampled over every inch of the farm. It would have been more efficient and caused his leg a lot less grief to take the ATV, but he'd abandoned that route after only ten minutes when he picked up on a strange, chemical scent. They were just a few days away from the new moon, so his nose wasn't exactly at Superman levels, but it was strong enough to know it was one of those scent-eliminating things hunters used. He might have thought some poor guy had mistakenly wandered onto their property if anything had been in season and it wasn't just a few feet from the house. Since he couldn't follow the trail if the scent was overwhelmed by the smell of gasoline, he jumped off the four-wheeler and started walking the property. Knowing someone would purposefully mask their scent and then sneak onto Alpha Pack property was bothersome enough, but when he came across a second scent, Charlie got worried.

The second trail was more recent, and unlike the first one, he could pick up on a hint of the original human scent beneath the ridiculous amount of perfumes. It was like someone had poured bottles of every artificially fragranced thing they could find in a tub and then taken a bath.

He had intended to call in some reinforcements, but he'd left his phone somewhere again, and he wasn't about to run back to the house and lose the trail, so he'd continued on. Now, three hours later with nothing to show for his efforts, other than a gnawing sense of hunger, he questioned the validity of that decision.

He was ready to give up when he recognized Jase's Escalade parked by the gym. He was a few feet from the door when it burst open and a girl spilled out, doubling over and emptying up the contents of her stomach onto the ground the moment she was outside.

"Maggie!" Talley called as she came running out behind her. The moment she saw Charlie, Talley squealed and raced past the girl, wrapping her arms around his waist and squeezing with more strength than he thought she had in her.

"Geez, Tal. I've missed you, too." When she didn't stop her attempt to crush his internal organs, he said, "You remember you have a boyfriend, right?"

As if on cue, Jase came out of the barn. It took him about three steps to get to Charlie. Instead of pulling his girlfriend off his cousin, he wrapped his own arms around Charlie.

"Not only is this weird and creepy, it hurts." Charlie thought his liver might be damaged, and he was confident he'd have bruises on his arms thanks to Jase.

Jase pulled back and then punched Charlie as hard as he could on the arm. "Where the hell is your phone?"

"I don't know," Charlie said, rubbing his shoulder. He wondered if he could grab an ice pack out of the fridge without Jase calling him a pansy. "I think it's..." During the course of becoming the meat in a Jase-and-Talley sandwich (which was even more wrong once he thought about it in those terms), Charlie had forgotten about the puking girl, but the sound of the barn door opening yet again pulled his attention back in that direction.

Joshua stood next to her, his hands tucked in his pockets and an aw-shucks-I'm-not-dangerous look on his face. The girl didn't look like she was buying it at all. In fact, she looked like a cornered animal, and Charlie knew from experience that when a smaller, less dominant animal was trapped by a bigger, scarier one, they generally did something dangerously stupid. He knew Joshua wouldn't hurt anyone unless they deserved it, but he also knew accidents happened. Charlie didn't like accidents.

"Who is your friend, Joshua?" The girl's head jerked up. Her eyes were so black Charlie couldn't tell where the iris stopped and the pupil began. It made her look even more shocked and frightened, which was saying something, because he thought she was about to completely freak out before he even saw her face.

"Charlie Hagan!" Joshua called out. "You live! Excellent!"

Charlie looked down at Talley, who was still semi-wrapped around his waist. "You thought I was dead?"

"No. No, of course not," she said.

Charlie raised an eyebrow.

"Okay, maybe a little."

"We only thought you were partially dead," Jase said in some crazy accent. "But you had to live for true love, so..." He shrugged. "We brought you back."

The new girl blinked her pretty black eyes. "Does he ever make sense?"

"Nope," Joshua said as Charlie said, "Not really." Talley was a little more generous with her assessment of "sometimes."

Since Talley had finally let him go, Charlie walked over to where the new girl was standing. "Since my so-called friends completely lack anything resembling manners, I suppose I'll have to introduce myself." He stuck out his hand and plastered on the smile he'd spent weeks perfecting. If you didn't look too horribly close, it could almost pass as real. "I'm Charlie Hagan."

"Maggie McCray," she said, her hand small and soft inside his own. "I know we just met, but I'm glad you're not dead."

The carefully practiced smile felt a little less practiced. "Well, it's good to know you don't want me dead, Maggie McCray. It seems like a rather auspicious start for our friendship."

Maggie McCray reminded him of the vibrant glass birds his mother collected. Part of it was the clothes she wore. The dress was old-timey looking, a bright yellow fabric that buttoned down the front, came to a cinch at the bright red belt around her waist, and then flared out to stop just above her knees. She was wearing a pair of bright green sandals, and her toes were painted a shocking color of orange.

Her clothes were so distracting you almost missed how she was quite possibly the smallest full-grown human ever. Charlie was a far cry from Liam-the-Giant-sized, but she still only came to his chest. Everything about her looked small and delicate and untamed, from those coal black eyes that tilted down slightly at the corners to the wild springs of short, tight black curls having a party on her head. Her dark skin looked soft and fragile, and for some reason Charlie couldn't help but think about how it would taste.

Probably because it looks like it belongs on an ad for fancy chocolate, he thought, trying not to stare at where said skin was trembling over the pulse in her neck. *Maybe this is how the vampire legend was born. Some idiot saw a hot girl with skin he knew would taste like heaven and was stupid enough to take a bite.*

Which was a completely inappropriate thought. This was the Seer who didn't approach the Alpha Pack when she first moved into their territory and then refused an audience with Scout at the hustings. He shouldn't be thinking about how tiny and pretty and tasty she looked.

The barn door swung open again, stopping him from doing anything really stupid, like licking the poor girl's neck. He barely had time to catch it before it slammed into the side of his head. He might have cursed about that, but he was too busy delighting in Maggie's wide-eyed awe of his Shifter reflexes. He didn't let himself think about how there would be even more wonder and surprise on her face if it had been Liam or even Jase standing there. He might not be the most dominant Shifter, but he wasn't exactly an Omega. If she wanted to think he was a scary Dominant, then he'd let her. It would do her some good to be afraid of him and everyone else in the Alpha Pack.

"Charlie, thank God," Liam said as he emerged from the barn the two of them had renovated into a place for the Alpha Pack to work out. Charlie knew he meant the words even though there was nothing in his voice that sounded like relief. Liam didn't say things he didn't mean. "I thought you were dead."

"You know, you all keep saying that. It makes a guy wonder."

Liam rubbed the back of his head. "You need to see this," he said. "All of you do."

Charlie could feel Maggie stiffen beside him, which was ridiculous because she was at least four inches away. "I've already seen, thank you."

"No, there's more." Liam rubbed the back of his head again and Charlie felt the familiar tendrils of dread sneak through his body.

"Whatever it is, it's Shifter business. It doesn't have anything to do with me."

"I'm sorry, Maggie, but you really need to see this."

"What do you See?" Charlie asked her.

"I don't."

"You don't what?"

"She doesn't See," Jase said.

"But Liam just said—"

"Little 's' see. Not big 's' See," Liam clarified. "Maggie is a Thaumaturgic. And an artist."

The last part sounded like an accusation, and Charlie wasn't the only one to pick up on it.

"What does that have to do with anything?" Luckily, Maggie sounded confused instead of like she was challenging the Alpha Male. That could have gone very badly.

"It means they left a calling card," Liam said. "A giant, painted calling card, and I need you to come and see it."

Maggie's eyes flicked over to Jase's Escalade.

"Running will just make you look guilty." Maggie wouldn't look at him, but the big, shaky breath she drew into her lungs let him know she heard him and was considering his words. "Liam isn't the kind of guy who would ask you to do something if he didn't really need you to do it."

He'd asked so very little of Charlie over the years and always for a purpose. Anyone else in Liam's position would have made Charlie run the gauntlet just for the satisfaction of seeing him do it. Hell, most people in Liam's position would have killed Charlie two years ago instead of treating him first as an ally and later a brother. There wasn't anything Charlie wouldn't do for Liam now, including making sure Maggie followed his orders. He would rather get her inside with the power of persuasion, but if he had to, he would resort to other means.

He really hoped the persuasion tactic would work.

"Come on," he said, once again plastering on that practiced smile. "How bad can it be?"

Black eyes met his. He thought she was going to say something, but instead she puked again.

CHAPTER 8

Maggie had missed the space-age kitchen the first time she'd been in the barn thanks to the distraction of the dead body. It was nestled off in a corner just inside the door. The new guy, Charlie, came back from the shiny Goliath-sized fridge with a bottle of water. "I also grabbed you one of these," he said, dropping a piece of cellophane-wrapped candy into her hand. "My mom swears by peppermint as a cure for unhappy stomachs. I don't know if it really works, but I thought it was worth a shot."

"Thank you," she muttered, appreciative of both the water and the mint. Her stomach wasn't really upset - well, not any more upset than the rest of her - but it would at least help with her breath. Maybe it was the real reason he'd handed it to her and he'd just made up the stuff about his mom using it as medicine so she wouldn't be embarrassed.

Maggie caught a flash of white out of the corner of her eye, which was all the warning she had before a large white wolf soared past her and plowed into Charlie's chest. "Oooaf!" Charlie stumbled back a few steps, but remained on his feet. "Hey there, Scout. Showing off for our new guest are we?" She licked his face a few times and he pushed her away, complaining about wolf saliva and doggie breath.

Maggie sucked a little harder on her peppermint.

They were standing outside the opening of the kitchen, so it only took a few seconds for him to walk over to the fridge, pull it open, and grab one of those giant containers of lunchmeat you can only find at one of those big box stores like Sam's Club or Costco. He pulled off the top and sat it down in front of Scout, who quickly devoured the entire contents.

"Anyone want to fill me in on what's going on around here? Not that I don't appreciate the whole Charlie Love Fest, but it's starting to freak me out."

Maggie couldn't believe he'd missed it since it was the only thing she could see. She was purposefully standing with her back to it, but every time she blinked, there it was, hiding on the inside of her eyelids. The back of her neck was staying all prickly as if it could feel the man's dead eyes looking straight at her.

"Vincent Barros is dead," Liam said from the kitchen where he was filling a Spider-Man themed popcorn bowl with water.

"Barros..." Charlie tapped his fingers against his thigh. "Pack Leader from Wyoming, right? He was supposed to talk to you guys about some territory issues, but never showed up."

Liam nodded. "He was murdered."

Charlie flinched, the first real sign of emotion she'd seen in him. Sure, he'd smiled and grimaced at all the appropriate places up until that point, but he looked like an elaborate robot programmed to do what was expected of him.

Input: Meet new person. Action: Smile, shake hand, and make polite small talk, complete with witty rapport.

Input: Discover new person is a Thaumaturgic. Action: Assess her from head to toe, determining the best ways to end her life.

It wasn't so much the memory of the dead body as the realization she might be the next body hanging from the ceiling that had her throwing up the second time.

Her stomach still quivered, but it was more from fear, embarrassment, and anger than a need to regurgitate the contents of her stomach, not that there was anything left to barf up. What she couldn't figure out was why she was so damn embarrassed. Sure, if she'd puked on the feet of a guy at school it would have been just cause for humiliation, but Charlie wasn't just some random attractive stranger. He was a Shifter, and that cold, dead look in his eye told her he wouldn't have any problem sending her soul to the afterlife. She felt certain hers wouldn't be the first he'd sent there, which was all kinds of disturbing. He couldn't be much older than her, maybe twenty or so, but he looked harder than anyone her age should. Even Liam, who was the exact sort of person you would avoid meeting in a dark alley, had more compassion and sympathy in his gaze than Charlie.

Of course, the humiliation might have something to do with the degree of attractiveness in said random attractive stranger. The Alpha Pack already looked like the pages of a fashion magazine exploded. Jase looked like he just stepped away from a pretty-boy photo shoot; Talley might actually be a plus-sized fashion model (Maggie was certain she'd seen her somewhere before); Liam was more action hero than pretty boy, but still the kind of person a camera couldn't help but love; and Scout was the epitome of high-end fashion model. A bit of make-up and some outrageous clothes and she was a double-page spread in *Vogue* just waiting to happen. Even Joshua was strangely fascinating to look at. It wasn't hard to picture him in nerd glasses and suspenders in some pretentious Target ad.

Yet even though she was standing in what could pass as the waiting room at Ford Models, Maggie couldn't keep her eyes off of Charlie. His bone structure was amazing. Sharp cheeks, a classic Greek nose, and a long, slim jawline created a play of highlights and shadows across skin which had obviously spent a lot of time in the sun. His eyes were similar to Jase's, a true grass green surrounded by dark lashes. But while Jase's eyes said, "Let's have fun," Charlie's eyes whispered secrets. They were terrible, horrific secrets, but they were secrets all the same, and Maggie was fascinated by secrets. Almost as fascinated as she was with his mouth.

It should be illegal for boys to have mouths like that. His lips were perfectly shaped, their lush softness was an intriguing contrast to the sharpness in every other facet of his being. Even pursed together in concentration they were beautiful, but when his smiled...

Dear God, when he smiled. Maggie could only imagine what would happen if he really, truly smiled. It would probably blind everyone on earth. That was probably why he didn't actually let loose and do it. He was saving the world, one fake smile at a time.

"And we know he was murdered how?"

Jase cleared his throat, his pallor taking on a decidedly green tone. "Because it's really hard to stab yourself multiple times by accident."

Maggie's stomach quivered yet again. She had only caught a glimpse of the body, and hadn't really paid enough attention to see how he died. Although, once she thought about it, she supposed all the blood across his midsection should have been a clue.

The only indication Charlie heard the other Shifter was a slight raise of the eyebrows. "Body?"

Jase pointed up, and Charlie's eyes followed the motion. There was no doubt the moment his eyes landed on Vincent Barros. His Adam's apple convulsed in his throat, making Maggie feel a little bit better about her own reaction.

"What the hell did they do to the body?"

Liam ran a hand over his face, and for the first time, Maggie noticed he looked more ashen than he had earlier. Perhaps dead bodies weren't as common around here as she thought. Or maybe it was the just the state of this particular dead body that had everyone so upset.

"It's been... posed," Liam said, his voice rough. "You all need to come upstairs." His fingers caressed the silvery white fur on top of Scout's head as she wound around his ankles. She was tall enough he didn't even have to bend down to do it. "Even you," he told the wolf whose pale blue eyes were focused on his face. "Care to come on two legs?"

Scout gave Liam's leg one last nuzzle and then trotted off towards the door leading outside. Liam stood and watched until she was out of sight, and since the rest of them didn't have anything else to do, they watched him.

That wasn't quite true, Maggie thought. Charlie still watched the dead body as if he expected it to get up off the chains holding it and do a dance. She couldn't decide if she thought it was brave or crazy to look at it for so long. She'd lasted all of two seconds, and that was two seconds too long, in her opinion. There was a chance she'd never be able to have a good night's sleep again.

"Let's go," Liam said, turning to lead the way up the stairs. Jase was close behind him, Talley's hand held tight in his. Joshua wasn't too far behind, and Charlie started to follow behind him, but he stopped at the base of the stairs.

"Maggie?"

She jerked back, startled to hear her own name.

"You coming?" he asked.

"No thanks." Was he insane? There was no way she was going up there. "I've had enough dead body for one day, thank you. I'll just..." What would she do? They were pretty far from the picnic area, but she wasn't opposed to walking. If everyone else was still there, surely someone would drive her back to school.

"Sorry, but that's not an option." Maggie jumped again, this time because Scout had popped up behind her like some sort of more-terrifying-than-usual Jack-in-the-Box. Scout was tugging on the edge of her shirt, probably because it was the only thing she was wearing. It was big on her - if Maggie was guessing she would say it belonged to Liam - but Scout was a tall girl. If Maggie tried hard enough she would be able to see the other girl's butt cheeks. "I've got to grab some pants out of the locker room," she said, although Maggie wondered why she bothered. It wasn't like everyone hadn't seen all there was to see of Scout when she decided to go all Alcide Herveaux earlier. "Wait for me. We'll go up together."

Maggie considered just making a run for it, and had almost talked herself into it when Scout emerged from a door on the opposite wall, a pair of leggings making her decent once again.

"I don't want to," Maggie said. It made her sound weak and the furthest from brave you could get, but she didn't care. She didn't want to see the body. Or smell it. She was pretty sure she could already smell the rot and decay, but she was telling herself it was just a figment of her imagination to keep the lining of her stomach where it was.

Scout stopped directly in front of her, which meant Maggie had to tilt her head back to see her face. Normally Maggie didn't get too upset over the fact she wasn't even five feet tall, but she hated how Scout could intimidate her just because God gave her legs the same length as Maggie's entire body. "Like I said, not an option." Cold eyes bore into hers and Maggie realized it probably wasn't just the extra seven or so inches that made Scout so intimidating. It could also have something to do with the way those teeth she was baring could turn into razor sharp Maggie-shredding weapons.

"I'm not one of you," Maggie said, trying to make her voice sound as mature and authoritative as possible. Just because she felt like a little kid facing off with the Big Bad Wolf didn't mean she had to act like one. "This isn't my business, and I'm not going to let you make it my business." The more she talked, the angrier she got. How dare they drag her out here in the middle of nowhere where she would be surrounded by Shifters and death? "I don't know what you want from me, but you're not getting it. I don't care who you are or what you can do to me. This?" She gestured her arms around wildly, trying to encompass everything from the multi-million dollar estate to the elaborate barn-turned-mega-gym to the Shifters and Seers who inhabited the place to the dead body upstairs. "It's crazy. It's not part of my world, and I'm not going to be dragged into it, no matter who or what you think I might be."

Maggie was so worked up her breath was coming in rough pants. Scout, on the other hand, looked bored.

"You're not part of this world? This isn't your business?" Scout leaned forward, her head hovering above Maggie. "You willing to put money on that?"

CHAPTER 9

It was even worse in person. Charlie wasn't quite sure how that was possible since it had been the most disgusting and disturbing thing he'd ever seen when he was looking at it through the window, but there was no doubt it was at least ten times more gruesome when you were actually standing in the room.

"Are we sure this it's Barros? I mean, he's kind of..." Charlie thought there was probably a word for how a person looked after Leatherface from *The Texas Chainsaw Massacre* got ahold of you, but his brain was too busy trying to talk him into turning around and walking away from this scene to think of it.

"It's him," Joshua confirmed, holding his phone up next to the dead man's neck. "The tattoo matches."

It was a testament to how screwed up all this was that no one asked Joshua where or how he'd pulled up a picture of Barros's tattoo so quickly.

"What do we know about him?"

Liam scrubbed a hand over the top of his head. "Not much. We contacted the Barros Pack when he didn't show at the hustings like he was scheduled to. They said he was coming to ask for some land bordering their territory and wasn't claimed by anyone else. Should have been a simple, no drama kind of thing. When I told them he hadn't shown up, they started calling hospitals and police stations, thinking he'd been in a bad wreck or something. They said he wasn't the kind of person to just flake on meeting with the Alphas, and the pack has no enemies to speak of."

"What about other enemies?" Even though he would rather go back downstairs, out the door, and walk straight to his bedroom where he might try to forget this day ever happened, Charlie knelt down in front of the body. Someone had cut off the lips and part of the ears. The bottom half of the body was wrapped in wire, and a hook had been inserted into each shoulder. The hooks were connected to chains coming off the ceiling. They held the top part of the body just a foot off the floor. To keep the head from flopping back, it had been fastened onto the shoulder. "This doesn't look like a pack vendetta to me. It looks personal."

"It looks crazy." Jase was holding onto Talley's hand so tightly her fingers sported stripes of purple and white. Charlie worried about sensitive Talley being near something so disturbing, but she seemed to be hanging in pretty well, considering the circumstances. Jase might have wanted it to look like he was clinging onto his girlfriend to comfort her, but Charlie could clearly see it was Talley who was keeping Jase upright.

Charlie had heard Scout and the Thaumaturgic coming up the stairs, but his heart still stuttered when the door opened. He took comfort in knowing the whole situation was at least affecting him on a subconscious level, because on the surface he wasn't feeling anything. It was like his brain knew the responses he should have - disgust, fear, anger - but he couldn't actually feel them. He felt as detached from the horror surrounding him as he did everything else in the world. He wasn't a psychologist, but he met with one once a week and was pretty sure this was one of those things that would make the good doctor decide to schedule a few extra appointments if he mentioned it.

"Crap." Scout threw a hand up over her hand and mouth. "It's just as bad in human form." Her hand muffled her voice, but Charlie could understand her. It was Scout. He always understood her, even when he really wished he didn't. "How long do you think he's been dead?" When no one answered, she looked around from person to person, meeting each of their eyes to indicate they should be bringing forth the information she wanted. "Seriously?" she finally asked when the Thaumaturgic just looked at her like she was a raving lunatic. "No one even has a guess?"

"Sorry," Jase said, "you haven't forced me to take a forensic biology class yet, but I'm sure you can fit that into your master plan for my life at some point."

Scout didn't give into the argument Jase was clearly trying to pick. "It'll be too late then," she said. "God, I wish Toby was here."

Five words. Five little words. I. Wish. Toby. Was. Here. Each one of them a knife in Charlie's soul.

Pain is better than nothing at all? Screw that. Pain sucks.

It wasn't the words themselves. Charlie thought the same thing at least a million times a day. It was the careless way they tumbled out of Scout's mouth as if *she* felt nothing at saying them. And that was wrong. Everyone should feel the same empty void as Charlie did anytime his brother's name was mentioned. It wasn't fair they were able to move on with their lives when his had stopped on that field in Minnesota over a year ago.

Joshua walked over, knelt in front of the body, and pulled a stylus from his back pocket. For reasons Charlie would probably never understand, it had a fuzzy pom-pom thing and googley eyes like kids use in arts-and-crafts projects stuck on the end. The contrast of the cheerful blue fuzz monster and the mutilated dead body was enough to tip the whole scene from unreal to surreal.

"Blood has congealed, but the body is still in rigor mortis," Joshua said, pointing to some dark purple spots on the man's arms. "If I was guessing, I would say he's been dead maybe twenty-four to forty-eight hours. All the... *work* was done to the body post-mortem."

Scout had wandered over to Liam and tucked her arm around his waist. His arm was slung over her shoulders. It looked very casual and thoughtless, but they were clinging to each other for support just as much as Talley and Jase were. Being Alphas meant they couldn't show their weakness and need for one another, even when surrounded by friends.

Well, friends and a Thaumaturgic who was standing on the other side of the room, her focus on the painting Charlie hadn't noticed until now.

"Does he actually know what he's talking about?" Scout asked.

"It's Joshua," Liam answered. "Who knows?"

"I know," Joshua said, standing back up. "I happen to be quite well versed in this sort of thing. I watched every episode of every season of every incarnation of *CSI*."

Scout closed her eyes on a sigh. "Joshua—"

"Which is what led me to taking a few classes in criminology and forensic science a few years ago." His smile was unrepentant.

While they were talking, Charlie made his way over to where Maggie was standing. She was either trying very hard to block out everything going on around her or was completely absorbed with the unsettling painting, which definitely hadn't been there when he'd sparred with Layne the night before. Either way, she had no idea he was behind her. He stood close enough to feel the heat coming off her body. She was so small he could easily look over her head to see all the disturbing details of their newly acquired piece of art.

"That's the biggest painting I've ever seen," he said, and felt a strange sense of satisfaction when she jumped at the sound of his voice. Her pulse quivered against the skin of her throat.

Maggie sent a sharp glance over her shoulder and then took a step forward. Away from him. "For the style it's actually really small. The canvas is only six foot by eight foot. DaVinci's *The Last Supper* was fifteen feet tall and nearly thirty feet wide."

Charlie took two steps forward. "Fifteen feet? It's a good thing they didn't go with that scale. It would have never fit in here. The ceiling is only ten feet high." Maggie tried to slide to the left, but he followed her. The step put him so close his fingers were brushing against her arms. Her skin was satiny smooth and he found himself raising his left hand slowly, purposefully dragging it against her bared flesh. She shivered, little goose bumps breaking out across her skin. "You seem to know a lot about art," he said, his voice a near growl.

"That's because she's an art major." Scout said from behind his shoulder. "She's very talented. I saw the doodles in her notebook the other day." Feeling crowded, Charlie tried moving away from the girls, but there wasn't really anywhere for him to go. He was trapped by Scout's body, the Thaumaturgic, and the wall. "If I remember correctly, it was a naked guy whose chest was ripped open. A girl wearing polka-dotted underwear stood beside him munching on his heart."

Maggie saved him from a claustrophobic meltdown by stumbling back until she was literally pressed up against the painting. Her eyes flicked over to the stairs.

"No matter how fast you run, we can run faster," he warned her in a low voice.

"I didn't do this." The way she was trembling reminded him of a cornered rabbit. The coyote inside of him wanted her to make a run for it. He was eager for the chase. "I... I'm not even a good painter. Give me a brush and some canvas and I'll prove it."

Charlie tilted his head, his focus once again captivated by the twitching pulse in her neck. "All that would prove is you're not stupid enough to show us you're a master painter when we're looking to hang one for murder."

All the color drained from her face, and even though he didn't think it was possible, she started shaking even harder. "I didn't kill anyone. Yes, I like to draw. And yes, sometimes it gets a little macabre, especially when I've had to endure the roommate from hell and her douchebag boyfriend, but I didn't do this," she said, thrusting a finger at the painting. "I didn't even know you guys were here until this afternoon, and even if I did, I couldn't have done that to that man. Look at me." It was a ridiculous request. Like he could look anywhere else. "Do you think I could carry a dead body twice my size? I couldn't even carry the painting."

"That just means you had help." The coyote urged him to pounce, but he held himself still, refusing to give into the animal inside of him. That way only led to death and heartache. He'd had enough of both to last a lifetime already. "Confess now, little rabbit, and we may be convinced to go easy on you."

"I didn't do it." The tremble had spread to her voice and a single tear streaked down her face. The sight of it caused an honest-to-goodness growl to build in his throat.

"Stop it."

His prey was suddenly blocked. He made a move to remove the obstacle, but the obstacle wasn't having it. Scout grabbed his shoulder, her nails digging into his flesh. "Damn it, Charlie. What the Hades is wrong with you?"

"I won't let her hurt you," he said.

Scout snorted. "She's five-foot-nothing, and if she weighs a hundred pounds dripping wet I'd die of shock. She couldn't hurt me if she wanted to."

He finally pried his attention away from his trembling prey. Scout was wearing her I'm-surrounded-by-morons face, her annoyance and exasperation so strong it seemed to be coming off of her in waves. How could she be so blasé? Had she already forgotten everything they had been through? The people they had lost?

"She's a Thaumaturgic, which means she's hardly helpless. Just ask Vincent here."

"I. Did. Not. Do. It." Maggie's voice still quivered, but it wasn't weak. Charlie's coyote perked its ears. His little rabbit still had some fight left in her. Good. It was disappointing when the prey just lay there waiting to die.

While Charlie and Scout were having their little standoff, the other members of the Alpha Pack gathered around. Liam stood just beside Charlie, his muscles tensed as if he was ready to strike. Talley moved up beside Maggie and was reaching for her hand, as if she was trying to comfort the girl. Jase, as always, was beside Talley. Joshua was ignoring them all as he examined the painting.

"She's on here," Joshua said, his face inches from the piece of canvas which nearly reached the ceiling. "Look." He pointed to one of the figures Charlie hadn't paid much attention to the first time. His attention on that section had been completely occupied by his own face contorted in pain. "She's right here. If she did this, why would she paint herself as one of the victims?"

"Vanity?" Jase guessed.

"Distraction," Charlie answered.

"I didn't—"

"I know you didn't," Talley said, squeezing Maggie's hand. "It's okay. Don't worry. The boys are going to believe you and stop being jerks now." He gaze swung to Charlie. "Aren't you?"

Talley's eyes were full of chastisement, and for a moment Charlie allowed a bubble of guilt to burst to the surface, but it quickly vanished. Sure, if Talley said the girl didn't do it, then she didn't do it. It wasn't exactly like she could get away with lying when Talley was holding her hand. Talley's position as a Soul Seer meant she could get into Maggie's mind and See all the thoughts and emotions floating around in there. Still, that didn't mean Maggie wasn't a threat. It just meant she wasn't this particular threat.

"I don't know her, and I don't trust her," Charlie said. "And I want to know how her face got on that damn painting if she really didn't know about us until today, because I know we didn't know who or what she is."

"Charlie..." The admonishment came from between Scout's teeth but her eyes were sad. He knew she was thinking he wasn't the friend she had grown up with and loved, but he couldn't find it within him to feel bad about that. The truth was, he wasn't that guy any more than she was the girl he'd fallen in love with all those years ago. Things changed. They had changed. And maybe he was less sympathetic than he'd been then, but the old Charlie had stood by and watched as people around him died. New Charlie wasn't going to let that happen again, even if it meant he had to be an asshat.

"The paint is still wet." Joshua's comment didn't match up with everything else going on in the room. At least, it didn't to Charlie. And the the-killer-is-in-the-house tone with which he said it didn't help matters any. "Not the whole thing," Joshua clarified. "Just Maggie." He touched the spirals of dark hair on the picture gingerly. "Not wet-wet, but definitely not dry. And it looks... different. Everyone else has so much detail there isn't any doubt who it's supposed to be, but not Maggie. I think they were in a hurry or maybe didn't know what she really looked like."

Scout shot Charlie one last behave-or-else look and walked over to stand next to Joshua. She leaned in close, her nose just inches from Maggie's painted form. After long, thoughtful consideration, she said, "I have no idea what I'm looking at. I'm pretty much the exact opposite of artsy." She straightened back up and put her hands on her hips. "Maggie? What can you tell us?"

"I didn't do it."

Scout sighed, the youth and weariness in her face contrasting each other even more than normal. "Yes. We know that. What we don't know is anything about art.

Could you please give us your expert opinion?" Maggie hesitated, and Scout's face hardened. "You do realize you're in this now, right? There isn't any going back to school and pretending everything is normal. Your face is on this painting. Somewhere out there, there is a murderer who knows who you are and that you're different than normal humans." She nodded towards the body still posed a few feet away. "Do you think whoever did that is going to take mercy on you just because you didn't ask to be here? Do you think they're going to care that you would rather be a normal girl doing normal girl things?"

Maggie blinked back the tears threatening to fall from her eyes.

"Listen, I get it," Scout said. "I've been there, done that, and have the souvenir scars to prove it. And I can promise you one thing, trying to hide from the evil in this world isn't going to make it go away. The only way to win is for the good guys to fight back, and for me to fight, I'm going to need your help. So, what can you tell me about this painting?"

Maggie shook her head slowly. Charlie was already opening his mouth to put in his own words of encouragement when she spoke up. "Sorry, but I don't know much. I'm into ceramics and drawing. Oil on canvas really isn't my thing."

"But you know something about it, right?" Talley asked. "I mean, you know it's oil on canvas. I'm not sure all of us knew that already."

Jase raised his hand. "I did."

The corner of Talley's mouth kicked up. "With the exception of Jase, of course."

"I had to take an art appreciation class," he said like a five year old explaining how he knew stop signs are red.

"For the love of all things shiny, if Jase is our resident art expert, then please," Scout folded her hands together, "please help us. You're are only hope Maggie Wan Kenobi."

The entire room seemed to hold a breath waiting for Maggie's reply.

"I'm not familiar with the work," she finally said, "but I think it's a replication of a classic. I'm going to guess around the seventeenth century or so. They were all about big, religious paintings back then." She walked over to where Scout stood, taking a path that deliberately veered far away from Charlie. "I think it's supposed to be Lucifer and his followers getting kicked out of heaven."

Scout took a step back and tilted her head. "So... if I'm looking at this right, that makes me the devil, right?"

"You should have taken that Jesus's sister thing and ran with it like I told you," Jase said.

"You only like that scenario because you think it makes you Jesus," said Joshua.

Jase assumed Scout's tilted head pose. "Sure beats being Beelzebub, although I think Reverend Jessup may have called that one a long time ago."

Charlie hadn't really considered the Lucifer aspect of the painting before, but since Maggie mentioned it, it made sense. The angel thing was pretty much a given with all the winged babies hanging out in fluffy clouds. The main guy - if a person with that dress-like thing, those long, golden curls, and a face that would make Anne Hathaway look butch could be considered a guy - had something like a fifteen-foot wingspan and a giant sword. But he wasn't really using the sword. Instead, he was doing some crazy ballerina stance on Scout's shoulder.

The top part of the painting was all bright and clean and heavenly. On the other hand, the bottom part was, if Maggie's theory was correct, quite literally hell. A red glow came from the bottom of the picture, and smoke billowed up from it. In the smoke was a tangle of bodies, their faces contorted in fear and pain. It was a disturbing image on those merits alone, but when one of those terrified faces looked just like the guy you saw in the mirror every morning, it crossed right on over into Crazy Freak Out Land.

"It's what Gus saw," Charlie said, realizing why the whole scenario seemed familiar. "Do you think—?"

Talley shook her head. "No way. I Saw Gus. She couldn't have done anything like this."

"I don't think whoever did this has ever seen any of you in real life before," Maggie said, bringing everyone's attention back to her, including Charlie's. She wasn't shaking any more, which disappointed the coyote but relieved the man. "They got your bodies all wrong."

Scout lifted an eyebrow in the perfect imitation of Liam's do-you-take-me-for-an-idiot face. "Well, they did give me a penis."

"I think it's a tentacle." Joshua got so close his nose brushed against the canvas. "Yep. That's a tentacle. You don't have penis, just a kraken between your legs."

"What kind of person does this?" Talley asked. "How does someone get so broken they could do something like this? What would make them hate us so much?"

Joshua continued examining bits and pieces of the painting in that up-close-and-personal way of his. "Maybe it's not about us."

"Those sure do look like our faces," Liam said. "Makes me think it *might* be about us."

"Well, obviously it's about us, but that doesn't mean it's *about us* about us."

Jase looked at Talley. "Is he being absent-minded-professor confusing or I-dropped-acid-in-the-70s-and-I'm-having-a-flashback confusing?"

"The first," Talley said. "I think."

"He's saying this might be a movement against the Alpha Pack, as an institution, not necessarily Scout, Liam, Jase, Talley, and Charlie," Charlie said, pointing out each of them in the painting. "He's saying the Shifters of the world may have an enemy, and that enemy just declared war." Maggie's near-black eyes showed only the smallest trace of fear. "Now, let's see... Who are the enemies of Shifters and Seers?"

"I didn't—"

Maggie's words were cut short by the sound of a body being slammed against something solid. The body belonged to Charlie, and he was surprised to see Joshua was the one who had him pinned against the wall.

"That's enough," Joshua said, all traces of flaky genius gone. "Thaumaturgics aren't your enemy, and this girl most certainly is not. You have been rude and cruel and it will stop now. She is under my protection, and I will not allow you to continue to frighten her for your own sick amusement. Do you understand?" Charlie couldn't say anything. He was too in shock over both Joshua's newfound aggression and his own actions. “Do you understand? Answer me, Charlie Boy.”

“I understand,” he forced out. He craned his neck as much as Joshua’s hold would allow. “I’m sorry,” he said, meeting Maggie’s gaze. “I’m normally not so...” What was the word for what he’d become? Ass seemed too civil by far. “It’s been a bad day.”

Maggie wouldn’t look at him, but she nodded her head in acquiescence, which he supposed was the best he could hope for, all things considered. He really didn’t know what it was about her that got under his skin. He wasn’t normally known for torturing people just because he could. Back when he actually noticed girls, he’d been fairly popular with the prettier sex. His little black book wasn’t quite as thick as the one Jase tossed out the window when he finally got the one girl he truly wanted, but he’d always had someone to take to ballgames and movies. At the time, he was a “sweet guy.” He knew because every single one of those girls took the time to tell him so. Now? Well, no one was telling him he was sweet, but he thought that was because he hadn’t been on a date in...

Crap. When was the last time he had a real, honest-to-God date? It had to have been the year he was at college. He’d dated a girl semi-seriously for a while, but his heart hadn’t been in it even then. She was supposed to be his one last wild, carefree fling before settling down with Scout. His grand plan had been to wait until she graduated high school, and then he was going to let her know how it was going to be. The two of them, forever and always. But then she’d gone and fallen in love with someone else and everything changed. Charlie’s forever and always had died one Sunday night by the lake under a full moon.

For that first year, he'd had plenty of excuses to not date. None of those who currently served as the American contingent of the Alpha Pack was really going out for dinner and a movie while they quietly and then not-so-quietly battled the former Alphas. But what about the past twelve months? They had been busy, but not too busy. Everyone else had started living real lives, but not Charlie. He hardly left the farm, and he certainly hadn't taken the time to go out and find himself a girl.

Maybe that was it. Maybe he was just out of practice. Almost all of his interactions were with other Shifters these days, and while they may have appeared to be human on the outside, inside they were different. He didn't think so when he was younger, but he knew the truth now. He had an animal inside of him, and that animal had instincts and desires that were as far from human as you could get. He'd become so accustomed to being around others like himself he'd forgotten how to be around normal people.

He glanced at Maggie again. She was watching him warily, and he felt the animal's satisfaction. He tried to tamp down the reaction, but instead of locking itself into a box with everything else he'd tried not to feel for the past two years, it only flamed higher.

Fine. If he couldn't control the coyote around her, he simply wouldn't be around her anymore. "I think it's time we get Maggie back home." And away from him. "She's a civilian, and scenes like this aren't for the innocent."

Charlie felt better already. No one would want the poor girl to have to hang around, especially after the way he'd treated her. Joshua would probably jump at the opportunity to get her out of there and back to the normal world.

Charlie's first indication that things weren't going to go quite so smoothly was the way Liam was aggressively rubbing his hand over his head.

"I'm sorry," Liam said to Maggie. "But I'm not going to be able to let you leave."

CHAPTER 10

Maggie was a prisoner. Sure, they dressed it up all pretty, giving her a room in the giant mansion and making speeches about how it was all for her safety, but underneath it was still an orange jump suit and leg shackles situation.

"It's only for a few days," she told herself, unpacking the overnight bag Jase and Talley had helped her grab. Luckily, Reid hadn't been in the room at the time, probably off doing naked things with her boy toy. At Jase's instruction, Maggie scrawled out a long, rambling note about having to stay with a friend for a few days who was scared to be in her apartment alone. Maggie tried to explain that Reid would know it was a complete and total lie, but in the end, Jase's argument of *"for God's sake, she's not your mother"* won.

Instead of a closet, the room had one of those big wardrobe things that, when the circumstances were right, contained a hidden magical kingdom. The dark, heavy wood on the doors was etched with a detailed forest scene. It would have been nice and serene if there hadn't been a wolf peering menacingly around one of the trees. Inside, Maggie found a bunch of satin-padded hangers. "No wire hangers... ever!" she intoned dramatically.

She nearly jumped out of her skin at the sound of a male chuckle. She wheeled around to see Scout and Charlie standing just inside her door.

"Sorry to interrupt, Joan," Scout said, "but we need to go over a few things with you."

Maggie draped the straps of her favorite dress over one of the ridiculously expensive hangers, focusing super-hard on the task so she wouldn't have to look at Charlie. "Things?"

The room they'd given her was bigger than her dorm room, big enough there was a little sitting area in front of a large, tiled fireplace. Scout indicated one of the leather wingback chairs with a tilt of the head. "You mind? It's been a long day."

"It's your house," Maggie said, smoothing non-existent wrinkles out of the dress which now hung all alone in the impressive armoire.

"It is, isn't it?" There was a thump, and Maggie turned thinking something had fallen, but it was only Scout dropping herself rather ungracefully into the chair. "I keep forgetting that. I feel like an adult is going to walk in here at any moment and ask me what the Hades I'm doing in their house." Scout looked around the room as if she'd never seen it before. "That is my floor," she said. "And those are my ugly curtains. And that..." She tilted her head as she regarded a framed picture sitting on the mantel. "What is that?"

"I believe it's the cast of a Disney show. The one where the kids have to raise themselves because the mom is too self-involved and the dad is too clueless," Charlie answered.

"Angel?"

"Angel."

Scout's smile was sardonic. "Well, that is definitely *not* my framed picture, but the rest of it..." Her hand twirled above her head to indicate the entirety of what surrounded them. "The rest of it is mine. Well, it technically belongs to the Alpha Pack, but since I'm the Alpha Female, I get to lay claim, I suppose." She threw her legs over one arm of the chair, leaning back into the not-so-cushiony cushion. "But this room, Maggie, I'm giving to you. Do with it as you please." Scout's eyes darted back to the mantel. "Especially if what you please is to get rid of that thing. Feel free to just toss it in the trashcan. No one is going to care."

"Angel will care," Charlie corrected.

"As I said, no one who gets an opinion on these matters will care."

Maggie didn't know who Angel was, but if Charlie's face was anything to go by, Scout was underestimating or ignoring just how important her opinion was.

"Thanks," Maggie said. "But I don't really care how the room looks. I don't plan on staying long enough to redecorate or anything."

Scout and Charlie exchanged a look and Maggie felt her stomach relocate itself.

"I only have enough clothes for three days, max," she said, knowing it was a lame and stupid excuse, but she was grasping for whatever she could get. She couldn't stay here. She wouldn't. She didn't trust the Shifters, and Charlie..

Her eyes darted over to the guy sitting on the edge of the antique table by the door to her room. Her stomach decided to once again change locations, the effort causing her pulse to speed up. She'd been wrong before. Charlie wasn't some emotionless robot. He felt things. Angry, homicidal things, and they were directed at her. He terrified her more than all the other Shifters combined.

"Listen, I know things were a little crazy and confusing earlier, but someone wants you dead," Scout said. She was still sprawled out across the chair, looking for all the world as if she had nothing more to worry about than scheduling her next manicure. "I don't know what kind of Thaumaturgic power you're packing, but I'm going to guess if it had any combative ability whatsoever, you would've used it on us already, which means you need our protection."

Maggie's chin tilted up. "I can take care of myself." After all, she'd been doing just that for the last few years anyway.

"Whoever this is took down a full-grown Shifter. A wolf Shifter who happened to be a Pack Leader," Charlie said. Maggie went back to concentrating on putting away her clothes so she wouldn't have to look at him, but she could feel his eyes boring into her. "He wasn't shot from a distance, and Liam didn't smell chemicals or drugs. The best we can guess, he was stabbed." A floorboard creaked, and Maggie looked up to find Charlie standing just a few inches away. She made the mistake of looking up into his cold, green eyes. Her lungs forgot how to work, and she worried she would actually pass out at his feet before they remembered how to do their job.

At least it would be better than puking on him again.

"These people know what they're doing," he said, leaning towards her ever so slightly. "Do you want to die that way? Do you want someone to do that to your body? Because I promise you, if you leave here, and they find you, there isn't anything you're going to be able to do on your own to stop them."

"Why do you care?" The words were out of her mouth before she had time to stop and think about how saying them might be a not-so-great idea.

Something flashed in Charlie's eyes, but it was gone before Maggie could figure out what it meant. "I care because it's our duty to protect."

"Shifters and Seers," Maggie said. "Your duty is to protect your own. I'm not one of yours. I'm the enemy, remember?" He'd certainly known back in the barn. It took all of her will power to not tremble in front of him again. She might not be some strong, fierce Shifter like Scout, but she wasn't going to be a timid victim either. She'd already decided, no matter who the enemy was - some faceless killer or a member of the Alpha Pack - she wasn't going to show fear. She would face it head on and damn the consequences.

Assuming those consequences didn't include her untimely demise, which she supposed was a real possibility.

Not for the first time, Maggie prayed she would wake up in her dorm room and realize this was all a crazy dream inspired by accidentally inhaling too many paint fumes.

"We don't give a crap if you're a Thaumaturgic." Maggie had almost forgotten Scout was still in the room, which was insane. She was the freaking Alpha Female. How could someone forget her? "And we care because we're decent human beings. In general, we think people shouldn't go around killing one another. It's bad form."

"Your kind has been hunting down and killing Thaumaturgics for centuries, yet you don't care whether or not I might be one? I'm sorry if I'm having a little trouble believing you."

Charlie had backed off just a bit while Scout was talking, but he was still standing close enough Maggie could hear the little puff of air escaping in a nearly-silent snort. "What do you know about what has happened in the Alpha Pack over the past year or so?"

Maggie didn't feel the need to answer. Of course she didn't know anything about what had been happening in the Alpha Pack. It wasn't exactly like they sent out a newsletter to the supernatural community to keep everyone abreast of what they were up to.

"Things have changed since Scout and Liam became Alphas," Charlie said. "We don't kill little girls just because they might Change one day, and we don't give a damn about other supernaturals. We've got enough problems of our own to worry about your shit."

It wasn't exactly an olive branch, but Maggie didn't doubt his honesty. She couldn't imagine Charlie ever saying something just to make her feel better, and if he would, she hoped he'd be a bit more diplomatic in his attempt.

"I can't stay," she said, although even she could hear the fight gone from her voice. "I don't belong here."

Scout laughed. "This is an eighteen-hundred acre horse farm that cost *millions* of dollars. None of us belong here." She dropped her feet off the arm of the chair and swung her body around, bringing her elbows to rest on her knees. "Stay with us, Maggie. Talley says you're good people, and she's never wrong about this sort of thing. I've done a lot of crap in my life, and have seen a lot of people die, and I just can't do it anymore. I can't let you leave knowing you might die and it will be my fault for not keeping you safe." Maggie and Scout were about the same age, but at that moment Scout's striking pale blue eyes looked much, much older. "Please. Let us protect you."

Maggie looked around the room, from the finely detailed crown molding to the king-sized canopied bed. She'd never been in a room this nice in her entire life, and if she took Scout up on her offer, it would be hers for a little while. If she left, what would she have? The tiny room she shared with Reid? And would she even be able to function out there knowing some crazy killer knew who she was and had thought about what she would look like in the throes of death? Sure, she wasn't completely comfortable surrounded by Shifters, and Charlie did something truly terrifying to her insides, but she was starting to believe they wouldn't hurt her.

"All of my stuff..."

"Joshua will take you to get some more clothes and stuff tomorrow," Scout said. "Just get what you need, and don't worry about shampoo and stuff that we can run and grab from Target."

Maggie tried to mentally calculate how much it would cost to buy a complete overhaul of toiletries, hair products, and make up. She stopped when she started feeling queasy.

"I have a break in between my classes tomorrow," she said to distract herself from all the money that she didn't have to spend. "I'll stop by and grab a few things then."

"Yeah, about that..." Scout looked at Charlie, who shifted from one foot to the other and turned his attention to carpet. "You can't go to class."

"I can't—" There was a ringing in Maggie's ears, which had to explain why she thought Scout had just said she couldn't go to class. "I have to go to class. I'm on scholarship. I'm an independent study student."

"Can't you just study independently here?"

Maggie caught her tongue just before it told Charlie to go have sexual relations with himself.

"In order to keep my scholarship and my position in the independent study program, I have to keep better than a 3.0 grade average and attend more than 80% of my art classes. I *have* to go to class tomorrow."

"The campus isn't secure. Trust me. We've done what we can, but it's a public place filled with over a thousand students. There is no way." Scout shrugged back against the chair. "I think it would be best if you just held off on school until after this is all over."

Maggie shot an icy look Scout's direction.

"Are you quitting?"

"Well, no. I'm the Alpha Female. It would be seen as a sign of weakness, and—"

"So you can keep going to class, but I have to become a drop out?"

"It's not that big of a—"

"No." Maggie felt like she was trapped on one of those merry mixer rides from the carnival. She was off balance, unable to get her bearings, and every time she was slung toward one of the mirrors surrounding the ride, all she could see was a distorted, warped version of what her life was supposed be. "I can't quit school. I *won't* quit school."

Charlie looked at her like she was some hysterical child. "Is school really more important than your life?" he asked more than a little condescendingly.

"School - this school, this program - is my life." Steeling her nerves, Maggie met Charlie's eyes. "Whatever the risk is, I'm willing to take it. I won't drop out."

"Dear God, my parents would love you," Scout said, which caused Charlie to throw a questioning look over his shoulder.

"Come on. '*School is more important than life*'? I think dad might actually have that tattooed somewhere."

"You're not helping."

"And you're not listening. I'm not Sarvarna, which means she's not a prisoner here." Maggie wasn't sure who Sarvarna was, but the way Charlie flinched at her name gave her some idea what type of person she was. "Maggie wants to keep taking classes, so we're going to let her."

"And when she goes missing and turns up three days later strung up in our barn, what then? Are you going to be able to shrug it off and say it was her choice?"

No one said anything for a long moment. Scout was staring at the arm of the chair, her lips pressed together, her face a study in human emotions. Charlie stood staring at Scout, the robot once again in control. And Maggie looked back and forth between the two of them, wishing like hell she could get the image of her own body carved and posed out of her head.

Finally Scout broke the silence with a sigh. "Liam is sticking around until we catch whoever is behind this mess. He can shadow her while she's on campus."

"I'm sure the campus police will be cool with some large, scary-looking guy just skulking around campus. No way will it raise any red flags and get us unwanted attention."

"Then we'll just get him enrolled in all of her classes." Scout shook her head as if agreeing with herself over such a splendid plan. "That could totally work."

"Sorry, but it won't."

Scout shot Maggie a look to remind her she was talking to one of the most powerful Shifters in the world. "Yes, it will. We're the Alpha Pack. We have connections."

"Unless your connection is with Hendrick Stroud, it isn't going to work." And while Maggie didn't doubt the Alpha Pack's connections extended throughout the world, she felt certain the mercurial art genius wasn't one of them. "Most of my classes are art labs in Rosa Hall, and only independent study and grad students are allowed inside. Stroud is the only art prof who isn't mentoring an independent study student right now."

"Hendrick Stroud..." Charlie's eyebrows darted down. "Like the guy who illustrated one of those new runs of *Batman*?"

Hendrick Stroud was a world-renowned artist, and the four issues of *Batman* he'd illustrated were some of the best selling comic books of the last few years, but still Maggie was surprised Charlie knew who he was. "Yes, that Hendrick Stroud. Sanders recruits some of the best artists in the world to be on their staff. It's what draws in the rich kids. And they'll do anything to keep their rockstar artists happy, including letting them get away with only accepting one independent study student every five years. Stroud just graduated his last one in May, so it'll probably be another four years before he picks out another."

"So, he teaches like illustrations and stuff?"

"Yes, he's the drawing professor."

Charlie paced a couple of steps, his hand squeezing the back of his neck. "I'll do it," he said, looking over where Scout sat.

"You'll do what?"

"I'll go talk to this Stroud guy and get registered for all of Maggie's classes."

Maggie tried to trample down the strange fluttering in her chest. Spend all day, every day with Charlie?

Oh hell no.

"Were you listening to me? It's not happening. Stroud won't accept you unless you're some sort of undiscovered genius."

"You can go tomorrow," Scout said to Charlie. "I'll get Liam to cover her for the day, and then you can pick up on Tuesday."

"Seriously, guys. You heard me say this isn't going to work, right? I mean, I am talking aloud and not just in my head?"

"You'll need to reassign some of my duties here if I'm going to be hanging around campus all day."

"Joshua?"

"He'll whine like a baby that you're making him stay awake in the daylight hours."

"True." Scout shook her head slowly as a wide grin spread across her face. "Which is exactly why I'm making you tell him."

"I hate you," Charlie said, his words carrying the exact opposite of malice.

"You love me. I'm your queen." On that announcement, Scout sprang from the chair in a move so quick and graceful it looked like a special effect. "Well, I suppose my work here is done. Maggie, give Charlie a copy of your schedule. Liam will meet you downstairs in the morning to shadow you until Charlie can get everything worked out."

"And when Charlie can't get everything worked out?" Which he wouldn't. Maggie didn't feel confident about too many things at this point in her life, but on this fact she was certain. There was no way Charlie was weaseling his way into the world she'd been working towards for years in just one day.

"It's Charlie," Scout said pulling her hands over her head and stretching her body back into a perfect crescent. "If he says he can do it, he can do it. He's pretty awesome that way."

"But Stroud—"

"You got anything else for me, Boss Woman?" Charlie turned so his back was to Maggie. She took a moment to entertain the idea she might have actually turned invisible and mute over the last few minutes.

"Carry me to my room?" Scout asked, releasing her body from the odd angle. Somehow she even managed to make crumbling in exhaustion look graceful.

Charlie rubbed the back of his neck again, discomfort breaking through the carefully constructed robot mask. "Yeah, I don't think your mate would like that too much."

It sounded like Scout muttered, "Like he would notice," but since Charlie didn't react, Maggie decided she'd imagined it.

With Charlie refusing to assist her, Scout made her own way to the door. "You coming with?" she asked him, holding it open.

His eyes met Maggie's, and for a moment she worried he would stay.

"Yeah," he finally said. "Gotta go run down Layne. It seems we've both gotta get ready for school tomorrow."

CHAPTER 11

Charlie hadn't been on a college campus since he dropped out three weeks before finals over two years ago. He'd had every intention of being back in class on Monday when he drove off that Friday afternoon, but then life (and death) got in the way. And even though he'd gone in expecting to leave with a degree, the fact that he never actually finished didn't bother him.

Until now.

"I feel like an old creeper," he said, leaning over the back of one of the many benches decorating the campus.

Liam didn't look up from the game he was playing on his phone. "You're twenty, which makes you the same age as everyone else."

It shouldn't have been a surprising bit of information, but it was. He supposed it was true - after all, he would be a senior now if he'd stuck with it - but watching a couple of guys kick around a soccer ball, he just couldn't see it.

"They seem younger."

Liam put down his phone and made a point of looking around. "I don't know. I'm not sure more carefree and less embittered are necessarily the same thing as younger."

"Hey, I'm not bitter."

Liam snorted as he picked his phone back up. "Keep telling yourself that, sunshine."

Charlie would've argued the point, but he knew it was useless. It wasn't because Liam was Alpha. Sure, some people might agree with everything he said just because they felt the need to completely submit to the title, but

Charlie wasn't one of them. The two of them started building a friendship after Liam's brother Alex died, and Toby's death brought them even closer. They understood each other in a way no one else could. And one thing Charlie understood about Liam was he didn't feel the need to argue a point with you when pointed silence did such a marvelous job on its own.

Since Liam's eyes were still glued to the screen of his phone, Charlie leaned over to see exactly what level of candy he was crushing and was surprised to see a tiny map covered in red dots.

"Infrared?"

"Yeah, it's reading the heat signatures of everyone in a hundred yard radius. We're far enough from the new moon that even the least dominant of Shifters should be showing a little warmer than normal."

Charlie took a closer look, and sure enough, two dots right next to each other were a bit brighter than those around them.

"I always knew I was hot." His statement only got an eye roll from his Alpha. "I'm guessing this is a Joshua original?"

Liam zoomed in on a new dot moving into the area, and then zoomed back out when it was obviously a human.

"One of these days I'm going to figure out exactly who that guy is and what all he's done in his long life," Liam said, referring to the Immortal who rarely spoke of his past but always seemed to be able to pull the most random, unexplainable knowledge out of his ass, like how to create a phone app that could read heat signatures.

Charlie walked around the bench and sat down by Liam. "Don't count on it. I'm pretty sure he was part of the

CIA for a while. You're not going to get anything out of him he doesn't want to share."

"Which is exactly why I want to know so damn bad. I hate secrets. They make me stabby."

Charlie thought about pointing out how some of the phrases Liam was picking up from Scout made him sound less manly, but decided against it. For one, he wasn't really feeling up to Liam proving his masculinity through fisticuffs. And for another, it would take all the enjoyment he and Jase got out of laughing at him whenever he spouted one off.

Liam once again zoomed in on a new dot. When he didn't immediately zoom out, Charlie looked over his shoulder.

"It's just a touch brighter than the others. Looks like someone just has a fever to me," he said, wondering how accurate Joshua's new toy was.

"Yeah, probably..." Liam zoomed in a bit more and then looked at the building in front of them. The dot appeared to be just around the corner. "Want to take a walk?"

Charlie followed Liam around the building, making note of every person they passed. Sanders didn't have a lot of students, but it also didn't have a very big campus. The entire school covered about one city block, which meant the lawns and sidewalks were filled with students busily rushing from one place to another or just hanging out between classes. With that many people, Charlie couldn't pull out individual scents, so he had to rely on observation and gut instinct to decide whether or not there were any rogue Shifters lurking about.

"So, we're still thinking it's an inside job?" Charlie asked, immediately dismissing an overweight guy who tripped over a crack in the sidewalk.

After Charlie left Maggie's room, where he'd somehow managed to not apologize for his previous actions like he'd meant to and ended up signing on to be her full-time bodyguard instead, Liam called a meeting of the Alpha Pack. Scout laid out what they'd found in the barn, from the body of Barros to the painting they'd found.

"Obviously, there are some members of the Shifting community who don't agree with how we're doing things," Liam said. "Thankfully, they were kind enough to leave us a hit list so we'll know where to concentrate our efforts."

"Not true." Charlie had thought Aunt Rachel was asleep until she spoke.

"Which part?" Jase asked. "That's not a hit list, or it's not a group of unhappy Shifters?"

Unfortunately, Aunt Rachel's Sight wasn't an exact instrument. As a Truth Seer, she could detect flat-out lies with ease, but other truths were a bit trickier. They'd rephrased each of the statements in as many ways as they could imagine, but her sight remained dormant. They'd argued about which was more likely to be wrong until they were all so sleepy they could barely keep their eyes open. When they'd finally agreed to call it a night, they were no closer to coming to a decision than they had been hours before.

"Shifters is the only answer that makes sense," Liam said, not for the first time. "Who else knows who, what, and where we are?"

He paused at the edge of a grassy area and looked at his phone again. His eyes roamed the space until coming to rest on a girl whose pale coloring, bloodshot eyes, and chapped nose were obvious even from ten feet away.

It seemed the answer to, *"How accurate is Joshua's new toy?"* was, *"Freakishly accurate."*

"Do you ever thank God that Joshua is on our side?" Charlie asked.

Liam nodded. "Every single day."

There were more students on this side of the building, most of them sprawled across the grass in a style of clothes that ranged from I-think-I'm-a-hippie-but-I-really-just-smoke-pot to I'm-not-a-hipster-because-hipsters-are-passé. It didn't surprise Charlie at all to see Rosa Hall written on the top of the building.

He wondered what Maggie did there. He added, *should have asked her what type of art she does* to his growing list of things he'd done wrong the night before. It was wedged under *forgot to apologize, purposefully scared her*, and *threatened her life*.

"Maggie is inside?" he asked, hating himself for the effort it took to sound nonchalant. What did it matter if he was interested in where she was? They were supposed to be guarding the girl. Of course he was interested in her whereabouts.

"Yeah, she's--" Liam zoomed in on a section of the phone screen, zoomed out, and then focused in on a different section. "She's..."

"Liam, please tell me you haven't lost the Thaumaturgic." Because if he had, then Charlie was going to have to give into these feelings of panic that were tingling in his chest.

"Wow, I'm so glad I've got you two around to keep me safe."

Charlie turned towards the familiar voice. She was once again wearing a brightly colored grandma dress, but today the colors were muted by a coating of white powder that seemed to cover the majority of her body.

"You're filthy," he blurted out before realizing how incredibly rude he sounded.

"Thank you for noticing," was her reply, given with a sarcastic smile.

Damn. So much for making a better third impression.

"So, how quick did Stroud shoot you down?" she asked as her hands danced across her dress, sending white powder flying into the air.

"He didn't."

"He didn't what?"

"He didn't shoot me down." Charlie reached into his back pocket and pulled out his new student ID, making sure Maggie could see the gold stripe running across the top indicating his status as an independent study student. "We're now officially study buddies."

Charlie didn't think eyes as dark as Maggie's could be very expressive. They were so black they couldn't bleach out like Scout's did when she was angry or darken like Talley's did when she was sad. There was such a small difference between the iris and pupil it would take considerable effort to see if the center was expanding or contracting. But despite the disadvantages caused by their color, Charlie could see everything Maggie was thinking when he met her eyes.

He tried not to be offended at her shock and disbelief. It's not like she really knew anything about him, and Stroud had been a hard sell. It wasn't difficult to see why someone would doubt the man would be willing to take on what he'd termed "an extra headache."

"How much did that piece of plastic cost us?" Liam asked.

"Don't worry. We can cover it."

Maggie's obsidian eyes narrowed along with the rest of her features. "You paid him off?"

"You're angry," Charlie said, rather stupidly. It was amazing actual physical daggers weren't flying out of her eyes.

"The faculty is only required to accept one independent study student every five years."

"So I've heard."

"You didn't just buy yourself a spot, you sold someone else's." The top of her head barely reached his shoulders, but he felt like she was looming over him. "Someone who has spent hour after hour, day after day, year after year for a chance to study under one of the greatest artists living today. Someone who deserves the chance to make their dreams come true. And you've just...," her tiny body shook with fury, "*wasted* it."

There was a time when Charlie would have let her words get to him. Guilt and empathy for the unknown person he'd wronged would have left him feeling sick until he made it right. But that was before he'd taken up an eighteen-month residence at the bottom of the pit of human emotions. He'd found his way back out into the light of day, but he'd emerged a changed man. In order to not feel the pain, he had to give up the ability to feel much of anything at all.

All in all, he thought it was a pretty good trade. Charlie was on close, intimate terms with pain, and he would choose muted emotions over revisiting it any day of the week.

"Fortunately for you, I value human life more than someone's chance to have some arrogant ass sneer at them while he devalues their talent and hard work." He leaned forward, crowding into Maggie's space. "If you're going to point a finger at me, you might take note of the three that pointing back at you. I wouldn't be here if you had taken our advice and just took a semester or two off."

In the move he'd made to keep from feeling like Maggie was lording over him, Charlie had moved into a position in which Maggie had to tilt her head back completely to look him in the eyes. Too late, he realized it was the same position they would be in if he was about to kiss her. And once his brain went there, he couldn't seem to reign it back. His gaze was stuck on the dusky rose of her lips, and he became overly aware of the scent of lilacs and vanilla coming from her skin. He licked his lips without thought and saw on her face the moment she too realized the position they found themselves in. A blush darkened her satin cheeks. As he watched the color spread from her high cheekbones to the long column of her neck he imagined what it would be like to follow the same path with his lips.

Holy inappropriate thoughts, Batman.

"Don't you dare push the blame off on me." Why did her voice have to be so low and raspy? That certainly wasn't helping matters. "My life was perfectly calm and uneventful until you guys brought attention to me."

"Calm and uneventful? That sounds like a grand old time. I'm sorry you had to give it up."

"It may not have been the nonstop party that is being a member of the Alpha Pack, but it was safe."

Charlie's coyote paced beneath the surface, savoring the way they drew even closer to one another as they argued. It wanted to pounce, and Charlie was having trouble keeping it leashed. He wanted to tell her to run. He didn't know what would happen if he let that side of himself out again, but he knew for certain she wouldn't survive it intact. But no matter how much he wanted to, he couldn't get the words past his lips.

"Sorry to interrupt the foreplay you two have going on there," Liam said, breaking the spell, "but you should know we're being watched."

CHAPTER 12

Maggie opened her mouth, but couldn't speak. Her brain was stuck on the word "foreplay."

"Don't turn around," Charlie muttered. His face inched impossibly closer to hers and her breath ran away to the same place her voice was hiding. "Just keep concentrating on my lips like you have been."

Her face heated at his words. She had *not* been staring at his oh-so-perfect lips.

Okay, so maybe that was a lie, but it was only because she was concentrating on all the ridiculous crap coming out of them. It certainly hadn't been an act of *foreplay.*

I don't suppose you would consider opening up and swallowing me whole? she asked the ground beneath her feet. But like everyone and everything else over the past few days, it acted as if it hadn't heard her.

She looked up, expecting to meet Charlie's cool gaze, but he was focusing on a point over her shoulder. Liam was standing beside him, his eyes glued to the tiny screen of his phone.

"What do you see?" she asked no one in particular.

Charlie answered. "Girl. Average height. Thin with obvious surgical enhancements up top—"

"And rainbow hair."

His eyes dropped back to hers. "You know her?"

Instead of answering, Maggie turned around and searched the crowd until she caught sight of her roommate. "Reid," she called out, waving her hand frantically as if she was thrilled to see her, which was hardly the case. But since they'd already been spotted, it was best to get it over with.

"Mags, I've been so worried about you," her roommate whined, wrapping her thin arms around Maggie's neck. "Where on earth have you been?"

Hanging out in a million dollar house with a couple of psychotic were-creatures.

"Staying with a friend. Didn't you get my note?"

"Yes, but—" Reid froze the moment her eyes landed on Liam.

"Reid, this is Liam. He's..."

"A friend," Liam supplied.

"A friend," she agreed, trying to hide the incredulousness in her voice. "And this is Charlie. Charlie..."

Maybe they should have covered the fine art of lying with her before they sent her out in public with two secret bodyguards.

"Friend of Liam's," Charlie said, kicking the sides of his mouth into the Charlie-bot's imitation of a smile. "I just transferred in and discovered Mags and I have almost all of our classes together. She agreed to show me the ropes."

Maggie was fairly certain she was feeling hurt over something other than the way Charlie had categorized himself as Liam's friend and not hers, but she couldn't figure out exactly what it was. Maybe she was mistaking hurt for annoyance.

"Liam," Reid said, obviously transfixed by the attractive Alpha Male.

"He's dating Scout Donovan," Maggie said, both to share what she knew her roommate would consider squee-worthy gossip and to warn her off. She had a feeling Scout wouldn't react well to someone making googley eyes at her boyfriend.

If anything, Liam's normal glare grew even colder. "We're not dating."

"Oh..." Maggie thought back to how the two had interacted and wondered what she was missing. They had certainly seemed to be a couple. "Sorry, I just thought you were together."

He flicked her a look that seemed to suggest that she was an idiot. "We are together."

"But not dating?" Maggie was confused. "You're engaged?" Nineteen seemed awfully young to be making that kind of commitment, but more than one of her former classmates were set to tie the knot in the next year, and they'd just graduated high school. Some people were just crazy like that.

"No, we're not engaged." Liam, who normally seemed pretty reserved and in control, looked like he was about to have a celebrity-level meltdown. "We're ma—"

"Making plans to be engaged," Charlie interrupted, his smile even tighter than normal. "Not Liam's idea, obviously, but Scout is very into Southern traditions."

Being from Tennessee, Maggie thought she knew a bit more about Southern traditions than anyone in Kentucky, but she let it slide. Whatever the deal was between Liam and Scout, it wasn't really any of her business.

Reid acted as though she hadn't heard a word of what any of them had said. She was still looking at Liam like he was Robert Downey, Jr. wearing a giant "free for the taking" sign around his neck, and Maggie wasn't the only one who noticed. Charlie's eyes flicked back and forth between the girl and Liam, while Liam looked like he was ready to turn tail and run, which made Maggie giggle. The Alpha Male was scared of Reid, the girl who complained about how heavy her MacBook Air made her backpack?

"Liam, this is Reid. She's my roommate."

"Nice to meet you." Liam offered his hand. Reid looked at it for a full second before taking a step backwards.

Three sets of eyebrows - Maggie's, Charlie's, and Liam's - all rose in unison as if the action was choreographed.

"I have class," Reid said, her voice coming out thin and shaky. "I have to go." Frantic eyes met Maggie's, making her feel a certain kinship with the girl for the first time. "Call me later?"

She didn't even wait for Maggie to agree before she turned and began plowing her way through the crowd.

"So, that's your roommate," Charlie said.

"Yep."

"She's..."

"Intense?"

Charlie snorted. "That's one word for it."

"She has sex with her boyfriend while I'm in the room," Maggie admitted, the words spilling out of her mouth on their own. "And she doesn't clip her nails over a trash can. She just sits in the middle of her bed and lets them fly all over the place."

The corner of Charlie's mouth lifted, and for the first time, she thought his amusement might be genuine. "You know, after all of this is over, you can still stay with us. I would hate to know I saved you from one horrible fate just to drop you back into another."

"I'm sure the Alphas would love to become a half-way house for college kids with horrid roommates." She couldn't stop the grin that spread across her face.

"Liam doesn't care. The more the merrier."

Liam didn't comment. He was too busy staring off in the direction Reid had disappeared, his eyes narrowed and nostrils flared.

"Liam? Do we have a problem?"

Charlie's voice broke Liam out of his trance, but instead of looking at his pack mate, he turned to Maggie.

"What do you know about your roommate?"

Maggie thought back to the nonstop chatter she'd learned to tune out an hour after moving in to the dorm. "She's an only child. Her parents are fabulously wealthy and live somewhere up around Louisville. She's majoring in Business Management," the default degree for the rich kids who would never actually have to work a day in their life, "and fancies herself a unique soul, but has Top-40-highest-grossing-movie tastes. And she really, really likes to be naked. A lot."

"Seriously," Charlie said. "The room is yours."

"Does Reid have a last name?" Liam asked her.

"Nope. It's just Reid, like Cher or Madonna." She caved to Liam's death stare in a fraction of a second. "St. James. Reid St. James."

"Louisville area is the Fields Pack, right?" Liam asked.

"Yeah, they stretch all the way over to Cincinnati and up to Indianapolis," Charlie said, "but if you go just a touch south, you're in Orman Territory."

Liam rubbed the back of his head. "Dig around. See if she's associated with either pack in any way."

Maggie felt the cold fingers of dread travel up her spine as Charlie cocked his head to the side and inhaled deeply through his nose. "Did you get something off of her?" he asked.

"Not exactly. Something just seemed... wrong."

"On it." Charlie pulled out his own phone and started taping and flipping his way through multiple screens. "I've got Lennon and Salinger on Mandel. What do you think about pulling in Mitchell to start digging into this?"

Liam seemed to consider it for a while and then nodded. "Yeah. That'll work." He checked the time on his phone. "I'll make the call since you two have class in ten minutes."

"Maybe I should wait until tomorrow—"

Liam cut Charlie off with a look. "Or you could go ahead and start today."

"But I'm not going to wait until tomorrow, because I really need to just go ahead and jump in there," Charlie finished with mock sincerity.

Maggie barely listened as the two Shifters discussed the finer points of her security detail and where they would all meet up later. She was too distracted by the idea that Reid might have something to do with everything going on. It didn't make any sense... except for the way it kinda did. Reid's obsession with Scout. Her reaction to Maggie being "tapped" for the "secret society." And the way she'd been held transfixed by Liam. Maggie expected Reid to see him as a hot guy, and so she'd read the situation as poorly hidden lust, but what if she was wrong? What if Reid had known who Liam was and was frozen in fear, much the way Maggie had been the day before when she'd realized she was standing in front of the Shifter's Alpha?

Thank God the Alphas had given her a place to stay. There was no way she could go back to their room and sleep knowing there was a chance Reid was mixed up in all of this.

"You okay?"

Maggie snapped out of her my-roommate-is-going-to-stab-me-with-a-rusty-knife thoughts to realize Liam had already gone.

"Sorry," she said. "I was just..."

How to end that sentence?

"I guess I've got to get used to being around an artist who exists on a different plane than us regular folk."

Maggie normally abhorred all artist stereotypes and corrected anyone who assumed she was scattered or unreliable just because she was creative, but she let it slide with Charlie since he was being civil for the moment and there was no telling what might set him off next.

Their next class was just across the quad in the Grafton Building. As they wound their way around the other students, Charlie stayed right at her back, one hand placed on her hip, guiding her. The day was warm, but Charlie's hand was even warmer. It nearly swallowed her slender hip, and Maggie found herself relaxing into his touch. She'd been on edge all day. Someone out there knew what she was and wanted her dead. Sleep exhaustion from a night of tossing and turning in an unfamiliar bed with visions of mutilated corpses dancing in her head had left her paranoid and jumpy. Every look tossed her way was an enemy sizing up the best way to overcome her. Every shadow was a mad man with a knife. And it didn't help that the creepy kids' song from the Freddie Krueger movies was stuck in her head.

Knowing Liam was nearby had helped. He was, after all, the most badass of badass Shifters. But Liam kept his distance, watching out for her from afar. As she walked across campus, sat in class, or worked in the studio, she had to remind herself he was out there somewhere, making sure she was safe.

There was no forgetting Charlie. His presence engulfed her, the heat of his hand warming her whole body. The fingers flexing and shifting to lead her in the direction he thought was best were strong and sure. He might not have been the Alpha, but he wasn't exactly a weakling. Whatever was out there, whoever might mean her harm, would more than meet their match if they took on Charlie Hagan. Of that, Maggie had no doubt.

It only took a moment for Charlie to get everything settled with Chase once they got to class. She had muttered something about rich kids thinking they didn't have to come to the first week of class, but Chase was somewhat cordial as she showed Charlie around the studio. The studios in the Grafton Building were much bigger than those in Rosa Hall. Rosa was reserved for independent study and grad students, whereas Grafton had instructional classes. Chase's room had ten wheels and two massive gas kilns as well as enough worktables to accommodate a class of twenty students. Thankfully, this beginner's class wasn't that large. Charlie made the unlucky thirteenth student.

"We all mixed our clay last week, but you can use some pre-made stuff for now. Just be sure and have my TA show you how to mix your own. You'll be tested on it later." Chase slapped a handful of clay on the table in front of Charlie before spinning in a ballet-worthy move and facing the class. "We're taking on the wheels today, children." Half the class cheered while the rest looked a little terrified. "Grab your putty buddy and scurry along to your designated torture devices. The first one to let an f-bomb slip is the daily loser and shall be forced to wear The Hat of Shame."

Since it was just the second week of classes and the room was filled with freshmen, everyone just sat there looking dumbfounded. "Shoo," she said, flicking her fingers at the students. "Be gone with you now."

Charlie started to raise his hand, but Chase was already turning towards him. "Okay, pretty boy. People who decide to show up for class a week after everyone else miss the opportunity to get putty buddies. But because you're so woefully behind the rest of the class, you're getting my TA for the day. She can catch you up." Maggie should have been expecting it, but she nearly fell on her face when Chase grabbed her shoulders and thrust her in front of Charlie. "Be gentle with her," Chase instructed the Shifter. "This one is precious to me." And with that statement, she flounced off to explain to a set of students that "center of the wheel" did not mean "three inches to the left of center".

"You're the TA?" Charlie asked after Chase demonstrated to the whole class the correct way to slap the clay around.

Maggie hefted Charlie's allotment of premixed clay and curled her lip. The tubes were convenient, but it wasn't anywhere near as good as what she'd spent the last few hours mixing over in her studio. There were too many impurities and not enough plasticity. She hadn't used the stuff since she'd first started throwing when she was maybe five or six.

"I'm Chase's independent study student. She's letting me earn some extra cash by TA'ing this class."

Charlie watched her intently as she pushed the heel of her hand into the clay over and over again. "You do realize she's a little bit crazy, right?"

"When the Queen of England commissions you to make a vase for her, you're eccentric. Crazy is much too gauche for a true artist," Maggie said, dividing the ball of clay she was working on in half. "Have you ever kneaded bread?"

"Needed bread? Well, I get really hungry for a sandwich on occasion. It feels like a need, but I'm sure it's really more of a want."

He was not amusing. Not at all. Maggie had to be fighting a grin for some other reason.

"Knead that," she said, pointing at one of the new piles of clay. "I'm getting the water."

One side of Charlie's mouth pulled up and Maggie felt something flutter inside her. She hadn't forgotten how beautiful he was, you couldn't overlook something like that, but she hadn't remembered how devastating he was when he wasn't being hateful. "You know, I kinda like this new, dominant Maggie. Are you sure you're not one of us?"

"Positive." And if he was going to keep looking at her with a tiny spark of humanity dancing in his eyes, it would be prudent for her to remember that.

CHAPTER 13

Charlie was still picking clay out from underneath his fingernails hours later.

"How is playing with mud considered a class?" He ran his hands under the faucet for the millionth time. "Seriously, I'm going to get a grade on my ability to use a turntable to make a bowl?"

"So what you're telling us is that you suck at ceramics," Jase said, peering over Talley's shoulder as she checked on the contents of the oven.

"I'm telling you it's a stupid class."

"Maggie told me everything Charlie tried to throw collapsed in on itself," Talley the Traitor said, transferring a pan of cookies from the oven to the counter. Jase immediately grabbed one and popped it into his mouth. No one paid attention to the howl of pain or litany of four-letter words that followed. The idiot did the same thing every time someone baked cookies, which around Fenrir Farm was almost nightly. "She's worried his giant hands have too much Shifter strength in them to do something as delicate as ceramics."

Jase grabbed a carton of milk out of the fridge. "Giant hands, you say?"

Charlie felt his face grow red as Scout lifted one of those hands into her own. "And they're practically radiating with strength. I don't know how he grabs onto a doorknob without twisting up all the metal on accident." She blinked her mocking eyes at him. "It must take all your concentration to not destroy everything you touch."

"I hate you all," Charlie said through gritted teeth.

"You adore us," Scout said, dropping his hand. "But it's not your feelings on your bestest friends in the whole wide world I'm interested in." She leaned in and dropped her voice to a conspiratorial whisper. "What do you think of our little Thaumaturgic?"

"She's hot," Joshua answered, scooping up a cookie with one bare hand, and then tossing it to the other hand, and then back again. "Almost as hot as these cookies." He dropped the chocolate-chipped treat on the counter and blew on his fingertips. "Damn, Tal. What did you do to these things?"

"I cooked them. In an oven. At three hundred and fifty degrees."

Scout grabbed a cookie off the tray and cocked an eyebrow at Jase and Joshua as she bit in. "I want to know what *you* think, Chuck," she said around a mouthful of sugary and buttery goodness.

"I think you probably just burned your fingertips and lips in an attempt to be a showoff."

"I did no such thing." But she obviously had, because she grabbed the gallon of milk out of Jase's hand and took a giant chug, making sure to wrap her fingers around the part where droplets of cool condensation were gathered. "Come on. Spill it. What do you think of Maggie?"

Charlie threw his legs up on the edge of the giant wood-planked table and leaned back until his chair was propped up on the back two feet. "If she's involved with whoever is behind the murder then she's one of the best actresses I've ever met." He noticed another bit of dried clay on the corner of his finger. How on earth was that even possible? "I still think it's a good idea to stick close to her. For someone to know what she is and that she'd been contacted by us, it has to be someone close."

"Like the roommate," Liam suggested.

"Like the roommate." Charlie had questioned Maggie more about Reid as she attempted to show him how to make a bowl instead of a giant lump of grayish nothingness. She'd tried to laugh off the suggestion Reid could have been involved, but he could tell she was trying to convince herself as much as him. Her face was an open book, every thought and emotion she had was written in big, bold letters all over it. Charlie gave it a lot of thought last night as he lay in his bed, waiting for his customary four hours of sleep to come and take him under, and decided her openness is what brought his coyote to the surface. The animal half of a Shifter revels in instincts and emotions, and Maggie McCray was a smorgasbord of emotions. After being caged for so long, Charlie's coyote gloried in seeing and creating those emotions he could no longer feel.

A folder landed next to Charlie's feet. "The roommate checks out," Joshua said. "I started pulling everything I could find on her when we first approached Maggie. Mitchell double-checked my findings today, and everything adds up." He flipped the folder open and picked up the first sheet of paper. "Reid St. James. Eighteen. Daughter of Sandy and Calvin St. James. We traced her family tree back three generations, and there isn't a Shifter or Seer hanging out on any of the branches. She's just what she appears to be - a kid with more money than sense."

Jase made the requisite comment on Joshua's use of grandpa-phrases while Charlie thumbed through Reid's folder. Joshua hadn't been kidding. He had a ridiculous amount of information on the girl. Birth certificate. Report cards. Transcripts of online chats and text message exchanges.

"Damn," Liam said from over Charlie's shoulder. "I really thought we were onto something."

Charlie picked up a print out of Reid taken from a security camera time stamped over three years ago, wondered how on earth Joshua managed to get ahold of it, and then decided he'd really rather not know. "Yeah, me too. I guess we're back to square one."

"Not necessarily," Joshua said.

"Can I do it?" At the tilt of Joshua's head, Jase leaned across the table, his eyes aglow. "Guess who didn't return to their pack like they were told and is still checked into a flea-bag motel in Lexington?"

Charlie sat up and let his feet fall to the floor. "Mandel?"

"Ding, ding, ding! We have a winner!"

Liam was already moving towards the back door.

"But he's not there," Scout added, stopping Liam in his tracks. "From what I can tell, he hasn't been there in days."

Liam turned his head slowly, as if someone had slowed down the film for dramatic effect. "You went to his room?"

"I went to the room he's been paying for, but I'm telling you, he hasn't been there in days." Scout broke a cookie in two and popped half of it in her mouth. "Actually, I'm not sure he was ever there. I couldn't really catch a scent, but you know how those old, crappy motel rooms are. It's impossible to pick up on anything other than old smoke, old booze, and old... *funk*."

"Who went with you?"

Scout hooked her thumb to the right, towards Talley, who raised her hand.

In the wild, submissive coyotes will flatten themselves to the ground and press their ears back to their head when a more dominant coyote or wolf unleashes their anger. Shifters in human form didn't have the same control over their ears and getting themselves to the ground would require too much motion. The point was to avoid the alpha's attention, so Charlie, Jase, Talley, and even Joshua dropped their heads and averted their eyes, becoming so still they hardly breathed.

Scout popped the other half of the cookie in her mouth.

"What?" she asked when it became apparent Liam was going to just stand there and growl instead of actually saying or doing anything.

"You went looking for him *alone.*"

Charlie risked a glance out of the corner of his eye. Scout had one leg tucked up underneath her in an attempt to look casual and at ease, but the line of her spine and flare of her nostrils said she was as tense as the rest of them. But unlike the rest of them, she would do battle with the big bad wolf if she had to.

"I wasn't alone." She reached for another cookie and Liam tracked the movement with his eyes. "Talley was with me the whole time."

"Talley is *Seer*. Seer, Scout. Not a Shifter. Not a fighter."

"It's not like I took Mischa or Lizzie. I took Talley. She's the Stella Polaris and can outshoot Dirty Harry. As far as back-ups go, she's pretty damn capable."

If Talley hadn't been cowering in fear due to the Alpha tension in the room, she would have taken the opportunity to remind them she didn't consider herself the Stella Polaris, but as it was, she was too busy staring at her bellybutton and clinging onto Jase's hand to do much of anything else.

Liam prowled over to Scout's barstool and leaned over her, bracing his hands on the counter behind her. "Do not ever, *ever*, do something that stupid again."

"Stupid?" Scout's eyes narrowed until only a sliver of pale blue could been seen behind her lashes. "How is going to gather evidence on a potential murderer *stupid*?" She pulled her shoulders back and jerked her head up, forcing Liam to lean back a bit. "Protecting the Shifters and Seers of the world is our job, or have you forgotten?"

Even though Scout looked like she would enjoy breaking a bone or ten, Liam refused to back down.

"Being reckless and getting yourself killed are not in the job description."

"I wasn't being reckless!"

"You went alone!"

"I. Was. With. *Talley*."

Liam's growl sounded more wolf than human. "Don't ever do something like that again without telling me and taking backup." Scout started to correct him once again. "No," Liam said, cutting her off. "Talley isn't backup. Joshua. Charlie. Jase. They're backup. Talley is not. We don't place Seers in danger. They're sacred."

Scout took a deep breath, and when it came out between clenched teeth, she took another. "One," she said, her voice considerably quieter, but still carrying a tremor of anger, "Talley was an excellent choice of backups. Don't ever give me this take-a-boy-instead-of-a-girl sexist crap again, or I swear, I will show you what women are capable of. And two, where the Hades do you get off telling me what I will and will not do?”

“I’m your mate!”

Scout rolled her eyes. “Of course you are.”

Every muscle in Liam’s body visibly tensed. “*‘Of course I am?’* What does that mean?”

Charlie realized at some point he’d stopped playing the role of the submissive Shifter and was watching the scene unfolding before him, and he wasn’t the only one. Everyone else was looking on with expressions ranging from uncomfortable to horrified.

“It means,” Scout took another deep breath, this time holding it for several seconds while she quickly batted back some tears with her eyelids. “It means ‘of course you’re my mate and want to protect me, but you’re overreacting.’ Seriously, Liam, we were fine. I promise.” When his expression didn’t change, she pressed on. “You know I wouldn’t ever knowingly and willingly put Talley in harm’s way. If you don’t believe anything else, believe that.”

“I’m your mate,” Liam repeated, but this time it sounded more like a question.

Scout answered it by placing a hand on the side of his face and giving him a small, fragile smile. “I know,” she said.

“Scout—“

“Joshua, what kind of information have you and your tech geniuses gathered on our not-so-good Mr. Mandel?”

It was perhaps the most unsubtle redirection in the history of time, but Charlie couldn’t have been happier. He loved his Alphas and felt closer to them than most members of his family, but there were just some moments you shouldn’t share with others.

What he'd just witnessed was one of them.

"Ummm..." Joshua cleared his throat, and shook his head as if trying to clear the giant Etch-a-Sketch of his brain. "The only credit card activity since Saturday has been on the motel room. No restaurants, stores, or anything, but he did remove the maximum allowance from the ATM twice on Friday."

"Has anyone seen him?" Liam asked.

Joshua shook his head, and then, realizing Liam wouldn't see the motion since he was still in some kind of hypnotic eye-lock with Scout, said, "No. No one at the motel will admit to seeing him, and he's refused maid service. Lennon is going over security footage from some places in the area, but no sign of him yet."

"How many members of his pack came to the hustings?" Jase, who was staring at Scout and Liam staring at each other, asked.

"It was just him and Imogen," Charlie answered. It was his job to keep track of who attended each hustings. For days before the event, he met with every person seeking an audience with the Alpha Pack, getting information on who they were and what pack they were associated with. He remembered Mandel and Imogen clearly. A guy didn't easily forget a girl who looked like Imogen. "Even her mother stayed back home. I got the distinct impression they didn't agree with his reason for coming here."

"Well, then kudos to the Mandel Pack for being decent human beings." Scout finally broke eye contact with Liam in favor of seeking out her best friend. "Did you get a chance to See him the other day, Tal?"

"I tried to track him down after the hustings, but he was already gone."

Scout fell back against the counter. "So, now what?"

"We wait," Joshua said. "Send someone to keep an eye on his house and the motel, and Lennon and Salinger will keep following his digital breadcrumbs. He'll eventually slip up, and when he does, we'll catch him."

"Do we put the word out that we're looking for him? Declare him an enemy of the Alpha Pack or whatever it is we do?" Scout asked.

Liam considered it for moment. "Let's hold off," he decided. "If he doesn't know we're on to him, he might get sloppy."

Joshua grabbed a handful of cookies off the counter. "I'm going to go work on the heat signature app some more. It needs a few tweaks, and then I'll be able to equip all of your phones."

"We're going, too," Jase said, also grabbing a handful of cookies. "*Someone* signed me up for a class at eight in the freaking morning." He shot a glare Scout's way. Scout widened her eyes in an attempt to seem innocent. "What? It wasn't me. It was Talley."

Talley patted Scout's shoulder as she made her way to the door. "Nice try, Your Majesty. But I think he was sitting there when you said, 'Oh, look. An interpersonal communications class at the butt crack of dawn. Jase will absolutely hate that,' and then erupted into evil laughter as you hit the enroll button."

"Hmmm... That does sound vaguely familiar."

Jase expressed his feelings on the matter by flipping her off. Scout responded with the grace and maturity one came to expect from the Alpha Female and stuck out her tongue.

“I’m going, too,” Liam said, sliding his phone into his back pocket.

“Going?” All signs of amusement melted off Scout’s face. “Going where?”

Liam ran a hand over the back of his head. “The gym. I need to decompress.”

“But you’re coming back?”

There was a long pause where Charlie had to look away from the angst-ridden scene before he died of discomfort.

“Yeah.”

“Tonight?”

“I’ll just be a few hours.” Liam bent down and placed a kiss on the top of Scout’s head. “Will you be in your room when I get back?” he muttered in her ear so softly no one else should have been able to hear it. Unfortunately, Charlie possessed the same super-hearing as all Shifters and heard every word just as clearly as if Liam was whispering in his own ear.

The two shared a few more tender moments before Liam left through the backdoor, saving Charlie from attempting to disappear to save himself from having to watch two of his best friends making out. Once he was out the door, Scout’s entire body seemed to curl in on itself.

“You okay there, Scout?”

“Peachy.”

Charlie might have considered believing her if she wasn’t swiping tears out of the corner of her eyes as she said it. Since he was already up and moving towards the cabinets, he wandered over to where she was sitting and tapped her nose twice. “Yep,” he said. “It’s growing.”

Scout clapped her hands together in front of her chest and batted her eyelashes. “Gee, Jiminy. Do you reckon one day I might be a *real* Alpha? One who can make her own decisions and everything?"

"Depends. Are you going to quit turning into a jackass on occasion?"

"Wait a minute. I wasn't the one—"

"What Liam did was have the good graces not to mention in front of half the Alpha Pack how we have operating procedures. Operating procedures you helped draft and approve. Operating procedures you and Talley completely ignored today," Charlie said as he dug through the cabinet until he found glasses boasting the faces of Batman and Superman.

"I didn't—"

"You did. And then you acted like it was stupid for your mate to be concerned about your well-being."

"He said—"

"You could have gotten hurt. Or worse. Do you have any idea what that would do to him, Scout? Do you?"

He did. Because Charlie wouldn't be able to survive it either. He'd understood Liam's righteous indignation, because he'd felt it, too. Scout had been a part of Charlie's life since before he had memories. She was as close to him as a sister, if not closer. Scout owned a piece of him, and he her. He'd watched her come close to death a few times too many to be okay with her going out and chasing it down like she was immune.

His hands shook as he poured milk into the two glasses. She couldn't die. She just couldn't.

"Here," he said, thrusting the Batman glass towards her so she wouldn't see how the milk sloshed around as he held it, but she refused to take it. Instead, she just stared up at him, her lips doing a strange dance as she chewed all the skin off the inside of her lips.

"Charlie?"

"What?"

"You're ummm...." She grabbed a paper towel and offered it to him. When he took it, she pantomimed wiping the corner of her eyes. Charlie copied the motion, and...

God. Damn. It.

He was crying like a freaking baby, twin rivers rushing down his cheeks. When the hell had that happened? And how could he have not known?

The water in the sink was cold as he splashed it on his face. He repeated the motion until he couldn't feel his hands or face anymore, and still he leaned over it, watching the continuous cyclone chase itself down the drain.

"How is the new therapist working out?"

Was it possible to drown yourself in a sink? Someone once told him you could drown in a teaspoon of water, so surely he could manage it in a ridiculously deep sink.

"Charlie? Are you okay? Should I call someone? If you're new guy isn't working out, I'm sure Judd's dad—"

"The new therapist is fine." Charlie lifted himself off his elbows. There weren't any towels lying around, and he hadn't quite figured out the drawer system in the massive kitchen, so he used the bottom of his shirt to dry off his face. "Sorry. The past few days have been a little intense."

Scout was the only one who knew Charlie was so screwed up he had to see a psychologist on a regular basis. He'd started seeing someone after the accident that killed Liam's brother and left Scout with foot-long scars across her stomach. They'd helped at first, but his therapist wasn't a Shifter. It was hard talking about the crap he was dealing with without actually talking about the crap he was dealing with. When he'd run across a certified psychologist who was loyal to the new Alphas at the last hustings, Charlie went to Scout and quietly asked if she could pull some strings. Three hours later, he was one the phone with the guy setting up regular sessions.

Even though Scout had gone through her own round of therapy once upon a time, he still felt embarrassed when she brought it up. How big of a loser did he have to be to need the help of a shrink when everyone else around him was able to deal with everything on their own?

Charlie climbed up on the barstool across from Scout. She had her chin propped on her fists, and he mirrored the pose.

"When did we sign up for this?" she asked. This close he could see how red her eyes were and the dark circles underneath she was trying to hide with make-up.

"I'm not sure we did. I think we were drafted."

Scout let her fists fall onto the table, and her head followed. Her face was buried in her arms, making her words come out all garbled, but he still understood her perfectly when she said, "I want to quit."

It had been a long time since he'd seen Scout look so defeated. Sure, being Alpha Female wasn't exactly the life she'd always envisioned for herself, and it was a hell of a lot of work and responsibility for someone so young, but she'd met the challenge with all the grace and strength he knew she was capable of. Even Charlie, who could remember Scout in her awkward and gangly middle school years, started thinking of her as the eternal, invincible Lilith, the living embodiment of the moon. But at that moment there was no denying who she truly was - an over-worked, over-stressed girl in need of a friend.

Well, he might not be much good for anything else, but Charlie could at least do that.

"Talk to me," he said, reaching out to hold onto her fingers.

"Muffle, muffle, muffle."

"Head up. Mouth moving. Come on, Scout. You can do it."

She lifted her head just enough so her chin was resting on the inside of her elbows. "I don't want to talk."

Charlie gave her an I'm-not-leaving-until-you-say-something look.

"Fine." She pulled back, dragging her fingers from his grip so she could push short strands of hair back from her face. "Let's talk... about Maggie."

They were in the middle of a murder investigation and she wanted to talk about Maggie? He might have agreed if she wanted to talk about the way she was related to the case, but Charlie could tell by the smug expression on Scout's face that was definitely not the direction this conversation was going.

"New topic," Charlie said for no other reason than he really didn't feel like talking about the Thaumaturgic to anyone, least of all Scout. The girl set him on edge, and while most other people wouldn't notice, Scout would.

A quirk of lips. "Fine. I think Liam regrets that we're mates."

"Scout, that's stupid. Liam adores you."

"Maybe. But he doesn't love me—"

"Of course he does."

"He's never said so. And we've never had sex."

Milk surged down Charlie's windpipe, and the subsequent coughing fit was so violent he knew he'd be able to feel it in his abdominal muscles the next day. "Maggie is very talented," he wheezed once he was able to get the words out.

Scout leaned back in her chair and crossed her hands over her chest, a self-satisfied smile spread across her face. "Talented, huh? Tell me more."

He thought about refusing, but worried Scout might bring up her sex life again. It was a well-played move. He would do or say almost anything to not have that conversation.

"She's doing her independent study in ceramics, but she can do anything. It's like she doesn't even have to try." After spending an hour watching his lump of clay collapse in on itself over and over again, they'd gone back to Rosa Hall. Maggie made him use his ID to open the door and was noticeably surprised when it worked. Since he'd just been through the torture of his first ceramics class, Charlie believed he knew how the whole throwing process worked. Even though he hadn't been successful, several of his classmates managed to have bowl and vase-shaped objects by the end of class.

What Maggie did wasn't anything like what he'd seen the previous hour.

After preparing all of her materials, she sat down at the wheel, not even bothering to put an apron on over her bright yellow and red dress. It only took her one try to slap the clay on the center of the wheel, and thirty seconds later, he saw a plate magically appear out of the mud. Two minutes later, she was taking it off the wheel and grabbing the next ball of clay. By the end of the hour she had four dinner plates, four salad plates, and four bowls, and each was the exact same size and thickness of the others in the set.

"She sells dishes online," he told Scout, "and they're like the coolest dishes ever. She does this whole superhero thing, and she can imitate any comic book artist's style. She made this cup with Miles from *Ultimate Spider-Man* on it, and I swear to you, I thought it was official Marvel licensed merchandise."

If possible, Scout's smirk grew even more pronounced. "She paints comic book superheroes?"

"Onto cups. And bowls. Convex items. Or is that concave?"

"Convex," Scout said, pointing to the outside of her glass of milk. "Concave," she said, pointing to the inside.

"Well, then, she paints on the convex side of cups and the concave side of bowls. It's amazing."

Charlie's earliest memory of Scout was of the day the three of them - Scout, Charlie, and Jase - decided to break into Gramma Hagan's refrigerator and steal the cake she was supposed to be taking to that night's pack meeting. They couldn't have been very old, probably around three or four, and their sneaking abilities were bad at best. They didn't realize it at the time, but when you're a kid in a house full of Shifters, someone is always listening to what you're up to, even if they're on the other side of the house. But by some miracle, no one was paying careful attention to the trio of mischief-makers that day. Once the three of them managed to get the ginormous cake to the middle of the floor, Scout smiled at her two cohorts, pride over a job well done and giddiness over the feast before them lighting up her entire face.

That same smile spread across her face as she looked across the counter at Charlie.

"What are you up to?"

"What? Me? Nothing."

"Scout..."

"It's just..." She shrugged. "I'm happy to see you interested in someone."

He felt his face heat, which was even more embarrassing than being called out about Maggie. He wasn't some twelve-year-old boy who was just accused of having a crush on one of the cheerleaders. He was practically an adult, for God's sake. So what if he was interested in Maggie?

"You came to this conclusion when exactly? Maybe yesterday when I was threatening to kill her?"

"Do you have any idea the number of times I've threatened to kill Liam?"

"It's not the same." Scout had never thought she might have to kill Liam, whereas there was a time yesterday when he thought he would watch Maggie draw her last breath. "And if that was the criteria for deciding whether or not someone is interested in another person, then Talley may need to worry about Jase's feelings towards Joshua."

But Scout wouldn't be dissuaded. She leaned up on her elbows, the challenge of the Alpha in her eyes. "You look at her."

"I look at lots people. I'm looking at you right now."

"No you're not. You're looking through me, just like you've looked through everyone since Toby died." A flash of white pain in his chest made him want to lash out at her, but he reined it in, refusing to fall into that rabbit hole of emotion. "But when Maggie is in a room, you can't look away. It's like she's a magnet, one of those cool, super-charged magnets bad guys use to steal the Eiffel Tower or moon or whatever."

"She's a Thaumaturgic, an unknown in a situation where lives are on the line. Of course I watch her. It's my job to protect you and this pack."

"Keep telling yourself that, Chuck," Scout said. "Maybe one day we'll both believe it."

CHAPTER 14

For a house big enough to park a jet plane inside, there was absolutely nowhere for Maggie to draw. She supposed she could have stayed in her room, but something about the dark wood and heavy furniture made cabin fever set in at an alarmingly fast pace. She'd grabbed her sketchbook and pencils hoping to find a nice, quiet place to think, but it turned out nice and quiet were foreign concepts at Fenrir Farm. She'd thought she had hit the jackpot when she found Mischa and Imogen quietly watching *The Help* in the den, but despite the absolute silence and mile of couch separating the girls, Maggie got a strong we-want-some-alone-time vibe from the possibly-maybe-a-couple couple.

After wandering around some more, and getting hit in the head with one of the cardboard tubes Jase and Joshua were using as swords as they chased one another up and down the hallway, Maggie finally found an empty room. Like every other room in the house, it was obviously decorated by someone obsessed with Victorians. The walls were covered in a dark red satin, the carpet was think enough to double as a mattress, and the oversized desk and chairs taking up the majority of the room were carved mahogany. The only concession to modern times was the Chihuly hanging from the middle of the ceiling.

Within minutes she was so absorbed in her own thoughts and the charcoal flying across the paper she didn't hear the door open.

"Are you supposed to be in here?"

Maggie jerked back, causing the spinny-swively chair to almost topple over backwards. Her shriek would have made a Beatles fangirl proud.

"Jesus," the newcomer said, his hand covering his ears. "You know most of us have dog-like hearing, right? I think you just busted my eardrums."

"Sorry." She tried not to look at the errant streak of black stretching across the page she'd been working on. "I'm Maggie," she said, forcing her eyes back to the guy who was still standing in the doorway looking at her like she was one of the less interesting exhibits at the zoo. "I'm staying here for a couple of days."

"Yeah, I know. Even the Omega gets informed when a Thaumaturgic moves into the house."

"Omega?"

The new guy ignored her question, plowing on as if she hadn't said anything at all. "So, you guys are supposed to be like Seers, right? Like you have your one special thing you do, but instead of Seeing stuff you can like control it or whatever?"

"I've never said I was a—"

"So, what is your thing? Can you shoot fire out of your fingertips or breathe underwater or what?"

Maggie caught herself before explaining how it didn't exactly work like that. Thaumaturgics couldn't control their element so much as converse with it.

"Which Hagan are you?" she asked instead. She was pretty sure she hadn't met this one before, but she knew he had to be one of Charlie's relatives. She'd met a handful of them and they all had the exact same green eyes.

"Makya. Alpha Pack Omega."

"Omega. Right. Of course." Maggie thought over everything she knew about Shifters, and still came up with nothing. "What exactly is an Omega?"

The sigh escaping Makya's lips said he couldn't believe she was stupid enough to not know this.

"Omega. Lowest of the low. Servant of the Alpha Pack. See also: *whipping boy*."

"Oh," Maggie said, her face growing warmer and warmer by the second. She wasn't quite sure what to say, but that didn't keep her mouth from moving and words spilling out. "I didn't know. I don't really know anything about Shifters, other than they exist. I don't suppose you have a handy brochure or instructional video to get me caught up on all the terminology and everything?"

Makya snorted. "God, don't let Scout hear you say that. She's been threatening to make Marie and Michelle write one. She wants to call it *There Really is a Monster at the End of this Book*."

"I need something more self-helpy. How about *The Secret (to Living with Shifters)*?"

"*The 7 Habits of Highly Successful Shifters*?"

"*How to Befriend Seers and Influence Shifters*?"

"*Shifters are from the Moon, Seers are from the Stars*?"

Maggie wrinkled her nose. "That doesn't make sense."

"Preaching to the choir here, sister." Makya said as he unfolded a wand-like device with shredded rags on the end and began dusting the bookshelf on the wall behind her. For the first time, Maggie noticed the bucket of cleaning supplies he'd brought with him. He wasn't kidding about that whole Omega thing.

Knowing Makya wasn't one of the powerful, scary Alpha Pack Shifters made it easier for Maggie to relax.

"I'm just afraid I'm going to say or do the wrong thing," she confessed as he moved down to the next shelf. "Everything here has its place, and there are these rules everyone seems to know but me, and I'm like this idiot child, running around trying not to accidentally stomp on anyone's toes."

Makya looked over his shoulder, his eyes narrowed on Maggie as if he was trying to figure something out.

"Okay, this is what you need to know," he said with a sigh, turning around to face her. "One, keep Scout happy, which is basically impossible, because Scout is only happy when she's miserable. But she's the Alpha Female, and Liam, who is the Alpha Male, would move a mountain with a teaspoon if she asked him to, so it's Scout you have to concentrate on.

"Jase and Talley seem like happy-go-lucky people who do nothing but touch each other all the time, but they're both hella powerful. Jase can be ruthless and determined when he thinks something is important, and Talley is supposedly the Stella Polaris."

"Stella Polaris?" Maggie asked, wishing she had a glossary to keep up with all these crazy names the Shifters gave to everything.

Even though Makya wasn't quite as heart-stopingly gorgeous as Jase and Charlie, there was something about him and the rest of the Hagan men a girl couldn't help but notice. Maybe it was the clean lines comprising their slender but muscled Shifter bodies. Maggie traced Makya's biceps with her eyes as he reached up to scratch the back of his head. "Literally, the Stella Polaris is the North Star," he said, oblivious to her ogling, "but in Talley's case, it means the most powerful Seer on the planet."

The words Talley and powerful didn't seem like they went together, but neither did Jase and ruthless. Maggie wondered if Makya actually knew what he was talking about.

"What about Charlie?" she asked, trying to sound nonchalant and failing miserably. "What do I need to know about him?"

It took a few minutes for Makya to answer. He tried to play it off like he was too busy messing with the stuff in his cleaning bucket, but Maggie could recognize a stalling technique when she saw it. It only made her more eager to hear what he had to say.

"Charlie is..." Makya sprayed a thin coating of lemon-scented cleaner over the table. "I don't know. Hard, I guess." He nodded his head slightly, as if agreeing with himself. "He's always been more serious than Jase, but after his brother... You know about his brother, right?"

She hadn't, but once she gave it about half of a second's thought, she thought she might know where this was going.

"Toby Hagan was Charlie's brother, wasn't he?"

"Big brother. Pack Leader. Idol. They all apply."

Maggie tried to work through everything she'd learned from news reports after Scout's rescue and look at it through the filter of knowing they were Shifters.

"Toby didn't die rescuing Scout from domestic terrorists, did he? It was some Shifter thing?"

All the color seemed to bleed out of Makya's face, and Maggie wondered what his own connection to Toby had been.

"He was rescuing Scout, in a way, but it wasn't domestic terrorists," he said, his voice rougher and quieter than it had been moments before. "Scout and Liam were making their bid to become Alphas and things went bad. There was a big fight, and Toby didn't make it." Wetness shone in Makya's eyes, and Maggie had to blink back the answering moisture in her own. "After that, Charlie was different. I thought he would be angry and..." The deep breath he drew into his lungs sounded shaky as he exhaled. "He acted like he didn't even care. I don't know if he even cried at the funeral."

So that was the birth of the robot. Maggie tried to imagine what he had been like before his brother died. Was he fun and flirtatious like Jase? Sarcastic like Scout? Angry like his nephew Layne?

The door slammed open and Charlie stood there as if they had conjured him. His eyes darted accusingly back and forth between Maggie and Makya as if he'd heard their conversation.

Which he probably did, Maggie realized. Shifters and their supernatural hearing. It was going to take some getting used to.

"We need you," Charlie said to Makya without so much as a hello. "We're ready to bury the body."

He said "bury the body" the same way Maggie might say "eat a brownie".

"The autopsy?" Maggie asked, knowing they'd flown in someone from Romania to examine Barros's body. It all seemed wrong and under-handed to not call in the cops, but Talley assured her it was best to let the Shifters take care of their own. Maggie didn't consider burying a man next to a bunch of horses caring for one's own, but she held her tongue. They were going to find whoever did this, and then she was going to go back to her normally scheduled life.

"He was drugged," Charlie said. "Somebody must have slipped something in his food or drink and then attacked after he wasn't able to fight back. Actual cause of death was a stab wound. Like Joshua suspected, the arts-and-crafts portion was done after he'd been dead a while."

So no new information, other than maybe the drug thing. Maggie wasn't surprised. Actually, that was wrong. She *was* surprised, just not because the autopsy didn't uncover any important clues. What she couldn't believe was the Alpha Pack, who was nothing more than a bunch of college-age kids who had trouble ordering pizza on occasion, had been able to keep a dead body away from the authorities and media. Every day Maggie expected to see cops pulling up the long drive, lights flashing, but so far it hadn't happened.

Slowly Maggie became aware of something going on between Makya and Charlie. Their eyes were locked on one another, but not in a sexy slash-fanfiction kind of way. It was more like a really intense stare contest where the first person who blinked died.

"Robby and Joshua are waiting for you. You should go," Charlie said, his tone casual despite the obvious tension in the air.

Makya stepped forward, his eyes still locked on Charlie. "I will go because I want to. Because I chose this. Don't make the mistake of forgetting that."

And then Makya was gone with the quiet clink of the door shutting closed.

"That was—" Charlie turned towards Maggie, and she completely forgot what she was going to say. "Umm... What was that?"

Charlie's intense gaze traveled over her body, and she felt herself blush at the inspection.

"What were you doing in here with him?" he asked, his voice hard and severe like it had been when he was accusing her of killing Barros.

Maggie squared her shoulders and tried to hide how he was affecting her. She would will her hands to stop shaking and her voice to remain even. He wasn't going to push her around just because he was big and scary.

"I was drawing. He was cleaning." She forced herself to meet Charlie's eyes. "Not that it's any of your business. I'm here as a guest, not a prisoner or an Omega."

Charlie placed one hand on the back of her chair and the other on the table in front of her. She knew there was nothing behind her, but she felt pinned in all the same.

"Let me tell you what you need to know about Makya." His warm breath fanned over her cheek, causing goose bumps to shower down Maggie's spine. "He wasn't chosen as Omega because he's the weakest of our kind. He took the position as punishment for betraying his family. So if you're looking for a bad guy around here, he's it. Don't trust him. Don't feel sorry for him. And if you know what is best for you," he leaned impossibly closer, and Maggie tried to convince herself her heart was racing from fear instead of something much more disturbing, "you won't let me catch you alone with him again."

And then Charlie pushed himself away from her and followed Makya, although this time the door rattled in its frame as it slammed shut. Maggie took a deep breath and sent up a plea to the universe that the Alpha Pack would find their murderer soon, because she wasn't sure how she was going to survive if she had to be around Charlie Hagan much longer.

CHAPTER 15

It was with no small amount of shock that Maggie realized she was getting used to having Charlie around all the time. The scary, growling Charlie hadn't made a reappearance, and she found Robot Charlie oddly soothing. They spent the majority of their time in Rosa Hall where Maggie worked on stuff for her Etsy shop while Charlie messed around on the computer. It would have been peaceful if they could've locked the door to the studio. Unfortunately, there wasn't an actual door, which meant fifteen different types of music was constantly waging war on Maggie's eardrums and every independent study and grad student who wanted to come in to rant about their professors or rave about their newest project could just saunter right on in. Since neither she nor Charlie really encouraged this behavior, Maggie wasn't quite sure how hanging out in the ceramics room became the cool thing to do. She suspected it had something to do with Pepper, the girl who had been working on her MFA in ceramics for the past two years, although she couldn't be certain since the girl hadn't bothered to show up at the studio since school started.

Whatever the cause, Maggie's workspace wasn't the quiet, serene place she wanted it to be. Chaos reigned in Rosa Hall, and whenever Maggie felt as though she was going to be buried beneath it, she would look to Charlie, who seemed oblivious to the mayhem erupting around him. He was completely unflappable, merely raising an eyebrow when one of the glassblowers got his man-purse too close to the flames and everyone ran around screaming their heads off as if the building was burning to the ground. He became her Rock of Gibraltar, a breath of sanity in Bedlam.

Friday night Maggie found herself playing an elaborate board game in which Scout, Joshua, and Liam had to try to escape her and Layne's zombie. It was a long, drawn-out game. The clock declared it after midnight when she gleefully defeated the last of the townsfolk with a roll of double-sixes. As she climbed onto her massive Tempurpedic mattress thirty minutes later, she found herself already dreading moving back into the dorm, whenever that might be. She and Charlie had picked up the rest of her stuff earlier in the week, telling Reid she had been accepted into one of the secret societies and was moving in with one of the other members. Reid had cried and begged her to stay in a big dramatic scene, and in the end, Maggie had promised her she would have lunch with her at least twice a week so they could "stay close".

Because, obviously, ignoring each other for ten days built the sort of bond nothing could sever.

Maybe if they found the killer she could talk Scout into letting her stay somehow. Like maybe she could do all of their laundry in exchange for room and board. Of course, that meant they would have to fire the current laundry woman, but since she was a rather cantankerous woman who kept referring to Maggie as "that mixed girl," she didn't feel any guilt in wishing her out of a job.

A few hours after drifting off, Maggie was ripped from sleep by a scream that would make Wes Craven's heart stop in his chest. Without thinking, she bolted from her bed and out the door. A second scream came not two seconds later, and she took off down the hall towards the master bedroom. Her hand was just an inch from the door when a large, warm body encased her from behind and pulled her back a few steps. The only thing keeping her from shattering the night with high-pierced shriek of her own was the hand clamped over her mouth.

"Shhh.... It's me," a voice she knew all to well said in her ear.

She stopped trying to scream, but she still struggled against the arms holding her fast against his chest. Now she was closer, she could hear the crying and pleading. Someone was being tortured and Charlie was letting it happen.

"You can't go in there." His voice was soft and steady, as if he was trying to calm one of the volatile Thoroughbreds living on the far edge of the farm. "Scout is having a night terror. If you go in there, she'll think you're trying to attack her and retaliate."

As if she was in on the conversation and wanted to prove the point, Scout chose that moment to scream, "I will kill you!" at the top of her lungs.

"Someone needs to help her," Maggie said once Charlie dropped his hand.

"Liam is in there. He'll take care of her."

Something crashed against the wall next to the door.

"Are you sure?"

She wasn't struggling anymore, but Charlie still had his arms wrapped around her. Maggie became aware of how very little her thin nightshirt did to cover her. The heat from Charlie's bare chest penetrated straight through the flimsy material and soaked deep into her body, pooling up in the pit of her stomach. They were pressed so close together the hair from his legs tickled the backs of her bared knees.

If it wasn't for the constant sounds of distress coming from inside Scout's room, Maggie might have taken more than a second to think about the way her insides were turning to jelly.

"Does this happen often?" she asked to distract herself.

Charlie's chin brushed across the top of her head. "No. Only when Liam's here."

She leaned to the left an inch, turned her head, and looked up Charlie. "Liam isn't normally here?"

He looked down at her and Maggie felt every nerve inside her body fizzle. She wasn't even sure what fizzling was, but she was certain her nerves were doing it. But before she could short-circuit, Charlie turned his attention back to the closed door.

"He's here when he can be, but the Den is in Romania. He has to stay there most of the time." There was a fluttering sensation on Maggie's right side, which is how she realized Charlie was stroking her waist with his thumb. Suddenly, it felt like he was stroking other, much less decent places. "When he's gone, Scout doesn't do more than catnap. She's up all hours of the night, video conferencing with him or spending way too many hours in the gym. But when he comes home..."

"She sleeps." Maggie wasn't sure if she felt sorry for the couple, or if she was annoyed at Liam for not caring enough about Scout to stick around and at Scout for letting Liam control her life so completely.

Something shattered inside the room, and then another scream pierced the air.

"No, Scout. Wake up. You can't. Not here," came Liam's voice from inside the room.

Another scream, this one succeeding in raising all the tiny hairs on the back of Maggie's neck.

"Shouldn't we—"

The door banging open cut off her words. Liam stood in it, his massive physique silhouetted by the light spilling into the hallway. Scout was draped across his arms, and even with the bad lighting, Maggie could see her skin rippling. As she watched, the bone beneath Scout's eye visibly shattered.

The only thing saving Maggie from falling to the floor was Charlie's arms tightening around her waist.

"Help me get her outside. Now."

This time, when Maggie surged forward, Charlie let her. She held doors open so Liam and Charlie could carry Scout's mangled body through them. Her breath came in short, painful gasps as she opened the door leading from the corridor to outside. Liam and Charlie struggled down the front steps and laid Scout on the grass. Seconds after her body touched the ground, a white wolf stood, looking like something out of a beautiful nightmare, despite the tank top and boxer shorts it wore.

"Are you going to let me get those off of you?" Liam asked, kneeling down in front of her, his hand moving slowly, palm up, just like the lady from the pound taught Maggie to do when approaching an unknown dog.

Scout answered the Alpha Male by letting loose a low growl.

"I think that's a no," Charlie said. He was standing next to Maggie, and without thought, she slipped her hand into his. He gave her fingers a squeeze, the action doing more to calm her nerves than she thought possible.

"Be careful," Liam said to the wolf, who was already loping towards the back of the house. "And for the love of God, come back."

Liam's heartache was palatable, and if he was anyone else, Maggie would believe he was getting ready to burst into tears. If she hadn't been tethered to the spot by Charlie's hand, Maggie would have left him to it, but since she wasn't about to pull away from the warmth and strength Charlie provided, she just stood there and watched as Liam tried not to fall apart.

"What the hell was that?" Charlie asked once they could no longer see the white dot moving swiftly over the ground.

Liam rubbed the back of his head so hard it was a wonder he didn't lose skin in the process. "I don't know. She was having one of her normal waking nightmare things, and then..." He paced away as if he didn't want to drop an f-bomb right at their feet, then paced back and stood right in front of Charlie. "I heard what you told Maggie," he said. "Is it true?"

"Is what true?"

"Does she only do this when I'm here?" Liam's Adam apple rose and fell with an audible swallow. "Am I the reason this happens?"

Charlie slowly shook his head. "Man, it's not like—"

"I should leave," Liam said, pacing again. "She keeps telling me you guys can handle this and I should just go back to the Den." He stopped and rubbed his head again. "She doesn't want me here. I make her miserable."

"Listen, I think—"

"She still loves you, you know," Liam said. Maggie, who had been trying to pretend like she wasn't listening, snapped her head around so fast she made herself dizzy. "You're a good guy. Hell, if none of this had happened you two would probably be engaged by now. Maybe I should just—"

"No."

Liam had wandered away again, his back to Charlie and Maggie, who was trying to pull her hand out from Charlie's grip, all desire to touch him diminished at Liam's words. At Charlie's refusal, Liam turned just enough that he could look back at them, his eyes shining under the moonlight. "Did you see her? Did you see what I've done to her?" His lips pressed together tightly, and Maggie willed him not to cry. Men like Liam weren't supposed to cry. They were supposed to growl and glare and try to fix all the world's problems with their fists. Crying was not part of that equation. "I can't keep doing this to her, Charlie. She deserves better."

"You're right," Charlie said and Maggie considered kicking him. "She does deserve better. Scout Donovan deserves a mate who loves her."

Liam froze, the anger of an Alpha chasing the unshed tears from his eyes. "I do love her."

"Does she know it?"

"Of course she does. I'm her mate."

"Yes, she's painfully aware of the fact that she's your mate, but does she know you love her?"

Liam didn't respond.

"Listen, I don't know why on earth I'm in the middle of this, because God knows I don't want to be, but here are the facts: You love her. She loves you. You're both too damn stubborn to talk about it, but if you don't, you're going to lose each other. So do all of us in this house one big freaking favor, and tell her you're in love with her and can't live without her, and then spend the rest of your life proving it. Because, I promise you, if I ever found someone to love like that, they would never, ever doubt how I felt about them." His eyes flicked to the right, and for a moment Maggie thought he was looking at her. And then she saw the same thing he did, a white wolf coming out of the tree line.

In that moment, Maggie McCray began to hate Scout Donovan a little.

CHAPTER 16

Rosa Hall was eerily quiet on Saturday mornings.

"Do we really have to do this today?" Charlie asked, carrying a giant tub of clay over to the table. "Why can't this be a Tuesday morning activity?"

"Because we have classes on Tuesdays, and I can't leave the kiln my first time firing it." She checked the gauges on the side of the kiln and adjusted the airflow. "I've got to stay with it until it's done."

"Which will be when exactly?"

Maggie lifted a shoulder and glanced at the clock. "I'll try to have you home before midnight, princess."

"Midnight? We're going to be here all day? Do you understand the concept of a weekend?"

Maggie picked up a bowl someone had left on the shelf, frowning at a nick in its exterior. She ran a thumb over it, making the surface perfect once more.

"Weekend. Also known as Saturday and Sunday. Two days in which a person must try to accomplish the myriad of things they can't get done Monday through Friday."

"You realize you might have some sort of pathological workaholic problem, right?"

"I have ambition." She tilted her head at his feet, which were propped up on a stool. At her lifted eyebrow he raised them, allowing her to pass back over to the other side of worktable. "If you need to look it up on your phone, I understand and will try valiantly not to judge. At least not out loud."

Charlie glared at her over the top of the copy of Michael K. Vaughn's *Saga* clenched in his hands.

Input: Someone insults your vocabulary and laziness.

Output: Look annoyed.

Except, Maggie wasn't fooled by Robot Charlie. He wasn't annoyed. Annoyance requires unmet expectations and an emotional investment in another human being. Charlie didn't have expectations or emotional investments of any type, at least not when it came to her.

This morning when she'd gone downstairs to grab a cup of yogurt she'd found herself alone with Charlie in the kitchen. After everything that happened the night before, she'd expected things to be different between the two of them. She wasn't sure how they would change - maybe things would be awkward due to regret or embarrassment, or maybe things would continue to shift in the direction they'd begun the night before - but either way, she was braced for something, and instead got the same old nothing as always. No inability to make eye contact. No flushed cheeks. No apologies. No secret smiles. No lean-in or accidentally-on-purpose touches. No "we need to talk." Just the same "good morning" they'd been passing back and forth for a week.

That was when she knew last night hadn't meant anything to him at all. Well, obviously the night held meaning, but not because of her. It was all about Scout for him, and from what she could infer from everything she'd seen while living with the Alpha Pack, it had always been about Scout for Charlie.

"If I ever found someone to love like that, they would never, ever doubt how I felt about them."

Maggie felt certain Scout did know. It was in the way she went through her day always expecting him to be there, knowing he would tell her whatever she wanted.

The tiny seed of dislike planted the night before grew a bit at the realization. Scout knew how Charlie felt and took advantage of it, but she obviously didn't feel the same about him. Anyone could see no matter what their current issues might be, Scout loved Liam with her whole heart. Maggie might not know a ton about Shifters and their customs, but she knew mates were something beyond a normal human relationship. Scout wasn't going to leave Liam for Charlie, yet she kept him hanging around.

It shouldn't have mattered to Maggie how the Alpha Pack felt about each other or how they treated one another. However, knowing that didn't stop the little ball of anger fueled by disappointment to form in her stomach.

What was so damn special about Scout anyway? So what if she was some badass who looked like a supermodel, had access to millions of dollars, and could change into a white wolf in the blink of an eye? Did that make her any better than Maggie?

Unfortunately, Maggie knew it did. And that was the problem. If Scout Donovan was Charlie's ideal, then there was no way he would ever be convinced to turn his attentions towards Maggie.

Not that I would want his attention, Maggie lied to herself. *I haven't got time for some stupid college fling. And even if I did, I like my men to be men, not robots. Who would want to start a relationship with someone incapable of human emotions?*

She tried desperately hard to ignore the tiny part of her brain screaming, *"Me!"* but it was nearly impossible. She tried to tell herself the voice just wanted him because she knew she couldn't have him. When she couldn't make herself believe that, she tried the only-because-he-touched-you-and-you're-touch-starved argument. That didn't work much better. Maggie was well acquainted with things she couldn't have, and chose instead to focus on the things she could obtain and how she was going to get them. And touch-starved wasn't ever a phrase she would ascribe to herself. Sure, she needed a hug every now and again as much as anyone else, but human contact wasn't something she normally craved. Some dirt beneath her feet and a breeze tugging the strands of her hair did more to refresh her soul than any kiss had ever managed.

Maybe that is just because you haven't kissed Charlie yet.

The mutinous part of her brain was getting louder. To quieten it, she turned her attention to her clay. Her initial intent had been to throw her NCECA piece, but she was too morose at the moment to even consider it. When it came time to throw that piece, it would require all her heart and soul, both of which were a little distracted at the moment. Instead, she forced herself to concentrate on making the mass as square and even and smooth as possible, knowing the result would be so perfect someone would accuse her of trying to pass off mass-produced as handmade. She was just slicing off the final row when a familiar voice broke through the calm and quiet.

"Mags! Yay! You're here!" Reid came bouncing into the room, her bangs now a pattern of alternating blue and pink stripes. "I was worried I would be so bored all day, but now I get to talk to you." She slung her arms around Maggie's frozen body. "God really does love me best of all."

"Hey, Reid," Maggie said, tapping the other girl's back with the very tips of her fingers, hoping Reid wouldn't have a meltdown when she realized her black D&G shirt now had grayish fingerprints all along the back. "What are you doing here?"

"My boyfriend insists on working today, and I insist on spending the whole weekend with him, thus..." She spread her arms. "Ta-da. Here I am."

"But you're not supposed to be in here. At all. This building is off limits to anyone who isn't an independent study or grad student."

"So?"

"So you could get Davin in tons of trouble, even kicked out of the program."

"As if." Maggie rolled her eyes. "Anyway, you're one to talk. You've got your boy toy here, too." She shot a pointed look in Charlie direction.

"Charlie is not my boy toy," she said, refusing to acknowledge the blush spreading across her face. "He's an independent study student. Drawing."

To prove the point, and that he was listening, Charlie waved his stylus in the air.

Reid snorted indelicately through her nose and hopped up onto the table, next to Maggie's clay, which made it impossible for Maggie to actually do any work.

"I thought you needed like charcoal pencils or something to draw," Reid said, fingering the edge of one of the coasters Maggie had just cut out. Maggie clenched her fists so tightly she could feel her practically nonexistent nails biting into her skin. "He's playing on the computer."

"It's called digital art," Charlie said, not looking up from his screen. "Welcome to the twenty-first century."

Reid flattened the corner of a second coaster and Maggie quickly reviewed the signs of a brain hemorrhage, hoping Charlie would recognize one when she finally succumbed.

"You're getting dust all over your jeans," Maggie said through clenched teeth.

Lifting her left butt cheek off the table, Reid examined her jeans, which weren't just dust-encrusted, but also had a splotch of paint on the pocket. "Oh well," she said with a shrug. "These are old jeans anyway."

"They're from Anthropologie." And they probably cost over two hundred dollars a pair. Maggie's own jeans were a pair of Levi's she'd picked up at the Goodwill for less than five dollars, and she would've still be a little panicked over ruining them.

"They're from last year. I was going to toss them anyway."

Maggie considered asking Reid if she would just give them to her. There was no way Maggie could wear them, the leg was roughly the length of Maggie's entire body, but even with the paint stain she could maybe get enough off of them on eBay to make up for the batch of coasters Reid was *completely ruining*.

"Is Davin going to get upset that you're spending all your time hanging out with us instead of with him?"

As if conjured by Maggie's question, Boyfriend appeared in the doorway. His hair was pulled up in a knot on the back of his head. Maggie had seen movie stars pulling off the same look in gossip magazines, but on Boyfriend it looked more repressed librarian than relaxed badass. The shirt he wore had both arms cut out, along with most of the sides, and his jeans had holes so large and so high that everyone who saw him knew his blue boxers were fraying along the edge.

Maggie decided she might be more scandalized at this point to see him in a turtleneck and slacks than walking through the middle of town without a stitch of clothing on.

"Hey, babe. What are you doing in here?"

Reid finally hopped off the table and flung herself at her douche of a boyfriend, wrapping her arms around his sweaty body as if he'd just returned from a two-year stint in the Middle East. "I found Maggie!"

Boyfriend's mouth tightened. "I didn't realize she was lost."

"You're so funny," Reid giggled, playfully slapping his chest.

Maggie was saved from having to watch the resulting sloppy, visible-tongue kissing by her phone. She was temporarily confused when she saw Charlie's name pop up on the screen, but then she read the message.

"Isn't Mr. Comedian ridiculously wealthy? Couldn't he at least afford an outfit?"

She hid a smile as she texted back. *"And cover that beautiful body? It would be a crime against humanity."*

Her phone beeped again before she could even put it back down. *"When are they going to stop kissing?"*

"It could be hours."

"You are never living with her again. I promise."

Instead of texting back, Maggie moved her hand from her chin to down in front of her chest in the American Sign Language sign for "thank you". Charlie responded with a subtle upturn of those dangerously beautiful lips and repeated the gesture.

Freaking Charlie Hagan. Why did he have to go and be so damn cute when she was trying her hardest to not have a crush on him?

Eventually Reid and Boyfriend took their make-out fest down the hall to the metalworking shop, finally leaving Maggie and Charlie to work in peace. With the exception of Reid and Boyfriend returning around noon with a pizza, which might have been the first time Maggie had ever been happy to see the two of them, no one else came into the ceramics studio. A few other students came in and worked in the other studios, but they were amazingly subdued, their presence only marked by the occasional soft-spoken conversation. Yet, despite the lack of external distraction, Maggie found it impossible to concentrate. Her mind kept flying off in different directions, thinking about everything from the ongoing murder investigation to life with Shifters to how nice Charlie looked in his faded Incredible Hulk t-shirt as the sun coming through the window cast him in a natural spotlight. She spent most of the day sketching instead of working with the clay, knowing it would be pointless to attempt anything. It would've come out as confused and erratic as her thoughts.

"Too bad we don't have an x-ray machine," Maggie said to Charlie not long after lunch. She was adjusting the gas yet again, praying she wasn't screwing anything up. She'd never worked with a gas kiln before, having only had access to the tiny electric one at the community building growing up.

Charlie looked up from the screen his eyes had been fixed on for hours. "We need an x-ray machine?"

"For the painting," she explained.

"The painting. Of course." Charlie sat the computer down on the table. "Maggie, dear, is there a chance you've inhaled a few too many fumes today?"

"*The* painting." Really, how many other paintings could she be talking about? "If we had an x-ray machine we might be able to see whose face was face painted beneath mine."

"There is a face beneath yours?"

Maggie looked thorough the peepholes, wishing she could manipulate the flames so she could get a clear view of her pieces. She was abnormally uneasy about this firing. She didn't know if it was because she was using a new kiln for the first time or if all the craziness of the last week was making her feel anxious over every aspect of her life, but she wanted nothing more than for time to fast-forward to tomorrow night when she could get her pieces out and make sure they were okay.

"Of course there is a face beneath mine. We already covered this. My face was probably added no more than forty-eight hours before we found it. The paint was still wet, remember?"

Charlie's eyes followed her as she moved around the kiln, removing bricks and squinting into the haze.

"And you think they painted it over another face?"

Maggie slid the last brick home. "Of course they did."

"And you didn't think to mention this to someone before now?"

"Let me say, yet again, I thought we already had this discussion." Maybe Robot Charlie and Angry Charlie were two different personalities who didn't share information well.

"We discussed that your face was painted last, not that it was covering up an old one." Charlie pinched the bridge of his nose, an uncharacteristic display of annoyance. "Maggie, you've got to stop hiding information from us."

"What are you talking about? I'm not hiding anything."

"Really? Then what is it you can do, Thaumaturgic?"

Maggie swallowed down something that couldn't have been guilt. Nope. No guilt. Definitely not that. After all, it wasn't exactly like she was the only one who thought it was a bad idea to tell the controlling group of her people's natural-born enemies what she could do. After Scout and Charlie left her room that first night, Joshua had found her, and they had a little talk, Immortal to Thaumaturgic.

"Their knowledge of what I am and where I come from is very basic," Joshua said. "It's not that I don't trust the people in this house. I do. More than I've ever trusted anyone else in my life, which has been considerably longer than this handsome face would have you believe." He was sprawled over the same chair Scout had occupied earlier, which made Maggie wonder if it was the chair or if every member of the Alpha Pack had horrible posture. "But they're still the Alpha Pack, and the Alpha Pack is an institution which has had a long history of not cooperating with other supernaturals. And one day, whether it's in a hundred days or a hundred years, Scout and Liam's Alpha Pack will be gone, and another will take its place. Scout and Liam I trust, but their successors? Maybe I will, but there's a chance I won't, and I won't risk the lives of the other Immortals on that chance. So, I keep an air of mystery when it comes to my race, and I suggest you do the same."

And so she had. Everyone from Jase to Liam had asked her what it was she could do, but she'd kept her mouth shut, just as Joshua had suggested. It hadn't been hard, and no one had pressured her for an answer after a single attempt, although she felt certain they were working together to wear her down. But somehow with Charlie it was different. He was altering his entire life to protect her, yet he didn't even know what he was really protecting. And stupid feelings of jealousy aside, the two of them had formed a timid sort of bond over the past week. Friends may have been stretching it a bit, but whatever friend-type relationship a girl and robot could have, they were building one of those. He was like her very own C3PO, just not as shiny or British.

"It's not like you've spilled all the secrets about Shifters and Seers to me." It sounded defensive because it was. "Are you going to tell me what Talley can See?"

Charlie crossed his arms over his chest, a challenge in his eyes. "Thoughts and emotions. She can also catch small glimpses of the future."

Maggie nearly dropped the vase she was moving in a bout of nervous organizing. "Two sights? But I thought they were only supposed to have one talent, like us." Not that she was admitting to being a Thaumaturgic.

Except she kinda just did.

Damn it.

"Talley is special. Joshua thinks she's the Stella Polaris."

Maggie watched thousands of particles jump up to embrace the afternoon sun streaming through the window as she ran a duster over a stack of bowls she was pretty sure had been there since Lindsay Lohan was known as that cute red-headed kid from Disney movies. If he was willing to tell her about Talley, how much more would he share?

There was only one way to find out.

CHAPTER 17

"So, Talley knows what is going on in my head at all times?"

He knew it was coming, and quite frankly he was a little surprised it had taken this long, but he still hesitated. Liam had told him to give her whatever she wanted to know. The Thaumaturgics didn't have a central ruling body like the Shifters and Seers did, so there was no one for her to leak their information to. She had the full trust of the Alphas, and even without Talley's gift, Charlie knew she wasn't the kind of person who would do anything to harm the people who were trying to protect her. They may have only known each other for a week, but it had been a fairly intense week. Still, he didn't want to start down this path. He knew all too well where it would eventually lead, and they were just getting to the point where she didn't look at him like he was a monster. He hated to prove he was everything she initially thought and more.

"She has to be touching a person to See them," he told her. "And then she only Sees what she wants to, with the exception of Immortals, Thaumaturgics, and their offspring."

Maggie climbed onto the table next to him. It was too close. From this distance he could smell the lavender and vanilla mingling with her distinctly Maggie scent, which reminded him of open fields on an early summer morning. The smell had his coyote, who he'd been fighting extra-hard to keep at bay, sitting up and taking notice. It would appear rude and be completely cowardly to get up and move to the other side of the room like he wanted, but he did manage to put some space between them by leaning his chair back on two legs and propping himself against the wall.

"How are we different?" she asked, not realizing she'd admitted to being a Thaumaturgic for the second time in just ten minutes.

"Immortals and Thaumaturgics are harder for her to See. Joshua has to be projecting pretty hard for her to get anything at all. With you, she says you're a little more open naturally, but still she only gets a surface glimmer." The full truth was Talley could glean more off Maggie than she ever thought possible for a Thaumaturgic who wasn't actively projecting, but he wasn't going to tell her that. Talley's feelings were too easily hurt by people who avoided her touch. "It's the reason we knew we could trust you. Talley said she could See you weren't lying."

"And here I thought she was just one of those touchy-feely people. Instead, she was just trying to rummage through my head."

"Oh, no. Talley definitely is one of those touchy-feely people. Sometimes she's just hugging you because she likes hugs."

He hoped she would leave the discussion there, but his hope fizzled as she pulled up her feet and arranged her legs in crisscross-applesauce style, bracing her elbows on her knees. There was no mistaking her I'm-in-this-for-the-long-haul pose.

"And the visions of the future? What are they like? Can she give me tonight's winning lottery numbers?"

"No, her visions are sporadic and more of the bad-things-are-coming variety than fabulous-wealth-and-riches." The worst part was, once she Saw something, it would happen. There was no changing that moment, though they'd found they could prepare for the moments after. "As far as I know, they've all been about Scout."

Because he was paying so much attention to her, he saw Maggie's eyes tighten ever so slightly. "It always comes back to Scout, doesn't it?"

"She's the Alpha Female. The first Shifter Alpha Female in over a thousand years. It's kind of a big deal."

"So loyal," Maggie said, and it didn't sound like a compliment. "What did she ever do to earn your undying faithfulness?"

"She forgave me."

"For what? Forgetting to bow down when she entered the room?"

"For killing the boy she loved."

There it was. He laid it out there, and now it was hers to do with what she would. He couldn't change or forget the past, no matter how much he wanted to. The night his coyote sent Alex's wolf over the edge of a cliff would forever be burned into his brain, a nightmare he created and could not escape.

It took so long for her to respond he eventually had to draw a breath. She tilted her head and watched as he fought to keep his emotions at bay.

"You didn't mean to do it," she finally said. "It was an accident."

Accident. It's what everyone had been saying from the beginning, but he knew better. He went out that night enraged Scout had chosen Alex over him. He couldn't remember the details, but when he was human again, Scout was in a hospital bed and Alex was dead. Liam and

Scout had both forgiven him, but he would never forgive himself. He would die with Alex's blood on his hands.

"You don't know," he said. "You weren't there."

"But I know you." Some unnamable emotion shot through him at her declaration, but he quickly buried it. "You wouldn't hurt someone on purpose unless they deserved it."

"And you know this how?"

He held his breath as she leaned in close, and then two fingers trailed lightly over the tips of his lashes. "Because sometimes even Robot Charlie can't keep the truth out of your eyes."

She hadn't even touched a place with nerves, but his whole body felt her caress. It was a remembered sensation. His body knew how her small frame fit against his, of the warmth and softness that was her skin. There was no quelling his coyote now. Something about her had spoken to that side of him since the moment he first saw her, and her touch was quickly becoming an addiction to his more primitive side. Last night, when she'd pulled away to go to bed, it'd taken everything Charlie possessed to not to prowl after her. The coyote demanded more touching, and it was only through the discipline Charlie had been subjecting himself to for the past year that he was able to walk away.

"Why it happened doesn't matter," he said, his voice rough. Maggie moved away from him, but it wasn't helping. His teeth ground with the effort of putting the coyote back in its cage. "Some mistakes shouldn't be forgiven."

"What a completely horrible thing to believe."

"The truth is often horrible."

For some absurd reason, Maggie smiled, a bright, full smile that almost managed to chase away the ghosts now haunting him.

"My grandmother would have loved you," she said. "She was an eternal optimist, a true believer in goodness and light and all that stuff." She hopped off the table. "Basically, the exact opposite of you."

"And she would love me… why?"

Maggie walked down the aisle, looking back and forth beneath the two tables. She stopped near the end and pulled out a large plastic container. "My grandmother loved many, many things. Hot chocolate on cold winter nights. The way dogwood trees bloom in the spring." She popped off the lid and began peeling back the plastic sheets beneath. "The one thing she loved more than anything else, though, was arguing." She flashed another smile his way as she grabbed a wire cutter. "She would have had field day with you, Charlie Hagan."

"I'd like to meet her," he said, surprised he actually meant it. He could just imagine what Maggie's grandmother would be like. A little woman with a big smile and lots of attitude.

The pause was small, hardly noticeable, but Charlie caught it, and he knew what it meant. He paused the same way every time someone asked him about Toby.

"Grandmother died last year." Another pause, this time to blink back the moisture shining in her eyes. Once she had control of her tear ducts again, she took a deep breath and flashed another smile, although this was much more subdued. "Which is why I'm doing this as my final project for the year."

"This being…?"

She thunked the clay onto the wheel. "It's a show-and-tell. You'll have to wait." He watched as she flitted around the studio, getting everything she needed ready. He'd grown accustomed to seeing her in her brightly colored dresses, which somehow made her outfit of jeans and an old, faded t-shirt seem almost more revealing even though considerably less skin showed. By the time she planted herself on the other side of the wheel he was fighting once again to keep his coyote under control.

It only took seconds for a shape to start to form. Charlie had watched other people throw clay in class. When they sat at the wheel, they used their hands to guide and shape the mud to create a bowl or vase or whatever. Not Maggie. When Maggie's hands glided over the mud they weren't doing something so basic as moving the clay to suit her needs. No, Maggie's hands merely danced along as the clay formed itself. They didn't guide and shape so much as coax and encourage. It was beautiful to watch.

"I've been wondering something about last night." Charlie's head jerked up, his cheeks flushing. How long had he been sitting there hypnotized by her hands?

"Last night?" *Why, yes. I did enjoy touching you. Can we do it again soon? Like maybe now?* "What about?"

She pushed the clay up, adding height. "What happened with Scout? It looked like she couldn't Change. Her body was trying to, but she couldn't do it until she was outside. Was it the moon? Because I thought you guys only did that under the full moon, but last night was like a half-moon or something. It seemed to be enough to help Scout, though."

"Most of us do only Change under the full moon," he said, making an executive decision to let her in on some lesser-known facts about the Alpha Pack. She was living with them and could learn most of this by paying attention. Anyway, he needed to think about something other than the way those jeans hugged her body. "Scout and Liam are special. Liam can Change anytime he wants, but it's still the slow, painful process we all go through. Scout on the other hand..."

"Is all, 'Poof! I'm a wolf.'"

"Exactly."

"Except she couldn't last night."

"No, she couldn't do it last night," he said. "She's completely asleep during her night terrors and has no idea what she's doing. I'm sure she thought she was in a massive field or thick patch of woods, but she wasn't, so she didn't have any energy to tap into."

A lip started to form at the top of the vase. "Energy? From the moon?"

"From the ground."

For the first time since she started, Maggie's eyes left the wheel to meet Charlie's. "The ground?"

"Yeah, we pull energy from the ground when we Change. It's all the conservation of energy, E equals MC squared stuff."

Maggie's focus went back to the clay as she began slowing the wheel. "Energy from the ground. That's interesting."

Charlie didn't find it so much interesting as deathly boring, but then again, he'd grown up a Shifter. Everything about their world he took for granted was new to Maggie. He could see the way she ate up every morsel in her expressive black eyes.

"Well," Maggie said, taking a deep breath, "here comes the moment of truth." She ran a wire cutter under the vase and lifted it off the wheel, her measured breaths the only sound in the room as she crossed over and sat it on the table. "Oh my God." She spoke in a whisper, as if she thought too much noise would shatter it. "I did it." Her smile was so joyful when she turned to him that Charlie felt the corners of his mouth tilting up in response. "Come look!"

There was no way he could resist. He was out of his seat and by her side in seconds, borrowing a bit of speed from his coyote.

"Oh, wow," he said, immediately regretting the way all of his words came out bland and bored anymore. "This is amazing. I swear, I can almost see through it."

Maggie ran a finger over the lip. "Once it's fired, painted, glazed, and fired again, you'll be able to."

"Really?" Charlie knew just enough from his one week crash-course in the world of ceramics that was a very big deal.

"If the Grolley is as good of a porcelain as I've been told, then..." Those expressive eyes traveled over the vase and then back to him. "Yeah, I think it's going to work." If possible her smile spread even further across her face. "I'm going to paint the inside with cobalt. Oh, here." She turned and yanked up her shirt, causing Charlie to clench his hands so tight there was a chance a bone may have snapped in two. "This is the pattern I'm going to use," she said, referring to the blue rose pattern tattooed on her side.

"I think my mom has some dishes with that on them," he managed to ground out.

"Yeah, well..." Maggie shrugged. "It's something that was important to my grandmother."

"Which makes it important to you."

"Exactly," she said, dropping her shirt. If she noticed the way he was growling the words at her, she didn't show it. "So, the plan is to paint that on the inside. Then, if God loves me as much as Reid thinks he loves her, when you hang a gallery light right over the top, you'll be able to see the pattern from the outside."

"So, what you're telling me is I'm currently looking at what will become ceramics answer to the Mona Lisa?"

Maggie bit her lip and tilted her head to the side, eyes narrowed on the vase. "No..."

"I'm telling you, Maggie. I don't know—"

"Not this one," she said, picking it up with considerably less care than when she'd taken it off the wheel. "I'm going to throw another one. A thinner one."

Charlie's experience with perfectionism was vast. He was, after all, a member of the Alpha Pack. Perfectionism and control issues where pretty much standard issue. But no one took it to the extreme quite like Maggie.

"Are you insane? That one is so thin I don't know how it's not collapsing in on itself as it is. No one can throw thinner than that."

She placed the Vase of Impossible Thinness on a wire shelf beside some other will-probably-never-make-it-to-kiln pieces.

"I can," she said, turning back to him.

"How?" It had to be impossible, but then her eyes met his, and he knew. As long it was made out of clay, Maggie could do anything.

“It’s a natural talent,” she said with a smile he couldn’t help but return.

CHAPTER 18

Charlie spent Sunday morning patrolling the grounds of Fenrir Farm with Layne. Because of his newfound course work, Charlie hadn't spent much time with his nephew. And even though Layne didn't seem to mind, Charlie felt a bit guilty about it all the same.

It took an ungodly amount of effort to get Layne awake, dressed, and outside. More than once Charlie considered just leaving him behind, but he knew taking Layne out was important. It wasn't just the substitute-daddy-and-me time Charlie's psychiatrist assured him Layne needed. Following Maggie's advice from yesterday, Joshua had shown up at two in the morning with a mobile x-ray machine. Because he's Joshua, he knew exactly what to do, and two hours later Charlie's gut clenched as he looked at a ghostly version of Layne's face.

"What do you see?" Charlie asked as they stood on the northern edge of the Alpha Pack's property. When Layne didn't answer, Charlie reached over and plucked an earbud out of his ear and asked again.

"I don't know? Like, trees and grass and shit."

I wouldn't have to teach him how to protect himself if I went ahead and killed him myself.

"Look closer. How can someone get onto the property here? Is there anything out of place? Has anyone besides us been through here recently?"

Layne's gaze never left Charlie's face.

"For the love of God, just look."

Still staring at his uncle, Layne gave a sigh of overwhelming boredom. "The fence is low enough even a four year old could climb over it, and for reasons I don't understand, it's not electric. Anyone who wanted could crawl right on over and slit our throats in the night, but no one has been over recently because the ivy hasn't been broken or smooshed. Are we done now?"

Okay, so maybe Layne didn't need Charlie to show him the ropes.

"What about smells? Do you catch anything off?"

A smirk lifted one corner of Layne's mouth making him look like a carbon copy of his father. Charlie ran his palm over the sudden discomfort in his chest.

"Well, you smell like a loser. It's called body spray, man. Buy some."

"New flash, kid. The commercials lie. Reeking isn't sexy. I would tell you to ask a girl, but since none of them will actually talk to someone as pathetic as you..." Charlie shrugged off the end of his sentence, and Layne responded by flipping him off.

And winner of Parent of the Year goes to... Anyone but Charlie Hagan.

"Maybe this was a bad idea." He hated to admit defeat, but this was pointless. Layne obviously knew how to keep his eyes open when it actually mattered, and all the two of them were going to accomplish together was pissing each other off. "Come on," he said, turning back towards the house. "If we hurry, we can get a pizza before I have to take Maggie back to campus this afternoon."

Five steps later, he realized Layne wasn't following him. He turned back around to find his nephew standing with his nose practically pressed against a tree. His eyes were closed, and his hands were balled into fists at his side.

"Layne...?"

"There is something here. It's all messed up, but I know this scent. It's... it's..." His eyes snapped open. "Is this a test?"

Charlie shook his head as he walked back to where Layne was standing. He was about a foot away when he too caught the weird chemical smell of a scent blocker.

"It's old. From last week," he said. "I found it the day we found Barros's body. I've had Robby look into it, and he says it's our neighbor. Apparently the guy is a nature photographer who doesn't understand property lines. He trampled all over the farm trying to get the perfect shot of a red-tailed hawk."

"But the smell..." Layne took another deep sniff. "It's familiar. I know this person, and it isn't the guy next door." Charlie didn't say anything as Layne continued to try to place the scent. He stood back, giving him the space he needed. Part of Charlie hoped he actually teased out something to prove Robby wrong. Charlie's gut didn't like his cousin's explanation, and like Layne, he found something familiar beneath the scent-blocking chemicals.

Layne's eyes once again snapped open, but this time all the disdain and ire normally shining out from their green depths were gone and replaced by a sheen of vulnerability.

"It's dad," he said quietly, and then again with more conviction. "It's dad, Charlie. I can smell dad."

Damn it. Just... Damn. It.

"Layne, you know it can't be your dad."

"I know it's not actually him. He's been dead over a year now. I've kinda noticed." Despite his harsh words and the valiant effort he put into appearing apathetic, Layne still looked like a sad, scared little boy. If Charlie didn't think it would earn him a black eye, he would've hugged him. "I'm saying the smell underneath is the same, like how yours is the same as his. But this is different."

"Different how?" Charlie had never noticed a similarity in his and Toby's scents, but he'd never been particularly good at sniffing out the subtle nuances of different smells. Layne, it seemed, didn't have that problem. He'd just been Changing for two years, but signs of being a Dominant were already starting to show. Not surprising since he completed his first Change at eleven, two years earlier than either Charlie or Jase. "Different like another Hagan?"

Layne took another deep breath and released it on a growl. "It's too faint, and the scent blocker is screwing it up. I can't tell."

Charlie scrubbed a hand over his face, trying to think. Robby was convinced the scent originated with their idiot neighbor. If it had been one of the guys from Romania, he would do his own digging around, but Robby was a Hagan. He'd been one of Toby's closest friend, and Charlie knew for a fact the guy wouldn't ever put his family or his Alphas in danger. If Robby said the scent didn't represent a threat, then it didn't.

Still, Charlie couldn't shake the feeling something was off.

"I'll talk to Liam," he told Layne. "If there is anything we're missing, he'll find it."

That night found Charlie back at the studio with Maggie. He was actually happy to be returning to the tiny room with its industrial floors, cinder block walls, and inch high layer of dust coating every possible surface. It was beginning to feel like home.

"Here we go," Maggie said, unlatching the door of the kiln. She opened it about an inch and then stopped. Her eyes were squeezed shut and her chest was rising and falling with slow, deliberate breaths. "I can't look," she finally admitted.

"What? Why not?" Charlie hadn't actually fired any ceramics before, but he didn't expect this to be a big deal. What could have possibly gone wrong? "You know they're going to be perfect." It was one of the benefits of being able to manipulate clay with Thaumaturgic skills.

"I don't know. I just have this really bad feeling—"

"Like maybe you're over-stressed from an extremely emotionally taxing week? That kind of bad feeling?" Charlie knew all about that feeling. Liam had given him a long, heartfelt talk about it earlier.

Maggie gave him a tiny smile. "Yeah. Kinda like that." She rolled her shoulders and stretched her neck as if preparing for a fight. "My brain is just being stupid. Nothing happened in the kiln." She threw open the door. "That would be—"

Maggie froze, her face twisted into a mask of horror. He had to physically move her aside to see the damage for himself.

"What the hell?"

It looked like a bomb had gone off. Debris was everywhere. The lucky pieces were riddled with holes. The unlucky pieces were completely shatter.

"I... I..." A single tear dripped down her cheek. "Oh, my God. Oh. My. God. Who would do this?"

"How did this happen?"

"Wet clay. It had to be wet."

"Wet clay?"

"Mine was all dry. I know it was. And Chase has been doing this for twenty years. She knows you can't put wet clay in a kiln. It'll explode, and..." Instead of finishing, she fished her phone out of her pocket and started pacing.

"Chase?" Because he was a Shifter and the moon was growing in the sky, he could hear their teacher's confirmation, and Chase swearing the only thing she'd put in there was two little turtles she was making for her nephew. He could see both turtles had mostly survived, although they were missing their heads. Maggie asked if the mysterious Pepper might have put something in, and that was when they learned she was in jail on a drug charge.

"What were the little balls supposed to be?"

Maggie stopped pacing. "Balls?"

"Yeah, the balls of clay you placed on each shelf. Are they supposed to be something, was it wadding, or were you testing air flow around your pieces or something?"

"I didn't—" She closed her eyes and Charlie could almost see her thinking through different scenarios. "It was an experiment," she finally said. "And it went all kinds of wrong. I'm sorry, Chase, but your turtles are kinda dead."

Chase tried to tell Maggie it was no big deal and her nephew would probably prefer a box of Legos anyway, but Maggie insisted on apologizing for a full five minutes and paying her for damages, which Chase estimated to be a grand total of five dollars. The moment the call was over Maggie slumped down onto the floor and buried her face in her hands.

"Someone sabotaged your pieces on purpose," Charlie said.

"Fifteen hundred dollars."

"Five. Five dollars." Charlie squinted at one of the little turtle figurines. "And that's for the two of them together, not each. Although, looking at these things, I think she might be swindling you." He picked one of them up, trying to figure out if paint would make them look less or more like turtles instead of six circle of various sizes stuck together, seemingly at random. "Are you sure Chase knows what she's talking about? I mean, I would expect the person who is supposed to be teaching me ceramics to actually know how to do ceramics, at least enough to make a kid a turtle."

"My pieces. The dishes." Maggie looked up, and even though he hadn't heard so much as a sniffle, her cheeks were wet with tears. "My stuff was worth fifteen hundred dollars." She wiped her cheeks and stood. Charlie had the urge to hug her, so he shoved his hands in his back pockets. "It was a commission," she said, walking over to stand beside him. "It was going to be a complete set of Hulk dinnerware. The buyer was going to pay me fifteen hundred dollars, but they had to be shipped by next week."

Tears ran down her cheeks again. Somehow the silence with which she wept made it all the more heart-breaking.

"I can't get it done now. I'll have to message them and let them know." She used the back of her hands to dry off her cheeks, although it didn't do much good. New tears took the place of the discarded ones almost immediately. "Do you think there is any chance they'll not write a horrible review about my lack of professionalism?"

"We can fix this." There had to be a way. He couldn't stand much more of her quiet tears.

"I can't. Once the clay is set, it's set. Even I can't undo what the fire has done."

"So you make new ones. Big deal. You can have that many plates and bowls thrown by midnight."

She picked up a plate that was almost usable. "But I have to fire them, and I can't do that until Saturday."

"Why not?"

"Because I have to be with it all day, and I have classes Monday through Friday. You should probably remember that since you're taking them with me."

Charlie curled up one side of his mouth and raised his eyebrows. It was a practiced look, one that was supposed to say, *I'm-about-to-talk-you-into-doing-something-wonderfully-naughty*. He'd perfected it as a teenager trying to get to second base with whichever girl would give him the time of day, but he hadn't put it into practice in a very long time.

"Maggie McCray, haven't you ever heard of the concept of skipping?"

She swiped her cheeks again, this time succeeding in getting them dry. "It's only the third week of school. No one skips during the third week of school."

"Why not? It seems like a perfectly good time to skip, if you ask me. We've got a few weeks before our first exam, so we're probably not going to miss anything they won't cover again." He could see his logic wearing down her defenses. The spark of hope he saw in her eyes turned his half-smirk into a full-on smile. "Come on, Magpie. We can do this. I'll clean up this mess while you throw, and then tomorrow we'll stay here all day and fire."

"The clay won't be dry enough—"

"Can you make it dry enough?"

"Maybe." She ran a finger around the rim of the plate she was still holding. "No, I mean..." She lifted her lashes and met Charlie's eyes. "Yes. I can do it."

"Well, then," Charlie said, grabbing a bowl out of the kiln and silently cursing himself for not realizing earlier that it would be hot, "let's get started."

He made Maggie start throwing while he emptied the kiln and took care of the mess. Two plates and one bowl came out undamaged, and Maggie brightly said that she could paint those on Monday while firing the other pieces. Once the kiln was empty, Charlie sat and talked to Maggie while she worked. He told himself it was just because he'd left his computer at home, thinking they wouldn't be gone long, but he knew he would have done the same thing even if he had it and an entire stack of new comic books with him. The coyote had woken up at the first sign of her distress, and it was becoming increasingly difficult to subdue him. So, instead of fighting it, he indulged that side of himself by talking to her, coaxing smiles and laughs when she began to feel overwhelmed.

It was nearly midnight when they made their way back to the parking lot on the other side of campus. They were both too tired to talk, but it was a silence Charlie welcomed. His coyote had settled, but for once he didn't feel empty in its absence. Instead, he felt content for the first time in a long, long time. His therapist had been harassing him to go out and make friends outside the Alpha Pack, and he'd resisted, thinking he would never be comfortable around someone who hadn't trudged through hell beside him, but the exact opposite was true. He was comfortable with Maggie because they weren't haunted by the same memories. He didn't have to worry about what dark corner her mind had wandered into, and even though she might ask him something that would make him uncomfortable, it was only his discomfort he had to contend with. There was no shared pain threatening to break through the surface with a single thoughtless comment.

He'd parked the Humvee, his official work vehicle, on the edge of the lot, beneath a light pole. It was a good habit for anyone, but especially for people who were the target of a crazy psycho killer. Constantly being aware of your surroundings was another one of those good-for-everyone-but-especially-potential-horror-movie-extras things Charlie was very into these days, which is why he noticed there was no light shining down on the Humvee the moment it came in view.

"Maggie." His voice was barely above a whisper as he slowed his strides. She didn't ask questions. She just fell in step beside him, close enough he could grab her if need be, but not crowding him so much he couldn't move if he had to. "Taser in one hand; pepper spray in the other." She located both in her bag within a matter of seconds. Still, she didn't say anything. Her eyes showed fear, and the hands clinging onto the weapons Joshua gave her trembled, but she kept walking with an even, confident gait. "Remember, a Shifter's hearing is sensitive, especially with the moon getting closer to full every night. If someone grabs you, scream loud and high. You may be able to shattered his eardrum."

They were about ten feet away from the Humvee when the scent finally hit him. Strong. Chemical. A dozen perfumes piled on top of one another.

The exact same scent he'd been following on the day they found Barros's body.

Charlie steered Maggie towards a burger shack well known for their cheesy tater-tots and 24-hour operating schedule while punching an emergency code into his phone. Ten minutes later, Talley and Scout were standing at the edge of the booth they had procured.

"Liam has called a Bronies meeting across the street," Scout said, snagging the Cherry Coke Charlie had bought so they wouldn't get kicked out of the restaurant, which had a very strict no-eat-no-stay policy. "They need you, Apple Blossom. They need your pluck and good ol' southern common sense real bad."

Charlie looked at Maggie, who hadn't said much in the past ten minutes. He wasn't sure if it was because she was freaked out, or if she realized anything they said to one another might be overheard. He knew staying in the restaurant where she was surrounded by a crowd of college students clinging desperately to the last hours of the weekend was for the best, but still he hated to leave her alone. She wasn't a Shifter. She wouldn't know if there was a danger until it was stabbing a knife into her chest.

Even though she wasn't touching him, Talley saw the direction his thoughts were going. "You and Twilight Sparkle run along. Maggie and I will stick around and finish off your cheesy tots for you."

"Are you sure? What if something—"

"We're covered," Talley said, patting the purse where she kept her carry-and-conceal. "Anyway, Liam thinks whoever was there is long gone. The danger is less than clear-and-present."

Charlie had come to the same conclusion earlier, but he still thought it was best to be overly cautious. He was living with enough what-ifs and I-wish-I-would-haves already. He wasn't about to add onto the list if he could help it. Leaving Maggie with Talley, whose love of handguns was only a little alarming, seemed safe, but he still felt a bit like he was abandoning her as he slid out of the booth.

"Wait for one of us to come back and get you," he told her as Talley took his spot. "I'll text you to let you know what's up as soon as I can." And then, because he thought he might do something crazy, like kiss her, he turned around, linked his arm with Scout's, and said, "To Ponyville!"

CHAPTER 19

"Someone cut your brake line," Jase cheerfully told Charlie when they reached the parking lot.

"Someone human," Scout clarified since she could smell them underneath the stench of perfume. Once, when they were eleven, she had accepted Jase's dare to go through a department store and spray a sample of every perfume they had on her arm. She ended up with a headache for two days and they were both grounded for a week. The way her arm had smelled the entire drive home had been tame compared to the stench surrounding Charlie's Humvee.

"Two someones human," Joshua added. He was crouched down beside the driver's door, doing something with what appeared to be a make-up brush.

"Did you know our in-house Immortal has a fingerprint kit and knows how to use it?" Liam asked, either noticing where her attention had turned or picking up on her thoughts the way he sometimes did.

Not that he ever picked up on the *right* random thoughts. Or maybe he did and just ignored them. She really wasn't sure which way was worse.

"It's Joshua. He's like two hundred years old," she said, leaning against her mate as he wrapped an arm around her shoulder. "He's had like five lifetimes to learn all this crap. Try not to be impressed. It only makes his gigantic head even bigger."

"One," Joshua said, whipping out a black light, "I'm less than a hundred, thank you very much. And two, it's not arrogance if you're actually that damn good."

Charlie crouched down by Joshua, scenting the area around where Joshua was working. "Getting anything?"

"Other than prints I'm almost certain will match yours? No. It seems our humans know how to cover their tracks."

Charlie nodded, probably picking up the faint smell of latex Scout could tease out of the other scents surrounding the vehicle. "Which begs the question, how the hell do humans know how to cover their tracks from Shifters?" he asked.

"Oh, I know the answer to this one," Jase said, looking up from the video he was watching on how to repair a brake line. "Abram Mandel."

"Mandel is hiring out humans to do his dirty work?"

Scout mirrored Charlie's look of disgust. Since she'd spent the majority of her life as a plain, nothing-fancy-happening-here-under-the-moonlight human, she didn't think of them as inferior like some Shifters did, but she did think of them as very breakable. It was both cowardly and stupid to send humans to take on the Alpha Pack. Any one of them could easily take on several humans at noon on the day of a new moon and still come out on top.

"When Imogen heard what we suspected her dad of doing, she shared some information about his business dealings," Liam said. "It seems our fine, upstanding Mandel Pack Leader was working with the mob, so hiring out a couple of human thugs to make a few hits wouldn't be as hard for him as your everyday citizen."

"Are you sure there is really a mob?" Scout asked, not for the first time. The first time had been when Imogen came to find her and tearfully explained about the way her father managed to turn the Mandel Pack from one of the poorest packs in the country to one of the richest in less than a decade. Scout didn't have trouble believing Mandel was a ruthless bastard, but she was so unconvinced mobs were an actual thing in the real world she made Talley use her Seer abilities to confirm what Imogen was saying. "I thought mobsters only existed in the 1930s and had names like Babyface and Big Ugly. They ran booze and flirted with flappers. Now you can get booze at Wal-Mart and I haven't seen a flapper outside of Halloween in my life."

Liam looked down at her. "Haven't you ever watched *The Sopranos*?"

"No," Scout said, "but don't even try to convince me I should use HBO as evidence something exists unless you're willing to argue that Bon Temps, Louisiana, is overrun by hot vampires and the Stark family is out there somewhere preparing for winter."

A smile teased the edges of Liam's lips and a burst of warmth blazed through their mating bond.

My Liam. My mate.

"What was that all about?" she whispered.

His finger trailed down her nose and then lightly tapped the tip. "You make me happy," he said.

Thankfully, Jase interrupted that revelation with a muttered curse word. Otherwise she might have done something truly embarrassing, like throw herself into her mate's arms and cry like a baby.

"What is it?" Liam asked Jase, not taking his eyes off of Scout's. She imagined he was entranced by the little animated fireworks exploding there.

"I've got something." Jase was standing on the passenger's side of the Humvee, looking through the open door, his temper flaring.

Don't let it be a dead body. Don't let it be a dead body. Please, God, don't let it be another dead body.

If she would have been thinking, she would have realized she hadn't smelled a corpse, but she was too freaked out to be thinking, so it was with great relief she stood in the doorway and saw nothing more than a leather seat which would need to be replaced.

"Oh, look," she said. "Someone engraved my name on the seat. How lovely."

Not that she really tolerated being called a bitch, but since she was part canine, she figured she couldn't get too upset over it.

"That wasn't meant for you." Charlie shouldered past her. The muscles in his jaws flexed with barely contained rage as he took in the slashed upholstery. "You've ridden in this vehicle, what? Three times in the past six months?"

"If not me, then..." It took a second, but then she understood. "Maggie. You think this is for Maggie."

"I think whoever is doing this is gunning for her. Someone purposefully ruined all of the pieces she'd been working on this week, and now this."

"But why would Mandel care about Maggie?" Jase asked. "I mean, it's our guts he hates for dragging his daughter out of the closet in public and then releasing her from his pack, right? What does Maggie have to do with anything? She's just a cute, hippy-dippy art chick. She's about as offensive as sunshine and butterflies."

Scout snorted oh-so-indelicately. "What does the crazy Shifter traditionalist have against the Thaumaturgic we've taken into the protection of the Alpha Pack? Gee. I can't imagine."

Charlie cut his eyes over to where Joshua was... measuring grass? "Hack into the surveillance cameras. Pull footage from Rosa Hall from two nights ago and get every angle of this parking lot from tonight."

Joshua, who only took orders from Liam and Scout, and only when he was inclined to do whatever it was anyway, miraculously didn't give Charlie detailed directions on how to find his way to hell.

"Can't," he said. "This campus is one hundred percent Big Brother free. There isn't a single camera anywhere on the property."

The muscles in Charlie's jaws knotted. "Are you serious?"

"Sadly, yes," Scout said, laying a hand against his back. "We checked into it before I enrolled. At the time, it sounded like a benefit. No cameras meant no super-smart Joshua-wannabes would be able to hack in and get footage of me. We didn't think about what would happen if we needed to hack in and get some footage of our own."

"That," Charlie said, pointing at the car parked in the spot next to the Humvee, "is a Porsche Boxter. One of those runs about fifty grand. And guess what? Not even close to the most expensive car in this lot. You really expect me to believe there aren't cameras around here to make sure no one takes off with a car that costs more than most people's houses?"

"Chinoe's low crime rate is one of the major selling points for Sanders College."

His growl was the sort that made the bad kind of goose bumps break out from the top of your head to the bottom of your feet. The first time Scout heard it, she couldn't believe such a harsh and terrifying sound could come out of her Charlie. Even now, years later, she was amazed he was capable of something so animalistic.

But even as part of her instinctively shrank back, her lips threatened to curve up into a smile. She'd gone over a year without hearing that growl, and now she was hearing it for the second time in just over a week. She wasn't quite sure of what to make of Maggie McCray, but if she was making Charlie growl, then Scout was ready to do whatever it took to keep her around.

"Joshua," Charlie ground out, "tell me you're over there hacking into the Pentagon or White House or some shit like that and getting us some satellite images."

"Sorry, man—"

"You have got to be kidding me!" The crack from his fist hitting the ripped leather was like a gunshot splintering the night.

"I'll keep working on it," Joshua said. He looked to Scout, and she nodded her agreement. Joshua could do a lot with a computer and internet connection - he was basically the MacGyver of cyberspace - but not always without complications. Hacking into those kinds of sites could direct some very unwanted attention their way, but it was worth the risk. Even if it wasn't all of their lives on the line, Scout believed it was worth it to protect one innocent person. They could handle the fallout from a nosy government, but none of them could deal with knowing they could have done something to save someone's life and didn't because they were worried about getting into trouble.

"So, what do we do now?" Jase asked. "Listen, I know I'm in the minority here, but maybe this going to school thing is a little too risky right now. Why don't we all just... drop out?"

"No," Scout said at the exact same moment Jase's phone dinged. He was standing at an angle that meant with her super-Shifter sight, Scout could easily read his screen. It was from Talley and only contained one word: *"No."*

Jase scrunched up his eyebrows and squinted into the neon glow coming from across the street. "How did she do that? Can she hear my direct thoughts through our mating bond now?"

"I doubt it," Scout said.

"Then how did she know what I said?"

"It's because I'm awesome," came Talley's reply from several feet behind Jase.

At a time when not a whole lot of things were funny, watching Jase jump up and do a 180-degree twist in the air while yelping like a little girl was somewhere beyond the line of hysterical. Scout thought she was going to pull a muscle or pee her pants before she stopped laughing.

"What the hell are you doing?" Jase bellowed. "There is a psycho-killer running around cutting brake lines and slicing uninspired insults into the seats of locked vehicles. You're supposed to be sitting *safely* in the freaking restaurant across the street until I come and get you."

There was a time when Talley would have attempted to fold in on herself, mutter an apology, and promptly cry at such an outburst from Jase, but that was before they mated. Now, Talley knew Jase loved her, no matter what. It gave her a level of confidence that made Scout proud.

"One, Maggie was supposed to stay in the safety of the restaurant. Not me. I was there as her protection. Two, I'm just as much a member of the Alpha Pack as you are, so I get to sit in on whatever dangerous middle-of-the-night meetings I want. And three," she shoved her phone into his face, "Some guys were creeping on us. Liam said it was safe out here, so we left."

Of course, Jase wasn't as easily defused by the mention of the Alpha Male as he should have been. "How do you know it's safe?" he demanded of Liam.

Liam, who could have been a complete jerk and told Jase it was none of his damn business, just shrugged. "The perfume is dissipating. I can smell someone coming from a mile away, so it's not exactly like they could sneak up on us now."

Jase turned his irritation back on Talley. "Why didn't you just walk directly across the road?"

"Because scaring you was funnier, right up until you got your panties in a wad." Jase continued to glare, so she pranced over and gave him the sort of kiss people should only share behind closed doors, especially if they're kissing someone's brother. "I'm sorry I scared you," she whispered, which meant everybody but Maggie and Joshua could hear it. "I know you're just trying to protect me. I'll try to be more considerate next time."

Maggie, who had materialized out of the shadows beside Talley, moved away from the couple as they began yet another completely inappropriate display, and walked over to where Charlie stood.

"I'm not dropping out of school," she told him. "I can't."

Charlie never seemed tall to Scout. Since she wasn't exactly short for a girl and he was an average-sized a guy, there were only a couple of inches separating their height. But Maggie was roughly the size of a ten-year-old. She had to tilt her head almost completely back to look him in the eye, but she still managed to look fierce. It made Scout like her even more.

"I know," Charlie said, clenching his hands as if he was thinking about using the ruined passenger's seat as a punching bag again. "We'll figure something out. I promise."

And because she had known him forever, and because she'd spent the majority of her life studying him, she saw it. Charlie *was* going to find a way to make sure Maggie could stay in school. Not just because he promised, but because it meant something to her. Because Maggie cared, Charlie cared.

At the next available opportunity, Scout was going to give Maggie the world's biggest tackle-hug.

"I can set up surveillance on all the vehicles, but I'm not sure about being able to get onto campus," Joshua, who was now lying on the ground with his head beneath the Humvee, said. "I can give you one of my dual-recording iPads to put in your studio, and I'll have the feed sent both to my computers and the control room at The Den. I'll make sure someone keeps an eye on them."

"Someone is going to be watching me all the time?"

"Someone is going to be watching out for you all the time," Charlie told her. "And just until we run down these assholes and make sure they can never hurt anyone again."

Maggie wrapped her arms around her middle. Even from a distance, Scout could see the way her small frame trembled. "Did someone try to kill us tonight?"

"Yes."

A single tear slipped free of Maggie's eye, but before could trail down her face, Charlie's thumb was there to brush it away. Scout waited for a pang of jealousy that never came.

"She'll either be his salvation or damnation."

Scout agreed with her mate, but unlike Liam, it didn't worry her. Because either way, the shell Charlie had become since Toby's death would finally shatter and her friend would join the land of the living once again.

CHAPTER 20

By the time Halloween rolled around, Maggie had stopped thinking about the Alpha Pack as *The Alpha Pack*. She still felt awkward around Liam, and Scout wasn't exactly what someone would term as "friendly," but she was starting to feel like part of the group. It was a new experience for her. In high school, she'd always had a few friends, but when it came to actual groups, she was always on the fringes. Growing up dirt poor is hard enough for anyone, but when you're too white for the black kids, too black for the white kids, and there aren't even any other Asian kids around to tell you how you don't fit in with them either, it becomes something of a trial. Maggie had never felt like she truly belonged anywhere before, so the fact she was starting to feel that way with a bunch of crazy-rich Shifters and Seers was somewhat astonishing.

Still, with the exception of being a target for a wannabe serial killer, life was pretty nice. Joshua kept track of her every movement off the farm with his unsettlingly advanced tech toys, but as long as she was on the Alpha's property, she was able to go wherever and do whatever she wanted without someone looking directly over her shoulder thanks to their newly upgraded surveillance system. When she started feeling suffocated, which happened about every other day, she would just take off for a walk outside with her sketchpad and give herself a chance to breathe. The rest of the time, she was surrounded by people who didn't mind her being around. And when it came to Joshua, Talley, and Layne, who decided she was the best board game player in the whole house, they actually seemed genuinely happy she was there.

The only time she felt like a prisoner instead of just another member of their pack was during the full moon. Those nights, she was forced to stay in her room while coyotes and wolves took turns patrolling the house. She would spend the entire night sitting by her window, watching the Shifters below and listening to the cries and howls filling the night. Even knowing it was the same people she'd been with every day, the sight and sound terrified her. If someone was to ask her why she stayed awake those nights, she would have spouted off something about worrying one of Mandel's human thugs would try to attack the house when he knew the Shifters weren't there to protect them, but that wasn't true. Mandel hadn't made a move since the night the Humvee's brakes were cut, and any idiot who thought he could get past a pack of wolves and coyotes deserved to be torn to shreds.

No, the real reason Maggie refused to go to bed on full moon nights could be summed up in one word: Charlie. Over the past two months the two of them had formed the kind of friendship that involved a lot of hoping and longing for something more. Well, at least it did on her end. On Charlie's end, there was mostly a robot, but she made it her goal every day to make him flash a real smile at least once, and as time marched on, she was finding success more and more often. It wasn't really enough to be called encouragement, but Maggie didn't let that stop her from hoping and longing.

Maggie had stayed up on the night of the first full moon because she was being nosy. She'd only ever seen Scout in wolf form, and she was curious about the others. Mischa had swung by her room around midnight and stayed until the early hours of the morning, pointing out who was who while narrating what was going on outside her window as if it were a show on *Animal Planet*. After she'd seen a glimpse of everyone except the one coyote she wanted to see, she'd asked Mischa where he was and got only, *"Charlie is off fighting his demons"* as a reply.

Mischa told her how in their animal forms, Shifters are ruled more by emotion and instinct than human reason, but Maggie could have figured that part out for herself. It was most obvious in Liam and Scout. The two of them were always so controlled and hesitant in their affections towards each other in human form, but the moment they were both on four legs it was another story. They danced around one other, nipping and rubbing their sides together so often it bordered on obsession. They were like the wolf version of Jase and Talley.

Watching Liam and Scout made Maggie wonder what Charlie was like when the robot exterior fell away. Even if he was fighting demons, Maggie wanted to see it. She wanted to see the passion and the fury she knew was raging beneath his surface. So, every night the full moon hung in the sky, Maggie sat at her window and waited to see the real Charlie Hagan, and every time she was disappointed.

The latest disappointment had been two nights before Halloween. Maggie was still a little depressed over missing a glimpse of Coyote Charlie yet again. She debated on asking him to come into the yard near her window, but she kept chickening out. Didn't he deserve one night a month when he didn't have to be her bodyguard? That was, after all, the only reason the others roamed into the yard. They took turns "guarding the fort", making sure the house, the

Seers, and the single Thaumaturgic inside stayed safe. Just because Maggie didn't want to go a single night without seeing him didn't mean he didn't desperately desire a night without her.

"Where is your costume?"

Reid strode through the door of the studio wearing a vinyl nurse's uniform showing what had to be an unhygienic amount of skin. She and Boyfriend were around more often than not, and while Maggie couldn't say she enjoyed their company, she was definitely getting used to it. It was that, or go crazy.

"I'm being festive," Maggie said, indicating her outfit with a hand. "Purple tights. Orange skirt. Black spider-web top. If that doesn't say Halloween, I don't know what does."

Reid came into the studio and hopped up onto one of the stools. Or at least, she tried to. Turns out, it's kind of hard to hop when you're wearing skin-tight vinyl.

"Festive isn't the same as in costume, and you have to be in costume to trick-or-treat. It's, like, the rules or whatever."

Maggie sat her cobalt carbonate on the table and began digging for the brush she wanted to use. "I'm not trick-or-treating."

"What do you mean you're not trick-or-treating?"

"I mean I'm not dressing in a costume and going around campus to beg professors for candy." It was some weird Sanders tradition that was supposed to be raising money for juvenile cancer research, but Maggie couldn't quite figure out how it worked since the only money exchanging hands was the fortune their professors were paying for all the chocolate they would be passing out.

"Charlie and I are going to have a nice, quiet evening in the studio."

"All you two ever do is have nice, quiet evenings in the studio. I can't believe you haven't put a cot in here and just moved in at this point."

There were nights when Maggie had seriously considered it. She'd managed to get the Hulk set out in time, and the buyer had been enthusiastically impressed. So much so he'd ordered Captain America, Batman, and Goon sets as Christmas gifts. With all the assignments from her professors, her regular orders, and the vase project, she felt like she was working around the clock and still not staying caught up.

"Sorry, Reid, but I have to work tonight. You know what they say."

"All work and no play makes Maggie a big freaking loser?"

"No, Maggie has to pass all of her classes or she's going to get kicked out of college."

Reid rolled her eyes, which was made all the more dramatic by the entire stick of kohl surrounding each eye. "Who says that?"

"The good people down at the scholarship office." Finally locating her favorite brush, Maggie was ready to get started, with just one exception...

"So, I guess you and Davin are going to be leaving pretty soon..."

"Maggie McCray, are you kicking me out?"

"No!" *Yes.* "I just, you know, didn't want you to be late."

"It's okay," Reid said, sliding off the stool, an act leaving Maggie in the loop on Reid's continued position on underwear being an inessential part of a person's wardrobe. "My feelings aren't hurt too badly."

"I'm sorry, Reid. I've just got so much work—"

"Well, if you wanted to make it up to me, maybe we could hang out some this weekend."

"Sure!"

Please God, let something better pop up on her calendar.

"Great! I'll grab a pizza and come to your place on Friday."

Maggie tried to stop the sigh escaping her mouth, but it was impossible. "You know you can't do that. I'll get in trouble. They're really hardcore about stuff like that." Which Reid knew, because Maggie had to tell her at least once a week. She was pretty sure the only reason her old roommate was still talking to her was because Reid thought Maggie could get her an invite into her "exclusive, secret society." Too bad the Alpha Pack was the sort of thing you had to be born into.

"You," Reid said, jabbing her finger into Maggie's shoulder, "are no fun and a horrible friend."

"I'm sorry."

"Save it." Reid leaned across the table and grabbed one of the granola bars Maggie had brought along as supper. "Oh, chocolate chip. My favorite." She stuffed the stolen treat into the plastic pumpkin draped over her wrist before turning on her heel and sauntering out of the door without so much as a goodbye.

"Thank you so much for your assistance," Maggie said once Reid was out of earshot. She took a deep breath to steady her hands before carefully removing the vase from its resting spot on the shelves. The second one she threw had been even thinner than the first. She wasn't quite sure how it was holding its shape. If it worked, she really did have a chance at gathering the type of attention she needed to move up in the art world. "I do so appreciate how chivalrous you are. It's nice to know I can count on you to save me from unwanted awkward conversations."

Wanting to see if her sardonic chiding made the corners of his lips twitch in the slightest, she turned to where he was messing around with his computer only to freeze mid-turn.

Because Charlie wasn't looking at his computer at all.

"What are you doing?" It came out way louder than she'd meant for it to, but she couldn't help it. He was looking at her sketchbook.

Her sketchbook.

"These are amazing," Charlie said, oblivious to the hurricane of emotion swirling on her side of the room.

"You can't look at those." She was across the room in a few quick strides. She ripped the sketchbook from his hands, not caring if the pages ripped. Embarrassment burned her cheeks.

"Maggie, you should show these to people. You're incredible. You should be working for Marvel or something."

"You don't just look through someone's sketch book without asking." Her voice was high and shaky. "It's private. It's... it's..."

Maggie was pretty sure dying of embarrassment was a real thing because she was in the process of doing it.

As if noticing her distress for the first time, Charlie threw his hands up in surrender. "Whoa. I'm sorry. I didn't know."

"It's how I think. When I have trouble processing, I just draw it out, and it helps. But it's personal. It's private." She was rambling incoherent nonsense and she knew it, but she couldn't make herself stop. "The reason there are so many of you is because I can't finish them. The eyes. They're all wrong. I can't draw your eyes." She felt something wet splash onto her cheek, which made her even angrier. Why was her body's natural reaction to extreme emotion of any sort tears? "You shouldn't have looked at this without asking!" The last words were practically a scream, and she could only imagine the look of crazy on her face. From Charlie's reaction, it was quite impressive.

"I swear to you, I didn't know it was supposed to be private."

He reached for her and she jerked away, unable and unwilling to take comfort from him. The last thing she wanted was his pity. As if this moment wasn't horrible enough. He couldn't have looked at that sketchbook and not known everything. She put everything she thought and felt into those pictures. He knew every piece of her soul, including the piece of it that ached for his attention.

Ached for his touch.

Oh God.

A fresh wave of embarrassment threatened to leave her face in ashes.

"Maggie, tell me how I can make this right."

"You can't." He couldn't unsee what he'd seen, and now there was no way their relationship could go back to the way it was. She hadn't realized how much she treasured the comfortable companionship until she knew it was forever destroyed. Now she would be self-conscious of her every word and action, knowing he was gauging the level of her obsession. She knew without a doubt there would be no more hard-worn smiles. Over the past few months, she hadn't completely figured Charlie out, but she knew him well enough to know he wouldn't do anything to encourage her. No more smiles or late night conversations about comics. No more early morning donut runs or shared orders of fries. Their relationship would become that of protector and protected, and Maggie's heart would break a little more with every passing day.

God damn him for looking at that book.

"Maggie—"

"I have work to do," she said, turning her back to him so he couldn't see how crushed she truly was. Like this situation needed to be any more awkward and humiliating. "This vase isn't going to paint itself." And maybe, if she tried hard enough, concentrating on it would keep her from digging herself into a pit of self-pitying despair. Doubtful, but there was the smallest of possibilities, and Maggie was going to cling to that with everything she had.

Charlie didn't say anything more to her as she crossed back over to her side of the studio and settled in to start on the section she was painting tonight. She was only able to do a few inches a day, the intricacy of the design and the small space her hand had to work in making it impossible to do too much at once. She was getting ready to make her first stroke when Charlie sat his computer in front of her.

"*Calisthenics*? I haven't read that in ages," she said, struggling to keep her tone normal. Problem was, she couldn't remember what normal sounded like. "It was huge for about five minutes, but then the guy who was writing it, H.C. Charles, stopped posting on a regular basis and everyone went back to reading *Homestuck*. Still, it was a pretty cool webcomic. Did you just now start reading it?"

Instead of answering, Charlie leaned over and made a few clicks and keystrokes. When he pulled back again, Maggie was looking at a screen prompting her to create a new post.

No. Not her.

H.C. Charles.

"I was afraid if I used Hagan someone might figure out it was me, so I just reversed my name. H for Hagan, C for Christopher, and then Charles. H.C. Charles. Me, but the opposite of me." He rubbed the back of his neck, his eyes locked on the screen instead of Maggie. "It's lame, but I was like sixteen. I thought I was being deep and artistic."

"You're H.C. Charles." Maggie hit the back button, taking the computer screen back to the public page, and began scrolling through the panels. *Calisthenics* was an alien story, which normally wasn't her thing, but she'd been drawn in by the art. The minimalist style and sparse use of color was a beautiful backdrop for a story that ended up breaking her heart on a weekly basis. "You didn't buy your way into your independent study did you?"

"Not with money." Charlie still wouldn't meet her eyes. "But I did have to tell him who I was. It was the first time I ever told anyone. I thought after all these years it would be nice to finally have someone give me credit, but it just made me feel like I'd cheapened it somehow."

Maggie stopped scrolling on a panel where the main character, Chuck, was getting hit by his father. Even though Chuck was an alien done in classic alien style - oversized head, giant black eyes, and tiny mouth - Maggie could still see he was modeled after Charlie.

"No one else knows you did this? You were like an internet celebrity."

Charlie shrugged. "I didn't really see much of that. Once it started getting a lot of readers, I turned off the comments and tried to ignore the stuff people were writing about it online." Finally, he looked at her. "I wasn't doing it to get famous. I just needed to process. I needed to think, and this was how I did it." A corner of his mouth lifted. "Of course, I didn't really realize that was what I was doing until a much better artist pointed it out to me recently. I just thought I was getting back at everyone who was making my life hell by airing their dirty laundry on the internet."

"What about Jase and Talley? What about Scout? Don't they know...?" Surely they had to know. Most of the time it was like four bodies sharing one brain.

"They don't even know that I draw or write or anything. I've never been comfortable sharing it with people I know. It just seems like something that should be personal. Private." Maggie's chest constricted at the sound of her own words being repeated back to her. He was doing this, laying his soul bare, to make things right between them.

Maggie realized she might be in danger of falling in love with Charlie Hagan.

"What about the rest of it? Did they know about that?"

She probably shouldn't have asked, but there was no way to take it back now.

"They knew Dad..." He picked at a chip in the table, looking less like the fierce Shifter warrior she'd come to know and more like the vulnerable young alien from his comic. "They knew we didn't get along and he sometimes hit me." He peeled back a piece of flaking paint, embedding a splinter in his finger in the process. He pulled the tiny dagger of wood from his flesh and watched as a drop of blood formed. "They didn't know how bad it was, but they knew enough to try and keep me out of the house and away from him as much as possible. It's the reason I have custody of Layne. My parents wanted him, but Scout threatened to banish my dad if he didn't convince social service Layne was better off with us."

Maggie could see how life had been for him. An alcoholic father who constantly put him down and told him he was worthless and emphasized the point with his fists. A mother who wouldn't stand up for him, preferring to drown out the yelling and tears by turning up the volume of the show tunes she turned to when things got tense. And all of this he had to endure while pretending everything was okay, while seeing how easy life was for Jase and Scout, whose parents loved and cared for them. He'd spent his teen years feeling like a failure and an outsider.

She understood why the robot existed now. How could one person deal with that much hurt? And it wasn't like things had gotten easier for him once he was able to escape his craptastic home life. Maggie didn't exactly know how Scout and Liam rose to power, but she knew it was messy. She knew Charlie had been seriously injured and almost died. She knew his brother had died in some epic Shifter battle. And she knew he carried around the responsibility for Alex's death, whether he deserved the guilt or not.

Charlie is off fighting his demons.

And he had so very many to slay.

In that moment, she hated the other members of the Alpha Pack for making him fight alone. No one should have to wage wars on that scale by themselves. Maggie had no armor or sword of her own, but she was ready and willing to fight by his side if he would let her.

"You're amazing," she told him, too overwhelmed to be embarrassed by how much the awe in her voice gave away.

"At best, I don't suck, but thanks," he said, misunderstanding what she found amazing. "Stroud has me working on a new comic. He wants me to 'stretch myself as an artist', but I don't really have anything left to stretch. *Calisthenics* was the absolute edge of my skill set."

"I doubt that." Unlike Charlie, Maggie had spent her whole life devoted to art. He was obviously untrained, and his art lacked polish, but there was so much raw talent there it took her breath away. Under Stroud's guidance, Charlie could become the kind of artist whose name was whispered with reverence in comic shops and cons. "*Calisthenics* is good, but you could be better. And I know you, Charlie Hagan. You're not going to just coast by. You're going to work your ass off to make sure this new comic makes fan girls weep in the streets over its sheer amazingness. Hearts will break. Panties will burst into flames. And anyone who knows a damn thing about comics will hate themselves for not having done it themselves."

"So much faith." He stepped forward so his jeans were tickling the insides of her knees. "How do you do it?"

"Do what?"

His thumb was warm as it traced across her jawline. "Live in this world and still believe there is good in it? That there is good in me?"

"How can you live in this world and not see the good in it? How can you not know who you really are?"

With every breath they were drawing closer and closer together. Maggie's entire body buzzed and tingled in anticipation.

"Who am I, Maggie?"

"You're Charlie Hagan. Stratego of the Alpha Pack. Creator of one of the most well-regarded web comics of all time." She breathed in the scent of him. Cinnamon and male. "You're a fighter of demons and protector of innocents." Unable to stop herself, she finally did what she'd been dreaming of since she first met him and placed her lips against his. It was just a fleeting caress, but she felt it deep in her soul. "You're beautiful," she said, knowing it wasn't a strong enough word to describe him.

Charlie closed his eyes as if he could hide from her words. His forehead tilted down until it rested against hers. Maggie felt his breath warming her face and once again gave into temptation, turning so she could gift him with another peck against the corner of his lips.

"I can't be what you need me to be." The whisper sounded as if it had been wrung out of him.

A pronounced ache settled in her chest, but she wasn't going to let this fragile thing they were starting end here and now. She wasn't a quitter.

"Then I'll take whatever you can give me."

CHAPTER 21

Monarch, Tennessee was one of those small, depressing southern rural towns whose nicest buildings were a Wal-Mart and McDonald's.

"Left on Vine, and then a right onto Third," Maggie directed, her fingers tapping out a nervous rhythm on her thigh.

Taking Maggie home for Thanksgiving was the absolute least Charlie could do for Maggie, but he'd almost failed at even that, thanks to his Alphas.

"I understand wanting to see your family and all that jazz, but in case you've forgotten, there is still a killer on the loose who wants to see her dead," Scout had said when he brought it up.

As if he could forget. The painting remained stretched out on the wall in the gym where he worked out on a daily basis. No one had seen any reason to move it, and this way they could all sit around and study it whenever they thought they had a clue, which was less and less often. There had been no more direct attacks since the brake line was cut on the Humvee, and there had been very little information on Mandel coming in over the past three months. Liam had even gone so far as declaring Mandel an enemy of the Alpha Pack, but still they had very little to go on. A map was taped up next to the painting, thumbtacks marking places where people had reported seeing him.

So far, the map boasted only three thumbtacks.

Charlie didn't know if it was because Mandel was hiding so effectively, or if it was due to a lack of support for the new Alphas. Either way, they weren't getting much help from the general Shifter population, and they'd already used every resource they had at their disposal. At this point, it was a wait and see game, which was turning into a whole lot of waiting with no seeing to show for the effort.

In the end, Charlie had won the argument. It wasn't more than a quick pass-through anyway. It couldn't be. The full moon was Thursday night, so they were driving down on Wednesday afternoon and would be on the road again tomorrow. Luckily, Maggie's family didn't seem to mind turning the holiday into an eat-lunch-and-run event. His own parents would have had more than a few unkind words to say if he suggested doing the same thing at their house, which was one of the many reasons he wasn't going there.

"It's two driveways up. The one with the red car in it."

He turned in behind an old Mustang. It was one of the hatchbacks from the early 90s that didn't look so much like a sports car as a really small and confused family car. The paint was originally red, like Maggie had said, but one of the doors was now black and the bumper, which didn't look like it was exactly the right size, had been spray-painted blue.

Charlie finally understood why Maggie seemed so relieved when he'd suggested taking the truck he'd inherited from his grandfather instead of the Humvee.

"So, this is it," Maggie said, her voice quaking.

He didn't know how to respond. He would have said it was nice, but they would both known it was a lie. This was obviously the wrong-side-of-the-nonexistent-tracks side of town, and Maggie's house wasn't one of the nicer ones on the block. Some effort had been taken to keep the yard clean and neat, and the roof wasn't half-caved-in like one of the neighbors, but that was about as positive as you could get about the tiny house with peeling paint and taped-up windows.

"I guess I should have mentioned we're dirt poor, huh?"

Maggie's face was flushed with embarrassment, which made Charlie feel like a complete ass. Like it mattered where she lived.

"You should ask Liam about the first place he lived in Timber." She gave him one of her I'm-not-falling-for-this looks. "Seriously. I'm still not sure how a guy his size was able to walk around without the whole thing collapsing around him."

A shadow appeared in the window. The curtains moved back just enough for a sliver of a woman's face to be seen, her eye narrowing on the truck and its occupants.

"This was a bad idea," Maggie said. "Let's just go back home. Or to Scout's parents. Or Vegas." Her eyes were pleading when they met his. "Please? Anywhere but here?"

Charlie responded by opening the driver's door and sliding out into the crisp November air. Almost immediately the front door of the house swung open and a tiny little Asian woman darted down the stairs.

"Maggie Mae!" she squealed, arms stretched out as she sprinted around to the side of the truck where Maggie was dragging herself from the passenger's seat. "I've missed you, sweeting."

"It's nice to see you, too, Mother," Maggie replied drily.

"And you!" Maggie's mom, whose name Charlie thought might have been Lynn, turned in a dramatic sweeping movement. She clasped her hands to her chest as her eyes roamed all over Charlie's body in a way that made him want to find a trusted adult and tell them someone's mommy made him uncomfortable. "My goodness, Maggie Mae. You've certainly outdone yourself in the boyfriend department."

"Charlie isn't my boyfriend, Mother." New splotches of red having nothing to do with the cool wind whipping around them spread across her cheeks. "I've already told you that more than once."

Lynn draped an arm over Maggie's shoulder, which only served to highlight how dramatically different they were. It wasn't because Maggie's skin was so much darker or her hair was a wild, kinky mass of curls while her mother's dark hair was so straight and shiny it seemed to be made of glass. No, the major differences between Maggie and her mother had nothing to do with the physical traits she inherited from her father.

Standing there, Maggie looked like... well, like Maggie. She was wearing gray wool tights, a pleated black skirt, a vintage CBGB t-shirt, and a purple pea coat. Even if he couldn't see anything but the outfit, he would know it was her in a room filled with a hundred people.

On the other hand, her mother was wearing a pair of skinny jeans, an Abercombie shirt he would have thought came from the kid's section if Abercrombie & Fitch had a children's section, and a pink jacket with "pink" spelled out in pink rhinestones on the back, just in case you were confused as to what you were seeing. Basically, she looked like a million other teenage girls in the world. Problem was, she wasn't so much a teenager as the mother of a teenager.

"Sweetie, if you're waiting for something better to come along, just give up now, because you are not going to get any better than that."

Charlie squirmed under another all-over perusal, and Maggie threw a hand over her face, muttering something about how dying of embarrassment would be a welcome relief at this point.

Realizing she wasn't going to get anything other than uncomfortable looks from the two of them, Lynn gave a dramatic sigh. "Well, I suppose it's a good thing you two are 'just friends.'" She added an eye-roll to the sarcasm and air-quotes. "You're going to have to share a bed while you're here, and I'm definitely not ready to be a grandma yet."

Maggie tensed under her mom's arm. "What do you mean we have to share a bed? Charlie can sleep on the pullout."

"We don't have it anymore," Lynn said, dropping her arm and giving Maggie the freedom to move closer to the truck. Charlie could see the desire to jump in and drive away in her eyes.

"What do you mean we don't have the pullout anymore? Did it break?"

Her mother played with the zipper on her jacket. "I sold the couch."

"You sold the couch."

"I needed the money."

"For what?"

Lynn shrugged. "Stuff. Like the electric bill."

"Mom, I pay the electric bill. Try again."

Lynn turned to Charlie, all batting eyelashes and pouting lips. “Do you hear how she talks to me? Is that any way for a child to speak to her mother?”

It is if you don’t realize you’re supposed to act like a mother.

“Don’t worry about the sleeping arrangements,” Charlie said instead. “I’ve got a sleeping bag. I can just crash on the floor somewhere.”

Maggie’s eyes met his from across the bed of the truck. “I told you this was a bad idea,” she said. “Let’s just go.”

“Leave? What? You can’t leave, Maggie Mae. You just got here.” A tear trailed down the side of her face, but instead of making Charlie feel sorry for her, he kind of wanted to shake her a few times and tell her to get ahold of herself. “I’m sorry I sold the couch. I know you worked really hard to get enough money to buy it, but the brakes went out on the Mustang again, and it’s the only way I can get to work. I had to do something.” She surged forward and grabbed onto her daughters hands. “Please don’t leave me, baby girl. I miss you so much it hurts.”

Maggie closed her eyes and took a deep breath before finally giving in and wrapping her arms around her mother. While they embraced, Charlie went ahead and got their bags out of the truck.

An hour later, Charlie was looking at the pictures covering the wall of the living room when an older man saddled up next to him, a can of Budweiser in one had. The smell had Charlie’s stomach working itself into knots. Beer had always been his father’s drink of choice.

“Who are you, Charlie Hagan?” Maggie’s grandfather asked. Charlie had been introduced to the burly man when he’d entered the house. Even though he hadn’t lived in

Scotland since he was five, Barron McCray still had a touch of an accent. According to Maggie, he clung onto it for dear life, out of fear that once he lost it he wouldn't be able to ramble on about *"the way things are done in Scotland"* for hours on end any longer.

"Charlie Hagan, sir," Charlie said, even though the man obviously already knew his name. Still, what was he supposed to say? If Maggie had asked, he would have had a million different answers. *"I'm the guy who thinks of you twenty-four hours a day;" or "I'm the guy who doesn't deserve your friendship but is damn grateful he has it anyway;" or "I'm the guy who can rip the door off of a car if the moon and mood is right, but would rather run and hide than talk to your grandfather."* "I go to school with Maggie."

Mr. MrCray studied Charlie's expression in the reflection afforded by the glass in all the picture frames. "I want to know what you are to my granddaughter."

"I'm her friend," Charlie replied automatically, although even he wasn't stupid enough to think that was the right word for what they were to one another. She wanted more. It was obvious when they were together, leaned against one another on the couch as they watched whatever BBC nonsense Jase and Talley were forcing on them or while they were bent over a project one of them was working on. In those moments Maggie would look at him like she was waiting for something to change, for their relationship to finally make that final shift. As if he had something more he could give her. As if he was holding part of himself back. What she didn't understand was there was no more of himself left to give. The part of him she wanted was gone forever, and it was only when he was with her he regretted losing it. Because in those moments, he wanted to give her everything he'd once been and more.

Charlie looked around for an escape route, but there was nowhere to go. He could hear Maggie humming in the shower where she retreated to hide from her family, and he silently begged her to hurry up and save him.

"What are you doing with your life, Charlie?"

"Ummm... I go to school?"

The old man narrowed his eyes. "You plan on staying there your whole life?"

"God no." While it wasn't nearly as bad as he imagined, Charlie was looking forward to the day he didn't have to sit through a lecture ever again. "I'm going into the service." Because being in the Alpha Pack was technically a type of service, right?

Mr. McCray rocked back on his heels. "I was in the army for eight years. It's how I met my wife." He pointed to an orange-hued picture of a young man in a uniform with his arm wrapped around a woman who looked almost identical to Maggie's mom. "I was stationed in Japan. She worked at a little store just off the base, and I thought she was the most beautiful woman I'd ever seen. I made excuses to go to that damn store every day. Sometimes I would beg the other guys to let me go buy their smokes or magazines for them just so I could see her."

"Your strategy obviously worked," Charlie said. There were several pictures of the couple scattered across the wall, and in all of them, they were clinging onto one another as if they were the only things worth having in this whole world.

"It did. We got married right before I got shipped back to the States. I couldn't leave her there, and luckily, she felt the same way."

They didn't speak for a while. Mr. McCray seemed to be lost in his memories while Charlie tried to figure out where this conversation was going.

"I may be an old man, Charlie, but I'm still a man," Mr. McCray said, breaking the silence when Charlie was getting to the point that he was thinking about just walking away. "I know what you're thinking about when you look at my granddaughter—"

"We're just friends."

The old man turned, his eyes drilling into Charlie. "You seem like a good kid, Charlie, but she deserves better than you." And with that he drained the last of his beer and shoved past Charlie into the kitchen.

Charlie's gaze went back to the wall of pictures and stopped on one of a Kindergarten-aged Maggie, her hands caked in mud and a blinding smile on her face. Mr. McCray hadn't told Charlie anything he didn't already know. Maggie did deserve better than what he could give her. He'd been saying the same thing for a month now. But knowing that didn't stop the growing ache in his chest or the desire to prove the old man wrong.

CHAPTER 22

"Mom, where is the turkey?" Maggie asked the next morning. She picked up a gallon of milk, and when the stuff on the inside didn't move, she tossed it into the garbage can, making a mental note to drag it out to the curb before the whole house started smelling like homemade cheese. "Please tell me you didn't leave it in the freezer."

Lynn McCray looked up from her Nora Roberts paperback and took a puff of her Salem Light before answering. "I didn't get a turkey."

"What do you mean you didn't get a turkey? It's Thanksgiving, Mom."

"Why do you care? You don't eat meat."

"But I like the smell of turkey cooking." It reminded her of her grandmother. Thanksgiving had always been a favorite holiday of Taeko McCray. As an immigrant, she had a sense of national pride missing in most natural-born Americans. The Fourth of July and Thanksgiving were always cause for massive celebration at the McCray residence, Grandmother always making every effort to make sure every tradition was followed. "And how am I supposed to make gravy for the mashed potatoes without the broth from the turkey?"

Lynn flicked her foot-long ash into a red Solo cup. "We don't have potatoes either."

Maggie stood up slowly, praying this was another one of her mother's attempts at a prank. "We don't have potatoes?"

"Do you know what they want to charge you for just a couple of potatoes? I could buy a whole ten pound bag for that."

You cannot kill your mother. You cannot kill your mother. You cannot kill your mother.

"Mom, what exactly are we supposed to eat for Thanksgiving dinner?"

Lynn took another puff of her cigarette and flicked over the page of her romance novel. "I think we have a tray of salisbury steak in the freezer, and there is a can of peas and carrots in the cabinet."

When she was a kid, Maggie would sometimes imagine what it would have been like if she'd lived with her dad instead of her mom. Unlike Lynn, who had dropped out of school after giving birth to Maggie in the tenth grade, Luke Norwood graduated high school and then went off to college. When she was young, Luke's parents would invite Maggie to their house out in Sherman Hills, the nice subdivision on the edge of town. She would sit on their matching leather furniture and go out to dinner at nice restaurants where you didn't have to stand in line to place your order and someone else cleaned up your mess after you were done. Mr. and Mrs. Norwood always bought her really nice Christmas and birthday presents, and generally made some effort to treat her like a granddaughter even though their son hardly acknowledged her existence.

Sadly, that all changed when she was ten and Luke got himself a wife and a real kid. Maggie had a few moments of proper angst over the whole ordeal, but it didn't take her long to begin to understand. She wanted to go off and start a new life and forget all about her mother as soon as possible, too. She couldn't blame him or his parents for starting fresh, even if it meant she was coming out a loser in the whole situation.

But even when she'd grown up and knew there was no way it was ever happening, Maggie would still sometimes fantasize about the Norwoods coming to take her away to live in their nice, clean, middle class world. It became a coping mechanism, which is how Maggie found herself standing in the middle of her mother's kitchen in the early morning hours of Thanksgiving, imagining sitting around the Norwoods' large oak table, helping her younger siblings spoon sweet potato casserole onto their plates. Her father would ask how her classes were going and her stepmother would be polite to Charlie without trying to undress him with her eyes.

"I'm going to the store," Maggie said, opening her eyes. Maybe they would get lucky and the deli would have some pre-made Thanksgiving meals. She woke up at dawn to start cooking so they could get back to the Alpha Pack before the full moon rose, so the chances of getting the good stuff before all the other last-minute shoppers got in there and started throwing elbows was pretty good as long as she left now.

"Grab me another pack of smokes and a case of Mountain Dew."

No, I'm not going to enable your quest to kill yourself slowly.

"Sure, Mom. Anything else?"

Another puff. Another turn of the page. "Yeah, you better grab some paper plates while you're there so we'll have something to eat on."

"It's Thanksgiving. We eat off of Grandmother's china."

Lynn didn't say anything, and Maggie's body went icy cold for one full second before blazing with unbearable heat. She couldn't stop her hands from shaking as she went over to the pantry and opened the door to find the bottom shelf empty.

"Mom, where is the china?" Her voice didn't shake or screech or bellow. She wasn't sure how that happened. It probably had something to do with adrenaline. In tense situations some women could lift cars off their infant children, and others could speak in a calm and controlled manner when they were mere seconds away from painting the walls with blood.

Lynn mumbled something around the cigarette in her mouth.

"What?"

"Gold Brothers." Lynn threw out like a challenge, and Maggie wanted to meet that challenge so bad the bones in her hand threatened to snap from the force of the fist she was making. But she knew yelling at her mother wouldn't do anything but bring on a poor-pitiful-me cry fest that would end up making Maggie feel guilty, and at the moment, Maggie was too pissed off to do anything to dull her righteous anger.

"How much?" When Lynn didn't answer Maggie fought the urge to throw something, preferably her mother. "How much will it take to get it back?"

"You don't understand." Lynn put down the book and pulled another cigarette out of the pack. The lines that formed around her mouth as she took a pull on the cancer stick didn't completely go away when she opened her mouth to let the smoke roll out, making her look much older than her thirty-five years. "You don't know what it's like to be an adult and have all these bills and responsibilities."

Maggie considered pointing out how she did understand since she'd been paying most of the bills and taking on the majority of the responsibilities for the past five years.

"Just tell me how much money it's going to take to get it back, Mom."

Lynn's eyes narrowed on Maggie before darting to the window.

"Three hundred."

Maggie closed her eyes and once again she was in her grandparent's house, surrounded by normal people doing normal family things. But it didn't work. Instead of calming her, this time it only fueled her anger. Why couldn't she have that life? It should have been hers. It wasn't fair.

Without another word to her mother, she stormed out of the kitchen and into the living room where Charlie was hunched over his computer. The sound-eliminating earphones strapped over his head gave her a profound sense of relief. It was bad enough she had to live the conversation, she didn't need to also endure the embarrassment of knowing he had overheard.

She waved a hand in front of his face and almost teared up at the blazingly beautiful smile he shot her as he uncovered his ears. Over the past few weeks, Robot Charlie had made fewer and fewer appearances. The smiles Charlie gave her now weren't practiced or calculated, and the difference was heart stopping. Every time he graced her with one, which was becoming quite often, she felt the urge to throw herself at his feet and swear lifelong fidelity. She would follow him to the ends of the earth for one of those smiles.

"Walk me to the store?" She could have gone by herself, the Food Giant was only two blocks away and she seriously doubted anyone was going to attack her in Monarch, but the truth was, she needed to be near him right now. Her life seemed more normal and balanced with Charlie around.

"We won't be gone long, will we?" Charlie asked as he stuffed his feet into his shoes. "I promised your granddad I'd help him with the gutters before lunch."

Maggie grabbed her coat and tossed Charlie his. "You're going to work on the gutters on Thanksgiving?"

"Well, they're in pretty bad shape—"

"No. Just... no." It was like everyone was conspiring to make this the least Thanksgiving-like Thanksgiving since the Pilgrims and Native Americans shared some corn-on-the-cob a few hundred years ago. "This is Thanksgiving. You can watch the Macy's Thanksgiving Day Parade and the dog show, or you can go outside and throw around a football, but you will not be messing with the gutters."

"Mags, your granddad can't do it himself, and we're leaving right after lunch. It won't take long. I'll be done by the time Santa rolls through Time Square. Promise."

"We're leaving today." She knew they were leaving after lunch, had known it all along, but it wasn't until he said it that she realized what it meant. "We're leaving today, and Gold Brothers won't be open. I can't... I won't be able to..." And then, because there was no force on the earth that could have stopped her, she burst into tears. It was the first time she'd really cried in front of him since the day someone ruined her pieces of pottery, and she was just as embarrassed as she'd been then. But unlike the first time, Charlie gathered her into his arms and held her against his chest as the tears streamed down her face.

Her heart couldn't decide if it wanted to burst from finally being in Charlie's arms or crumble from knowing she couldn't get her grandmother's china back.

"Tell me what is wrong," he whispered into her hair. "Whatever it is, I'll fix it." One of his hands came down to cradle her face. His thumb worked as a windshield wiper on her cheek, brushing the nonstop flow of tears away. "Come on, Maggie. Tell me what's wrong. These tears are killing me."

"My grandmother's china. It was... it was important to her."

"The pattern on your side?" he guessed, and she nodded against his chest, crying too hard to answer.

For years Maggie's grandmother had made dinnerware for a small company specializing in handmade ceramics. For years she'd made expensive plates and bowls for other people, her family ate on chipped Dollar store dishes. The company didn't offer employee discounts, and they sold them for more money than they paid Maggie's grandmother in six months.

"She bought it piece by piece. It took her fifteen years to get it all."

Once Maggie was old enough, she helped, saving up her money so she could buy a cup or salad plate at Christmas. Every year her grandmother would gasp in surprise. Maggie might have thought it was an act if she hadn't also cried every year.

"Grandmother left it to me, Charlie. Me. It was mine, and she... she just got rid of it like it was nothing." Her voice broke on a sob, and she pressed herself even tighter against the hard warmth of Charlie's chest. "God, I hate her sometimes."

"What did she do? Break them? Throw them out?" His voice was quiet, but she could hear the anger he felt on her behalf.

"No. She took them to the pawn shop."

Charlie pulled back just enough that he could look down at her. "The pawn shop? So we can get them back?"

Maggie knew she should answer him, but she was too hung up on the whole part where he looked into her eyes and said "we" as if there was a "we" instead of two people who hung out together all the time, sometimes sitting so close she might explode from desire, but mostly not even doing that much.

"I've got some money saved up. For some reason, Liam insists on paying us, and since he also insists on paying for our house, food, and everything else, I don't really have anything else to spend it on." He brushed away the last straggling tear with the back of his hand. "I'll fix this, Maggie. We'll get them back, and we'll take them home with us so she can't ever do this again."

God, if he didn't stop Maggie was going to start bawling all over again.

She shook her head, forcing herself to move out of the comfort of his arms. "No, it's done." She tried for a smile that didn't quite take. "Let's just go find some food, eat lunch, and get the hell out of here," she said. "The sooner, the better."

Maggie thought that was the end of the discussion, but she should have known better. Charlie had told her he would fix it, and he wasn't the kind of guy who went back on his word. Still, she had no idea what he was talking about when he announced he had good news the moment she emerged from the grocery store, bags of food in hand.

"Is it that barbecued turkey is an acceptable Thanksgiving Day lunch option and you love German potato salad even more than mashed potatoes and gravy? Because that would indeed be good news."

"Even better," Charlie said, grabbing two of the bags from her. "We're staying until tomorrow."

Maggie nearly tripped over a crack in the sidewalk. "Charlie, that is not better news. Did you hear the part where I want to get the hell away from my mother as soon as humanly possible?"

"All I heard was someone with a broken heart asking for help."

"Charlie--"

"It's all taken care of. Mr. Ryker said they were still there, and he'll open his doors at nine in the morning." His smile was smug. "See? I fixed it. Maggie's heart can be whole again."

And it was. She could feel it in her chest, coming back together, bit-by-bit. And the glue binding it all together was Charlie. Beautiful, damaged Charlie Hagan who she couldn't resist anymore. She'd tried so hard for so long, but with one smug smile, he plowed over her safeguards and she fell, head-over-heels in love with him. It didn't matter that he didn't want her love. Who she loved wasn't his choice to make. It was hers. It didn't matter he might not ever be able to love her back, she was going to love him with everything she had anyway.

"What about tonight?"

Charlie shrugged. "There is a park practically in your back yard. Not ideal, but it'll work."

"And Scout?"

She hated bringing her into this moment, but there was no way around it. You couldn't talk about Charlie, and who and what he was, without bringing Scout into the conversation.

"It's fine," he said with a twitchy little shrug, which made Maggie think it was anything but. Her doubt must have shown on her face because he said, "It's okay, Maggie. I got Mommy's permission. She said I can sleep over at your house."

She hit him when she really wanted to hug him. "I was just checking. I didn't want Her Royal Cranky-Pantsness to throw the smack down on me. I am small, and I break easily."

"Tiny? Yes. But I don't believe for one second you're fragile, Maggie Mae McCray." His eyes held a mischievous glint. "Maggie Mae. *Maggie. Mae.* How is it I didn't know your middle name until yesterday?"

"Charlie..."

"I mean, all the opportunities I've missed of being able to wake you up and tell you I have something to say to you."

They were back at the house, and Maggie wheeled on the top step to block his passage to the door. "Charlie Hagan, I swear to whichever deity you believe in, if you even *think* about bursting out into song, I will end you."

He hummed the first few notes and Maggie lunged. He caught her easily, but the bags in his hands meant he had to lock his arms tight around her to keep her captive.

My body pressed to Charlie's chest not once, but twice in less than an hour. I suppose there are things to be thankful for today.

"See," Charlie said, his eyes locked on hers. "You're fierce, not fragile."

"But you caught me."

His gaze slid to her lips. "I will always catch you."

It was not the point she was making, but she didn't care. Since he was holding her up off the ground, his lips were in strike range, and before she could talk herself out of it, she was brushing her own against them. "Maggie," he whispered against her mouth, and she took it as a sign of encouragement. Her tongue hesitantly reached out to feather along his bottom lip, and he rewarded her with a growl.

"Charlie." She whispered it against his lips like a prayer, and maybe it was.

"Maggie--"

"Shhhh..." She silenced him with a nip at the corner of his mouth. "Just let me..." Her tongue laved the spot where her teeth had just been. "Have my moment." Then she settled her lips against his with purpose. He hesitated for the briefest of seconds before parting his lips and giving her complete access and control. Control she relished. Never before had she taken charge of a kiss like this, and she found the power dizzying. Or maybe it was just the feel of Charlie's velvety tongue sliding against hers making the world tilt and twirl.

She became so lost in Charlie she forgot the world around her, including the bag of groceries in her hand. Cans hit the metal railing with a loud thwack-thwack-thwack. Charlie jerked back, releasing her gently, but quickly, back onto the ground. His eyes were wide and panicked, as if a shower of bullets had shattered their perfect morning instead of cranberry sauce and creamed corn.

"I'm sorry."

All the warm fuzzies floating through Maggie's body frosted over. "You're sorry?"

"Maggie, don't..."

Don't what? Don't think about the way I just had my greatest and worst life experience in a matter of seconds? Don't think about all the ways you're going to continue to break my heart now I've decided to love you?

Maggie turned her back to him, bending down to pick up the cans she'd dropped so he wouldn't see how she was fighting to keep her eyes dry.

"I told you before, Maggie. I can't give you what you want."

A can of green beans had rolled beneath a decrepit chaise lounger, which gave her a perfect excuse to literally crawl under the nearest piece of furniture as she said, "You want it as much as I do."

At least, he'd never said he didn't want her, and he certainly had seemed to be getting into that kiss there at the end.

"What I want doesn't matter." His voice was further away than it should have been, and Maggie crawled out from her hiding spot to find him leaning against the railing at the other end of the porch, his back turned to her as he seemingly addressed the neighbor's house. "I told you before, I can't be what you want me to be. I can't give you what you need. What you deserve."

"What if what I need, what I deserve, is you?"

His head dropped to his chest. "It's not."

"How can you possibly know what it is I need? Do you have some secret Seer power I don't know about? One that lets you See a person's needs and desires? If so, I'll listen, but otherwise, you might want to take my word on this."

Charlie closed his eyes as if trying to shut out her voice of reason. The jingling music from a Black Friday ad poured through the window that was always open two inches, even in the middle of a snowstorm, because no one could get it down. The peppy bells and horns were so at odds with what was happening on the porch Maggie might have laughed if she wasn't so close to screaming.

When Charlie's eyes opened again, she knew her battle was lost. The spark of life was gone, leaving only the robot with his carefully considered responses in its place. She knew nothing she said at this point would matter. There was no bringing him back once he made the conscious decision to shut himself off.

That didn't mean she wasn't going to try.

"Charlie." The porch was small, so it only took a few steps to reach him. She placed her hand on his chest, the contact sending a surge of heat from her fingertips to other, less exposed parts of her body. "Please. At least try."

He looked at her hand as if he didn't know what it was, and then placed his own on top of it. Her rush of hope quickly died as he pulled her hand away from him and placed it back at her side. "Don't make this any harder than it has to be."

There are many bad emotions in this world, and in that moment, all of them settled like a stone in Maggie's stomach. Too many of them. She didn't know what to do with it all. She wanted to scream and cry and rail against him while either beating the hell out of him or clinging onto him for dear life, she wasn't sure which yet.

In her whole life, Maggie had never felt as comfortable, as happy, as *complete* as she did with Charlie. The hours they spent working together, side-by-side in silence, were among the most content in her life. And the times when they weren't so silent? When she was trying to coax a smile on his all too perfect lips or he was making her laugh with his latest rant about a favorite comic? She hadn't known that kind of joy really existed in this world. Charlie Hagan, the impossibly talented boy whose life had been filled with trials and tragedies should have been the poster child for sadness, but instead, he'd taught Maggie the meaning of happiness.

Of course, what she was feeling now was the exact opposite of happiness, and he'd taught her the true definition of that emotion, too.

Why? Why did he have to be such a complete ass about this? Why couldn't he see how good they were together?

"Scout." She hadn't meant to answer her own question aloud.

Charlie opened his eyes, his eyebrows drawn together in confusion. "What about Scout?"

She shouldn't ask, but she found she couldn't stop herself. "Do you love her?" Charlie flinched ever so slightly. He started to open his mouth to say something, but Maggie stopped him with a shake of her head. "No, don't answer that." *Because I really will shatter if I hear you say it.* "It's okay. I know. I understand. It's... fine."

Except it wasn't really, but he didn't need to know how hard she was fighting to hold herself together. She'd already done a bang-up job of making everything crazy awkward. There was no need in adding a hysterical, heart-broken, jealous, rebuffed, wannabe girlfriend on top of everything else.

Charlie had sat his bags of groceries on the chaise lounge at some point during their little drama. Maggie was reaching for them when he said her name. She knew he was going to apologize again, and she couldn't take it. This part, the one where he was telling her he could never feel the same about her as she did him, was an experience she didn't want to have again in a million years, but the part before that, the one where she felt as though he was hers for a brief moment, was worth it. One day she would be able to look back on today and only remember the way his lips had felt against hers, and she would be damned if she let him spoil that moment by being sorry it happened.

"Good news," she said, preventing him from saying another word. "I got the last thing of sour cream in all of Monarch." Maggie pulled the tub from the bag as if he wouldn't believe her without proof. "That means I get to make my famous corn casserole. You're going to love it."

There was a tense moment as she looked up into his eyes, begging him to let it go and just move on with their day. It took more heartbeats than Maggie was comfortable with, but finally he relented.

"I love corn casserole," he said with a robotic smile. He reached out and took the bags from her once more, careful not to make contact with her fingers. Maggie told herself it wasn't a big deal, although her heart argued the point. "Do you need help? Not to brag, but I can open a can of cranberry sauce like nobody's business."

Maggie tried for a smile and failed. “It’s okay,” she said. “I’m good on my own.” And one of these days she would be again.

CHAPTER 23

Lunch was a disaster. The turkey Maggie bought wasn't so much barbecued poultry as shredded leather covered in red, liquid sugar; the potato salad tasted like it may have been left over from Labor Day; and thanks to a heating element in the oven that didn't quite work right, Maggie's corn casserole was still wobbly in the middle after baking for over an hour.

The worst part was watching Maggie fight back tears as she sat the paper plates on the table. She'd flashed him the fakest smile he'd ever seen when she pointed out the blue flowers decorating the edges. "This way, if you squint real hard, you can make yourself believe they're the real thing," she'd quipped as if it didn't tear apart her soul to say it. It made Charlie want to strangle her mother, who spent most of the preparation and mealtime on her phone, recounting to every person she'd ever known some fight she'd had with her boss.

As he poked at the corners of his corn casserole, which was actually really good if you could find a cooked bite, Charlie tried not to think about how different the day was going for Jase, Scout, and the rest of the Alpha Pack. Gramma Hagan's tiny house would be filled to the point of bursting. The air would smell of his gramma's cooking and laughter would float up and down the hallway. Jase and Scout would try to steal some type of dessert from the kitchen before the meal was served, and would be caught by Gramma Hagan, who would scold them as if they were still small children instead of two of the most powerful

Shifters in the world. Joshua and Angel would be at war, both of them taking extreme delight in annoying one another. After a meal of the best food on earth, the TV would be turned to a ballgame and the tables would be cleared so an epic card tournament could commence.

It sounded perfect, and for most of them, it was. But not Charlie. Charlie would have spent the day watching the bottle of bourbon grow emptier by the hour, tensing every time he accidentally found himself in the same room as his father. He would talk to his mother, never quite looking her in the eye because he was too busy looking for signs his father had finally turned his violence toward her. He would always be aware of the seat in the corner no one sat in because they knew it belonged to Toby. He would be too blinded by Layne's anguished outbursts to see the joy and love filling the room.

At least at Maggie's house he didn't have to pretend to be swept away by the spirit of the holiday. No one jabbed him in the side when he went so far into his thoughts he forgot where he was. No one looked at him as if they were expecting him to fall apart anytime the smile on his face faltered.

After dinner, he'd climbed onto the roof with Maggie's grandfather, despite her protests. It was getting colder outside, and he wasn't particularly fond of heights, but freezing his butt off in a position where he could easily fall to his death was preferable to staying inside where he would have to face the temptation of her. Pushing her away had been the hardest thing he'd ever done in his life, and it was taking all of his self-control to not gather her up in his arms and beg for her forgiveness.

You want it as much as I do.

She was wrong, of course. He wanted it more. He hadn't realized how badly he wanted it until she was in his arms, fitting perfectly against his body. At the first brush of her lips he'd been gone, swept away in sensations he hadn't felt since before his life had taken a turn for the impossible.

No, that wasn't quite right. The way Maggie made him feel was beyond anything he'd experienced before. It was like every press of her lips pushed a little more light into the darkness where he existed. It was exquisite and beautiful, and he had to stop it before she realized how broken and empty he was on the inside. It took more will power than he cared to admit to sit her back down and once more gather the shadows around him.

She didn't understand that he did it to protect her. Maggie was full of life and light. She created things so amazing and beautiful it made him ache. She was fierce and brilliant, but fragile all the same. Her emotions weren't just attached to her sleeve. Instead, they cloaked her whole being with nothing standing between them and the hard world. Nothing to stand between them and the damage he could - the damage he *would* - do to her.

So, he walked away. He knew he'd hurt her, could see it in those black eyes that reflected everything, but it was better to hurt her a little now than completely destroy her in the long run. Because that's what Charlie did. He destroyed everything he touched.

It was late afternoon when he finally decided to call the roof done. With Mr. McCray's help, he'd reattached most of the gutters and patched a few places the shingles had abandoned for greener pastures. He'd actually been done more than thirty minutes ago, but he'd lingered until the last possible moment, making sure there was no time for him to go seek out Maggie before he had to succumb to the pull of the moon.

"Are you insane?" the object of his every thought chided as he descended the ladder. "It's almost dark."

He looked to the spot where the sun was making its final stand on the horizon. "I have enough time to get to the park still," he said, grabbing the ladder and moving past her to return it to the storage shed.

"I've been thinking about that," she said, trudging behind him. "I don't think it's a good idea. It's not like there are acres of woods or anything. You won't have room to run."

The small cluttered building caused her to stand too close. With nightfall rapidly approaching, his senses were becoming more acute by the minute. Each breath was filled with the scent of her. He could hear the steady melody of her heart and feel the heat of her flesh.

"It'll be fine," he told her, the words coming out more clipped than he'd intended.

"You don't understand. If people see a coyote running around Monarch, they're going to freak."

"Trust me, no one is going to see a coyote tonight."

"And if they do?" Her heart rate changed as her scent altered ever so slightly. Charlie turned, expecting to catch a glimpse of her slow-to-burn fury but finding eyes filled with fear instead. "Charlie, someone could shoot you. People around here own guns and like to use them."

Charlie stuffed his hands in his pockets to keep them from reaching out to her. "No one is going to shoot me. I've done this before."

"You've Changed in the middle of city park before? Really?"

Well, no. Not exactly.

"I've Changed lots of places."

"But not here. Not in *this* neighborhood with *these* people."

His shoulder twitched. It wasn't much more than a fluttering, but like a tremor before a major earthquake, it was a warning of what was to come. Soon. Too soon. It was getting darker much quicker than he anticipated.

"Maggie," he said, placing his hands on her shoulders and moving her aside, "if you don't let me go, I'm going to Change in the middle of your backyard. Don't you think the park might be a bit more convenient?"

A second tremor rippled across his left cheek, and Maggie saw it, her eyes widening with understanding.

"Oh, God. I'm sorry, Charlie." She jumped in front of him again, but only to pull open the door of the storage shed. "Go," she said, ushering him outside. "There is a shortcut to the park if you can get over the fence. What am I talking about? Of course you can get over the fence. I could do it when I was a ten year-old kid, and you're a full grown Shifter." She was rambling, and if he wasn't terrified of dropping to the ground in front of her at any moment, he might have stood there longer just to hear what else she might say.

As it was, he took off in the direction she pointed as quickly as possible. He vaulted the waist-high fence without breaking his stride. Three minutes later, he fell to his knees, giving in to the pain.

CHAPTER 24

She should have stayed home. He didn't want her there, but an hour after the sun finished setting, she found herself stumbling through the Monarch City Park anyway. Her toe slammed into the tail of giant concrete dinosaur who had successfully camouflaged himself against the cloudy night's sky and she recited every curse word she'd ever learned. For at least the twentieth time in the last five minutes she wished she had her phone and its handy-dandy flashlight app, but it had been missing, along with her mother, when she'd decided to come in search of Charlie.

Stupid, idiotic, arrogant boy. She felt her way up the length of the brontosaur, trying to remember where his friend the T-Rex was. *When I find you, I'm going to explain the myriad of ways you're wrong about absolutely everything, and there isn't a damn thing you're going to be able to say about it.*

She could forgive Charlie a lot, God knew he had a right to be in possession of a few issues, but she would never forgive him if he went off and got himself killed because he insisted on staying in town so she could get her grandmother's china.

I can't give you what you need.

Charlie Hagan lived in perpetual state of being wrong.

A muffled cry came from her right, so quiet she would have never heard it if she hadn't been listening so intently to the sounds of the night, hoping to hear a coyote slinking through the park. She froze, her ears straining to hear the noise again, and after a few silent seconds, it came. She was halfway across the park before realizing investigating strange sounds in the middle of the night wasn't necessarily the smartest thing in the world, but then a soft whimpering reached her ears and propelled her forward once again.

Maggie didn't know what she was expecting, but nothing could have prepared her for what she found. Behind an out of control mimosa tree, Charlie was crouched on the ground, his skin rippling and spasming as bones cracked and then knitted themselves back together.

"Charlie?" It came out as a whisper, her voice stolen by the horrific scene in front of her. His head swung towards her and she had to throw a hand over her mouth to keep from screaming. Where his mouth and nose should have been was a tangle of teeth and the beginnings of a snout. She watched in horror as two more sharp teeth ripped through his gums.

"Charlie, what's happening? What's wrong?"

Because something was most definitely wrong. She'd seen Scout Change a handful of times now, and even when she'd tried it inside the house it hadn't looked like this. Maggie knew it took longer for the others to Change, but Charlie should be in coyote form by now.

What was she supposed to do? She wasn't a Seer. She didn't know how to help him. She didn't even know what was happening. If he was with his pack, like he was supposed to be, they would be able to do something. Liam or Talley would fix him. Even Joshua probably had an answer, but not her. Charlie needed help, and anyone who could provide it was hundreds of miles away.

What had she done in agreeing to stay here?

With shaking hands, she searched her pockets frantically before remembering her phone was missing. A cry of despair ripped from her throat as hot tears trailed down her face.

"What can I do?" she asked as she sank to her knees beside the thing that was neither human or coyote. "Charlie..." She reached for him, and he leapt back from her touch, his foot getting tangled in the discarded shirt on the ground.

His shirt, which was laying next to his jeans, where he always kept his phone.

Moving slowly so she wouldn't spook him again, Maggie leaned forward until her fingers hooked into the waistband. Charlie watched as she pulled them back towards her. After what felt like ten minutes, the pockets were finally within strike range. Her trembling fingers snaked into one pocket and touched metal. Still moving like a basketball replay, she pulled out the phone buried inside.

"What the hell?" Forgetting there was a sorta-kinda wild animal in a lot of pain nearby, Maggie snapped her head up so quickly a sharp pain shot up her neck. "What is my phone doing in your jeans, Charlie?"

It was turned off, and she thought daybreak would occur before the thing finally powered up. When it did, it proudly told her about the fourteen voicemails, twenty-three text messages, and thirty-nine missed calls she'd failed to receive over the past two hours.

"Oh, Charlie," she said, scanning the text messages, unable to completely process what any of them said. "What have you done?"

Most of the messages were from Scout, who was now doing her own four-legged thing, but the last few were from Talley. She immediately pushed the callback button, silently begging her to pick up. Maggie nearly burst into tears when she heard the click after the second ring.

"How bad is it?" Talley said, bypassing her customary cheerful greeting.

"Bad," Maggie said, any relief she'd felt at having the phone answered already fading. For some reason, everything suddenly seemed even worse than it had just seconds before. She fought the urge to break down into tears. "Charlie isn't Changing. Something is wrong. He's..." *dying* "in a lot of pain."

"Is he convulsing?"

There was a loud snap, and Charlie's shoulders lurched up, rotating in their sockets.

"I think we're a little past convulsing."

There was a long minute of silence on the phone and then, "He's trying to Change?"

Isn't that what I said?!?!?

"Yes, and it's going very, very badly."

"You need to listen to me, Maggie--"

"It's not exactly like I'm playing Minecraft while we're talking here, Tal."

Talley continued in a calm, patient, Talley-like voice. "Charlie hasn't Changed since he got hurt really badly in a fight with the old Alpha Pack. We don't know why. At first we thought it was because his wounds were so extensive, but then he healed and... nothing."

"So he has to endure this every full moon?"

Maggie could hear the now-familiar sound of wolf howls and coyote barks through the phone. Unlike the rest of the Seers in the Alpha Pack, Talley always went out with Shifters on full moon nights. After a single visit to the shooting range with the Stella Polaris, Maggie completely understood why they trusted her to take care of herself.

"Are you sure he's trying to Change?"

"He currently has one hand and one paw." Although, paw sounded way too innocuous for the clawed mass at the end of his arm. Acid burned the back of Maggie's throat, her craptastic Thanksgiving dinner desperate to make a reappearance.

Talley cursed, using a word Maggie didn't think the mild-mannered girl knew, let alone would let slip past her lips. "Normally it's just some small seizures," Talley said. "We have a doctor come and keep him sedated the whole time. I..." Her voice shook. "I don't know what to do."

Up until this point, Charlie had been on all fours, but at that pronouncement, he collapsed to the ground as if he'd heard Talley's end of the conversation and knew no help was coming. Maggie didn't think, she just dropped the phone and went to him. There was nowhere she could touch. His body was too damaged, but she lay down beside him, her face next to his on the cool dirt, and that is when she felt it. Power, more power than she'd ever felt before, was gathered in the earth beneath Charlie's body.

From the moment Maggie's grandmother had passed along her powers of Thaumaturgy, Maggie was aware of what was going on in the ground beneath her feet. She respected the earth, and in return it gifted her with abilities most people couldn't imagine. Where most people saw dirt, Maggie saw life, energy, and power.

Life, energy, and power that was hers to command.

Life, energy, and power that Charlie needs.

It was all there, coiled up, ready to turn the man into the coyote, but it wasn't getting through.

"Charlie, it's there. Take it. Change."

He whimpered in reply, and the energy remained trapped in the ground.

"Charlie, please. Do whatever it is you guys do, and *Change*."

If anything, the invisible barrier between all that energy and Charlie grew stronger. She could feel it all there, humming beneath her. There was so much of it she could have leveled the entire city with a thought if she wanted. If she had to watch Charlie writhe in pain much longer, she might. Anything would be better than watching him suffer.

"Please. Please, take it. Please Change." She kept chanting the words, over and over, hoping he would hear. That he would listen. "Please, Charlie. Please Change."

His entire body trembled and a cry that could pull tears from a stone shattered the night. Maggie pressed her hands, palm down, onto the ground and felt the energy hum around them, and she knew what she had to do.

Her fingers flexed, sending ripples through the tightly wound energy eagerly awaiting her instruction. Could she do it? Could she push it into Charlie? Could she break through the shield he was trapped in?

There is only one way to find out...

Maggie pulled herself up on her knees, keeping her palms right where they were. As she moved, she called more energy to her, the power pulsing in a steady rhythm beneath her hands. She gathered it up until she had as much as she thought she could handle, and then she pulled in even more.

“Brace yourself,” she said, looking into the grass green eyes she had grown to love, and then she pushed the power towards him with everything she had. She pushed as sweat dripped down her neck and her breath came in short pants. She pushed as her arms began to tremble and then gave way beneath her. Even crumbled on the ground, her chest burning with the effort, she kept pushing. Her vision had gone blurry, but she could still hear the wet, crunchy noises and knew her job wasn’t finished, so she kept pushing until there was nothing left to push. The last thing she saw before everything went completely black was the face of a coyote inches from her own.

CHAPTER 25

Joshua wouldn't be able to save her. He had sworn to protect Maggie, but there was no way he could shield her from Scout's wrath. The Alpha Female had been ready to rip the Thaumaturgic to shreds by the time the sun began sinking back into the earth.

"She's kidnapped him!" Scout bellowed, stomping around her parents' kitchen, slamming cabinet doors as she gathered post-Change fuel.

Jase sat on the counter, unwrapping packages of lunchmeat and putting them into easier-for-four-legged-creatures-to-access Tupperware containers. "Maggie is a ninety-pound girl with the muscle tone of a slug. Unless she slipped something in his drink, I seriously doubt she's keeping him against his will."

"She didn't have to drug him," Scout said, turning on her heel and brandishing a sleeve of crackers like a weapon. "All she had to do was wiggle those fingers she's got him wrapped around. He's probably doing some sort of creepy marionette dance right now."

"You do realize Charlie is an adult, and if he wants to be Maggie's own personal Howdy Doody, then it's his choice, right?"

Scout gave Joshua a look that would have made a lesser man pee himself. As it was, Joshua wanted to crawl under the table. She might be sixty years younger than him, and he might technically be unable to die, but something told him the Alpha Female could make death seem like a welcomed friend. "One, he's not an adult, he's

Charlie. And two, it's not Charlie's fault she's a manipulative little witch." There was pop as the cracker sleeve relented to the power of the grip Scout had on it. "We don't even know what she does. Maybe she can manipulate people. Maybe she's using her crazy brain power to hold him captive." She threw the demolished crackers into the trashcan and grabbed her phone off the counter. "I'm going to try to call him again."

No matter how much Joshua defended Charlie's right to stay where he was, Scout remained convinced he was in need of rescuing. It didn't help when Liam and Talley started agreeing with her, although neither of the others blamed Maggie. Still, a small rescue party formed and was ready to head out when a phone call changed everyone's plan. Being the only Stratego not called by the full moon, Joshua was sent on a solo mission, one he would have accomplished a lot sooner if the interstate hadn't been closed for two hours just west of Nashville. He was beginning to make progress through the long lines of traffic when Maggie's call to Talley came through. He linked the car's GPS to the phone, and pulled into the park only forty-five minutes later.

"Maggie?" He listened for the horrific sounds he'd heard over the line when he'd intercepted Maggie's call to Talley, but only heard the typical late-night noises. He hoped she'd found a way to knock him out. He wasn't sure where he stood on the whole is-pain-still-pain-if-you-can't-remember-feeling-it debate, but he was certain anyone would rather be in a medically-induced coma than scream as their body parts rearranged themselves over and over.

He pulled up the signal from her phone onto his own and walked towards the flashing dot. He was closing in on the spot when a coyote jumped in front of him, blocking his path.

"Hey, Charlie," he said as casually as he could while looking at a mouth full of sharp teeth. "I see you made the Change after all."

Even though Joshua had never seen Charlie's coyote form, there was no question who was standing in front of him. If the similarities between this coyote and the one Jase turned into weren't enough of a hint, those grass-green Hagan eyes would have given it away. Still, Joshua was afraid, and he wasn't too proud to admit it. Charlie hadn't Changed in a very long time, and he'd been in a lot of pain for hours. There was no doubt there was more coyote instinct than human logic going on.

"Where's Mags?" There was no way Charlie would have hurt her on purpose, but on accident? With a wild coyote there was always the chance. And the longer they stood there with her not stepping out of the shadows, the more Joshua worried. "Did she go back home?"

Charlie growled low in his throat, his ears pressing back against his head. He stepped forward, forcing Joshua to step back. Understanding dawned slowly.

"Is she back there? Behind those bushes?"

Charlie forced Joshua back another step.

"Hey, bro. It's me. It's Joshua. You know I'm not going to hurt her, but if something is wrong, I might be able to help." The coyote didn't back off, but he didn't press Joshua further back either. "You can stay right by my side and start chewing on my face if I'm lying."

The standoff lasted a few minutes longer, but finally Charlie dropped his head. Joshua moved with exaggerated slowness around him and past the area of undergrowth.

Maggie was just on the other side, heaped on the ground like another piece of Charlie's discarded clothing. There was no blood or signs of injury he could see, but that didn't mean she wasn't laying in a pool of her own blood.

"I'm going to lift her up," Joshua told the coyote who sat next to her head, nudging her hair with his nose. "I need to check for injuries, okay?" He laid a hand on her shoulder, and when Charlie didn't try to snap off a few fingers, he used it to roll her over. The side she was laying on was as unmarred as the rest of her, but her skin was cold. Cold enough Joshua was surprised to find a pulse. "I'm going to have to get you off this freezing ground," he murmured to her, feeling a bit of a chill himself as the cold seeped through his jeans.

Joshua's eyebrows snapped together. It was cold out, but not freezing. Joshua had been completely comfortable wearing a cotton button-up shirt over his Kiss the Cook tee just minutes before, but the ground here felt like it was waiting for the snow to start. He looked at the girl in his arms again, the one whose secrets he'd known even though she never told him, and the coyote who looked ready to tear him from limb-to-limb for touching her.

"You talented girl," he said, a slow smile spreading over his face. "You beautiful, amazing, talented, selfless girl." He couldn't stop himself from placing his lips on her forehead, even with Charlie growling in his ear.

Never being around a Thaumaturgic who had drained herself before, Joshua wasn't sure how to proceed. After some debate with a Shifter who couldn't reply, he settled on pulling Charlie's shirt over her own clothes, wrapping her legs in his button-up shirt, and rolling up Charlie's pants and placing them under her head. He went back to the car to grab the blanket he always kept in the trunk, running through ideas in his head, but as he was heading back something grabbed his attention. He stood and stared at the ground for several moments, trying to figure out the difference. It wasn't something so obvious as dead grass and living grass, but somehow there seemed to be a line in the dirt so to speak. On one side, the grass looked weaker, less vibrant, and on the other, there was a luster that couldn't be hidden by the night sky. He knelt down and placed a hand on either side of the barely visible line and the temperature difference was obvious. On Maggie's side, the side with the barely-surviving grass, the ground was chilled to the point it hurt his hand to touch it. On the other, warmth reigned.

"I'm moving her," he told Charlie, who had stayed to guard the girl. "She's drained too much of the earth here." Proving he was starting to understand like a human a bit more, or that he could see Joshua's resolve and knew better than to get in the way, Charlie let Joshua lift Maggie off the ground and carry her out into the main part of the park. It was a risk, he knew it, but trees lined three sides of the open area, and the fourth spilled out onto the parking lot where only Joshua's car resided. Still, he hoped this would work quickly, before a friendly neighborhood police office came by and asked what exactly he was doing with an unconscious girl and a coyote.

When he put her on the ground, he didn't re-cover her. Instead, he exposed as much skin to the earth as he could, knowing that like Talley, Maggie's powers required touch to work.

Color didn't return to her cheeks for another thirty minutes, and Joshua worried it wasn't going to work, but finally her eyelashes started to flutter. "Charlie?" she forced out the moment she could, and in the space of a heartbeat, he was there, nuzzling her and letting her hands brush weakly through his fur.

"Miss McCray. How nice of you to join us."

The shock of hearing Joshua's voice had her sitting up a little too quickly for someone who had been completely out of it just moments earlier, and Charlie snapped his teeth at Joshua in warning.

"Here, let me help," he said, sliding an arm around her waist so she wouldn't fall back. "How are you feeling, Mags?"

Her eyes were unfocused as they looked up into his face. "What happened?"

Joshua smiled down at the girl even as Charlie gave him the coyote death glare. "Well, my dear, it seems you have bent the laws of physics to fix your boyfriend here. Quite the amazing feat, I must say. I'm very much impressed."

"Charlie..." she looked around frantically, her shoulders dropping with relief when she met the gaze of the coyote who sat by her side. Again her fingers went to his coat, brushing and easing away the aggression in his canine body.

"How did you do it?" Maggie froze mid-brush, and he clarified. "I mean, I understand what you did, but how did channeling all that energy turn our Charlie boy here into a real Shifter?"

Her eyes narrowed on him. "You know what I can do?"

"I'm Joshua. Information is kind of my thing."

She seemed to accept his answer, although somewhat reluctantly.

"There was something blocking him from accessing the energy from the earth. He couldn't complete the Change without it, so I gave it a push."

From the state of the ground in a twenty-foot radius from where he found her, Joshua was willing to wager it was one hell of a push.

"Something was blocking him?" He looked at the coyote in question. "Sure it wasn't someone?"

Maggie tilted her head in confusion. "But who would want to block Charlie? Who could even do that?"

"Who indeed." He met the coyote's green eyes, and the defiance there was all he needed to know he was right. Joshua had only ever known the broken Charlie, and had seen him break even further when they buried his brother, but looking into the eyes of the coyote, he finally understood the sadness and worry on the faces of all the other members of the Alpha Pack when they looked at their friend. The Charlie Joshua knew was missing something, and this was it. The coyote. The part composed of instinct and emotion. It was a wild thing, unpredictable and uncontrolled.

Joshua prayed he was here to stay.

Just hopefully not forever.

"Do you think he'll be able to Change back?" he asked. Traditionally, the human form was the one Shifters preferred, but he didn't know how much of Human Charlie was left in the beast who still lifted his lip to show off his impressive fangs every time Joshua was brave enough to look at him. If the coyote had taken over completely, was it possible for him to do the same thing the human side had done to him? Could he hold off the Change and silence the human voice in his head forever?

"I'm not going to let him hurt like that again," Maggie said, cutting off his thoughts. "When he starts Changing back, I'll make sure he finishes."

Charlie growled, and Joshua thought about doing the same.

"You're spent, kiddo. There will be no more magic mojo from you tonight."

She rose her chin defiantly and narrowed her eyes on him. "I will do what I have to do to get him through."

"This girl is under my protection as a Stratego and an Immortal," he told the coyote. "If you force her to hurt herself any further, I swear to God, I don't care who you are, I will take the vengeance of the Lord out on you, and there won't be a damn thing you can do to stop me."

The coyote lowered his head to the ground, but it wasn't a sign of submission. The pose said, *I agree with you, but don't think you can threaten me, asshole. I will pounce on you and have your windpipe stuck in my teeth before you can say, "Down, boy."*

Joshua reevaluated how much he wanted this Charlie to stick around.

Over the next hour Joshua found both Charlie and Maggie something to eat and even convinced Maggie to take a few bites while Charlie scarfed down an entire turkey. After finding out which house was hers, he broke in and grabbed her some warmer clothes. He was trying to talk her into getting a few hours of sleep before dawn came when his phone beeped.

Joshua knew something was up when he'd sent a text to Scout's phone to let her know Charlie was okay and got a "K" in response. Scout didn't do one-letter texts, and she certainly didn't do them over something as important to her as Charlie's well being. No response would have meant she'd Changed and was without opposable thumbs, but a one-word text? She was human and busy.

Not a good sign, and neither was the "we need your forensic expertise" message he was looking at now.

"You think you can handle the rest of this on your own, Mags?"

Two sets of eyes - one coal black and the other green as grass - looked up at him as if he was less than bright. "We're fine," Maggie said as if it was obvious. He thought about mentioning how she was in a coma when he got there and Charlie had spent over an hour in excruciating pain before that, but decided against it. Charlie was considerably calmer than when he'd arrived, but Joshua didn't think it was wise to taunt him.

"Well, if you're sure," he said, pulling himself up off the ground, "it seems I'm needed elsewhere tonight." He pointed a finger at Charlie. "You will do whatever you can to protect her, understand?" The coyote growled, and Joshua swung his finger to the Thaumaturgic. "And you will not over-extend yourself again."

"We're not children."

"I've got t-shirts older than the two of you."

"That's only because you're older than dirt."

He smiled at her gumption and leaned down to give her a kiss on the forehead just to piss off the coyote. "Take care of each other," he said, knowing they would.

CHAPTER 26

Maggie hadn't meant to fall asleep. Honestly, she didn't think it was possible. But once Joshua was gone, the night became quiet, and the fatigue she'd felt from draining herself earlier came back with a vengeance. She'd only meant to close her eyes and rest for a few minutes, but the next thing she knew someone was calling her name softly as warm hands caressed her shoulder. Early morning light stung her eyes as she tried to shake off sleep.

"Hey, beautiful." Charlie's face, his very *human* face, smiled down at her.

Maggie scrambled up. "Oh, God. I'm so sorry, Charlie. I didn't mean to fall asleep." Her hands brushed down his strong arms as if she might find a patch of fur or some other part that had gone wonky during the Change. "Are you okay?"

One hand came up to cup her cheek. His eyes were locked on hers, and in them was something she couldn't name, but it took her breath all the same. "I... I am..." He smiled, a bright, amazing, true smile, and then those gorgeous lips were on hers.

They'd only kissed two times before, and both times she'd kissed him. Not so this time. This was Charlie's kiss, and she was lost under the power of it. He nibbled at her lips, teasing her mouth open before taking it deeper. The heat of his mouth warmed her so much she forgot the frosty November chill that had numbed her fingers and nose. His hands roamed over her as if memorizing the curve of her shoulder and line of her back. Her own hands found their way to his bare chest, worshipping the silky warmth they found there.

"Maggie," Charlie moaned, his breath coming in hard bursts.

Feeling even more powerful than she had commanding the earth the night before, she trailed kisses down his neck and settled in at the place where it connected to his shoulder.

"Jesus," he muttered. "We've got to stop."

"Why?" she asked, moving to the other side.

His fingers dug into her hair, gently holding her in place. It took several kisses for him to answer. "Because we're in a public park?" It came out like a question, and at the word "public", Maggie knew the answer. She pulled back, not at all surprised her breathing was even more erratic than his.

"This probably isn't the best place for this, huh?"

He gave her another smile, and she marveled at how it transformed his face. She'd thought she'd seen glimpses of the real Charlie before, but now she knew better. "I can hear people waking up and moving around," he said as if it was perfectly normal to be able to hear inside people's houses. "Someone will be walking a dog or taking a morning jog soon, and if it's all the same to you, I'd rather not give them something to share with all their friends and enemies on the internet."

Maggie spent the rest of the day waiting for the robot to slowly start taking over, but it never happened. She'd been disappointed the night before when Coyote Charlie insisted on sitting obediently by her side instead of going off and showing her some of the wild emotion she'd been so eager to see, but it turned out seeing it in Human Charlie was even better. His smiles were dazzling, and his laughter was so rich and earnest she could feel it lifting her own mood somewhere beyond the stratosphere. When they'd gone to the pawnshop she discovered his anger to be a quiet and terrifying thing. Luckily, the guy working the counter felt the same and let them take her china for the originally quoted three hundred instead of the forty percent mark-up they tried to charge.

The transformation seemed magical, which made Maggie worry the spell might eventually break and leave her with the robot. It made her want to stay in Monarch forever, but she knew it wasn't an option.

"We need to go," Charlie announced, walking into her bedroom where she was looking for the copy of *Kabuki* she wanted to lend him. "How soon can you be ready?"

"My stuff is packed and ready to go." She didn't bother telling him it'd stayed that way since they arrived. Maggie didn't trust her mother to not do something stupid that would end with them storming out at a moment's notice.

Charlie crossed her tiny, crammed-pack room in two long strides. "I'm sorry," he said, his palm once again cradling her cheek. In the hours since sunrise, she'd discovered it was his preferred way to have a conversation with her. It was quickly becoming hers, too. "Something has come up, and they need us back at the farm."

"Is anyone..." She cleared her throat, unable to ask the question she'd been forming. "Is everyone okay?"

"As far as I know. Someone tried to run the Alphas off the road, and Joshua says they have some information they'd rather not share over the phone."

Maggie could tell he was worried about the same things she was. It might have been selfish, but she sent a plea out into the universe that everyone was alive and well, not for their sake, but for Charlie's.

The drive back to Kentucky was mostly quiet and done at speeds which should have gotten them carted off to jail for reckless endangerment, but they pulled into the long drive leading up to the house without seeing any flashing blue lights. Charlie sprinted around the truck, pulling open her door before she could get her seatbelt undone. Once she was out of the vehicle, he gathered her hand in his. It wasn't a particularly sexy touch, just two hands clasped onto each other, but it felt more intimate than any of the kisses they'd shared.

If she hadn't already seen their vehicles in the six-car garage, Maggie would've known the rest of the Alpha Pack was already back the moment they opened the door. For a group of people with super-hearing and animal-like grace, they were a noisy bunch.

They were making their way towards the living room when a small blond person stepped out of the kitchen and directly into their path. She looked to be around nine or ten. She stood just a few inches shorter than Maggie, although she seemed to be trying to make up for it with the mass of curls piled high on top of her head. Her blue eyes widened in alarm for about a half-second before she launched herself at Charlie's waist.

Once she released her hold she looked up at him with prepubescent ire. "You weren't at Thanksgiving."

"Sorry about that, munchkin," Charlie said, rubbing his hands over her tower of hair and causing her to shriek. "Maggie needed a ride home to see her family, and I figured no one would notice if I went missing."

The girl rolled her eyes, and instantly Maggie knew who she was. "Yeah, no one would notice. Especially not your gramma, who had to say, 'I wish my Charlie was here,' every five minutes." One hand went to her hip as she poked Charlie in the chest. "You should be ashamed of yourself, Charlie Hagan. Your gramma is old, and we're supposed to be nice to old people." Apparently finished with the scolding, she turned and brought her full attention to Maggie.

It is stupid to be scared of a child.

Still, Maggie had to force herself to hold her ground.

"Who are you?" the mini-Scout asked as if she already knew she wouldn't like the response.

"My apologies," Charlie said, affecting a British-like accent of sorts. "I shall give the proper introductions. Miss Angel, this is Maggie Mae McCray. Maggie, this is Angel Donovan, the third of the overly sarcastic Donovan siblings."

Angel cut Charlie a look, but her focus remained on Maggie.

"Maggie Mae McCray? That sounds like a nursery rhyme name."

"And Angel sounds like the sort of name belonging to a kind, loving child instead of the complete opposite, yet here we are," Joshua said, stepping into the hallway. The past twenty-four hours had been noticeably hard on him. His eyes were bloodshot and sporting dark circles, and his face looked even more gaunt than normal. He almost looked as old as he actually was.

"Ignore him. He's an idiot," Angel said, stomping on Joshua's toe. He let out a string of nonsensical words, letting the world know she'd hit her mark. "So... Maggie Mae..."

"Maggie works just fine."

"Are you are werewolf, Maggie Mae?"

Joshua and Charlie were just as shocked by the question as Maggie. "Werewolf? What kind of crazy talk is that?" Charlie asked in such an overly exaggerated fashion even the absolute last person on earth who might believe in supernatural creatures would take pause.

Joshua was a bit more helpful.

"Somebody has been watching Netflix without parental supervision again, hasn't she?" he asked, giving her head a condescending pat.

Angel ignored them both. "You don't look like you would be a werewolf," she said, cocking her head to the side as she studied Maggie. "You must be whatever Talley is."

Maggie couldn't think of a single thing to say. Fortunately, she didn't have to since Angel had grown tired of that topic and moved immediately onto something else.

"That dress. Vintage or retro?"

"Vintage?" Maggie hadn't meant for it to be a question, but this little girl was confusing. "It was my grandmother's."

Angel nodded her head as if Maggie had passed some sort of test. "I like it."

"Thanks."

"No problem," Angel replied before turning to Charlie. "Your girlfriend is nice and she dresses well. I like her."

Maggie started to correct her, but was cut off by Charlie's "Me too."

As far as declarations of love and conversations on defining the relationship went, it wasn't exactly what most people would define as romantic, but Maggie decided the words "me" and "too" would forever be the most swoon-worthy she'd ever heard. She was feeling all sorts of happy, warm feelings when Liam stepped into the hallway. He looked like he hadn't slept in days, and Maggie thought it may have been an accurate reflection as he looked at the odd gathering happening as if he was hallucinating.

"Charlie," he finally said, after rubbing a hand over the back of his head. "You guys are here. Good. We have a problem."

CHAPTER 27

Charlie's coyote was still incredibly close to the surface when he walked into the never-before-used meeting room where he'd once caught Makya talking to Maggie. He could feel the tension of everyone around him, and it kicked his own anxiety up to the point of becoming a distraction.

He wasn't used to feeling so much. For nearly two years he'd cut himself off from his coyote. It hadn't been a conscious effort in the beginning. After he'd been injured, his coyote knew he didn't have the strength to pull through the transformation, so he'd receded, leaving Human Charlie to heal in peace. But there was never any peace in Charlie's life. He began to purposefully keep his coyote at bay. He'd grown used to Human Charlie's muted emotions, and he couldn't handle the way his coyote cried out in grief and anger over the loss of his brother. So he pushed it back down into the closed-off part of his soul where it had hidden during his recovery. And he kept it there so long he didn't know how to let it out when he found himself in Monarch City Park, desperate to break free and be the coyote again.

Thank God for Maggie.

She was poised on the edge of one of the big, heavy leather chairs. He'd always known she was beautiful, but he hadn't realized how her beauty was the kind that would punch you in the gut, leaving you breathless. He'd admired her smile and laughter before, but he didn't know how it could make him feel all warm and snuggly on the inside. She was kind and talented, and after seeing the way she'd grown up, he knew her spirit was made of the strongest stuff on earth to have accomplished everything she had without turning bitter. She was amazing, and for God knew what reason, she wanted to be with him.

He would happily take the burdens of the coyote if it meant getting to feel all the feels Maggie gave him.

"Where is Scout?" Jase asked, plopping himself into the seat across from Charlie and throwing his feet up on the table. Other than the Alpha Female, he was the last one to make an appearance. The rest of the Alpha Pack was all sitting and waiting, most of them studying the patterns on the textured ceiling. No one had said a single word up until that point, the gravity of whatever this situation was weighing on all of them.

Jase had little time or patience for weighing situations.

"She's trying to force Angel to sit down and watch television instead of joining us." Liam got that far-away look in his eyes that said he was trying to connect to her through their mate bond. "It's not going well."

"Why exactly is the munchkin here?" Charlie asked. "I mean, I love the kid and all, but if we've got something going on, maybe this isn't the best place for her."

Jase tilted the chair back as far as it would go. "For the love of God, do not let Scout hear you say that."

"Gus... Do you remember Gus?" Liam asked.

"Seer who talks to dead people? Hated Makya on sight?"

Liam nodded. "Gus's sister had a vision of the Donovan's house burning to the ground."

The rage was like a literal punch to his stomach. Threatening the Alpha Pack was one thing, but going after innocent humans like Uncle Dustin, Aunt Rebecca, and

Angel? That crossed a line. A line with a pissed off Shifter looking for revenge on the other side.

Once Charlie could catch his breath again he asked, "Was it a this-is-going-to-happen vision, or a maybe-possibly-or-perhaps-just-a-metaphorical-vision vision?"

"Does it matter?" Jase asked, the muscles in his jaw jumping as he ground his teeth together.

Of course it didn't matter. Any threat to the Donovans was unacceptable.

If the homicidal look in Liam's eyes was anything to go by, the Alpha Male agreed. "Scout convinced her family to come back with us as a precautionary measure."

"And she already regrets it." Scout walked through the room and to her rightful spot next to Liam with all the regality of a queen. It almost made Charlie overlook her unbrushed hair and the giant mustard stain on her shirt. "I swear, whoever decided cute teenage boys should be allowed to have their voice auto-tuned and recorded should be shot. Repeatedly. In the ears." Even though the arms on the chairs made it difficult, her hand intertwined itself with Liam's. "So...," she said, looking around the table. "This is everybody?"

"Everybody over eighteen and under eighty," Marie said, and Charlie wondered at what could have caused them to fly in the Minnesota contingent of the Alpha Pack on such a short notice.

Scout glanced at Charlie's side of the table and met his eyes. She held the stare a few seconds longer than was comfortable and then a slow smile curled up the corners of her mouth. "Hey there, Chuck. Glad to have you back."

He dipped his head, acknowledging she was referring to more than his physical presence in the room.

Robby Hagan leaned forward onto his elbows. "While I'm enjoying this hi-how-are-y'all-doing business, I really wish we'd just get on to whatever it is you made us all haul ass here for. I had to cancel a weekend getaway with my girlfriend at the last minute, and it's left me kinda cranky."

Charlie didn't miss the "pity that" Marie's sister Michelle muttered under her breath or the way Robby's body tensed up when she said it. If he wasn't as eager to find out what was going on as Robby was, he might have asked them what that was all about.

"Mandel is dead," Liam said, cutting straight to the point.

Jase sat up, the legs of his chair thudding down onto the carpet. "Which is a good thing, yes?"

"Not so much," Scout said. "It appears he committed suicide... more than three months ago."

And it had been around three months since Charlie's Humvee was violated. "I'm still not seeing the bad part," he said. "Guy does some bad shit, feels guilty, and offs himself. Personally, I feel like justice is served. Day over. Let's go get some pie."

This time, Joshua answered. And since it was Joshua, the lights dimmed and an image flashed up on a screen Charlie hadn't noticed before. The picture was of a corpse mostly covered in leaves. From the way most of the flesh was missing, it had been there a while. "In the Mandel Pack, the wife of the Pack Leader is expected to lay flowers on the grave of the first Pack Leader to hold that territory on holidays. Lucinda Mandel went to the small cemetery yesterday and discovered her husband's body at the base of the former Pack Leader's gravestone. She immediately called the Alphas." Joshua punched something into his phone and the image on the screen changed. Now there was the picture of the corpse on the left side of the screen, and on the right side was a picture of Abram Mandel at the hustings where he'd asked Scout to force Imogen into marrying another Shifter. "I've done some preliminary tests, and I think it's safe to say Mandel hasn't been seen since he left the hustings because he immediately drove back to Mississippi, found himself a nice, quiet spot, and shot himself in the head."

"But you can't be sure?"

"No," Liam said, "we can't. And we might be inclined to believe he'd arranged for the murder of Barros and the attempt on you and Maggie back in September with the contacts he had, but then we came home."

The screen changed again. This time the picture was of the wall in the gym where the Painting of Death resided. Since Charlie had last seen it there had been an update. The word "soon" was painted across the canvas.

"Is that blood?" Maggie asked in a strangled voice. Taking a cue from his Alphas, Charlie reached over and placed her hand in his.

"Horse, not human," Scout answered. "We found the body of one of our thoroughbreds behind the gym. He'd been..." She swallowed so hard even Maggie, whose hearing was at a normal human's level, had to have heard it. "He was posed." Her eyes flicked up to the screen. "There are no pictures. It seemed disrespectful, and I'm pretty sure I would vomit if I had to see it again."

One disadvantage to letting the coyote have so much control was at times like this it was hard to focus enough to think things through logically. Rage, disgust, and fear created a red haze he had trouble fighting through long enough to ask, "How? How in the hell did someone get to our horses? We have the best security system in the world, a vet who freaking lives twenty feet from the barns, and the house is inhabited by Shifters. This place is more protected than Fort Knox, and yet someone has slipped by us *again*? Long enough to kill a four hundred thousand dollar horse, drain his blood, have a little arts and crafts time, and then get all freaky with the dead body? Are you serious?"

Liam scrubbed a hand over his face. "I know. It shouldn't have happened. We had two Shifters on the property, plus the vet last night. The vet woke up this morning with no idea what had happened over the past twelve hours. I caught the scent of a drug in his coffee cup. And the Shifters Changed back over halfway to Lexington. They called as soon as they could grab clothes and a phone. Turns out, someone started shooting at them last night, and their animal completely took eover and ran."

"And the security system we spent half a fortune on?"

"We're looking into it," Joshua said. "It looks like it was turned off for a few hours last night."

"That's not all." Scout nodded at Joshua, and the image on the screen changed to a blurry picture of a black sedan. "Early this morning this car started following us somewhere near the Versailles exit on the Bluegrass Parkway. Once we got off the parkway, it tried to run us off the road."

Jase leaned forward, eyes squinting. "License plate number?"

"Didn't have one."

"Did you get a look at the driver?"

"Wearing a mask."

Jase turned to his sister. "Like a ski mask?"

"Like a Pennywise the Clown mask."

All the color drained from Jase's face. "That's not funny."

"No," Scout agreed, "for once, it was not funny."

Charlie slowly became aware of a gentle caress against the base of his thumb and a softly whispered "it's okay." That was when he realized he was growling. It shouldn't have been surprising to anyone. They were just one night past the full moon, and everyone's animal was riding them hard. But a quick glance around the table assured Charlie everyone had noticed his reaction and was definitely surprised. Michelle's jaw was literally hanging open, Jase was staring with raised eyebrows, and Talley was smiling at him like he just announced there would be an extra Christmas this year.

Liam's expression didn't change much, but Charlie knew him well enough to realize he was on the Talley end of the reaction spectrum. "Maggie, Joshua told me what you did." Her eyes fell to the table as a blush spread across her cheeks. "The Alpha Pack is forever in your debt. Anything you should ever need, all you have to do is ask."

"I didn't do it for you," Maggie said, not looking up, "so you don't owe me anything. But I appreciate the offer all the same."

If he didn't think it would embarrass her, Charlie would have pulled her out of her seat and kissed her until neither of them could breathe. Instead, he said, "We can start by finding a way to eliminate this threat to her."

"What I don't get," Talley said, "is why they did nothing for so long and then came out with guns blazing now. Do you think they knew the body would get discovered this weekend?"

"Maybe they have day jobs and needed a four-day weekend to do their extracurricular creepy murdering stuff," Jase guessed.

"A day job... or a busy school schedule." Maggie worried her bottom lip as she thought it over. "Barros's murder and the stuff with Charlie's car happened early in the semester. No one had too much going on then, but when all the exams and stuff started, everything went quiet. But now it's Thanksgiving Break, and I don't know about anyone else, but I'm not doing anything school related."

"So... another art student," Charlie said. "Either an independent study or grad student. Someone with access to Rosa Hall." He swallowed down another growl. How many times had Maggie been in danger just by being in that building? How many times might he have walked right past the killer and not known?

"Maybe, but who? You're the only drawing student. Everyone else is into 3D stuff. And I have a painting class with most of those guys. None of them are capable of what is hanging in the gym."

"Students aren't the only people on campus." Joshua leaned up onto his elbows. "Sanders boasts some of the nation's best artists on its staff. I'm assuming they all have access to Rosa Hall?"

Maggie nodded, seemingly too shocked by the thought of one her professors being behind all this to speak.

Charlie started a suspect list in his head, but stopped on one name. "Stroud."

It made sense. A recluse with a reputation for a volatile temper. Charlie's interactions with him had been minimal. He didn't have him as a regular teacher, and Stroud had asked for everything to be sent back and forth digitally instead of face-to-face. They were only a month into the school year when Charlie started relying exclusively on Maggie for feedback. Charlie hadn't thought much about it before, but what if there was a reason Stroud didn't want someone with super-senses around? And why had he even offered the independent study position to Charlie in the first place? Charlie had been proud enough to believe it was because he was talented, but what if it was to keep an eye on him? What if he'd had Charlie and the rest of the Alpha Pack in his sights way before Charlie walked into his office?

"The painting isn't his normal style, but he has the skill to do it," Maggie said. "But do you think he's really capable of something like this?"

Jase snorted. "I've read *Midnight of the Mighty*, and I'm telling you, that guy is screwed up. I definitely think he could have done it."

Some other names were tossed around, but everyone kept coming back to Stroud. After about ten minutes of discussion, Charlie was ready to storm out into the night and hold the guy accountable, but Liam held him back.

"We're not making the same mistake we did before and focus on one suspect," he said when Charlie suggested an interrogation team pay the good professor a little visit. "We'll take our time, and gather evidence. We'll look at other options. And then, when we're convinced of who is behind this, they will find out that this Alpha Pack isn't as weak as everyone believes us to be."

CHAPTER 28

"It's perfect."

Maggie leaned back against Charlie's chest, enjoying the weight of his arms wrapped around her waist. The vase sat on the table in front of them, fresh from the final firing.

"I did it," she giggled. She knew eventually she would look at it with a critical eye and see things she could have done better, but at this moment she was reveling in the giddiness of having it finished. She'd spent so much time and exerted so much energy creating the piece she'd been too nervous to even open the kiln. Seeing her panic, Charlie made her leave the room. When she came back in, it was sitting on the table, a light positioned directly above it. Even from the door she was able to see the pattern clearly on the outside.

"I say we celebrate," she said, spinning in his arms so she could reach his lips. Even though she'd had open access to his perfect mouth for a week now, she still marveled over the way he let her touch him, and the way he responded. She thought the growls and pawing would fade with the moon in the sky, but if anything, Charlie was getting more... *interactive* as time went on. Not that Maggie was complaining. No, the only complaint Maggie currently had was the studio didn't have a couch where they could make themselves more comfortable.

Well, maybe not so much comfortable as lateral since Maggie didn't feel truly comfortable anywhere on campus anymore. Liam called in some more Shifters from the Den in Romania to help with the investigation. Every night they had a meeting to discuss their findings, and every night more names got put up on the suspect board. Everyone was getting freaked out, including Scout, which was enough for Maggie to get freaked out all over again.

Charlie's mouth left hers to travel to her earlobe and all thoughts about murder suspects and Scout scattered at the onslaught of full-body tingles running from the top of her head to the bottom of her feet.

"Good grief, you two. Get a room."

Maggie jerked back at the sound of Reid's voice, but Charlie didn't seem to care about how the situation looked. He allowed Maggie to put some distance between their faces, but he kept her body pressed tight against his.

"We have a room," Charlie said. "And we'd like to have it back. Good-bye, Reid."

"Ha ha. You're a funny, funny guy," she deadpanned as she walked over to the table where the vase was. "Ooooh. Pretty." She reached for it, and all the oxygen in Maggie's lungs disappeared. But before Reid could make contact, Charlie's hand clamped onto her wrist.

"No touching. It's fra-gee-lay."

"Wait a minute," Maggie said, smacking Charlie's hand away from Reid. She knew it was ridiculous, but she didn't like seeing him touch her. "I'm African, Chinese, and Scottish. Not Italian."

They both giggled at their own cheesy cleverness while Reid looked between the two of them, her forehead folded in confusion.

"Is there a chance you two were possessed by pod people over Thanksgiving? Maybe you body swapped with some really happy, touchy-feely people?"

"Hey. I've always been happy."

Reid smiled at Maggie indulgently. "Of course you have, sweetie. Those little lines around your mouth probably were from bad moisturizer."

"I don't have lines around my mouth," Maggie said, her hand worrying over the corners of her lips self-consciously.

"I don't *see* any lines." Charlie leaned in until his breath was tickling over her jaw. "Maybe I need to see if I can feel any. Hmmm... tongues are really sensitive. I should probably use that..."

"Charlie!"

Even Maggie didn't know if her squeaked exclamation was because of his boldness in front of Reid or because as he was moving closer to follow through on his threat all the lights went out.

"Okay, did I just go blind, or did it get tomb-like dark in here?" There was just enough light for Maggie to see a spasm of movement, which she took to be Reid's arms.

"Reid, don't move. You might hit the vase." But still she flailed about. Maggie heard a rustling of clothes behind her, then the sound of something being placed on the next table.

"Moved it to safety," Charlie muttered in her ear.

There are definite advantages to having a boyfriend with supernatural senses, Maggie thought. She literally couldn't see her hand in front of her face, but he was able to perform a ceramic vase rescue mission.

Charlie's phone buzzed in his pocket, and because it was the only light source in the room, Maggie couldn't help but look at the screen when he pulled up the message from Joshua.

"Power has been cut. Video feed gone."

"Most probable source is the basement."

"Backup is on the way."

Maggie's knees went wobbly. "We need to get out," she said to Charlie, not caring Reid was there and would think they were crazy. Crazy was better than dead any day.

She felt, rather than saw, Charlie shake his head. "Let me go see what is happening," he whispered into her ear. He kissed the spot where her pulse rammed against her neck with a techno beat. "Just stay put, and if you have to, use this." He slipped something into her pocket. The weight pressed against her leg, and a quick exploration with her fingers revealed a gun.

She might have felt safer if she had any idea how to use it. As it was, she was now worried about accidentally shooting herself in the leg.

"Stay," she mouthed, hoping his super-vision enabled him to see her in the dark.

"Are you guys seriously doing the nasty over there?" Reid sounded oddly offended and put out for a girl who was known to have sex with Boyfriend in hall closets and empty classrooms. "I swear, if my phone wasn't in the metalworking studio, I would totally be spot-lighting you right now."

There was a zipping noise, and then Charlie said, "Oh well. I guess if you feel that way about it, I'll put these clothes back on and go see if I can figure out what happened to the lights." Reid made a gagging noise, and Maggie's face shot up in flames. "Be right back," he said, giving Maggie's hand a squeeze.

Don't go! Someone might be down there! They might hurt you!

But Maggie didn't scream after him like she wanted, because it wouldn't have done any good. Charlie wouldn't give up, and he didn't care he could get hurt or worse. She could have followed, but what good would that do if someone really was out there? At best, she would fumble around and not help matters at all. At worst, she would get them both killed. No, the best thing she could do would be to sit there and hope he made it back safely.

Well, sit around, hope he made it back safely, and tattle.

"Charlie went off to find whoever cut the power. Hurry," she texted to the oh-so-convenient list she'd programmed into her phone that included every person who would storm in, kicking ass and taking names, if they knew Charlie was in danger.

Jase texted back a string of cuss words, Joshua said he was working on getting the power back, and Scout said they were still ten minutes out.

"Yo, Phone Hoarder. Pull up a light on that thing and let's get out of here."

Maggie jumped at the sound of Reid's voice. She was so busy with being trapped in the dark and freaking out over the way Charlie could be dying at that very moment, she'd forgotten she wasn't just stuck in the room, she was stuck with *Reid*.

She supposed it could be worse, although she couldn't come up with any good examples of how.

"We don't know what is going on. We might run into something if we left." As far as made-up excuses went, it was on the terrible side of lame, enough so Reid didn't even bother acknowledging it.

"Come on. This crazy darkness if freaking me out. The metalworking shop has more than one window. We'll at least be able to see each other."

Maggie didn't want to leave - she felt most comfortable in her studio and Charlie had asked her to stay - but Reid had a point. Standing around in the dark wasn't doing anyone any good.

Reid insisted on taking control of Maggie's phone, leading them through the building. Even though it was a weeknight, very few people seemed to be around. One of the glassblowers was leaned out a window, blowing the smoke from his joint into the alley between their building and the Admissions Office, and two of the dancers were doing some back-breaking stretches near the door where what little moonlight the night offered spilled in.

Maggie hadn't actually been in the metalworking shop since the first week of school. It was forever away from the ceramic studio, and since Maggie never actually sought Reid and Boyfriend out, she had no reason to traipse over there.

The first thing she noticed when walking through the door was the smell. It was an odd mixture of earth and chemicals. The earth was coming from a mound of fresh dirt sitting beside the forge, ready to smother out the flames. The chemicals...

Well, she wasn't really sure where they were coming from, but this was the metalworking shop. Who knew what those guys did.

The second thing she noticed was the crucifix.

"What in the hell...?"

It wasn't huge, maybe three feet tall, but it seemed to take up most of the room. As far as skill went, it was amazing. No doubt the artist had immense talent.

Too bad their art made Maggie want to throw up.

"What do you think?" Boyfriend flicked a piece of imaginary dust off the figure. "I know this isn't how it really works, but I was making a statement, you know?"

Maggie could only stare mutely at the figure on the cross. It had the body of a human and the head of a wolf. Into its stomach was carved the word "abomination". Instead of eyes, it had hollowed out sockets.

"Reid didn't like the cross. She thought I was comparing you guys to Jesus, but I explained to her how crucifixion is one of the most painful, humiliating forms of public execution, and she eventually started liking the idea. Didn't you, babe?"

Maggie glanced at the door, calculating if she could make it.

"Not happening," Boyfriend said as if reading her mind. "Even if you were faster than me, I can have a knife stuck in your back before you make it to the hall."

"Charlie–"

"Is locked in the basement. When Reid told me he'd wandered down there after I cut the power, I realized how much better it would be for you both to die alone."

Reid pulled a phone out her pocket and did her best *The Price Is Right* Showcase Showdown presentation. "Turns out I had it with me all this time. Silly me."

Maggie was dreaming. Or maybe the gas fumes were making her high. That had to be what was going on. No way was this happening.

"Why? How?" Reid. And *Boyfriend*. Maggie's mind went back to Barros's body and all the wires and tools used to pose him.

All the wires and tools a metalworker would know how to use.

"Why?" she asked again, panic and terror making her voice quake.

"Why? Because you're all an abomination." His words were even more disturbing because of the casual way he said them. "Because God never meant for you to exist." He raised his arms out to his side. "I'm merely trying to send you all back to hell where you belong."

"Us?"

"Your kind. Shifters and Seers," Reid said. "Can you imagine my surprise at finding out you're a Seer? I mean, I came to this school to eradicate the world of such demons, and they had gone and given me one as a roommate." She smiled, which made her look all the more crazy. "It was a sign. God is on our side."

"God? You're not even religious."

"Religious isn't the same as spiritual, Maggie. Of course, as one of the damned, you probably can't understand the difference."

Reid was insane. Like over-the-cuckoo's-nest insane. No way did Maggie believe this had anything to do with God. She was just using the big guy upstairs as an excuse to screw with people's lives.

And Boyfriend... disturbed was the word that came to mind, especially as Maggie watched him play with a wicked looking knife appearing from God only knows where. He'd always seemed off, disconnected in a way that spoke of anger, bitterness, and a whole host of ugly thoughts and emotions, but this was beyond anything she'd imagined.

They were bat-shit crazy, and they were going to kill her.

Bizarrely, the thing worrying Maggie the most was knowing Charlie would never forgive himself for not saving her. The robot would return, more cold and emotionless than before.

But at least he will survive, the part of her living in hope whispered, confident he could hold his own against them. *And maybe, with time, he'll heal. He's done it before, and he can do it again.*

"You realize they will find you, right? That even if you kill me here today, they will hunt you down and give your twisted minds a lesson in pain and torture? These aren't some backwoods coyotes you've picked a fight with. This is the Alpha Pack."

"A stolen title for a freak among freaks," Boyfriend said with a shrug of his shoulders. "I'm not worried."

"You will be," Maggie bluffed. "Soon."

Surely ten minutes had passed. She couldn't be certain because when the world goes crazy, apparently time perception goes MIA, but she thought ten minutes had passed. Liam or Scout was going to burst through the door any minute and save the day.

Any... minute... now...

"Oh, you're not waiting for your rescue party, are you?" Reid gave a mock pout. "Sorry, I may have sent them a message letting them know you were okay and they could go home."

The place where hope exists is somewhere between the breastbone and bellybutton. Maggie knew because she felt it die a quick but painful death.

"You don't want to do this," she pleaded, tears springing to her eyes. She knew she should be ashamed to beg for her life, but she wasn't. It was her life, after all. Without it, she was nothing, and Maggie didn't want to be nothing. She wanted to create. To love. To *live*. "Please. We can all just walk out of here, and I won't tell anyone. We'll call a truce."

Boyfriend sneered. "No truce. No walking away. And no more talking." He nodded to Reid. "Ready, Babe?"

Reid moved behind Maggie. "Ready."

Before she make a grab for the gun Charlie gave her, Boyfriend wrapped his arms around her midsection, immobilizing her. In the next second, Reid jerked back one of her arms and wrapped something around her wrist. The pain was so intense she couldn't process what was happening, let alone fight back. By the time they let her go, she found herself laying on the ground, her arms and legs bound with barbed wire.

A Zippo lighter flashed in Boyfriend's hand. "I'm disappointed to have to let go of my original vision, but we do what we must." He cocked his head thoughtfully at Maggie. "Maybe we could strap you to the counter and move your hands..." He put one hand to his head and reached the other one out as if trying to grab onto something. Maggie recognized the pose immediately. It is hard to forget how the body wearing your face in a horrific painting looks.

"We don't have time, baby. Next time."

"Next time." He nodded, disappointment coloring his eyes.

Reid knelt down in front of Maggie, who was using all her focus to keep from giving them the satisfaction of hearing her scream. "Bye, Mags," she said. "I hope you enjoy the way the flames feel licking your dirty skin. You're going to feel it for the rest of eternity."

And then they were gone. Maggie heard the snick of the lighter and saw the flash of light on the far side of the room. Unable to keep it in any longer, she screamed. She screamed as she used her knees and elbows to drag her body across the floor. She screamed as the world ignited around her. She screamed and screamed until she couldn't scream anymore. The flames were so close the heat of it was searing her skin. Through the smoke, she imagined she saw Charlie standing in the door.

Look at me, she thought. *Come for me. Save me.*

But he looked the other way, and when he spoke, it wasn't to call her name.

"Scout!" was the last thing Maggie heard before everything went dark.

CHAPTER 29

Charlie realized his mistake the minute the door to the basement closed behind him. No one was down there, which meant he'd left Maggie unprotected when the killer was God-only-knows-where. He caught Davin's scent just before the door clicked shut, and heard the lock slide home before he could make a grab for the handle. Since the door was metal and he was lacking both lock-picking tools and skills, he'd been looking for another way out of the basement when he'd heard Reid leading Maggie to the metalworking shop. He ran up the stairs, screaming for her to not go, but she hadn't heard.

That's when he started trying to tear the damn door down.

It was a contest to see which would give first - the door or his shoulder. Just when Charlie thought he was going to be nursing a shredded rotator cuff until the full moon, the door swung open.

At the end of the long hallway to his left he saw the door slam shut behind Reid and Davin's retreating forms. The coyote wanted to run after them, and Charlie's human half almost agreed, but as he turned towards them a flash of fire poured out of the metalworking shop, accompanied by a boom he could feel in his chest. The majority of the blaze was swallowed as quickly as it had erupted, and in its wake he heard Maggie's screams.

"Scout!" he yelled, not even realizing he'd picked up on the Alpha Female's scent until he was screaming her name. He pulled his shirt over his mouth, trying to keep from inhaling lungful after lungful of smoke. He got a supply of almost usable air and tried again. "Scout! Liam!"

He was about to charge in on his own when a white wolf leapt over a flaming beam and landed beside him.

God. Damn. It.

"You were supposed to be in human form." *And have a fire extinguisher.*

The Alpha Female gave him an apologetic look.

"She's in there. I heard her." The smoke was blinding and logic said no one could be in there and still be alive, but he knew there was still a chance. It was nothing more than a feeling deep in his stomach, but he trusted it.

Scout dropped her head, peered into the smoke, and then stared into the room. It only took a second for her white fur to disappear completely into the haze. When she'd gone about two or three steps, she let out a short, commanding bark. Charlie took it as a sign to follow.

Winding his way through the inferno, Charlie realized the fire wasn't as widespread as he initially thought. The good thing about metal is it's hard to burn. Flames still shot up from the wooden cabinets, but with Scout as his guide, he avoided the worst of it.

He spotted Maggie before Scout did, her green-and-black patterned dress bright enough to serve as a beacon. He shoved past the wolf, nearly losing his leg to a shear in the process.

He braced one hand on the dirt beside her head, and then froze.

What the...?

Charlie couldn't feel the heat of the flames from his forearm down. He leaned in next to Maggie's head, and when he built up enough courage to do it, sucked in a lungful of air.

A lungful of fresh air.

She was holding back the flames and smoke with the energy she was drawing from the earth, but she wouldn't be able to keep it up for long. She'd already drained herself to the point of unconsciousness.

Charlie slipped an arm under her legs and lifted her gently off the ground, careful not to jar the barbed wire wound around her delicate wrists and ankles anymore than necessary. The sight caused a white-hot rage to burn in his blood, and he vowed he wouldn't rest until Davin paid for what he'd done.

Maggie's body trembled as she coughed against his chest. Before he had her completely settled, Scout was leading the way back out. Charlie had been able to hold his breath most of the way in, but he was a Shifter, not a vampire. He tried to pull oxygen into his lungs, but since Maggie was no longer touching the dirt, there wasn't any to be had. His chest burned and little lights dance in front of his eyes, but he walked on. By the time he reached the door, his field of vision had narrowed to virtually nothing. He thought that was why he couldn't see the hallway, but as he began to crumble, he realized he was wrong. The fire had spread, and he wasn't going to be able to get them out after all.

CHAPTER 30

The world was upside down.

No. That wasn't quite right. Charlie was upside down.

No. That wasn't it either.

"I don't want to be mean when you're obviously having a bad day, but have you considered a diet?"

Charlie's eyes and brain finally adjusted enough to realize Jase had the top half of his body. Since his feet weren't dragging on the ground and there was no way in the world they were moving, he assumed somebody else was supporting those. A pillar of black smoke threatened to block the stars out of the sky above his head. He took a deep breath, and the resulting coughing fit making Jase say a few special words and tighten his hold.

"Take it easy, bro. You're going be fine."

Charlie licked his lips and opened his mouth—

"Don't talk. She's okay. Your Maggie is a fighter."

His Maggie. He shouldn't have liked the sound of that, but he did. She was his. And she was alive. Although, the sooner he saw the proof with his own eyes the better.

"Let's move him onto the stretcher." The voice came from over Jase's shoulder. The owner, a guy with silver hair and a blue EMS shirt, leaned into Charlie's vision just a second later. "How are you doing there, big guy?"

Charlie meant to say he was fine, but the coughing got in the way.

"He was only out for two, maybe three minutes," Liam said, outing himself as the person carrying Charlie's feet. "He's got some burns on his right side."

Burns? Huh. He couldn't feel those...

Wait. There it was. And dear, sweet Jesus, it *hurt*.

He made a mental note to thank Liam for pointing those out as soon as he could throw a punch again.

"Where is the other ambulance?" Jase asked as they slid Charlie onto the stretcher and started pushing him across some pavement. Since Charlie could only see the pretty patterns the ambulance's flashing lights were making on the black cloud of smoke, he didn't know exactly where they were, but he guessed they'd carried him as far as the main sidewalk winding through the center of campus.

"We sent it on with the girls in it," Mr. EMT said.

"Girls? As in both of them?"

Mr. EMT flinched slightly at the tremor in Liam's voice. Even the most human of humans felt an instinctual ripple of fear when the Alpha Male growled at them. If Charlie was able to talk, he would've told the guy it was Liam's I'm-freaking-out-with-fear growl, not his I'm-going-to-kill-you-and-make-you-like-it growl. Not many people could tell the difference, but Charlie and Liam were tight. Not to mention, Charlie was wanting to do a little freaked-out growling of his own.

"The blond one... Senator Harper's granddaughter?" One of Charlie's friends must have nodded, because he continued. "She gave us a lot of lip, but then someone mentioned the press was on their way, and she relented. I'm guessing she didn't want the world speculating on why she ran out of a burning building, carrying a girl while wearing nothing but an old Rolling Stones t-shirt."

Charlie turned his head to look, and sure enough, Liam was going around bare-chested.

“Her injuries?”

Even Charlie knew what HIPPA was and how it meant the guy wasn’t supposed to answer, but it was Liam, so Mr. EMT said, “None we could see, other than a second-degree burn on her foot, but they’re going to check her over.”

“And Maggie?” It was more of a croak than actual words, but Jase had his back.

“The other girl,” his cousin translated. “She’s going to pull through and be fine, right?”

“She’ll probably need to stay in the hospital a few days, and there is going to be some scarring, but she’ll be fine. No lasting physical damage.”

In the end, Charlie had to go to the hospital, too. The burning in his lungs and on his side were pretty bad, but nowhere near as excruciating as having to lay in the emergency room, looking at the water-stained ceiling tiles, while he didn’t know what was going on.

He tried to focus on what Liam and the others might be doing to locate Reid and Davin rather than Maggie. If he thought too hard about her, he would think about what she had looked like when he found her. About the way the barbed wire had bit into her soft, delicate flesh. About how she was crumpled, lying still and lifeless on the ground. About how he felt when he thought he might lose her forever. About the scars she might carry on the inside now. About how she too was somewhere in this hospital alone.

Did she know he was alive? Did she know he wouldn’t rest until they paid for what they did to her? Did she know he was about two seconds away from ripping all the medical crap off his body and going off in search of her?

“Don’t do it.”

Charlie's hand fell away from the IV at the sound of his father's voice.

"You're strong, but you're not Superman, son." As far as hallucinations went, this one was pretty vivid. Not only did he hear his father, but he saw him, too. The original Charles Hagan moved to the foot of Charlie's bed. In Charlie's eyes, his father had always seemed larger than life. Not so much anymore. Arms, which had once contained enough strength to send a boy flying into a wall, now looked too frail to lift a gallon of milk. "Let the doctors do their magic."

Charlie ripped the oxygen mask off his face. "What are you doing here?" He sounded like someone had taken a sander to his vocal chords, but he could talk. That was a bonus.

"My son almost died in a fire. What the hell do you think I'm doing here?"

After the battle with the old Alpha Pack left Charlie in a coma and then bound to a hospital bed for months, his parents had stayed by his side. They'd gone so far as to rent an apartment in Nashville where they wouldn't have to make the forty-five minute drive back and forth to their house. It was rare for him to look up and not see either one of his parents, his brother, Jase, or Talley in the chair beside his bed, no matter the time of day. But Charlie knew his father's presence was nothing more than a show. People were watching - the Alpha Pack was watching - and so Charles Hagan had put in his required appearances, but Charlie knew better than to mistake his performance as actual care and concern.

"How did you get here so fast?"

It had only been a couple of hours since the fire started, not nearly enough for someone to make the drive from his parent's house to the hospital in Lexington.

His dad concentrated on the machines monitoring his oxygen count and heartbeat as if he knew what they meant. "I was around."

"You were around?" But then he understood. The familiar scent he'd caught around the farm on occasion. The way all of the guards shrugged him off without looking him in the eyes when he asked why they continued to let "the neighbor" on the property. "You've been spying on the Alpha Pack? Are you insane? That can be considered an act of treason." And the punishment for treason was immediate execution. Charlie might have some very mixed feelings about his father, but he didn't want to have to stand witness as Liam ended his life.

His father shot him a you're-an-idiot look. It was one with which Charlie was very well acquainted. "I haven't been spying on the Alpha Pack. I've been watching out for you."

Charlie tried to make sense of that in his head, but it wasn't happening.

"What? Why?"

Charles, Sr., rubbed his top lip with his thumb. "You're my son," was his very short, non-helpful answer.

"Since when?"

"Since your mama birthed you, or more accurately, about nine months before that."

He knew it was weird, but Charlie had never thought of himself as his father's son. His father's disappointment. His father's punching bag. Those roles he'd filled, but Charles Hagan's son had always been Toby. He'd been fiercely proud of his first born. The two of them had a relationship Charlie watched and envied his entire life.

"Afraid I would screw up as a Stratego? Making sure you wouldn't have to barge in and save the family from public embarrassment?"

There was a flash of anger in his father's eyes, and Charlie found himself bracing for a blow. "You're my son. I miss you. I miss Layne." His father's fists clenched so tightly the loose skin Charlie had been eyeing earlier was pulled taunt. "One of my kids is dead, and the other keeps trying to get himself killed. He refuses to come home. I only get to see my grandson with one of the Alphas looking over my shoulder." He worked the muscles in his jaw, his eyes trained on the ceiling. "Your mother left me. I have nothing left."

Charlie questioned the working order of the hospital's equipment, because it said everything was fine, but he was pretty certain his heart had stopped.

"Mom left you?"

Charlie couldn't decide if he was happy she'd finally grown a backbone and done it, or if he was angry she hadn't found the strength to do it when he needed her to.

His father nodded, and Charlie thought there might be tears in the man's eyes. Not that it mattered. Charlie wouldn't feel sorry for him. Not after everything.

"Right after the hustings where we were ordered to give you custody of Layne. She said I'd taken everything from her she'd ever cared about." He swiped at his eyes with one hand and Charlie felt a stabbing pain in his chest. "She moved in with your Aunt Rosemary. I tried to tell her she could have the house, but she said she didn't want it."

"And so you started stalking me?" Charlie was grateful he was laying down. Otherwise he was pretty sure he'd have landed on his ass by now due to the way his world was spinning upside down. "How did you get away with it? I mean, I get that you got those idiots from the Hagan Pack to cover your ass, but Liam and Scout should have sniffed you out ages ago." His father's silence was all the response he needed. "They knew," he realized. "They knew, and they let you?"

"They knew. Scout told me that should I, and I quote, 'cause you an ingrown toenail's amount of discomfort' she would 'end me with as little speed and as much pain' as she was capable of."

Charlie sank back onto his pillow. As if his night hadn't been shitty enough, now he had to deal with his dad? Or this strange person who sorta, kinda, but not really looked and acted like his dad. When he was younger he'd dreamed of this moment, of a time when his dad would realize what an ass he'd been and come begging forgiveness. He'd always imagined it would be more satisfying. Then again, he'd expected the words "I'm sorry" to come out of his dad's mouth. All he had so far was finding out his dad had become a major creeper.

"I checked on your girl," his dad said, grabbing Charlie's attention. "She's going to be okay. She's got a pint of someone else's blood in her now and a few stitches, but they say her lungs look better than yours. You'll get to take her home soon."

"And Scout?"

His dad snorted. "Checked out against doctor's advice before even seeing a doctor. She and the rest of your friends have gone on a manhunt. If those morons who set the fire were smart, they'd go turn themselves into the police. There is a chance prison bars might keep Scout from turning them into human origami projects."

"I should be out there with them."

"Don't be stupid." Ah, there was his real father. Finally. The explanation about how he wasn't smart or strong enough to be of any use was coming in 3... 2... 1...

"You're hurt, and you got that way saving the girl. That's the most important thing. No matter what they do tonight, you're still the hero."

Okay, that was it. Aliens had gotten to his dad. Aliens or maybe demons. Demons who were actually nicer and better at being human than his father ever was.

"You know, I like her."

Charlie had no idea what his dad was talking about, but that seemed to be the theme for the evening.

"I didn't expect to, you know. When I first saw her, I didn't think she was good enough for you, and not because of her color."

"Dad, if you have to say it's 'not because of her color', then it's because of her color."

"No, it wasn't." His dad had his don't-even-think-about-arguing-with-me face on, and after many years of learning his lesson the hard way, Charlie didn't. He might not agree with his dad, but he wouldn't ever say so. "I'm not racist. I served with good men of every color in the Middle East."

"Of course you're not." *And you're not a child abuser either. Oh, wait...*

"She was just different than us, you know. She wore those weird clothes and was always wandering off to draw in her book. She didn't talk much, and she always looked like she would take off running if someone yelled boo at her."

"I like her weird clothes. And she's an artist. An amazing one."

"Yeah, well, I don't know much about art." His dad shifted uncomfortably as if he was embarrassed by that confession. "I just knew the girl was strange, and I didn't like her too much. But then I started seeing the two of you together, and I saw who you were when you were with her, and I changed my mind."

Charlie really couldn't think of anything to say to that, so he kept his mouth shut. He thought they would lapse into a nice, awkward silence, but apparently once his dad started opening up and sharing he couldn't stop himself from going on and on and on.

"Scout was never a good fit for you. I know you two thought you were going to grow up and get married and have a bunch of pups of your own someday, but I knew it would never work. Scout was always too strong for you. She didn't need you."

"Love isn't about needing someone." He didn't want to be with Scout anymore, hadn't in a long time, but his dad's words still pissed him off.

"Of course it is. Love is needing someone to be there to hold you together at the end of the day, because without them, you'll shatter into a million little pieces. And it's about them needing you to hold them together. You and Scout don't need each other like that. You can't hold each other's pieces together. But Maggie..." He smiled. Like a real, I'm-thinking-happy-thoughts smile. "You'd already shattered, but she found all the pieces and put them back together."

For once, his dad was right. Maggie had put him back together. She'd made him feel alive again. He needed her like he needed oxygen, and thanks to the events of the last few hours, he knew *exactly* how much he needed that.

The problem was, he didn't know if she needed him. She liked him. She was attracted to him and liked all the hands-on activities they couldn't do in the presence of others, but that wasn't the same as need, was it? And while his dad might be on the Norman Bates side of crazy, he was onto something with this whole mutual needing thing.

What happened when you needed someone and they didn't need you back?

There was a tap-tap-tap at the door and a blond doctor who looked a bit like she was manufactured by Mattel came into his room, electronic clipboard in hand.

"How are we feeling, Mr. Hagan?"

"Fine, thank you," he said. There was a time when he'd been afraid of doctors. They seemed so sterile and God-like in their lab coats with all their fancy Latin words, but after a few months of being trapped in a hospital bed, he'd figured out they were just normal people. Normal people who were into big needles and other torture devices, but people all the same. "How are you this evening?"

"I would be better if my patients didn't take off their oxygen and have conversations after being told to lay back and rest, but so it goes."

Her face couldn't have been more stoic if it had been made of plastic. Charlie tried for a laugh, thinking maybe she was joking, but when her eyes snapped over to him, he reached back, located the little plastic mask, and promptly slipped it onto his face.

"Your chest x-ray looks pretty good considering everything, Mr. Hagan," she said, scrolling through his chart. "You're a lucky man." She came over to his bedside and pushed a few buttons on the monitor. "You need to stay overnight for observation, but since I know you're not going to do that, I'm going to write a prescription for some inhalers and pain medication. They will come with directions. If you want to fully recover, I suggest you follow them." She glanced up to make sure he was paying attention. Charlie gave her a smile and a thumbs-up. If anything, she looked even more annoyed. "Stay away from cigarettes of all descriptions, including pot. Don't exert yourself." Her eyes flicked to his torso, which was bare since his shirt reeked of smoke and he refused to wear one of the paper gowns. Charlie might have felt a flush of pride over what he knew was a well-defined chest, but her gaze was so clinical he felt more like a lab rat than a piece of man candy. "No working out for at least four weeks, and then I want you to go slow with it."

Charlie nodded as if he planned on complying, which he did. Kinda. He would take it easy until the full moon when the Change would put everything, including his lungs, back to the way they should be.

Doctor Barbie turned her don't-even-think-about-messing-with-me look on his father. "I understand he's legally an adult, but I'm releasing him into your care. Watch him. Make sure he doesn't do anything to further injure himself." There was a slight movement at the corners of her mouth and eyes. In the world of Botox, it passed as a smile. "Your son is a hero, Mr. Hagan, and I have a soft spot for heroes. When he comes for his check-up in six weeks, I want to see him in top condition. I will be very upset if he isn't."

Charles, Sr., chewed on his lips, trying to hide a smile. "I'll do what I can, ma'am."

"You do that," she said. "The nurse will be by with his orders in a few minutes. Once she gets everything unhooked, you're free to go."

"Thank you," Charlie's dad said, reaching out to shake the doctor's hand. "Thank you for everything." There was a roughness to his voice, and when Charlie searched his eyes, he was shocked to see a sheen of tears there.

A sheen of tears, but not the bloodshot bleariness he was used to. The moment the doctor left he asked, "Dad, when was the last time you had a drink?"

Charles, Sr., scrubbed a hand over his face. "I don't know. A week after your mother left?" He sat in the chair next to Charlie's bed, seemingly fascinated with the tile on the floor. "I drank... God, I have no idea how much those first few days. I think maybe I was trying to drink myself to death. But then the booze ran out, and I sobered up and realized she was really gone. You were gone. And Toby..." He took a deep breath and pinched the bridge of his nose. "Toby is gone forever." He took another minute to collect himself before finally raising his eyes to his son. "I know I'm not perfect, and I don't expect anyone to forgive me, but I'm trying, Charlie. I swear to God, I am."

Charlie didn't know what to feel. On one hand, his dad was a dick. He'd made Charlie's life a living hell from the time he was old enough to understand fear. He could remember anxiously watching the door every evening when he was a kid, dreading the moment his dad stepped through. Charlie wanted to tell him he deserved everything he was going through and then demand he get the hell out of his room.

On the other hand, it was his dad, and no matter what had happened in the past, nothing could change that. Charlie wanted to hate him, but he didn't. He knew the pain of being lost and all alone in this world. It hurt so much he'd chosen to not feel anything at all rather than suffer through it. He knew the anger that ate away at you until it was all you knew. In many ways, he and his father were alike. It always terrified Charlie. He worried one day he would become his father, giving into to those urges to lash out and destroy. That fear had as big of a role in suppressing his coyote as the pain and suffering.

Charlie knew his dad hadn't been there to help him when he was in the gutter, but the point of being a good person was basing your decisions on what was right, not what you thought the other person deserved. His gramma had taught him that. *"If you're always being the better man, one day you'll find you're the best sort of man,"* she'd told him when he was younger and constantly getting into fights with Toby and Jase.

"Where have you been staying?" he asked his father, his mind made up.

His dad blinked, obviously surprised by the question. "One of the barns on the east edge of the farm. It used to be the main horse barn, where they kept the geldings. It has an apartment."

Charlie knew exactly what those barn apartments looked like, and hole in the wall didn't even begin to cover it.

"We've got plenty of rooms in the main house."

His dad did a deep breath and nose grip thing again and Charlie found himself working just as hard at fighting the stinging in his eyes.

"You shouldn't forgive me," his father said once he was able.

"And I don't," Charlie replied. "But I'm willing to work on getting there."

CHAPTER 31

"You're not a lawyer."

Scout leaned back in the hard metal chair, looking for all the world like she sat around in interrogation rooms on a regular basis. "And here I was thinking you were stupid," she said, her eyes roaming over Reid's gray pajama-style attire which had been accessorized with two matching silver bracelets.

"We have nothing to say to you," Davin spat at her, his face twisted into a sneer that might have been intimidating if it had been aimed at anyone other than the Alpha Female.

"Good." Charlie's voice was still raspy from getting a lung full of fire, but instead of making him sound weak, it added a rugged, I've-seen-a-lot-of-shit-and-lived-to-tell-the-tale edge. He was growing quite fond of it. "I don't want to listen to your whiney-assed voices anyway."

Reid's lower lip quivered, and her eyes darted around the room so quickly it seemed impossible she was actually seeing anything. "You can't be here," she said, her chest, her heart galloping like Secretariat in the final leg of the Kentucky Derby. "My lawyer will hear about this. You'll get into lots of trouble."

"Seriously?" Scout laughed. "I'm going to be in trouble? What is your lawyer going to do? Put me in time out?" She leaned forward and put her elbows on the table. "I'm the Alpha Female. What exactly do you think you or any other human can do to me?"

Reid visibly paled, but Davin just ground his teeth together.

"I think it's time you two had a seat," said Liam, who was leaned back against the wall next to the two-way mirror where several members of the Alpha Pack taking in the day's entertainment sat.

Reid immediately dropped into one of the chairs. Her boyfriend lasted about two seconds longer.

Liam's crossed arms were resting on his broad chest and one foot was propped on the wall, but instead of looking casual like he thought, he looked like a wolf lulling his prey into complacency before devouring them, which Charlie supposed was a fairly accurate assessment.

The Alpha Pack's inner-circle was together when the local news said the two prime suspects in the Sanders College fire were arrested. A chorus of curses filled the air, and then, because he couldn't do anything else, Charlie picked up the TV and threw it into the giant stone fireplace taking up most of the den.

Getting into the jail was an even harder task than they'd imagined. Liam pulled every single string the Alpha Pack could get their hands on just to get a few minutes alone with the psychos. It wasn't much, but it was what they had, and so they were going to make it count.

"Davin, you should know we've informed your father of the exact nature of your crimes," Scout said, moving things forward as quickly as possible.

"My father? Why the hell would he care? He's just some guy my mother whored around with nineteen years ago."

"Fair enough." Once they knew who was behind everything, Joshua ran a thorough background check. He'd discovered Davin Simonds was the non-biological son of

Kevin Simonds, member of the Simonds Pack in North Dakota. Simonds had three sons, but only two were listed at the Archives, because only two Changed during the full moon. Davin, who was the middle son, was discovered to be the product of his wife's affair when he didn't start Changing as a teenager. "How about I reword that," Scout said. "We informed the Simonds Pack of your crimes against the Alpha Pack. They have removed all associations with you, including financial support for your defense. I believe it may be time to talk with someone about a public defender."

Charlie had to give him credit. He didn't show any emotion at the words, even though they had to hurt. It was bad enough finding out your dad isn't really your dad, but to have the man who raised you turn his back on you would be like a punch to the gut, and Scout knew it. She'd been there, turned out by a pack she considered family, once before. For Scout, things had turned out okay in the end. Charlie didn't think Davin would be so lucky.

"You know, Davin, I get why you're here." Scout seemed to think about that and then clarified. "I don't understand why you think killing people and messing up their bodies is okay. I think that's probably a sign that you have a severe mental illness. But I understand how you got messed up in Shifter stuff. I understand you not liking us. What I don't get," she said, turning her attention to Reid, "is why you're here. We've checked everything everywhere. You have zero ties to our world. What did we ever do to you?"

It wasn't a rhetorical question. Before Scout and Liam took over the Alpha Pack some bad stuff had gone down.

The new Alphas were trying to right those wrongs, but it was hard to undo hundreds of years of evil.

Reid met Scout's eyes, her sneer making her plain face all kinds of ugly. "You think you're so special. You think just because you can turn into a wolf or coyote or whatever that you're better than the rest of us. Well, you're not. You're nothing but a freak, and you deserve to die. You all deserve to die."

"Why?" Charlie asked, even though he was supposed to stay silent during this interrogation. The only reason he was in the room was because he'd sat down in the chair reserved for Talley and refused to move.

"Why do we deserve to die? Because we're different? Because we have something you can't buy? Because we're special, and you're not?" He sounded calm and reasonable, but it was just because he'd been calm and reasonable for so long he knew how to fake it. But he wasn't that calm and reasonable guy anymore. The coyote was back, and it was pissed. Soon Reid and Davin would realize just how scary and evil a Shifter could be. "Was this like a reverse *Incredibles* plot? When no one is special then everyone can be?"

Reid's face blazed red, and Charlie thought it was more from embarrassment than the anger she was trying to project. "This is about doing God's work. It's about sending you demons back to hell!" By the end she was practically screaming. Her neck was veiny from the effort.

Charlie snorted. "I've got twenty-five bucks in my pocket that says you've never even touched a Bible."

Reid's skin tone crossed from red to purple.

"You are evil. God hates you."

"And you're a spoiled brat who is willing to kill people out of jealously. The entire world hates you. Even Davin probably hates you. He just put up with you because you could get him access to hundreds of thousands of security codes. How long were you dating before he started questioning you about your daddy's business? A month? I'm betting it wasn't even that long. Two weeks, tops."

Reid screeched and grabbed onto the table with her bound hands. She tried to flip it, but since this was an interrogation room, it didn't work. The thing was bolted to the floor for such occasions. When that plan failed, she went into a full on temper tantrum. She kicked out and thrashed around, the whole time making some horrible racket which was somewhere between screaming and crying. She didn't stop until Liam walked around the table and stood over her. He didn't do anything but stand there and look at her, but she finally put a lid on it and stopped her Linda Blair impersonation.

"Well, good. We've got all that settled," Scout said once the room was quiet again. "Motive has been established, unless you have something to add, Davin?"

Davin acted like he hadn't even heard her.

"Great. The next step is proving you did it." Looking like a complete badass city cop, Scout grabbed a small bag off the floor and threw it on the middle of the table. "We found this in Reid's room. It took him a couple of hours, but Liam matched every single one of those scents to the ones left at the crime scenes. And then we went to Davin's room." Scout shook her head, confused as to how someone could be so stupid. "Here's the thing. If you're going to kill someone and leave a hit list with the body in the form of a classic painting, you might want to get rid of your murder weapon and all the practice paintings you did. Don't just leave them sitting around your dorm room."

They weren't investigators, and they certainly weren't in the room legally, but they'd gone in, because it seemed like something they should do. No one had expected to find anything, but then they opened the door and realized they hadn't needed Joshua's forty-five minute lecture on how to find and collect evidence.

Davin had somehow managed to nab a single-occupancy room. A room he covered with photos of the Alpha Pack, copies of Luca Giordano's *The Fall of the Rebel Angels* (both the original version and various interpretations of the one still hanging in the gym), and a collection of knives and metalworking tools.

"I think it's safe to say we have some fairly compelling evidence, but since any of this stuff could have been planted, we've got one last nail in the coffin that is the not guilty plea I'm sure you would have entered if I'd given you a chance."

Reid crinkled up her forehead. "This isn't a trial."

"Au contraire, mon frere," Liam said from his newly reclaimed post on the wall. "This is the most important trial you'll ever face. This is where the Alpha Pack determines your guilt in crimes against the Shifters of the world. This is the trial where we decide your true fate."

Davin paled.

"Our final piece of evidence," Scout said, turning the conversation back to her carefully planned script, "is the testimony of Charlie Hagan, Stratego of the Alpha Pack." Her original idea was to read a written testimony he'd prepared on the way over, but since he'd bullied his way into the room, she turned to him instead. "Charlie?"

"They tied up Maggie with barbed wire and then set the room she was in on fire." Remembering how she'd looked when he first found her put a tremor of rage in his voice. "I request capital punishment."

"Thank you, Charlie," Scout said, reaching over and giving his hand a squeeze. The contact calmed his coyote.

"Are we ready for a verdict?" Liam asked, pulling himself off the wall to come stand beside his mate.

Scout nodded. "Ready."

"Reid St. James and Davin Simonds, we, the Alpha Pack, find you guilty of murder, attempted murder, and terroristic actions against the Alpha Pack." Liam's voice was so calm someone might think he was reading names out of a phone book instead of telling a couple of teenagers they were guilty of some of the most hideous crimes Charlie could imagine. "You are hereby sentenced to death by the hand of the Alpha Pack."

"What? No!" Tears began streaming out of Reid's eyes. "It was him. It was all him. I didn't kill anyone. All I did was tell him how to turn off your security system. I didn't kill that man. It was him." The last words were muffled by snotty sobs, which Liam silenced with one of his patented looks.

While Reid made a spectacle, Charlie watched Davin. Throughout the sentencing and Reid's dramatics, he didn't change expressions. He sat stoically, the only sign of life was the clear malice in his eyes.

So, this is what a sociopath looks like, he thought.

Was that what he would have become without Maggie? Would he have been able to shut out his coyote until he was no longer able to feel anything at all? Would he have committed hideous acts in the name of the Alpha Pack without ever feeling guilt or remorse?

Charlie shivered even though there was no draft in the room.

"There's a catch." Scout looked at Reid as she spoke. Her eyes would occasionally flick over to Davin, but only for a second. If Charlie didn't know better, he would have thought the other boy frightened her. "As long as you're incarcerated, we can't touch you." She waited for this information to sink in. Once Reid was looking at her prison wardrobe like it was the single best thing she'd ever seen, Scout continued. "If you want my advice, plead guilty. And if you're really looking to buy yourself a few years, confess to killing Vincent Barros. Because the longer you're in here, the longer you get to live."

They had Charlie's dad to thank for this sentencing. Neither Scout nor Liam was comfortable with killing someone, no matter how evil they were. They'd both been there, done that, and had the nightmares to show for it, thank you very much. But the Alphas couldn't appear weak, and letting a couple of murderers go would definitely be seen as a sign of weakness. So, a death sentence they received, but since they were under the watchful eye of the federal prison system, the Alpha's hands were tied. And it wasn't like they were letting Reid and Davin run around free. They would be in jail, where criminals are supposed to be.

"This isn't over," Davin said, his calm voice at odds with the chaos in his eyes.

Scout made a production out of looking at the time on her phone. "Actually, it is. Joe B's stops serving their lunch menu in thirty minutes, and I'm craving a breadstick like nobody's business." She jerked her head towards the window and seconds later the door opened, admitting two uniformed officers.

"You think you know what is happening, but you know nothing." One of the officers put his hand on Davin's elbow, but he didn't immediately rise. "We are legion. You can't hide from us. You can't stop us. And one of these days, we will rid the earth of your kind." The officer gave his arm a jerk, and he finally stood, but he kept his eyes on Scout the whole time.

"Well, that was fun," she said once the door slid shut. She slumped back against her chair as if she was suddenly very tired. Charlie understood. He felt a bit like collapsing himself. It had gone just the way they'd hoped, but it didn't give him the sense of closure he was looking for.

"What do you make of that 'we are legion' stuff?" Liam asked Scout as he stood behind her, gently massaging her shoulders. "Bluff or truth?"

"Does it matter?" Charlie asked. "This is our life now, isn't it? Dealing with people who want to see us dead just because we exist? If it's not some crazy kid from a Shifter family who is pissed because he can't Change, it's a dad who doesn't like our views on equal rights for women and gays. It will never stop." For them, there was no other option. It was what they signed on for when they became the Alpha Pack. And maybe they weren't as well informed about what the decision entailed as they could have been, but it was done. This was who they were and what their life was now.

But Maggie had a choice. And if she chose to stay with them, with *him*, then she would always be in the line of fire, both figuratively and literally. She would be dragged into the middle of a battle she didn't wage, and Charlie knew with a nauseating level of certainty he wouldn't always be able to protect her.

His mind flashed back to the sight of her trapped inside the fire and it hurt so much he couldn't breathe. It had been close. Too close. What if he wasn't in time the next time someone decided to take their hatred out on her? How would he survive?

Of course, he knew with complete and total certainty he wouldn't. Nothing would ever bring him back from losing her.

His only hope of survival was making sure she never got hurt again. And unfortunately, there was only one way to do that.

CHAPTER 32

Maggie zipped up her last tote bag and tossed it beside the others. It was only a tiny pile. She'd spent less than two hours gathering up everything and getting it all in suitcases, but she was completely exhausted. Her wrists and ankles, which boasted rings of stitches, were screaming at her for insisting on packing up all of her stuff by herself, but she kept soldiering on. Maybe she was being stubborn, but she didn't want anyone's help. She needed to do this alone.

"It survived."

Maggie took a second to get ahold of her emotions before turning around.

"It did," she said. "The fire stayed contained mostly to the south end of the building. Chase brought it to me in the hospital. She'd stuck a few sunflowers in it. I think it was her version of a joke." Her finger walked over the lip of the vase. Maggie knew she would have to pack it away next, but she was having trouble putting it out of sight. She knew it was crazy, but she felt like the vase connected her to her grandmother. Ever since Chase brought it to her hospital room she'd found herself talking to it the way she used to be able to talk to her grandmother. She figured she was still on the functional side of crazy since the vase never talked back.

"I'm glad it's safe." Charlie stood just inside the door, and from the glances Maggie stole, he looked like he was ready to bolt at any moment. The silence that followed was so painfully strained Maggie considered making a run for it herself.

It had been four days since Reid and Davin left her for dead. She'd lost a lot of blood and had some smoke inhalation, but it was the toll using her powers to keep herself alive had taken that kept the doctors and nurses checking on her constantly. She was so dehydrated and exhausted she didn't even wake up the first twenty-four hours. By the time she was thinking clearly enough to know what was going on, Reid and Davin were in custody and Charlie had sent her a text saying she was free now.

It was the only time he'd contacted her at all during her hospitalization.

"It's over. You're free now."

She'd thought he'd meant free from being afraid all the time, but when he hadn't shown up by the third day and Joshua was evading any questions she asked about him, she understood. She was free of the Alpha Pack. She was free from Charlie.

Maggie pulled the vase's crate out from under her bed, desperate for something to do other than standing there looking at him and fighting back tears. Of course, the moment she pulled it out she remembered how he'd looked as he carefully cut pieces of wood and foam, relying on Joshua's measurements to make sure the crate offered the most protection for the fragile piece inside. After he'd finished working on it, they'd snuck back to her room where she'd expressed her gratitude with kisses that lit her on fire from the inside out.

Two weeks later and here they were, back in the same room. Only this time, she worried about getting frostbite.

"My mom freaked when she saw this house," she said because someone had to say something. "She's downstairs with Talley and Jase now. I think Jase is afraid she's going to steal the silverware."

Charlie nodded. "I saw your grandfather. He said you were going back with them today."

She was. There were still a few days left before Christmas vacation officially began, but it turns out almost dying in an on-campus fire gets you a free pass on all of your finals. Maggie wasn't excited about going back to Monarch, but she was more than ready to get out of Chinoe. She needed a place where it was safe to fall apart without an entire houseful of people hearing and knowing why her heart was breaking.

She risked another glance at the door. Charlie was still standing in the exact same pose. She thought eventually she would get used to how he looked and how he affected her, but if anything, it only got worse the more time they spent together. Those grass-green eyes she could never get right when drawing him met hers and she felt the force of it in her chest.

"I'm going to miss you." She shouldn't have said it. It showed too much and left her too exposed, but she couldn't stop the words. She would miss him. They'd been together so much over the past few months she'd forgotten what life was like before. He'd become so interwoven with who she was there wasn't anything that wouldn't remind her of him. Every cup of coffee she drank, every comic book she read, and every laugh would carry pieces of Charlie to her. Maybe one day those pieces would stop leaving cracks in her heart, but it would be a long, long time.

If Charlie saw any indication of what she was feeling, he did a good job ignoring it.

"You got your life back," he said. "I'd say it's a pretty good trade-off."

"Funny. I kinda thought I'd been living my life all along."

"Not on your own terms. Not the way you were supposed to."

Unable to hold the stare any longer, Maggie walked over and eased the vase from its resting spot on the mantle and placed it into the crate. There was a moment of resistance, a second when she thought it might not fit, but then it was nestled safe and sound in the foam. It was ridiculous to draw parallels between the vase and her place in the Alpha Pack, but that didn't stop her from doing it.

"What if this is where I am supposed to be?" she asked the lid of the crate as she slid it home. "What if this is where I was supposed to be all along."

Only silence answered her, and she thought maybe he'd left, but when she looked back, he was still there. Watching her.

"If I wanted to stay, could I?" she asked, terrified to know the answer, but needing it anyway.

A flash of something Maggie couldn't identify flared in Charlie's eyes. "You would have to ask Scout."

Scout.

"Scout!"

It was the scene she saw over and over when she closed her eyes at night. It was the voice she heard anytime it got too quiet.

"Scout!"

She had been on the edge of death, ready for the fire to come and claim her, and Charlie's first thought hadn't been for her, but for Scout.

It shouldn't have mattered. The way he'd put a friend he'd known and loved his whole life before her shouldn't have made her feel hollowed out, but it did. It hurt because if the roles had been reversed, her first concern would have been him, because she loved him.

She loved Charlie Hagan, and he loved Scout.

"I don't want to stay," she found herself saying. The thought of sticking around, of watching Charlie watch Scout, was Maggie's new definition of hell. "Actually," she took a deep breath, forcing her words out through sheer will, "I would rather cut off my ties with the Alpha Pack completely."

Finally, something broke through Charlie's casual indifference. "What do you mean?" he asked, his eyes and lips pinched together.

"I mean..." God. What did she mean? "I mean, I'm done. I want out. I want what you said I have. My old life back. The one where I don't have to worry about who is trying to kill me this week." The one where she didn't have to have her heart broken afresh every single day.

"I'll let the others know," he said. "We'll keep our distance, and let you get on with your life."

No! Don't do that. Fight for me. Tell me you want me to stay.

Tell me you love me, too.

"Thanks."

Charlie finally stepped into the room, and for one beautiful second she thought he was coming for her, to tell her all the things she wanted to hear, but he stopped at her pile of luggage. “This everything?” he asked.

She nodded, disappointment paralyzing her vocal cords.

“I’ll help you carry it down.”

“Thanks,” she said, plastering a fake smile on her face. It held as she followed him down the stairs and out to her grandfather’s minivan. It didn’t waver as she told Scout, Liam, Jase, Talley, Layne, and Joshua goodbye. She even managed to hold it in place as she watched the farm fade into the horizon. It wasn’t until her grandfather merged onto the parkway that she let herself fall apart.

CHAPTER 33

"Happy Boxing Day!"

Charlie tossed the Dark Knight collector's edition Santa brought him on the floor and sat up. It was strange, but in all the years they'd been friends, he couldn't remember Scout being in his bedroom before.

"What is Boxing Day exactly?" he asked. "Am I supposed to put things in boxes? Throw some punches? You're the one dating a Canadian. Explain it to me."

Scout plopped down beside him, cocking an eyebrow at his Batman sheet set, which was on display since he didn't actually see a point in making his bed.

"I'm not dating a Canadian."

"I don't care what Liam says, he was born and raised in Canada. He's a Canadian. No matter how much he wants to be one of the cool American kids, he's not."

"Oh, I'm not saying that Liam isn't Canadian. He's so Canadian he drinks maple syrup instead of coffee. I'm saying, I'm not dating Liam." If she was looking for something to shock him, she clearly succeeded. He felt his spine pop from the speed with which he whipped himself around to face her. Scout took one look at his face and started giggling. "Oh, that was even better than I expected."

"What do you mean you're not dating Liam? He's your mate." People didn't just leave their mates.

Mates were the luckiest damn people in the universe.

"We're not dating because..." Scout waved her left hand under his nose, the rock on her ring finger so big and bright even the low lights of his room made it glitter and shine. "We're engaged."

"Engaged?"

"As in, to be married."

"You're engaged to be married?"

Scout laughed again. "Yes."

"I guess things are better between the two of you now?" The Scout and Liam from August were nowhere near getting engaged, and since then...

Well, since then he didn't really know. His focus had been completely on Maggie. So much so, he didn't really know what was going on with his friends anymore. He tried to work up some guilt over it, but that was all reserved for Maggie, too.

"Did you know," Scout began, stretching out across his bed, "that Liam Cole is in love with me?"

"Of course he is. You're Scout Donovan. You're comprised entirely of lovableness."

Scout snorted. "I'm comprised entirely of snark and disdain, but thankfully, those are qualities Liam loves in a girl."

"I'm happy for you," Charlie said, and he meant it. Scout had earned the right to be happy, and Liam made her happy. Even when he was making her miserable, it was a happy sort of misery. The kind you only felt when you were with someone you truly loved. It was much preferable to the misery you felt when the person you couldn't stop thinking about wasn't anywhere near you. That kind of misery was entire galaxies away from happy. "Unless you're moving to Romania," he said, amending his statement. "If you're moving there, then you have my sincerest apologies."

"You do understand if I have to move to Romania, then you guys have to, too, right? You did that whole swearing to serve and protect me thing."

"Even Jase?"

Scout's smile was completely evil. "Even Jase."

"So, we're not going to Romania?" Because there was a chance the next time the Alpha Female's brother stepped foot into the country, he would be sent to prison.

"No, but don't tell Jase yet, okay? One of the few true pleasures I have in life is torturing him." She looked so comfortable that Charlie stretched out beside her. She scooted over to give him room, and he wondered how many times they'd done just this. He could remember the four of them - Scout, Jase, Talley, and him - having long conversations while staring at Scout's ceiling when they were all still small enough to fit on one bed. "We're moving the Den here," Scout said once he was settled. "The farm isn't quite as big as what we have over there, but it'll work. We'll keep some of the operations in Romania, which means Liam and I will have to travel over there once or twice a year, but we're making the Alpha Pack an American operation."

"You're going to piss people off."

"People stay pissed off at me. I don't really care anymore. I'm going to do what I think is right and what makes me happy. If they don't like it, they can go screw themselves. I'm over it."

"And the people who think you're too young to get married?" He could think of two people who were probably sitting at the top of that list, and there was no way Scout was going to tell them to go screw themselves. She might technically be an adult now, but that wouldn't matter to

Rebecca and Dustin Donovan. They would ground her for the rest of eternity.

There was a huff of annoyance from his shoulder, letting him know he'd guessed right. "I'm too young to be in charge of an entire race of people, yet here I am." She kicked a pillow, launching it towards their heads, and snatched it out of the air just before it barreled into her face. Her elbow came dangerously close to Charlie's nose as she crammed it behind her head. "It's not like we're some idiot kids who don't know what we want. We're the Alphas. Even if we didn't love each other with all of our being, which we do, we're bound for life anyway. For us, a wedding is just a technicality and an excuse for me to wear a princess dress."

"A princess dress?"

She cut her eyes over at him. "I'm still a girl, Charlie. And I want to wear a freaking princess dress."

Charlie felt the beginning of a smile tempt the corners of his mouth. "Then you should have the most beautiful princess dress in all the kingdom," he said. "You deserve to be happy."

Her teasing eyes grew thoughtful. "You do, too."

"Scout—"

"How is everything going with your parents?" she asked, taking the conversation in a direction he wasn't expecting. It was a direction that had been the number one taboo subject for the past ten years of his life, but for once he was happy to talk about it. Anything was better than where he thought she was going.

"They're trying." The drive back from Chinoe had been strained and silent. His dad tried to start a conversation a couple of times, but Layne was too busy trying to permanently damage his hearing by applying super-loud rap music directly to his eardrums and Charlie was too exhausted to reply. They arrived home to find Charlie's mother already there, pretending like everything was normal. Things weren't exactly like the heartwarming end of a made-for-TV Christmas special - Charlie caught his dad eyeing the liquor cabinet and his mother silently crying a few too many times for that - but it was considerably better than most of his Christmases. Layne had even taken off his headphones and said a few complete sentences over the past few days, which was a sort of Christmas miracle.

"Are you really okay with everything? I mean, with having your dad around and all that?"

Charlie shrugged, although the motion was lost in the mattress. "I'm not going to say it's good having him around, but it's not bad either." In reality, the two of them hadn't really had much interaction since his dad relocated to the main house at the farm. Their relationship wasn't much different than it'd been when he was a teenager. For the most part, they pointedly ignored one another, acting more like cohabitating strangers than father and son. The only significant difference was the elder Charles Hagan didn't get drunk and start terrorizing his son every evening. "At least this way I'll know when he starts to fall off the wagon, and maybe I can stop it."

"Chuck, I need you to make me a promise."

"Anything, your majesty."

"If and when he does, don't blame yourself." He opened his mouth to say he wouldn't, but Scout cut him off before he could. "You carry the weight of the world on your shoulders, Charlie. The only problem is, you're not responsible for the world. Crap is going to happen, and you can't stop it. It's not your fault when things go wrong."

"I know that."

"Do you know your dad's alcoholism and general jack-assedness is one of those things you can't control?"

He rolled his eyes. "Yes, Scout."

"Good."

They lay side-by-side in silence for a long while. Being with Scout gave him a sense of peace deep down in his soul. At one time he'd thought that feeling of peace was love. And it was. But it wasn't the buy-a-ring-and-abandon-a-centuries-old-Den kind of love. The bond Charlie and Scout shared wasn't tied together with threads of passion, but ropes of familiarity and comfort. Charlie would do anything in the world for Scout. Her happiness and safety were more important to him than his own life. But his dad was right. She didn't need him in her life the way she needed Liam.

That wasn't really shocking. He'd known all along he wasn't what she needed. What was surprising was she wasn't what he needed either.

"I called her," Scout eventually said, breaking the silence and any feelings of good will towards her Charlie possessed.

He didn't have to ask who she called. It was the person Charlie fought like hell to not think about. The person whose loss he felt deep in his soul every minute of every day. The person who occupied so much of his brain he'd only been present in body as his family opened gifts and laughed around a dinner big enough to feed an army of Shifters the day before.

How was she? Were her wounds healing? Was her family taking care of her like they should? Did she have a good Christmas, or was she sitting alone on the couch eating stale potato chips and watching *A Christmas Story* for the fifth time in a row?

He wanted to ask Scout, but he didn't.

"You shouldn't have done that." They had to cut her free from the Alpha Pack. It was what she wanted and the only way to keep her safe.

"I can do whatever in the hell I want, thank you very much. I'm the Alpha Female, and she's my friend. I wanted to make sure she was okay."

"Okay?" The bed creaked out a protest as Charlie launched himself into a sitting position. "Is something wrong?"

Scout pulled herself up onto her elbows, her you're-a-complete-idiot look firmly in place. "Yeah, some asshole broke up with her after she suffered a traumatic injury. And to add another insult on top of that insult that was added to injury, he did it like a week before Christmas."

"You can't break up with someone if you weren't ever together in the first place." They'd never said they were together. So what if he'd felt connected to her in the very core of his being? There had been no promises between them. "And she was the one who chose to leave."

"Yeah, well, it was kind of hard for her to choose any other option with you pushing her out the door."

Charlie stood and walked the three steps to his door. Then he turned around and walked the three steps back to his bed. And then back to the door. And back to the bed again.

His coyote was restless.

Ever since Maggie helped him power through the Change, his coyote stayed close to the surface. No matter how hard he tried to push it back down, it rode him hard, making sure he felt every single cut, bruise, and scar life left on his heart. More often than not, he felt like Human Charlie was fighting a losing battle against the coyote's instinct. It got worse whenever someone mentioned Maggie. The coyote didn't like how he'd let her leave. That last day, when they'd said goodbye to each other for the last time, he'd had to physically hold himself back. The coyote wanted to throw her on the bed and kiss her until she couldn't think of anything at all, least of all leaving him.

The coyote was an arrogant prick who believed he could protect her. Apparently, Coyote Charlie didn't share Human Charlie's memories of how many times he'd failed to keep the people he cared about safe.

"I did what I had to do," he said, although he wasn't sure if he was telling Scout or the animal inside him.

"Why?" Scout asked. He stopped pacing, and she pulled herself up into a sitting position. "Why did you have to throw away the girl you loved, Charlie? Is this one of those self-punishment things?"

"I never said I loved her."

Scout lifted one shoulder. "Doesn't make it any less true."

Charlie closed his eyes, blocking out Scout and sealing his emotions inside where she couldn't see them. Of course he loved Maggie. She was amazing. She was talent, passion, hope, and courage all rolled up in one beautiful package that loved comic books. If Charlie had been asked to create the perfect woman, he would have made Maggie. He missed sound of her laugh and the way her skin felt beneath his hands with an intensity that scared him, but even more, he missed just being with her. They could talk for hours about nothing and it would still be one of the best conversations of his life.

"It doesn't matter. She's better off without me."

He heard the springs of the mattress creak, but he didn't dare open his eyes to see what Scout was doing.

"Says who?" she asked, her voice coming from just a few inches to his left. He risked a glance to discover her standing at his shoulder, her arms crossed over her chest.

"Being with me is like painting a giant target on her chest," he said. "We're Alpha Pack, Scout. And we're not exactly a conventional, well-liked one, either. People are going to constantly be coming for us. Whoever Davin was working with is still out there, and I doubt they're just going to sit idly by for the next thirty or forty years while we go about our business. One of these days, they'll strike again, and I don't want her in the cross-fire." He swallowed down the ball of emotion lodged in his throat. "I can't let anything happen to her, Scout. She has to be safe. I can't live with myself if she's not."

"And you think throwing her out into the world all alone without anyone to look out for her is going to keep her safe?"

"She won't need protecting if she's not with us."

"That's a bunch of crap, and you know it." Scout jabbed him in the chest with the Iron Finger of Death so hard he knew it would leave a bruise. "The world is filled with scary, bad shit. Just because she's out there in the 'human' world doesn't mean she's safe. She could get hit by a car or shot by some asshole with a daddy complex tomorrow just by being in the wrong place at the wrong time." Charlie felt like someone stabbed him with a knife dipped in acid, but Scout didn't stop. "And do you honestly think shutting her out is going to make people forget she lived with us for four months? She could still be a target, Charlie. The only difference is, this time you're not going to be around to help her when she needs it."

Scout was either going to have to shut up, or he was going to punch her in the throat.

"She deserves better than me."

"She deserves someone better than a guy who loves her as much as she loves him? Explain to me how that works."

Yep, he was definitely going to have to punch Scout in the throat.

"You don't understand!" He didn't mean to scream it at her like a petulant teenager, but it happened that way all the same.

"*I* don't understand complicated, angsty relationships? Seriously?" Scout took a deep breath, and when she released it all the annoyance and aggression bled out of her body. He felt the fight drain out of him as well, and then Scout was wrapping her arms around his waist. He hugged her back, fighting to keep all the moisture in his eyes where it belonged.

"I'll screw up. She'll get hurt because of me."

"She's hurting without you," Scout said. "I'm not the most observant girl on earth when it comes to relationships. I mean, I was completely blindsided by Jase and Talley, so that tells you a little something about how obvious these things have to be before I catch on. But even I can see how much you two belong together. Don't give up on what you guys could have without a fight, Charlie. You'll regret it the rest of your life."

"I love her," he confessed out loud for the first time.

"I know." She gave him a tight squeeze before pulling back to look him in the eye. "Now you just need to make sure Maggie knows it."

CHAPTER 34

Maggie looked at the email on her screen and counted the zeroes yet again.

Five. Five zeroes and no decimal.

The room tilted slightly to the left

Apparently Chase had taken a few photos of her vase and sent them out to different collectors before delivering it to the hospital. Three different people interested in purchasing it had contacted her, but none of them had been as generous in their offer as Mr. Tony Henson of Marquette, Michigan. She allowed herself a moment to think about all of the things she could do with the money, knowing the whole time it wasn't happening. The vase was one piece she would never sell. Too much of her heart was bound in that clay. It had started as an ode to her grandmother, but it ended up as so much more. It was the time she'd spent with the Alpha Pack. It was all the evenings she'd wrestled cramped hands while painting the intricate pattern while Charlie worked on his comic. It was a reminder that she was a survivor, that she could overcome whatever the world threw at her.

Her computer chimed, letting her know she'd received a new email. She clicked over, eager to see if someone was making an even more outrageous offer than the obviously insane Mr. Henson. Her heart rate doubled when she saw the name of the sender and her fingers shook as she clicked it open. The message only contained a link, and even though she knew clicking on random links was the best way to get your computer fried by a virus, she clicked it anyway.

Twenty minutes later she was so engrossed in a webcomic about a coyote who falls in love with a rabbit she nearly fell off her stool when someone knocked on the door.

"Just a minute," she called out, quickly sending Joshua a text message to let him know someone was at the door. He'd installed surveillance cameras all around the small office the Alpha Pack had ever so kindly turned into an off-campus studio for her as a Christmas/farewell gift. It was a fifteen minute walk from her dorm, but having it meant she'd never have to step foot into Rosa Hall again. The day she'd moved back to Chinoe, Joshua had shown up with an armload of equipment. A few hours later, she had cameras set up around both her new dorm room and the studio. He was supposed to patch the feeds to her computer and phone, but that wouldn't be finished for another few days. Since she was a bit skittish after her recent brush with death, Joshua told her he would monitor everything until the transfer could be made.

"Why is Joshua sending me a text message asking why I'm knocking on your door?"

The world completely froze at the sound of his voice coming from outside.

"Charlie?" She sounded like Minnie Mouse on helium. Awesome.

"Can I come in?"

She nodded and then realized he couldn't see through the door or undo the seven different locks she'd installed with the help of her drill and some YouTube videos. Her hands shook as she fumbled with the obstacle course of chains and tumblers. It felt like it took an hour for her to get the door open, but once it started swinging back she decided it wasn't nearly enough time. She didn't know if she could face him after all this time.

"Hey," he said, looking even more beautiful than she remembered.

"Hey."

He pointed at the drizzle falling from an ominous gray sky. "I don't know if this stuff is snow, ice, or rain, but it's really cold and nasty."

"Oh! Sorry!" She hopped back, nearly falling off of her platform shoes. He steadied her with a hand on her elbow, and she felt the shock of his touch all the way to her toes.

Charlie dropped his hand and wiggled his fingers as if he'd felt it too. "This is nice," he said, looking around the studio. "I like the way you've Maggied it up."

"Maggied it up?"

He nodded absently, still examining the tiny room as if fascinated with every detail. "The scarfs on the windows and covering the lamps. The artsy, high-brow comic book panels on the wall." He flashed her a full-fledged grin, which caused all sorts of fluttery feelings in her stomach. "The thin layer of dust covering everything."

"It's a ceramics studio. The dust is mandatory."

"Well, to me, dust equals Maggie."

It was a ridiculous statement, and not necessarily a flattering one, but it made Maggie's face burn with a blush all the same.

You're supposed to be angry and hurt, not gobbling up the scraps of affection he's throwing out like you're starving for them.

Except she was starving for them. For him. It was why she'd left the Alpha Pack in the first place. She knew she couldn't be around him without losing her heart to him yet again. But it seemed getting rid of the Alpha Pack was easier said than done. They'd all called or texted her over the break, Talley and Joshua both begging her to reconsider moving back to the farm on a daily basis. She'd kindly tried to explain she was cutting her ties with the Shifter world when Scout called her on Christmas day, but the Alpha Female told her in no uncertain terms there was no out.

"Once you're one of us, you're one of us. We're like a family. Even if you hate our guts, you're still stuck with us."

Maggie tried to be annoyed, but it was hard when people were throwing out words like *family.*

"I sent you something earlier," Charlie said, dusting off a seat before sitting down. "Did you see it?"

"I did. It's good." The art was a little rough around the edges, but there was no denying his talent. Charlie had a unique style that pulled the reader in completely and opened up the story in unique and amazing ways. "It's not what you've been working on for Stroud. When did you start it?"

"The day after Christmas," Charlie said, using his finger to push the dust on the table into a line. "I realized I hadn't given you a present yet, so..." His head stayed bent toward the table, but his eyes rose to meet hers.

"Charlie..." What was she supposed to say? What was he saying?

"I love you, Maggie."

Oh. That. That was what he was saying.

And that was the room spinning around her.

Awesome.

"Maggie, I don't mean to be pushy, but I'm freaking out a little right now. I'm going to need you to say something, *anything*. Just talk instead of looking at me like you don't know who I am."

"What about Scout?"

Charlie eyebrows folded in together. "What about Scout?"

"You love her, and I..." Maggie took a deep breath to steady her voice. "And I can't live with being second best. Not with you. I love you too much."

"Second best?" He got up and came over to where she was standing. His hand lifted hers off the table, which she thought was a really bad idea. It was the only thing keeping her noodle legs from dumping her butt into the floor. "You're right. I do love Scout." Those were not the words she actually wanted to hear. "But I don't love her like I love you."

Well, that was better.

"How do you love me?"

"Like Superman loves Lois Lane."

"Lois Lane? Not Wonder Woman?"

Charlie's face broke into a grin. "Definitely not Wonder Woman."

"Is this a Maggie-is-freakishly-short thing?"

A finger trailed down her jawline. "It's a Maggie-is-way-more-important-to-me-than-Wonder-Woman-is-to-Superman thing. He only ends up with Wonder Woman in storylines where Lois doesn't exist. When given a choice, he always chooses Lois."

His hand shifted so it was now cradling her face. His face grew more serious as his thumb trailed over her bottom lip.

"Lois makes Superman whole," he said. "That's how I love you. I love you like you're a part of me that's been missing. And I know I've screwed up everything, but I'm not going to give up on us, Maggie. I will keep trying over and over again to show you how much you mean to me in case one day you can forgive me."

She could have told him she forgave him the moment she began reading his comic or that he made her feel complete, too. But she didn't tell him either of those things because her mouth had much better plans. He shivered against her as her lips coaxed his apart, and then it was her turn to quake as his tongue slid against hers. They teased and tasted each other, exploring parts of one another they'd missed over the past month and discovering new ones. By the time they came up for air Maggie was sitting on the table, her legs wrapped around Charlie's waist. She dropped her head to his shoulder since her muscles had turned to jelly.

"I've missed you," she said against his neck.

Warm lips pressed into her hair. "I missed you, too."

Maggie burrowed further into Charlie's embrace, wishing this moment could go on forever. She had been an outsider her whole life, but with Charlie's arms wrapped around her, she finally felt like she belonged.

"Your room is still waiting for you at the farm," Charlie said, his fingers tracing lazy circles over the tattoo on her side. "A few Seers from Romania have already moved in, but Scout wouldn't let any of them take your room. And she had Makya put fresh sheets on your bed this morning."

Maggie pulled back so she could see his face, a list of reasons why her moving back in with the Alpha Pack on her lips, but she forgot every single one when she saw the hope lighting his eyes.

"We're ready for you to come home," he said.

Home. It should've sounded wrong, but it wasn't. Somehow Fenrir Farm had become home for Maggie. She missed the rolling hills and her ridiculously opulent bed almost as much as she missed her friends.

And if having the Alpha Pack as friends wasn't the exact opposite of how she saw her life going, she didn't know what was, but she wouldn't have it any other way.

"Maybe I should wait," she said, trying to be reasonable despite the urge to immediately run back to the dorms and pack up her stuff.

She saw the disappointment in the downward turn of Charlie's mouth, but he quickly shrugged it off. "If that is what you want. Just as long as you're back by February, it should be fine."

"February?"

"Yeah, we'll be having our next hustings on the day of the new moon in February. Liam is going to officially induct you as a Taxiarho."

"Taxiarho?" Maggie wondered how long this conversation could go on with her just repeating the last word Charlie said.

"Taxiarho. Official member of the Alpha Pack. The rank just below Stratego." The corners of Charlie's mouth tilted up slowly, no doubt in response to Maggie's state of complete and utter shock. "I'm guessing Scout forgot to mention how she officially declared you an Alpha Pack Potential?"

"I can't be a Taxi-whatever. I'm a Thaumaturgic."

"And Joshua is an Immortal." His fingertips slid down her arms until they were tangled with her own. The weight of his hands on hers helped ground her, which was a good thing since she felt like she was in some dream world where she was tapped to join the most powerful Shifters and Seers in the world and was loved by the strongest, most amazing guy she'd ever known.

If this was a dream, she didn't want to ever wake up.

"Pack isn't about who can Change or See," Charlie said, his eyes locked on hers. "Pack is about building a family and having a place where you don't have to hide who you are or what you can do." He lifted their joined hands, using them to wipe away the tear trailing down her cheek. "You belong with us, Maggie Mae McCray. Say yes. Say you'll join us."

She didn't say it, but only because she didn't trust herself to speak. Instead, she nodded her head, and then Charlie was kissing her, saving her from having to say anything more.

ACKNOWLEDGEMENTS

The first thanks has to go to Victoria Faye Alday, cover designer; Gwen Hayes, story editor; Leslie Mitchell, copy editor; and Sarah Pace-McGowan, Comma Police, for making me look good. The world would know what a bumbling idiot I am if it weren't for you guys.

Also helping me look smart was Johnny Jones, world's greatest high school art teacher and knower of artsy things; Amy Chase, talented ceramicist and cheese-fry sharer; Dr. Joe Lowery, mad(ly helpful) scientist; and Joe Peel of Clairborne Farms. Many thanks to you all for helping with my research.

A big heap o'thanks goes to Kathryn "Kitty Kat" Sills for doing all the frustrating formatting work so I don't have to.

As always, the Beta Fish were instrumental in both inspiring this book and keeping it cool. Thank you to Samantha Newman, Tori Story, Amy Orman, Tory Driskall, Claire Harmon, Tessa Northcutt, and Emily Dunbar for being awesome. And even though she's not technically a Beta Fish, Erin Lowery alway offers valuable feedback early on in the process, so thanks go her way, too!

Samantha Young, thank you for replying to my emails and not filing a restraining order.

And finally, thank you to my family for supporting and loving me, even when it's hard.

What can the future hold for a girl whose days are numbered and a boy whose life has no end?

INFINITE HARMONY

Shifters & Seers Book 2

Coming November 2014

ABOUT THE AUTHOR

Tammy Blackwell is a Young Adult Services Coordinator for a public library system in Kentucky. When she's not reading, writing, cataloging, or talking about books, she's sleeping. You can follow her on Twitter (@Miss_Tammy), write to her at Miss_Tammy@misstammywrites.com or visit her at www.misstammywrites.com.